Finding Vera

by

Kerry Claire

DEDICATION

For Vera, Tess, and Lola.

CONTENTS

FOREWORD

Finding Vera is a fictional novel based on real events. The canine points of view have been forged from years of study and observation, and the author has depicted Tess, Lola, and Vera, their relationships with each other and with the world around them, as close to reality as possible. Although the names and essence of Tess, Lola, Vera, Duke, Sarah and Wally are real, all other characters in this book are fictional.

PART 1:
THE ADOPTION – 2006

CHAPTER 1

VERA

Vera shivered and wrapped her long tail around her haunches, the tip of it kissing her nose. The day had been frigid and calm, prickling like ice through her coat, but tonight a gale shrieked outside, lashing her shed so forcefully that in the blackness of early morning, she trembled—a mingling of cold and loneliness and fear.

When the grey of a still and silent dawn crept through the doorway of her shed, Vera awoke and stretched luxuriously, front paws reaching out before her on the dirt floor, bottom high in the air. Then she rocked forward, extending her coltish back legs one by one, surveying the house where her people lived, the wildness of the forest beyond, and the field that spread out in every other direction. She no longer smelled the stench of mud and feces that matted her coat, but tested the air for the scent of squirrels, raccoons, feral cats.

Nothing there.

She sat and scratched at her collar, her hind foot finding the metal ridge embedded in the flesh of her neck. It had been there for as long as she could remember. Sometimes she fought to swallow, coughed from the irritation, or in a bid to ease the discomfort, danced back and forth in careful steps across the chain that held her captive.

Leaf! She pounced, caught it, and tossed it with reckless joy through the air. She snatched it again, wrestled it to the ground and dug furiously, feeling the earthy resistance of mud against her nails and pads, taking pleasure in the work of her shoulders. Then, on a whim, she wheeled around to chase a clod of soil that flew from under her paws. A surge of excitement dashed through her limbs, and she scanned for a squirrel—wanting to run, run, run like the wind.

A familiar sound drew her attention and she turned, threw back her ears, and relaxed into a smile. Food? Company? The images flitted through her mind, captured her imagination—she was so hungry for both.

A harsh voice sliced through the air. The words were meaningless, but the tone froze her thoughts and turned her skin to fire.

"You goddamned dog! What the hell are you doing?"

She fled to the end of her chain and shrunk inside herself, ears pinned to her skull, tail tight on her belly. She strained to disappear, to meld with the earth.

The man barreled up to her, loomed above her, hands clenched, boots alive. Fists flew at her ears, kicks pounded her hips, her ribs, her chest and she yelped and cowered and arced away—but the chain jerked her back, over and over.

She snapped and flailed and snapped again, panic powering her limbs. She grabbed his jacket, adjusted her grip, and surged forward. Her jaws found his arm and she bit down as hard as she could, latched on with shark-like ferocity, defying the kicks that ravaged her body. She shook her head in wide, powerful jerks and tugged with all her might.

"Fuck!"

The shout deafened her. A blow to her head knocked her loose, and she spun away, the smell of the man's anger burning her nostrils. She staggered, the world greyed and swam, and the muddy earth surged up to meet her. His footsteps receded, somewhere a door slammed, and then there was silence.

Confusion and fear seared through her veins. She crawled to her shed and collapsed, her body throbbing. She had no idea what had just happened, or why the man had attacked her, and his unpredictability terrified her. With utmost care she curled into a ball, her breaths rapid and shallow, the pain blinding.

The next morning, Vera sniffed the air in short explosive bursts from the safety of her shed, sifting through the currents for telltale scents. She swiveled her ears like antennae, searching for any faint sound through the breath of the wind. Footsteps. The man? She pressed herself to the back of the shed till her side screamed.

"Vera!" His voice cracked like a whip through the open doorway. She melted into the planks, but he grabbed the chain and jerked her forward. The collar bit at her neck and she coughed, a harsh, rasping sound that rose to a shriek. She locked her front legs, pushed against the dirt, lowered her head, and strained against him with all she had, heart wild in her chest. But hands seized her and then she was flying, all control lost, a kaleidoscope of sky and metal and legs before her, the thrash and struggle to land feet first. Too soon, she crashed onto the truck bed, numb and terrified and still. The vibration of an engine stirred her and then they were moving.

The sun warmed her, the rushing air revitalized her, and she stood to watch the world flow past as they drove. Yellow fields fanned out in every direction framed by white peaks on the horizon. She was terrified and exhilarated and overwhelmed. Her feet vibrated and slid on the slickness of the truck bed, and when the vehicle turned sharply, she crashed hard against the side. She couldn't think. She couldn't move. She stayed where she landed, exhausted.

CHAPTER 2

SOPHIE

Sophie readjusted her stethoscope, closed her eyes, and listened. She hoped to hear a gurgle, any hint of sound that would indicate movement in the girl's intestines.

Nothing.

She looked down at the young woman lying on the exam

table in front of her.

"Take one finger and show me exactly where it hurts," she said. The girl's index finger circled in the air, then dropped to the right lower quadrant of her abdomen, just as Sophie thought it would. "I know it's sore, sweetie, but I have to push on your tummy now, so try to relax." Sophie studied the girl's face and pushed gently on the spot the girl indicated, then released the pressure with a sudden upward motion.

"Ow!" Kathy's knees flexed into the fetal position and she whimpered, hands clenched over her belly.

"Kathy, I'm pretty sure you have appendicitis. We need to get you to the hospital for more testing. Is there someone who can drive you?"

Kathy stared up at Sophie, wide-eyed. "I can't go. There's no way I can go to the hospital."

For the next hour, Sophie tried to convince Kathy to go to the ER—her father was out of work and lack of funds gave her few options. It was only when the girl's white blood count came back from the lab elevated high above normal that she reluctantly agreed to have a friend drive her to the hospital. Getting patients the care they needed when they had no resources was one of the hardest parts of Sophie's job as a nurse practitioner.

The first week of winter quarter had been insanely busy, and by the time Sophie drove out of the college health clinic parking lot for her half day off, it was midafternoon, and she was starving.

Damn. She had meant to get out to the animal shelter to see Duke one last time. And now it was too late. He was already gone.

She felt a sense of regret when she thought about Duke. He had been only been a year old; a powerful black lab mix. She'd taken him on as a project dog four months earlier because of his challenges—and because as the volunteer dog trainer at the shelter, she always chose to work with the most difficult dogs. She had trained and walked him three times a week until the dog would do anything she asked—sit, down, stay, heel, and walk on a loose leash. But the minute she released him from the exercises, he'd be all over her: grabbing her with his paws, tearing her clothes, snapping at her face—behaviors she'd been unable to stop.

Then yesterday, he had started to spin in his kennel—a sign of severe kennel stress—and staff had decided to euthanize him. Today. Early this afternoon.

And now she was too late to say good-bye.

She had thought of fostering him, of getting him out of the shelter environment to see if his behavior would improve. But it hadn't been possible—not with Jake and their two dogs at home. Not with Duke's destructive tendencies. Short of living in a one-room apartment by herself and staying with him twenty-four hours a day, there was no way she could have taken him. As she pulled into her driveway, she swallowed hard. She had to let this one go. She had no other choice.

The moment Sophie cracked the door, a cacophony of barks assaulted her and a beautiful collie swept through the opening. Slender face raised, Tess greeted Sophie with exuberance; long, strawberry-blonde coat floating over white legs, ears folded back into a laugh. Behind her, Lola approached, heavy golden-retriever ears pulled into a grin, black eyes smiling.

"Hello, sweet Lola," Sophie said, fending off Tess's antics with her left hand. Lola stood still for a moment while Sophie stooped to stroke her broad head—then turned away, content to let Tess usurp the moment. Thankful for the distraction, Sophie dropped her bag and kicked off her low leather boots.

"Come on, girls! Time for couch cuddles." With the dogs at her heels, she strode into the living room and plopped onto the couch. "On stage!" she said, gesturing beside her. Both girls jumped up, one dog on either side. They vocalized with moans of pleasure while she rubbed and kissed their faces, running her hands through their coats, delighting in the sleek texture of their fur.

For a moment, Sophie felt the ache of losing Duke fall away from her, felt the intensity of diagnosing and treating fifteen patients at the clinic that morning dissolve. She drank in the rays of pale winter sunshine filtering through the large windows of the living-room. At this time of year she was thankful for the reds and golds of the large tapestry that accented one of the walls—it filled the room with a warm glow in spite of the stark world outside. For a moment, everything seemed to be suspended in time, and she took a deep breath. Then the girls leapt off the couch and Tess was barking, demanding, "What's next? It's time for a walk, for play, for the dogs!"

Sophie knew she shouldn't indulge the girls in this way. Her twenty years as a dog trainer had taught her that the best way to contain the dogs' enthusiasm when she returned home was to greet them briefly, then ignore all behavior until they were calm. But Sophie had tried this with Tess who had only become more excited and demanding at the inexplicable rudeness of not being greeted in the manner she felt she was due. So Sophie had relented and continued to support Tess's loud and boisterous welcomes. After all, Sophie thrived on them too, and except for the fact that Lola was often overshadowed, she was unconcerned. To remedy the problem, she always made a point to greet Lola first in spite of Tess's drama.

Sophie ran upstairs to change into jeans and a sweatshirt, and the girls tore past her and jumped onto the queen-size bed to watch—Tess bursting with anticipation, Lola more patient. Sophie glanced at her watch. Three-thirty. She shook her head as if to reset the hands. There was barely time to walk the girls before dark, but it would give her a chance to clear her head and start to come to terms with losing Duke before Jake got home.

She checked herself in the mirror. *Huh.* It always surprised her that her hair was more grey than dark now. She could color it—but didn't have the time or the patience, so she'd best just get used to it. Thank goodness it was still a thick mass of curls that spread past her shoulders. Her face looked more relaxed than it had at work, though it seemed like she'd lost weight—the lines around her mouth more visible, cheekbones more prominent. And her clothes hung loosely on her tall, lean body. Probably from all the stress at the shelter lately—to say nothing of work at the clinic. She splashed cold water on her face, grabbed a fleece jacket and headed downstairs with the girls close behind her.

She wrote Jake a brief note, threw on a jacket, leashed up the girls, and loaded them into the car.

LOLA

Lola sat poised in the back of the car as it rolled to a stop, anticipating what would happen next, and the moment Sophie lifted the hatchback, she soared. She knew she shouldn't leap without permission, but on this occasion—well, she just had to go.

A shout filled her ears, a hand brushed her face—and she was running, pads pounding the cool path, the breeze fresh in her nostrils, the scent of the forest flooding her soul. This was her life, her passion, and she veered off the trail, clearing logs and branches with abandon.

And then she stopped.

And listened.

Tess barked. The hatchback slammed. Deftly, Lola hopped back to the trail, trotted toward the car—and froze. She loved this part. There was something about the crouch, the slow, painstaking stalk, and the slam of shoulder to ribs that she found irresistible.

"Lola, leave it!" Sophie's voice rang out, loud and insistent.

Lola understood the message—but nothing could stop her now.

The collie trotted closer, stopped in her tracks, lifted one paw, and made eye contact. There was nothing threatening about Tess, and Lola knew there never would be. She felt powerful, totally wild and in control.

Lola sensed an alarm flicker through Tess and noted her heightened awareness. The collie turned away, yawned, licked her lips and sniffed the ground. But Lola, ignited by the thrill of the hunt, ignored Tess's appeal for peace and crept closer, fixed her eyes on the collie, and streamlined her body.

And then she charged.

She barreled toward Tess, every muscle driving her forward. The collie had curved back toward her now, was gripping the ground with her toes, her body braced, head turned slightly away. Lola steeled herself for the impact—shoulder to flank— she could already taste the grunt of shock from the collie, was already steeped in the glow of victory.

And then, inexplicably, Sophie stood between them. A monolith of reprimand she couldn't ignore.

She feinted, arced, careened around the woman, and still finessed a gratifying swipe to the collie's hip. Her sister stumbled, staggered sideways, and turned on her.

Tess

Tess regained her balance, shrieked, and threw herself at the golden with all the force she could muster. She had been through this before—the crashing blow, the pain, the unbearable rudeness of her sister—and she would not stand for it.

In a fit of anger, she grasped Lola's muzzle in her jaws and forced her to the ground, pinning her to the forest floor. She spewed her frustration in a flurry of growls, felt the power of the golden give way beneath her, and drank in Lola's submissive, obedient posture, so like the puppy she had once been. Finally, with a cascade of high-pitched reprimands and a chorus of indignant yips, she stepped back and watched Lola stand, shake herself off, and bound away.

Sophie

"Dammit!" Sophie muttered. At least Tess hadn't been injured this time. Years before, a similar attack had caused Tess to limp for months. They had tried everything to stop Lola from body slamming the lighter, finer-boned collie: blocking her, firm reprimands, a high-pitched sound deterrent, and keeping Tess on leash. But it had taken them a year to discover that the only way to stop Lola's stalk-and-attack behavior was to let Tess out of the car first and keep the golden leashed for the first five minutes of a walk. When Lola was finally released, she would trot off quite happily, and other than affectionate communication, would leave Tess completely alone.

Sophie made a mental note to refresh Lola's understanding

of "wait" when the hatchback was opened so she could release Tess first. Where that brutish behavior came from in two dogs so bonded since puppyhood, she didn't know. Surely, with Lola so dependent on her slightly older sister, and with their close, loving relationship, such slamming behavior should never happen. She shook her head and let out a sigh. She had to accept that, on many levels, canine politics could be complicated.

With the girls running ahead, Sophie picked up her pace and jogged after them, letting the late afternoon sunshine seduce her. The path meandered between huge trunks in shades of muted blue-green and grey, then angled its way down a steep hill toward the beaver pond through stands of maple, their massive boles glowing green with thick moss and cascading licorice ferns.

Expectation and happiness written all over her face, Lola charged back up the trail, slid to a halt in front of Sophie, and snatched the salmon cookie from Sophie's fingers.

"Good girl, Lu, now go play!" Sophie said. Lola raced off again to explore the woods. As she thundered past her sister, Tess stepped aside, gave the golden an affectionate snap, and bounded after her.

With the girls occupied, Sophie lost herself in the morass of the shelter. Where had she gone wrong with Duke? She had worked so hard with him. It had been impossible to spend time giving him TLC because he was so combative when touched, but she had done everything else she could.

Were there drugs that could have helped him? It was a moot point, really, because in the shelter, psych medications were not an option. With one part-time veterinarian and limited funds available to care for all the animals, anything more than basic veterinary care was impossible.

She had to admit, even if Duke hadn't started the high-stress spinning behavior that was his death knell, he was not adoptable. And if *she* couldn't imagine living with him, how could she expect anyone else to?

She became aware of Tess pacing beside her. She stooped and ran her fingers through the collie's ruff. What would she ever do without Jake and her girls? They were her light, her anchor, her sanity. Tess nuzzled her hand, and finding no cookies, trotted off down the trail.

Then Sophie remembered something. It burst into her mind with a brightness that took her breath away. Josie, who owned the doggie-daycare and training facility where she worked as a trainer, had mentioned a shelter program called "Open Paw." It had been started by Kelly Gorman-Dunbar in California, and it coached volunteers on how to encourage calm, good behavior while the dogs transitioned through shelter life. It supplied an outline of skills to teach the dogs to help them get adopted, and since Sophie already taught weekly classes to shelter volunteers, how hard could it be to implement such a program?

A spark ignited in her solar plexus—the same one that had kindled her marathon training each time; the one that had spurred her on through graduate school. She could do this, and in doing so, she would save lives. She would order the materials when she got home, then call Emma, the shelter director, and get permission to implement it.

"Jake? Are you home?" Sophie knelt to dry the girls' paws. They would offer up their front paws, but she had never been able to teach them to lift their back paws on command.

"Sophie?" She heard Jake's voice call down from the bedroom, but before she could respond, Tess took off at a dead run up the stairs. "Tessie!"

The rest of Jake's greeting was drowned in a volley of excited barks, and when Lola and Sophie joined them a moment later, Tess had center stage, cavorting and circling against Jake's legs. He teased her, scratched her back and face, and the collie grinned up at him, ears flicking up and down in hysterical delight. Lola walked to his side, stretched into a delicious greeting, and secured a few pats before she hopped onto the bed to observe.

Jake looked up from Tess, brown eyes smiling from behind round glasses, his curly salt-and-pepper hair framing a lean, tired face.

"How was your day, Sophie?" He folded his six-foot frame to

the floor and Tessie, delighted, stood on his lap and nuzzled his chin. He leaned back against the wall, weaving his fingers into her ruff. He looked strained, the lines in his face more visible than she'd ever seen them.

"I didn't get out till three, so I couldn't make it to the shelter in time. They euthanized Duke today." Sophie choked on the words, her voice sounding thick and foreign. She avoided his eyes and bit her lip, ran her fingers through her hair and pulled hard on the roots. Then she forced herself to look back at Jake.

"Wow. They euthanized him? God, you worked so hard with him. But I guess you can't save them all. Not there." He reached up and took her hand. His voice was low and soothing and with it, her carefully constructed poise melted.

The grief she had fought to contain all afternoon escaped in a long, shuddering sob. She wiped her eyes with a rough swipe of her sleeve. "I know. I got tied up at the clinic with a girl who most likely has appendicitis, so I couldn't leave." She shook her head, breathed in, rubbed her face, and reset herself. "How was your day?"

"I had another parent-teacher meeting with Johnny's mother this afternoon." His mouth twisted downward. "That woman's crazy!"

"Only six more months, babe. You can do it." She was relieved that her voice sounded almost level now, the quiver gone. She didn't want to think about Duke any more. She didn't want Jake to know how devastated she was. She slid to the floor opposite him.

"How was your walk?" he asked.

"Lola bashed Tessie again. She just jumped right out of the car before I got the leash on her. I blocked her, but she still clipped Tessie's hip."

"You need to be more vigilant," Jake said. "You space out a lot." His tone was light with teasing in spite of his weariness, oblivious to the warning glance that Sophie flashed him. He looked down and rubbed the collie's ears. She lay beside him, leaning against his leg, utterly content. "What's on for this weekend?"

"Tomorrow I need to go to the shelter. And Jake, I came up with this great thought." She began to pour out what she knew of the Open Paw program, an edge of hysteria driving her words.

Jake cut her off. "You need to really think about this. It'll take up a lot of your time, and you're already out there way too much. You know what you're like."

Unfortunately, she did. Especially when it came to the shelter. She was addicted, obsessed, unable to pull herself away—and this would drag her in even deeper.

"I have to do this, Jake. Don't try to talk me out of it." She threw him a challenging look, then deflected it to the collie.

"What about the girls? You spend less time with them than you used to already."

Shit. That was true, too. She bit her lip. She'd figure out how to do it all—she always had, though at fifty-two she didn't have the stamina she'd had even three years ago.

"Do you have time for a hike tomorrow before you go out there?" Jake asked.

Damn! She wanted to research the program before contacting Emma in the morning, but now she risked proving Jake's point if she declined.

"I'd love to!" She took Jake's hand and kissed it in a clumsy attempt to compensate. He always knew when she didn't mean what she said. "We'll have almost the whole weekend together, I promise."

Sophie checked her watch. "Time for the girls' dinner." She stood up, took a step toward the stairs, and a whirlwind of fur and noise accosted her.

"Is it that time, girls?"

Once Sophie started to prepare their dinner, however, the girls sat politely. And when their bowls were licked clean, they lay close by, paws resting on the hardwood floor, gold and red bodies relaxed side by side on the carpet of the adjacent dining room, waiting for "the next part".

When it was light in the evenings, Tess would lie by the glass doors of the dining room and gaze past the large deck to the meadow of tall grass and alder beyond. If she were lucky, she'd see deer grazing or a cat stalking mice, and with a shriek of annoyance, would do her best to chase them away. But when it was dark like tonight, she positioned herself right next to the kitchen, anticipating special bits of chicken or cheese that came her way once Jake and Sophie started cooking. Lola, on the other hand, never gave up her begging position, and gobbled tomatoes and bananas indiscriminately as well as any form of protein she was offered.

When dinner was ready, the coffee table set, and the fire lit, they settled into their favorite spots to watch the six o'clock news. Jake sat in a civilized manner on the couch, while Sophie parked herself on the floor and leaned against the couch with the coffee table in front of her. Lola ambled over and stretched out with a satisfied groan—her large head placed definitively in Sophie's lap, anchoring her in place. Tess wedged her lean body between Lola and the couch, head perched on slender white paws inches from Sophie's elbow.

This dinner ritual was a tradition with complicated origins, but it had to do with Lola's skill as Sophie's trainer, Sophie's willingness to be trained, and Jake's tolerant nature. The girls never begged—they never drooled or stared at Sophie—but lay patiently with their heads between their paws. For their good behavior, they were intermittently rewarded with small treats—at least, that was Sophie's interpretation.

After dinner, Sophie checked with the hospital to find that Kathy had indeed been diagnosed with appendicitis and undergone surgery. Relieved that the girl was safe and sound, she settled in for her favorite part of the day.

The rest of the evening was given over to quality time with Tess and Lola, followed by a good movie. Sophie loved evenings with her family. Their routines filled her with a warm, heady glow—she lived for a lot of things, but her evenings were sacred. Tonight, however, she was distracted—haunted by Duke. But at the same time she buzzed with possibilities.

CHAPTER 3

VERA

The next twenty-four hours were a blur for Vera. By the time the truck came to a halt, she was trembling in fear and pain, crouched in the corner of the truck bed. The man dragged her out, forced her into a crate and slammed the door. It reeked—a thick animal smell laced with a strange, acrid odor completely foreign to her. A few shards of light filtered through a grille at the top of the door. She had no idea where she was, and for a long time nothing happened.

Then she heard voices.

She tensed, hackles rising along her back, and when the door of her kennel opened, she froze. They placed a noose around her neck and strong, gentle hands lifted her out.

"God, she stinks!" A loud, unexpected voice startled Vera, and she sank back on her haunches. "Any paperwork on her?"

"No...just a second, here it is—'Vera' it says. No owner name. Eighteen months old. An outside dog—sure is skinny. And check out that tummy—at least one litter of puppies."

"Yeah, and looks like a shepherd mix. She's limping—left rear? Better have the vet check her out first thing tomorrow. And look at this collar. Jesus!" The tension eased at Vera's throat and she shook off. "Glad we checked these kennels one last time before we locked up." The voices settled into a low, quiet murmur. "How can anyone do this to an animal?" Their words tumbled past her, but Vera found the firm, quiet quality of their hands to be comforting along her back and neck, then they were walking.

One of the women led Vera away from the after-hours drop-off shed, through a door, and into a low building. She smelled chickens and heard them clucking somewhere nearby, but then the door banged shut behind her. She jumped away from the sound. She had never been inside a building before and she tucked her tail more tightly between her legs. Her back arched, her ears lay back against her skull, and her tongue flicked and flicked out of her mouth.

The building reeked of animals, and cages of chain link and concrete lined one side of the corridor. Dogs barked savagely at her from behind the kennel doors, and she plastered herself against the wall, staying as far away from them as she possibly could.

She'd never had much to do with other dogs. Occasionally, stray dogs had come to steal food from beside her shed, and she'd fought them off, raging and biting hard at their necks, ears, and legs to get rid of them. And there was the dog who had mounted her after a long and exhausting fight. Somehow she'd made it through the ordeal, but after that, she hadn't trusted dogs again.

The women finally led her into one of the kennels where she could see a bucket filled with water—but even though thirst burned her throat, she was too afraid to drink. Carefully, she curled up on a thick blanket, tucked her tail over her nose, and watched the hallway, statue still, panic careening through her limbs. One or two people passed her kennel, leading dogs that barked and strained at the leash, but no one noticed her. One of the women offered her a bowl of food, but the smell of it repulsed her.

A man took her outside and left her alone. It was almost dark, but she could see an expanse of gravel contained by a high fence. She stood still and silent, scenting the air, and after a while the man returned and took her back to her kennel. The lights went out and she lay in the dark, eyes and ears twitching. Finally she slept, surfacing frequently to the muffled sounds of sleeping dogs; a few whimpered, some snored softly, and from time to time the quiet was punctuated by a sharp bark. Outside, she heard the wind heave and sigh through the trees. She was numb.

The next morning, she awakened to a burst of light, the sound of footsteps, and the clang of kennel doors. The atmosphere exploded with the clamor of barking dogs as, one by one, they were led past the long row of kennels to the yard.

She'd hear the tap-tap-tap of nails on the floor, and the heavy step of the animal-care staffer's boots, then a flash of movement as the dogs passed her. Then they would disappear, their progress defined by the barking from kennels down the row.

She took in her surroundings. The front of her kennel was slightly larger than the door to her shed had been, and beyond that was the corridor. On either side of her were concrete walls, and in the back of the kennel was a small door just slightly higher and wider than her body.

She stood and stretched as was her custom, noting that her hips weren't as tight and sore as they had been the previous day. A sharp pain lanced down her side, but it dulled as she finished the stretch.

Out of habit she sat and scratched at her neck, again eliciting the sharp stab of pain—but something was missing—the collar was gone. She didn't remember it being removed, but nevertheless, it was no longer there. She scratched again just to be sure—the weight of the chain on her neck was missing too. This sudden awareness was at once liberating and unsettling; for as long as she could remember, these things had been part of her life.

When she finished stretching and scratching, she cautiously ventured through the door at the back of her kennel. The other side looked exactly the same as the front and she started to feel safer. The trembling in her core relaxed a little, and she curled up on her blanket.

Without warning, a figure appeared in the corridor and reached for her kennel door; Vera cowered. She'd always liked people—some intrinsic part of her was drawn to them. In spite of the numerous beatings she had sustained over her eighteen months of life, in spite of the neglect, she had always felt a lightening of spirit when she saw them. But time had taken its toll, and now she drew back.

"Vera, it's OK. I'm Jessie. I'm just taking you outside." Although the words meant nothing to Vera yet, she liked the soft, easy tone of the woman's voice; in fact she recognized it from the night before. The woman looped the slip-leash over her head and past her ears. It felt familiar, this pressure on her neck, so Vera stood and followed her out of the kennel, down the dimly lit hallway, past the row of barking dogs, and into an enclosure. In one swift movement the woman removed the leash, turned away, and was gone. Vera was alone.

Vera didn't really know how she felt. Everything was so new. Yet here she was—alone without the chain and with a thousand new and interesting smells to investigate. She walked forward and relieved her bursting bladder, then started a systematic inventory of her surroundings. The enclosure was bordered by a high fence. Across from her was a forest, and beside her was another yard identical to the one where she stood.

The gravel surface was rich with the scent of dogs, and nose to the ground, she slowly made her way around the perimeter, picking up the age and sex of more dogs than she could imagine. Her heart drummed faster, her paws danced with excitement.

The door opened and the same woman reappeared. Vera recognized her by her unique smell, the lilt in her voice, and her definitive movements. "Come on, Vera. You have to eat before you see the vet." Hearing her name, Vera flinched, but allowed herself to be leashed and led back to her kennel where she found a bowl of food. It smelled better than anything she'd ever tasted before, and this time she ate, hesitantly at first, then greedily, as the depth of her hunger overwhelmed her.

Sometime later, Jessie led Vera past the kennels to a room full of white light and angles, the air cut with a harsh scent she recognized from the crate the day before.

"Don't be scared, Vera. This is Dr. Sims," Jessie said in a quiet voice.

A tall woman with intense eyes stood across the room, watching her. The vet said a few words to Jessie, her voice bouncing off the brilliant walls, then she knelt down and reached out to Vera. The vet's eye-to-eye contact was excruciating, the hand monstrous, and Vera ached to retreat. She looked away and licked, plastered her ears against her skull, and bolted for the door. But the leash brought her up short.

There were more words, voices flecked with concern, and then Vera felt Jessie's firm hand on her back.

"Vera, come over here." Vera's eyes flashed to the sound of the vet's sweetened voice. But when the woman's hand retraced its path toward her, she cowered into Jessie's leg.

An unexpected movement caught Vera's eye, and she flinched as Jessie's arms grasped her chest and shoulders. To Vera's horror, Dr. Sims lifted her hind quarters. The excruciating pressure on her ribs forced her into motion again, and she kicked her back legs violently, almost pulling free.

"We're just putting you on the table, Vera!" Jessie's voice switched to a sharp, grating curse, and more on edge than ever, Vera froze. She clutched at the metal surface with her claws, the air rushed and rushed through her nostrils, her jaws clamped shut. She scanned the room for an escape. Her being convulsed, her side shrieked with pain. She couldn't think.

Then the vet was touching her. Everywhere. And although the contact itself didn't hurt, she had never felt so vulnerable. Her muscles burned and trembled, and now she was panting—harsh, raking breaths.

Jessie's arms held her in a vice-like grip, and at that moment, Dr. Sims' hand reached her left side. In a monumental struggle fueled by sheer agony, she broke free from Jessie's grasp, whipped her head around and bit the vet on the hand. Not a hard bite—Vera had learned to inhibit her bite in puppyhood. But it was hard enough.

"Ow! Dammit!" Dr. Sims jerked away. It happened in an instant, but Vera had accomplished exactly what she wanted—the hand causing the excruciating pain in her side was gone.

The women were talking again, an animated discussion, the vet's hands flying every which way, voices and words echoing through the room.

Vera felt something slip over her snout—she had no idea what it was, but it forced her mouth shut. She couldn't pant, couldn't open her mouth at all. Her nostrils flared and air hunger squeezed in on her.

Hands resumed their poking track down her side and at some point her pain reached a crescendo. A desperate, high-pitched whine culminating in a keening scream erupted from deep in her soul. It sounded strange to her, an unworldly wail she had never heard before. But it rose out of her until the hands retreated and Jessie's gentle touch broke through her panic.

"OK, OK, Vera, we'll stop for a moment," Dr. Sims soothed. And then to Jessie, "I think she has a couple of broken ribs—they don't seem to be displaced and her lungs are fine, so I don't think we need to X-ray. I still need to check out her hips if she'll let us. Let's get her down. Got her?" Vera listened, tried to understand the sounds following her name, but it became a jumble of squawk and babble, and after a moment, she was lost. Hopeless, completely overwhelmed, she stopped fighting and they lowered her to the floor.

As soon as they let her go, she ran to the far side of the room, her left side throbbing.

"She's definitely got a limp, but let's see how she does in the next couple of days. I'll try to examine her more thoroughly if she doesn't improve. Are you going to bathe her? If you do, be sure to keep her muzzled."

The words swam around her, scratched at her brain, and then she felt the leash tug at her neck and she was led to another room. Jessie stroked the side of her face—a firm, gentle gesture—and Vera melted into the hand, pressing her head into the cupped palm.

She felt herself being lifted by Jessie and another woman. This time, Vera didn't struggle—she was too tired, too worn down, and in too much pain. Her paws scrambled to find footing when she was placed onto the metal surface. A spray of warm water covered her fur, and Jessie's kind, purposeful hands began to massage her back, carefully avoiding the injured areas on her left side. She'd never felt anything quite like it before, and in spite of the bizarre, clinging sensation of soap filling her coat, and the trickle of water down her legs, she breathed more easily and felt her despair lift a little.

"Just look at all that dirt running down the drain, Vera!"

Jessie's voice was laced with reassurance, and she felt a flicker of excitement when the muzzle was removed and a large towel stroked her head, back and chest. She tried to shake off, but the sharp stab in her side stopped her.

Back in her kennel, she fled to her blanket and curled up, and feeling a modicum of safety in the confined space, she dozed—her ears alert for any change in the chaos.

CHAPTER 4

SOPHIE

The Whatcom County animal shelter was located north of Bellingham in an old building that was small, musty, and depressing. Still, the staff worked tirelessly to give the animals a good chance at life and helped as many as they could. A fundraising campaign for a new building had been underway for years, but Sophie suspected it would be several more years before they could actually purchase or build a new structure.

Sophie signed the volunteer list in the adjoining portable and checked the director's office—it was empty.

When she walked into the main building, two young women were staring at screens behind the reception desk.

"How's it going?" Sophie asked. "Is Emma around?" She had become familiar with the staff over the past two years, but it hadn't been easy. They were distrustful of volunteers on the whole, so for the most part, Sophie kept a low profile and focused on helping the dogs.

"No," one of them answered.

When she didn't offer more information, Sophie tried again. "Do you know when she'll be back?"

"Why? Is something wrong?" The chill in her voice was not lost on Sophie. The woman narrowed her eyes.

"No, I just want to talk to her about an idea I have for the dogs." Sophie tried to keep a friendly lilt in her voice, but felt her face flush. Why were these people so suspicious? For God's sake!

"Oh. She'll be out of town till the end of the week."

"Thanks." She forced her face into a tight-lipped smile, gritted her teeth and hurried back to the portable. Now what was she supposed to do? Wait till the end of the week? That wasn't an option. She'd talk to Donna, the volunteer coordinator. Maybe she'd have authority to tentatively approve the Open Paw program.

Donna was a lovely woman; gracious, thoughtful and always supportive of the volunteers. There was something magnetic about her, a sense that she could carry the world on her shoulders. Sophie liked her a lot.

But when she walked into Donna's office and introduced the idea, all she got was a blank stare.

"I can tell you right now, it's not going to happen," Donna said, her voice just as round and motherly as always. "I know about the program, but we have way too much going on to put any time or resources into something like that."

Sophie stared at her, shocked. The frown on Donna's face didn't fit with the tone of her voice. Sophie took a step back. She felt like she'd been slapped. Her cheeks lit up, her stomach contracted. "But it will help the dogs," she rasped. The words sounded inarticulate as they tripped from her mouth. "It will improve their lives. I can pay for the materials."

Donna didn't even pretend to smile. "Not going to happen, Sophie."

Sophie walked into the adoption room, completely deflated. A row of chain-link and cement kennels lined each side of the aisle, and dogs of all sizes stared up at her; some barked at the front of their kennels, while others, wide-eyed and frightened, cowered back as far as they could get. A few gazed up at her sleepily, tails thumping. She fed treats to the dogs who were quiet. If they barked, she'd turn away until they stopped, then instantly reward them.

"Sophie!" She turned to see her friend, Leah, approaching. "There's a new dog in the back. Have you seen her yet?"

"No. I just got here." She gave Leah a hug.

"She's really cute. A German shepherd. She came in two days ago. They think she may have a couple of broken ribs, so she needs to be kept quiet." Leah was a relatively new volunteer at the shelter, and a keen observer of volunteers and staff. She was small and strong and enthusiastic about learning everything she could about the dogs. "Come and see her."

Sophie followed Leah through the swinging doors marked "Staff Only" into the back of the building.

"There she is!" Leah pointed to a thin dog curled in a tight ball at the back of her kennel. Dark eyes stared at them from behind a jet-black mask, the dog's mouth a tight, closed line. Huge, black-trimmed ears tipped and swiveled in response to the kennel sounds around her. A broad, dark band traveled down her back turning pure black down the length of her tail. She was very striking in spite of her coarse, dry coat.

"Yeah, she's cute." Sophie sized her up. The dog was scared. Really scared. She reminded Sophie of a difficult dog she'd worked with recently and felt a flicker of interest in spite of her indifference to shepherds.

Sophie looked for a name on the packet of information hanging on the kennel door. "Vera," she said in a soft voice. "I'm Sophie." Vera's ears swiveled forward and her head tilted slightly to the side at the sound of Sophie's voice. "What's your story?"

Vera stared back. Her gaze softened somewhat and Sophie tossed her a few small pieces of string cheese through the kennel door. Vera ignored them. "She's not taking the cheese. She must be really stressed."

"Yeah," said Leah. "She's bonding with Jessie, though. I heard she's had a hard time. She should get adopted pretty fast, don't you think?"

"I hope so. Shepherds don't tend to do well in shelters—they get stressed out so easily," Sophie said. "Have you heard when they'll put her up for adoption?"

Leah bent down to toss Vera a liver treat. "She's going to have to heal first, so it'll be a while."

"She's got a beautiful face." Sophie smiled down at Vera's quizzical expression. It seemed like the dog was trying hard to understand what they were saying.

"Yeah, she does," said Leah. "I wish we could take her out." Her voice had a wistful quality. Sophie could relate. "If only..." seemed to drive many of their conversations.

Sophie found it extremely frustrating that volunteers were not authorized to interact with the dogs until the animals had been officially temperament tested, evaluated by the vet, and released from any legal complications. The fact that some dogs were held for months in the "stray kennels" at the back of the shelter while their owners were taken to court on a variety of neglect and abuse charges seemed criminal. But she knew this was the law and that the staff did their best to take special care of these dogs. It was out of her hands.

"Sorry about Duke. I heard about him this morning when I came in," Leah said.

Sophie gave her a wan smile. "Thanks. I'm going to walk Sarah now—maybe that'll cheer me up." Sophie tried to make her voice upbeat, tried to stuff back the surge of emotion that threatened to ambush her. In the adoptable-dog section, she found an extra-large front-attachment harness and a heavy leash, and headed for Sarah's kennel.

Sarah had been at the shelter for three weeks now and Sophie adored her. She was a ninety-pound mix of German shepherd, Rottweiler, and Airedale, and she was full of life. Sarah already fancied herself the queen of the shelter and considered Sophie her personal volunteer. Sophie would have adopted Sarah in a heartbeat, but she couldn't consider it with Tess and Lola at home. Sarah was a much better bet for adoption than Duke would have been, but her seven-year-old girls would be too overwhelmed by Sarah's energy. And besides, the last thing Sophie wanted was three dogs.

Sophie stood quietly outside the kennel while Sarah leapt and barked a frantic greeting, her head bouncing higher than Sophie's in her excitement. After about fifteen seconds, Sarah sat down and Sophie quickly fed her cheese through the chain link.

"Good girl, Sarah." Sophie placed her hand on the kennel

latch, eliciting another frenzy of jumping. Sophie removed her hand and spun away, and with remarkable speed and precision, Sarah sat. The next time Sophie opened the latch, Sarah remained seated.

Sophie beamed down at her, squeezed into the kennel, and was greeted by another round of hysteria. But Sophie was ready, and quickly held a piece of string cheese directly in front of the dog's nose.

"Sarah, sit!" Toys flew sideways from the beat of the dog's tail as Sarah sat, and Sophie stroked her whiskery face with a slow, firm pressure. "Good girl, sweetie."

Concerns forgotten, she slipped the harness over Sarah's enormous head and shoulders, snapped it firmly in place, and opened the kennel door.

CHAPTER 5

VERA

Vera lay in her kennel in a state of semiconsciousness. After a month, she had grown accustomed to the early morning sounds and routines of the shelter. The slam of kennel doors and the barking of dogs would awaken her, then she'd be led to the yard which she'd explore in minute detail. Returning to her kennel, she would find a bowl of food and fresh water. She saw a few people every day—sometimes male, sometimes female. They talked to her, and she began to enjoy their presence. Only Jessie spent time in her kennel or touched her, but no one seemed to be angry, or threatened to hurt her in any way. The days were predictable, and the predictability brought her a level of comfort.

On this particular morning, she stood and stretched as usual, anticipating the walk to the exercise yard. Her side and hip were no longer painful. Living in such an enclosed space, she tried to hold her urine for as long as possible, but if she needed to wait too long, she would walk through the small door and relieve herself in the rear part of the kennel. Today, however, the man was early. "Hello, Vera." She recognized him. Rob.

She stepped into the yard with confidence, nostrils flaring, and noticed the presence of another dog in the adjacent enclosure. She glanced over and sniffed the air to catch the dog's scent. Male. Young. He seemed uninterested in her and did not make eye contact, so she turned away and did her business then sniffed the gravel, losing herself in the new smells caught in the crevices between the stones from the night before.

Moments later, the man was back again. "Let's go, Vera. Time for your temperament test."

He led her back down the corridor and through a door she hadn't seen before. A strange woman stood motionless in the middle of the room staring at her. Vera stopped in her tracks.

"Hey, Christa," Rob said. "This is Vera. I didn't feed her."

The temperament test was a series of exercises that Vera needed to perform before she was put up for adoption. Its purpose was to evaluate the dog's response to direct eye contact, touch, stressors, and to root out any tendency toward resource guarding and aggression. It also evaluated the dog's initial response to other dogs.

As soon as she was led into the room, Vera could sense discord. It prickled across her skin, making each hair on her body bristle with discomfort. She studied Christa closely. The woman's eyes flicked toward her then held her gaze. She felt vulnerable. She felt like prey.

When Christa took the leash and sat on a chair in the center of the room, Vera pulled away as far as she could. The woman smelled of anger, frustration, and darkness, and Vera turned away, flashing the white crescents of her eyes in distrust. Her legs shook beneath her, and a boiling panic rose through her chest, poured through her limbs.

Suddenly, Christa's demeanor changed, and her expression brightened. She leaned back in the chair, turned her head away, and took deep, slow breaths. A soothing voice hummed out of her. "Vera," she said, "you're such a good girl."

Vera studied the new, welcoming posture, and finally her curiosity got the best of her. She took a few steps closer, stretched her nose forward, and sniffed the woman's knees, transfixed for a moment by the scent of dogs layered into her clothes. Another step forward, and Christa's hand connected with her face, chest and neck. Vera liked the gentle pressure that flowed down her fur, and she shifted her weight closer still.

Then the hands stopped moving: they were now enfolding her head and muzzle, one on either side—and when she looked up to better judge the situation, Christa's eyes made direct contact with hers. Vera struggled and averted her gaze—but Christa's grip kept her immobilized. In desperation, she wrenched free and turned away.

"See how stiff and tucked her body is with eye contact, Rob? I'm stressing her out, but she's still doing OK—at least she didn't bite me." The voice caught Vera off guard, and she flinched.

Christa stood up slowly and Vera felt the tension ease on the leash. With relief, she ran to a corner of the room where she buried her nose in the scent of a dog that lingered from days earlier; the faint odor blocked out the room, the people, the sounds. When she felt the pressure return to her neck, she was more relaxed, and followed Christa back to the center of the room without resisting.

"The next part is the 'tag test,'" said Christa. "I'll try to get her to play, then 'tag' her to see how she copes. Move that chair against the wall, but don't scrape it on the floor or you'll scare her." Vera looked up at the woman, startled by the sharpness of her tone.

Without warning, Christa let out a string of high, squeaky sounds and dashed across the room. A bolt of indecision ricocheted through Vera's head and she pricked up her ears and leapt forward in pursuit. But the woman had changed direction and ran past her—too close. The shepherd felt a sharp jab to her hip. She stopped, tail tucked tight under her belly, and crept toward Rob. But before she panicked, the woman took off again, squeaky and playful. Excitement flared through Vera. *Chase!* It felt so exhilarating to romp and bound. She raced after Christa, flew back as the woman changed direction. Then that hand hit her again. A shaft of pain lanced through her injured hip. The room blurred. She wheeled around, poised to fend off a further assault only to see the woman walk away.

"Vera, come," Christa called. Her voice was quiet again, her body angled away, her eyes soft and averted.

Vera took a step forward, then another, and eventually Christa was able to reach out and stroke her chest and ears.

The test continued, and with each exercise, Vera's gut churned harder and harder. Filled with confusion, she cringed and cowered. Christa offered food, only to whisk it away when Vera reached for her second mouthful; she was poked and prodded; and when Rob finally took the leash and stepped toward the door, Vera raced ahead of him, crowding the exit before he had time to turn the handle.

She dragged Rob down the passageway, and when she reached her kennel, she stopped and rooted herself to the floor, looking straight at her bed.

"I think you're gonna pass the test," Rob said. His voice was low and encouraging and she let it seep into her, let it calm her panic. "You can eat now if you want." But Vera fled to her blanket leaving her food untouched. She lay very still. She didn't even move when two dogs trotted past.

Moments later, Rob was back.

Vera balked at first, but his gentle persistence got the best of her and she followed him down the hallway and back to that room. He opened the door.

A dog! Her ears folded back and her tail wagged in eager anticipation. She sniffed the air. He was male. She stepped forward, taking in the light-colored, square face, the large, heavy ears, the sturdy chest. Her ears flicked forward. She stopped and stiffened, tail high, ready for anything.

But the dog was attached to Christa, and he sniffed the floor and wagged in an easy, friendly manner. She detected no threat in the loose body, but she was cautious. He glanced at her and looked away. Lifted a paw. Vera softened. He seemed all right, his presence uncomplicated.

"Good girl, Vera. This is Jackson."

She sniffed toward the dog again and took a step closer.

The dog became more of a magnet to Vera with each moment. She took in his scent, the loose posture, the relaxed tail. His language captivated and thrilled her, but she couldn't shake her underlying unease.

Then the dog made eye contact. His gaze hardened to lasers. His head lifted a degree, his body stiffened, and the soft tail froze. It happened in an instant, a fraction of a second, but Vera caught every nuance of his challenge.

Vera launched, lunged with all her might to fend off the attack before it started. Her scream shredded the silence. The power and fluidity of her movements shocked her and she was on the dog before she knew it, teeth grazing his muzzle. Christa stumbled backward, the dog wrenched away with her.

Rob scrambled, jerked the leash, and Vera fell, the slip leash a noose on her neck. She choked, struggled for breath, coughed.

"Vera!" Rob's roar filled the room.

Vera gripped the floor with her nails, body taut and shaking against the leash. She stared at the dog where he preened and glowed in the woman's arms.

Christa raised her head and turned to Vera, her mouth twisted, eyes slits, forehead a network of wrinkles. "Get her out of here!"

Dragging Rob behind her, Vera fled.

Alone in her kennel, Vera curled up on her blanket, back braced against the wall. Confusion dizzied her. The air was steeped in the fetid odors that had poured from Rob, but she had no idea that her fear and his stress were connected.

Her kennel door banged.

Jessie.

The end of Vera's tail twitched in greeting and she eased onto her side. The woman squatted beside her, and Vera absorbed the delicious, firm strokes that massaged her belly. They sat together for awhile, Vera basking in the calm warmth of someone she trusted.

Then voices shattered the silence. Vera sprang to her feet.

"...so that's it, Rob," Christa's voice as hard as steel. "Don't argue with me. She failed. She tried to attack my dog and I already told you, I'm not passing her. She's aggressive."

"But…" Rob looked down at Vera.

Vera fixed her eyes on him. His hands raked through his hair in frantic strokes, and she smelled confusion pouring from his skin.

"Can't we redo the test?" he pleaded. "She was so stressed."

"Nope. We need the kennel space."

Vera saw muscles flex in Jessie's jaw, saw tension line her eyes. "Why did she fail?"

"She went after Jackson," Christa said. "It was bad. If she'd reached him, she would have done some real damage."

"Yeah, but when she first saw him she looked friendly. She even looked OK when she walked toward him," Rob said. "You told me that meant she'd pass."

"What else did she fail?" Jessie thrust open the door, slammed it behind her, and stepped into the woman's space, forcing Christa back a step. Vera smelled the rage, and saw the conflict carved into the lines of their faces, their short tight mouths, their rigid bodies. It terrified her.

"She was freaked out and scared the whole time too," Christa said. "This dog is unpredictable." She glared at Jessie. "Don't you dare tell me how to do my job. C'mon, Vera, let's go."

Vera watched Jessie slide past Christa, run down the hall and disappear. Her heart slammed against her ribs, and the violent tremors in her legs made it difficult to stand. A leash was slipped over her head and pressure encircled her neck. *Escape!* She tensed to flee, but Rob blocked the door. She couldn't pass.

"You're really going to euthanize her *now*?"

"Get out of the way, Rob." Christa glared at him and he stepped aside.

Vera fought when Christa dragged her out and turned the wrong direction. This was not the way she wanted to go and she strained against the noose, desperate to go outside to the small, familiar gravel yard. But Christa held her tight and jerked her along. The woman's fury was like a dense fog in the air around her. Vera calmed, withdrew, wrapped herself in a world of silence and grey until the kennels vanished and the dogs disappeared. She seemed to be caught in an endless hallway with Christa's legs drumming and drumming beside her.

And then Christa stopped. A door loomed in front of them, and from the crack beneath it oozed an odor that forced Vera back to the present and shook her to the core. It was the unmistakable smell of death.

CHAPTER 6

SOPHIE

It was Sophie's afternoon off and she was late—again. Why did it always seem that she worked at a frenzied pace on Wednesday mornings so she could get out at noon, only to be detained by unexpectedly complicated patients? It happened every week. She had wanted to have a couple of hours at the shelter before going home to walk Tess and Lola before dinner.

Today, three weeks since she had first mentioned the Open Paw program to the director, Emma had finally agreed to sit down and talk with her. They were to meet at the shelter at two o'clock and she didn't want to be late.

When she arrived, Sophie headed straight to Emma's office, trying to look and feel confident. She had known Emma for three years. The first year, the director hadn't even acknowledged Sophie's existence. The second year, Emma had started talking to her and, Sophie thought, started to respect her for her dedication to the dogs. This year, they'd developed what might be called a guarded friendship.

Sophie was wired with anticipation. In spite of Donna's refusal to offer even the slightest hope for the program, Sophie had ordered the information and received the video tapes and book in the mail a week ago. She had reviewed all of the materials, and was ready to defend her cause. She snuck past Donna's office, feeling guilty about going behind her back, but felt she didn't have a choice.

"I've heard of the program. Tell me about it," Emma said

once Sophie was seated. The woman's direct stare was somewhat unnerving. She had placed the file she'd been holding on the desk and her hands were now still, folded in front of her. Sophie had Emma's full attention.

Sophie drew in a deep breath and presented her plan. First, she would teach staff and volunteers how to interact with and train the dogs according to Open Paw protocol. This would involve weekly classes on handling and obedience and would be based on positive reinforcement training. In addition, if they could get enough Kongs (a hollow rubber toy), the dogs would be fed with kibble-stuffed Kongs exclusively—to mentally stimulate them and fulfill their foraging drive.

Sophie's expectation of the program was that the staff, the administration, and the board would buy into it. There would be more to the program once they were all involved, but this was where Sophie would start.

"Sounds pretty comprehensive," Emma said. "I like parts of it, but we can't involve the staff or the board—or the administration at this point. I'll support it, but that's all I can do." Her mouth clamped shut and her eyes returned to the folder.

"But the whole shelter needs to buy into it," Sophie argued. Her pulse quickened, her words tumbled faster. She leaned into Emma's space. "The dogs' behavior won't change if the volunteers are treating them one way and the staff another. And without the support of the administration, there's no way the staff will buy into it."

"That's all I can do for now," Emma said. "I know from experience that implementing programs in a shelter environment needs to be done slowly." Her voice seemed to soften, but when Sophie searched Emma's face for some sign of vulnerability, she couldn't find it. The woman's face was a mask. Perfectly made up. Perfectly unreadable.

Sophie swept her bangs from her forehead and tried to match Emma's level of determination. "Why can't we at least get the support of the board? I'd be happy to do a presentation for them." She could hear herself speaking louder now, her voice rising. Her mouth was desert dry. "And what about feeding solely with Kongs? That's an integral part of the program—makes the dogs forage for their food, stimulates them mentally. Keeps them sane."

"The board has too much on its plate right now. And I don't agree with the Kong-feeding part of the program. Of course you can give them stuffed Kongs, but I don't believe that the dogs should work for their food—some of these dogs have been starving their whole lives and they live for that bowl of food being placed in front of them twice a day."

Sophie silently agreed with this point, but there was no way she was going to acknowledge it. Foraging seemed like a perfectly reasonable way to challenge and stimulate the dogs—anything to relieve the boredom of the kennel. She shifted in her seat.

"Volunteers can stuff the Kongs we have, but we can't afford to buy more. And I'm not going to ask the staff to stuff them. They have enough to do. Thanks for coming in." Emma turned her attention back to her desk, hands busy shuffling and straightening her workspace.

Sophie stood and kept her poise. Part of her felt defeated, but at least Emma hadn't thrown out the idea completely.

She took her outline back to the car, trying to feel positive. From her own experience as a nursing supervisor, she knew that things sometimes had to be implemented at glacial speed. But when it came to the dogs' mental wellbeing, she found herself in a state of outrage. Why didn't Emma see this as a priority, especially since Sophie would be doing most of the work?

She checked her watch. Today she just had time for a quick walk with Sarah before heading home to hike with the girls. She'd need to put some thought into how she'd proceed with the project.

She squared her shoulders, grabbed a harness and leash, and headed for Sarah's kennel.

CHAPTER 7

SOPHIE

Sophie found herself in knots for the next two days at work. She tried to focus on what was at hand, but she was distracted. Thursday crawled by. She was desperate to get home to organize her approach at the shelter. She recognized this stage of obsession in herself, but she rode the wave and enjoyed the thrill of starting something new, something that would have an impact. She loved starting and organizing programs. And from the projects she'd supervised and implemented as a nurse, she knew she was good at it.

After work, she took the girls for a short romp, then settled down at her computer to sketch out a more comprehensive timeline for what she could accomplish, what she would include in each class, and how to get word out to the volunteers. Being a volunteer herself, she didn't have authority to access volunteer email addresses and phone numbers. She'd have to negotiate that aspect with Emma.

She was working out a class schedule when she felt a touch on her thigh. She looked down to see Lola's pale form standing beside her, tail sweeping from side to side, black eyes raised to hers in the blue light of the computer screen. The room swam in darkness. It must be later than she'd thought. She caressed Lola's ears.

"Sorry I'm so distracted, baby girl. I promise I'll be better." She stretched, and realized Tess was at her side too, woofing and shaking off. Lola spun around and led the way downstairs to the kitchen.

Sophie turned on the lights and prepared the girls' dinner, forcing herself to focus on the task at hand and, most importantly, on her own wonderful dogs. Tomorrow she'd go back out to the shelter and start to solidify her plan. She was psyched.

Friday afternoon, she marched into the shelter at one o'clock. For once she had at least two hours to spend with the dogs—as long as she was home by three thirty, she'd have time to walk her girls before dark. She posted the class schedule on the volunteer information board, checked Emma's office—it was empty—and made a beeline for the kennels.

She scanned the list of adoptable dogs. Yes, Sarah was still there. And she was delighted to see that Vera's name was listed for the first time. For the last month, she'd gone by Vera's kennel most days when she was at the shelter and tossed her bits of string cheese, chicken, or steak—whatever special treat she'd had at home for Tess and Lola. She had begun to form a relationship with the dog. Now Vera would come to the front of the kennel when she saw Sophie approach. This was good—the scared, traumatized dogs needed all the help they could get, and she could see that Vera was improving.

Sophie hurried between the double row of kennels and found Vera on the left. "Hey, Vera. You finally made it up for adoption! You must be all healed." She tossed Vera some string cheese and the dog gulped it down.

Vera's paperwork hung on the front of the kennel, and Sophie leafed through it to see how her temperament test had gone. Her volunteer sheet had a couple of entries on it: "Scared. Couldn't harness her," summarized the volunteer comments. That meant the dog hadn't been outside of the shelter compound in over a month.

To her surprise, the temperament test score showed that Vera had barely passed. It stated that she was fearful and distrustful of humans, which didn't surprise Sophie. But it also said that she was dog-aggressive. There was a handwritten note at the bottom of the page, partially scratched out and re-written, stating that she had been stressed when the test started. "*At first she showed interest in the neutral dog—but after about 30 seconds, she lunged at the dog aggressively. Because she looked OK at first, I'm going to pass her but she should be retested in a couple of weeks.*"

Sophie had just finished reading the report when Leah appeared, struggling with a medium-sized pit bull. He barked frantically at the dogs in their kennels while Leah tried to keep him close to her. Sophie opened his kennel door.

"Thanks," Leah said. She asked the dog to sit, removed his harness, and tossed treats on the floor to direct him away from the door while she escaped. "He's got so much energy and he's so strong. We saw squirrels when we were out and he went nuts. Just about pulled me over."

"We should try a gentle leader on him next time. Have you heard anything about Vera? She almost failed her temperament test." Sophie turned back to look at the shepherd. Vera's gaze was fixed on her.

"No, I hadn't heard that. You should talk to Jessie. She's here today. She might know something."

Walking through the stray area, Sophie glanced at the dogs. One was hidden behind a blanket, and an older golden retriever with a silver muzzle looked confused and anxious. Sophie wondered what they were thinking and she swallowed hard. Sometimes this place really bothered her.

She found Jessie tucked in the dingy laundry room folding towels. "Have you got a minute?"

"Sure." The woman glanced up, a halo of dark hair framing a ruddy, cheerful face.

"Do you know anything about Vera's temperament test? I saw that she almost failed. Maybe I can help."

Jessie motioned her around the corner. "I probably shouldn't tell you this, but Christa came this close to euthanizing Vera," she whispered, holding up her thumb and index finger a centimeter apart.

Sophie's stomach lurched. It felt too soon to lose another dog she'd bonded with. She'd visited Vera each time she came in, and had seen a lot of improvement in the shepherd. "Why?"

"She said that Vera didn't warm up fast enough—she was apparently scared to death through the whole test."

"But that's not enough to fail her. She'll get better over time."

"I know, but then Vera went crazy in the dog-meets-dog part of the test. Christa used her own dog and he can be pretty touchy—so it doesn't surprise me. But Christa was really upset."

"I guess I can understand that." Sophie imagined her own distress if a large, aggressive dog came after one of her girls.

Would she really want that dog out in the world at large? Still…
Vera seemed so sweet and vulnerable. "What happened?"

"It was crazy. Rob said that Vera looked pretty friendly with
Jackson at first."

"So technically, she should have passed?"

"Yeah. I found Dr. Sims and Emma in the clinic."

"And they stopped her?"

"Well, it just so happens that Vera's a universal blood donor—
she's donated blood twice already." Jessie gave Sophie an impish
smile. "They get really excited about these dogs because there
aren't many around—it's great for the community and it makes
Emma look good as the director. So they stopped Christa just as
she was taking Vera into the euthanasia room!"

"Great timing!" Sophie said. "Thank God you were there."

Jessie looked down at the floor and pushed a strand of hair
behind her ear. "Yeah, some dogs really get to me and Vera's one
of them. I want her to have a chance. Anything you can do to
help her would be great."

Sophie walked back past the long row of kennels and through
the double doors to where Vera was curled on her blanket. The
dog had probably been scared and stressed and felt threatened in
some way. However, Sophie wasn't at all sure it was a good thing
that Vera was working as a blood donor—a process that meant
regular visits to the veterinary blood bank in town where she'd
be sedated and have blood drawn every two weeks. She was too
scared. But if it kept the dog alive long enough to get adopted it
had to be a good thing, she told herself.

CHAPTER 8

VERA

Vera's new kennel looked just the same as her old one—a
chainlink front, a small door through the rear wall, a concrete
floor and sides, and a walkway in front. New odors drifted
past—strange and varied human scents mixed with the smell of
new dogs. She lay very still and observed the dog across from

her. He watched her too, and whenever a human or dog passed, he stood up and barked at them, then lay down again. She found his behavior puzzling—but it kept her alert and engaged. A couple of people walked slowly down the aisle outside her kennel and made eye contact, their words tumbling around her. She heard her name, but then they moved on.

Suddenly, the treat lady stood in front of her. Sophie. Vera looked up.

"Hello Vera. How's my girl?" The soft voice calmed her—there were no edges to the sound. Treats fell like rain around her and she gobbled them down, the flavor and odor an oasis of comfort.

With a flash, the woman stepped inside. The space was cramped, and Sophie's uninvited presence crushed in on Vera. She crouched in the back of her kennel, tucked her tail, plastered her ears back on her skull, and waited.

But nothing happened.

Sophie kept her distance—she didn't stare or reach out or bend toward her, and with those magical treats falling all around, the lead ball in Vera's stomach started to melt.

She took a step closer. The scent of dogs and a myriad of other odors floated from the woman's clothes. Every time Vera took a step forward, Sophie threw food behind her, and to Vera's relief, she could turn away in spite of her curiosity.

A thread of boldness stitched its way through her belly and in a final, daring move, she walked right up to Sophie and sniffed her legs. They smelled of female dogs, and food, and the air outside. She still turned away to retrieve the cheese tossed behind her, but felt herself drawn back—again and again.

When Sophie's hand appeared in front of her with a mound of treats in the palm, she reached forward and gulped them down, stayed where she was, and looked up. Sophie smiled at her, eyes soft and half closed. The treats were replaced, and as she licked, she felt long, firm strokes flow from her head to the top of her tail, over and over.

"Vera, let's go for a walk." The woman straightened. Vera didn't understand the words, but from the tone of voice, she knew that something was about to happen. She watched Sophie's hands, expecting more treats, but instead, they revealed something like a collar—a harness. She'd seen it before when a stranger had lunged at her, brandishing it before her like a weapon.

This time though, it held still. Vera sniffed it cautiously, inch by inch. It, too, smelled of dogs. Sophie held a piece of cheese on the other side of the opening. She really wanted that cheese. She weighed the risk and finally reached her nose forward just past the strap, grabbed the treat, and pulled back.

She had survived.

She tried it again and then again, and finally her head pushed all the way through. She felt a feather weight on her shoulders, felt Sophie's light touch on her chest, and with a snap, a band tightened on her ribs.

"That's my girl," Sophie said. "It's not going to hurt you."

The band settled—there, but not tight. Odd, but not threatening. She composed herself, looked back at Sophie, and smiled.

When Sophie attached the leash, Vera knew they were going outside. But instead of turning left to go to the yard as she had anticipated, Sophie turned to the right and they walked out the door, through the front office, and into the parking lot beyond. Vera's ears flicked forward, her nostrils flared, and her tail arched above her back.

She was ready.

Sophie

Sophie felt a rush of excitement as she walked Vera out of the shelter. She had anticipated this for weeks. The shepherd pranced across the parking lot, wove her way between a network of puddles, then burst headlong onto the grassy verge— and sniffed.

"Vera! What're you doing? Slow down." Sophie caught up to her, her arms wrenched. She made a mental note to try a gentle leader next time.

Sophie studied the dog. She had put on some weight over the past month. Her coat was still dull, but she had dramatic markings—especially in the natural lighting. And she was eager and full of confidence.

Then the dog took off again, charging up the driveway to the road, Sophie hanging on for dear life. Vera's ears were forward, her nails clawing the pavement, her tail and nose high in the air.

Sophie struggled, anchored herself to the spot—and waited. But Vera leaned forward, strained against the leash, and locked herself in opposition.

"Vera!" Sophie tried to keep her voice soft and coaxing, making an effort to hide her frustration. But a couple of minutes later her arms ached, her back hurt, and still this dog pulled forward—and they'd barely started the walk. "Dammit, Vera!" The words that escaped her lips were now sharp and irritable. She gritted her teeth, reset her stance, and waited for Vera to choose to turn back to her.

Just as she was about to give up and drag the dog to her side, a car tore around the corner and sped toward them. Reflexively, Sophie jerked back on the leash. Vera fled to the side of the road, and leapt into a nearby ditch where she cowered.

"It's all right, Vera. It was just a car." Sophie stretched her shoulders and shook out her arms now that the leash was relaxed. The rapid changes in Vera's emotions were astounding, but the dog had probably never seen a car drive past her before. What kind of life had she had, for God's sake? For some animals—perhaps many—the shelter was the best experience they'd ever had. Sophie shuddered.

Patience. She needed to be patient.

They walked on again, and when Vera pulled ahead, Sophie made a U-turn and walked in the opposite direction. Sometimes Sophie felt a sharp tug on the leash when she turned. But occasionally, the dog would mirror Sophie's movements and stay close beside her—which Sophie rewarded with praise and multiple small pieces of cheese. At first they didn't make much progress down the road, but after about ten minutes, Vera started to understand the dance and stayed close beside her with every turn.

"Since you're such a smart girl, Vera, let's go further down the road." Sophie headed off at a brisk walk and Vera stayed next to her, matching her pace. Sophie was shocked at how quickly this abused, neglected dog was learning to walk on a loose leash. It normally took multiple sessions of training to accomplish such a feat.

A truck flew toward them, but this time Sophie shoved a piece of cheese right in front of Vera's nose as it approached, and lured her head away from the road when it passed. When the dog started to turn back toward the moving vehicle, Sophie fed her a handful of treats, one after another. By the time she finished eating, the truck was gone.

After fifteen minutes of working on loose-leash walking, Sophie couldn't help herself—she needed to know how much Vera knew from her previous home. She didn't want to push the dog too hard, but Vera might enjoy it.

"OK, Vera, let's try something else. Can you sit?" Nothing happened.

With clear, intelligent eyes trained on Sophie, Vera cocked her head to one side.

Sophie tried again. "Vera, sit." She said it slowly and distinctly. Still nothing happened. "Oh my God, Vera! You don't even know what 'sit' means! Didn't they teach you anything?"

By the time they reached the end of the road, Vera still strained at the leash from time to time, but Sophie buzzed with excitement at her progress. She continued to feed Vera treats whenever a car passed, hoping she would form a positive association between the traffic and the treats. She was a smart dog, and it made sense that her ability to learn quickly would help with her anxieties.

At the end of the road, they turned into a field of long, wet grass and Sophie flinched when icy water oozed through her running shoes and soaked her feet.

"OK, Vera, I'm going to teach you to sit—it's kind of wet, but there's nowhere else to practice." Sophie held a small piece of cheese right in front of Vera's nose, then moved it back toward her tail. The dog tracked it carefully. But when her head could strain no further to reach the treat, she took one step back and plucked it with delicate precision from between Sophie's fingers.

Sophie smiled. "Well that didn't work, did it, girl? Let's try again."

This time, as the cheese traveled from Vera's nose toward her tail, her rear legs crouched, and then she sat. "Jackpot!" Vera gobbled up the cheese, then jumped to her feet. Sophie laughed, but her hand flew to her mouth to stifle the sound when Vera flinched. "Let's try again."

They repeated the process five more times.

"Let's try 'down.'" Sophie lured Vera into a sit. The dog's haunches sank to the grass as if in slow motion, gaze riveted on the food. Sophie lowered the treat inch by inch toward the ground and Vera's nose followed it. She was so close, front legs almost extended fully in front of her on the grass—and then she jumped to her feet and snapped the treat from Sophie's hand. Sophie suppressed a giggle, but "Vera!" popped out of her mouth too loud before she could stop it. She bit her lip, took a new treat and repeated the exercise. This time, Vera made it all the way.

"Down!" Sophie said in triumph when Vera's elbows made contact with the grass. "Good girl! Let's do it again."

By the time they left the field, Vera was doing sits and downs easily—as long as she followed a treat—and Sophie was ecstatic. This dog had potential. Lots of potential. She was going to make it, in spite of her tenuous temperament test. Sophie just had a good feeling about her.

They headed back toward the shelter. Vera was calmer, not tending to pull as often as she had on the way out, and Sophie was just starting to space out and think about what she should make for dinner when she saw Leah approaching with another dog.

"Hey Leah! Who do you have there?" Sophie called. Vera yanked at the leash. Sophie hesitated, remembering that Vera had been reactive toward the dog in the temperament test. However, that dog would have been female, so if this one was male, Vera might be all right.

"This is Sammy," Leah shouted back.

"How does he do with other dogs?" They were rapidly approaching each other.

"I've seen him with a couple of female dogs," Leah said. "He's really calm and mellow and he has good body language." They were now only about thirty feet apart.

"Let's see how they do in a parallel walk." Sophie stopped. She could see that Vera was eager to meet the other dog—maybe too eager. Leah stopped too, easily holding her dog in check.

"How do you want to do it?"

"I'll turn Vera around, and you and Sam can walk slowly up beside us on the other side of the street. Come on, Vera, let's go." She felt her shoulder wrench, and was brought up short. Vera had anchored herself to the spot.

VERA

Vera's heart pounded. Her paws danced on the road, and she strained to get closer to Leah and the other dog. She recognized them by their scent and by the rhythm of their movement. Leah had fed her treats through the kennel door for weeks, talked to her, and soothed her. And she'd seen the dog in the play yard, mirrored him through the fence with glances and look aways, arcs and play bows. And they had once gone nose-to-nose in greeting.

Excitement spiraled up from her core and burst from her throat in a high-pitched yip. She whined, she leaned into the leash, she clung to the pavement. But Sophie pulled against her, and no amount of turning back, no amount of gripping the ground seemed to help. Then, like a dream, she saw that Leah and the dog were following, and not only that—they were closing the gap. Anticipation tingled from her nose to her tail, and she trotted after Sophie.

A moment later, Sam was on the other side of the street. He glanced at her and looked away, then repeated the look. He stopped, buried his nose in the grass, and snorted and sniffed with unbearable intensity.

In that moment, she knew she needed to get to him, knew it more acutely than anything else in the world. She barged across the road and pressed herself against Sammy, her nose working beside his, their breath mingling between the sweet-smelling blades.

Dog! Dogdogdog! She felt joyous, playful, overwhelmed. She poked him with her nose, woofed, leapt away, then bounced back again. Sam looked at her with soft, blinking eyes then resumed his investigation.

She lost herself in his thick, male-dog smell and the hypnotic sound of his pads on the pavement. She took in his black coat, his heavy ears, his confident, relaxed stride. Her head spun from the novelty of his nearness and she paced on the road beside him, warmed with a deep calm.

Sophie

They were halfway back to the shelter when Sophie noticed a new volunteer with a dog she hadn't seen before, walking toward them. They were still about two hundred feet away, so there was plenty of time to plan their strategy—and Sophie wasn't worried anyway. Given Vera's reaction to Sam, she was confident that the dog wouldn't be an issue for Vera. Still, it was the end of a long, challenging walk, and that could make another new situation difficult for her.

"What should we do?" asked Leah, her words fast and strained.

"Can you tell who it is?" Sophie squinted through her glasses. "I don't recognize them."

"I think the dog is Joey, but that volunteer is pretty new and she doesn't have great control," said Leah, slowing her pace.

"Yeah, as if I do!" Sophie said. "Let's pull over to the other side of the road and I'll feed Vera treats as they go by."

The space between them was narrowing rapidly, and Sam was still unconcerned. Vera, however, was on alert—she stood on her toes, tail high, eyes locked on the dog. Step-by-step, the strangers grew closer. Sophie grabbed a handful of treats from her fanny pack and held her fist in front of Vera's nose. But rather than being lured away by the treats, she shoved Sophie's hand aside with her muzzle and leaned forward.

"Vera!" Sophie urged. "Come!"

But Vera, who had been responsive just moments before, completely ignored her and strained toward the other dog, every muscle rigid.

Sophie knew what was coming. In a desperate effort to direct Vera's attention away from the dog, she grabbed the leash with both hands. Treats sprayed everywhere—peppering the dog's eyes and nose, scattering on the ground. The woman closed in, chatting on her cell phone—paying absolutely no attention as her dog dragged her to their side of the road. And Sophie was no closer to removing Vera from their path.

"Stop!"

The volunteer frowned and interrupted her conversation. She glanced in their direction—but continued walking.

At that moment, Vera detonated: deafening, violent, and unbelievably strong. Sophie threw her weight backward, but the other dog retaliated, dragging the woman closer. The cell phone clattered to the pavement. The woman screamed. The dogs roared and shrieked, teeth flashed, paws grappled the air.

Sophie hauled back again, turned, and with the leash straining over her shoulder, leaned into Vera's resistance with all her might. In a final effort, she dragged Vera off the road, past the woman and the barking dog, and back toward the shelter. She broke into a run, adrenalin surging.

So this was why Christa had wanted to euthanize Vera! She had sounded freakishly scary, and Sophie had almost lost hold of the leash.

The rhythm of her steps calmed her down and she forced herself to think. Would she be able to fix Vera? She considered it for a moment, slowed her pace, took a deep, cleansing breath, and looked at the clouds—then back at the dog. She was pretty sure she could, especially after watching Vera with Sam. But taking in the svelte form of the shepherd trotting ahead of her, Sophie wondered what Vera would have done had she reached the other dog. She bit her lip hard enough to focus her mind, then forced herself to discard any doubt. Of course she could turn Vera around. She was absolutely sure of it.

CHAPTER 9

SOPHIE

The next several months were a whirlwind for Sophie. She was torn between work, the pressing needs of the shelter, and quality time with Jake and the girls. Everything was scheduled to the minute, and she found herself working late into the night on outlines and handouts for the new Open Paw classes until her vision blurred.

Still, in spite of all the work she was doing—promoting and teaching classes each week, arranging for volunteers to stuff Kongs, answering volunteer emails, making follow-up calls to recent adopters—the resistance she met in implementing the Open Paw program was unyielding.

After that first walk with Vera, she'd taken on Vera and Sarah as project dogs. She worked tirelessly with Vera on her dog-directed reactivity and had made significant progress. By mid-March, Vera could greet and pass dogs on the road without any reaction at all, and the staff had introduced Vera and Sarah in the yard. These were developments that filled Sophie with optimism.

However, by the end of April, no potential adopters had shown any interest in either dog. They had started barking at anyone who walked past their kennels, and although this was not an unusual behavior in shelter dogs, they were so large and violent that they scared people off. Sophie hoped that as the Open Paw program took hold, this reactivity would fade.

But in spite of teaching the volunteers to pay attention to the dogs only when they were calm and quiet, there were enough inconsistencies with the staff—who Sophie had still not been given permission to train, and the public, who knew no better—that there was minimal improvement in their behavior, and dogs were still being euthanized.

She understood the need for euthanasia. She really did. Dogs who were not adoptable due to aggression, and those who were severely kennel stressed and had no other options deserved a way out. Isolating dogs in their kennels indefinitely was just too cruel to fathom. Still, the whole point of the Open Paw program was to prevent escalating kennel stress in dogs who were susceptible by teaching them to be relaxed and keeping them mentally active and stimulated, thus minimizing the strain of confinement. Lack of cooperation from the administration was making her desperate.

By mid April, Sophie decided that she needed to have something special in place for Sarah and Vera. They had now been in the shelter for five months, and Vera's behavior was deteriorating—she was more reactive again on walks and was otherwise withdrawn.

Sarah, on the other hand, was still outgoing and joyous on walks—playful, focused on Sophie, and delighted to please in her own boisterous way.

In a further effort to help the dogs, Sophie decided to put two more programs in place: Canine Good Citizen (CGC) training for dogs who had been at the shelter for longer than two months, and mobile adoptions where she and Leah would take two adoptable dogs out into the community where the public could see them in a less stressful environment. If the dogs had earned a CGC certificate through the American Kennel Club, possibly more people would consider adoption. She was already a CGC instructor and evaluator, so she didn't think it would add much more to her load.

She decided to start training Vera and Sarah for the CGC test immediately, and planned to put together some materials for mobile adoptions to present to Emma later that month. With some alternate goals to distract her from the inertia of the Open Paw program, she felt somewhat hopeful.

But then, the week after she put her plans into action, she was hit with a severe case of the flu. Over the days that followed, it morphed into pneumonia, and in a state of anguish, Sophie found herself homebound.

CHAPTER 10

VERA

Vera didn't know how long she'd lived in the shelter. It had been so long that every day ran into the next and now she felt a chronic, burning anxiety fed by the constant clamor of dogs and unbearable boredom. Each day was the same, and what had at first been reassuring, was now excruciating. She had a playmate the staff called "Sarah" for a short time each day, and their romps had helped to ease her distress.

But now, even that wasn't enough. Vera found some relief by barking at people and dogs who passed her kennel. At first, it gave her a sense of control and satisfaction. After all, she barked—they walked away. Then it became a game for her; then more than a game, almost an obsession. The most recent escape she had found from the ever-present, searing distress was to race around and around her kennel.

When that no longer helped, she leapt up one wall, bounced on the floor and bounded up the opposite wall, spinning and spinning—bounce, up, bounce, up, bounce, up. And while she spun and leapt, she barked and barked as loud as she could. It numbed her mind and settled the shrieking anguish in her veins. Her whole focus was to get out of the kennel either to play with Sarah, or to walk with anyone who would take her.

She had a few favorites among the dog walkers. She liked Leah a lot. She probably saw more of her than anyone else. Leah sat with her and murmured and stroked her tummy. And they would go for long walks and runs on the road. She liked Sophie too, but Sophie was more aloof, and always challenged her with new things. She liked this because it helped to distract her, but it was a different type of relationship than she had with anyone else.

"Hello, Vera," Sophie said. "Leah's taking you to class today." Vera stopped spinning and sat, taking in the tall figure before her, the smile, the wrinkled brow. There was something different about Sophie today. Sophie spoke a few more words to her, and although Vera didn't understand, she recognized the uncertainty in Sophie's voice. Puzzled, she caught the treats that Sophie tossed—then the woman was gone, and barking and spinning reclaimed her.

When Leah led her outside, she saw Sarah standing by Sophie. She barked a greeting, pulled over to her friend, and nuzzled her muzzle and ears; there were other dogs and people close by, but they were no more than an impression, a presence on her radar. They were of no consequence.

She watched Sarah demonstrate the exercises beside Sophie. Vera knew these words now—sit, down, come, watch me, take it and leave it—and executed them perfectly, taking pride in understanding the words, in earning the praise, the treats, and the genuine delight that erupted from Leah when she succeeded. She felt the spring sunshine warm on her back, and whenever Leah stopped asking her to do things, she rolled over on the wet pavement, belly exposed, and drank in the soothing pleasure of Leah's hand on her fur. With Sarah nearby, she felt complete.

With a start, Vera heard Sophie's voice soften and trail into the distance. She sprang to her feet, realizing in a panic that Sarah was heading across the parking lot without her. She surged forward, dragging Leah behind her.

SOPHIE

"I guess they want to walk together." Sophie laughed and waited for Vera and Leah to catch up. With Leah beside her, the dogs surged ahead. The day was brilliant around them, full-throated robins lacing the air with songs of spring. "Did you see Vera spinning and leaping in her kennel today?" Sophie was aware of the somber tone in her voice, but in spite of the sunshine, she couldn't lighten it. "I'm worried sick. When Duke started spinning, they euthanized him the next day." It was her first day back at the shelter after her three-week illness, and she was still feeling vulnerable. Her eyes stung and her throat closed up.

"Shit," said Leah. "That's right, they did. What should we do?"

"I've been planning a mobile adoption program." Sophie explained what she'd been working on at home while she recovered. "Would you go with me?"

There was a moment of silence. Vera barked and lunged at a bird that had landed a short distance away.

"Sure, sounds like a good idea—if we can get permission," Leah threw Sophie an ingratiating smile. "You talk to Emma, though—she won't listen to me."

Sophie sucked in a lungful of air. "Emma's probably sick of me with all the Open Paw stuff—but I'll try."

The dogs walked on, shoulder to shoulder, Vera pulling ahead every now and again. They investigated the scents of the grass and earth together and Vera pointedly sniffed the spots where Sarah urinated—every time.

"Maybe *you* should adopt Vera," Leah said.

"No way! Tess and Lola would call the ASPCA to report us." And, Sophie reflected, testing the idea out for the first time, the girls would be way too stressed if she and Jake were to adopt a third dog. Besides, in the planned community where they lived, the covenants only allowed two dogs per household. "Maybe *you* should adopt her."

"Oh, right! My cats would die. They'd leave if I brought home a dog."

"OK, then. Let's go back and I'll see if I can talk to Emma," Sophie said.

Sophie went straight to the director's office. She was not at all confident about this. Mobile adoptions would require a whole new level of trust, and she had pushed Emma so much in the past several months.

Emma's door was open when Sophie walked into the portable. "Emma, do you have a minute? I need to talk to you about Sarah and Vera."

The woman looked up from her desk. "Sure. I hear Vera's not doing well. Once a dog starts spinning in its kennel, it's really not humane to keep it here anymore. You know that, right?" Sophie cringed, but forced herself to continue.

"Emma, what if Leah and I took Vera and Sarah out into

the community? We could make them vests that say 'Adopt me! WHS', and walk them in the most popular parks. We would advocate for them and hand out adoption packets. Plus, it would help to keep them sane by getting them out of the shelter environment." She threw out her ideas desperately. "I've put a lot of thought into it, Emma. I'm working on a proposal at home, but with Vera in her present state, I thought I'd ask you now. If I hadn't got sick…"

"I don't know, Sophie. It's a lot of work, and I think Vera has just about run out of time. No one has shown any interest in her. Is it really fair to her to keep her here any longer? You have to think about that. Sometimes euthanasia is the compassionate thing to do. There are lots of things worse than a peaceful death. We see it here all the time."

Sophie swallowed to suppress a sob. "So you're saying 'no' then."

"I'm not saying 'no', but I'll give Vera another two weeks, and if she hasn't been adopted by then, we'll need to euthanize her." Her voice was gentle, but the words stung like daggers. "I'm sorry, but I feel that it's in her best interest and it's really our only choice."

"What about fostering?" Sophie asked.

"We don't have any fosters who will take a big dog right now."

"Can you check?" Sophie fixed her eyes on Emma's, trying to force her into agreement.

"We don't have anyone, Sophie. Now, I have work to do." Emma looked down at her desk and started shuffling papers.

Sophie fled from the portable, tears of rage pouring down her cheeks. She had to come up with a solution. She just had to.

CHAPTER 11

SOPHIE

"It's such a beautiful day." Jake's hand rested on Sophie's lap and he gave her leg an affectionate squeeze. She absorbed his warmth and support, but she couldn't claw her way out of the morass she found herself in.

They were driving along Lake Whatcom Boulevard with Tess and Lola. The magnolias and rhododendrons were in full bloom, and the grass was the brilliant green that only appears in springtime. Tess let out a series of sharp, piercing barks when they pulled into the North Shore Trail parking lot. The girls loved this trail. It was one of their favorites.

"Easy, girls!" Sophie tried to sound upbeat. Tried not to feel so devastated. "Stay close. We'll let you off in a minute." Once on the trail, she unclipped Tess and watched the collie bound off, followed by Lola who fled like a pale golden wraith deep into the shadows.

"What's going on, Sophie? You're so quiet." Jake put his arm around her and pulled her against him, pressed his lips to her hair. "Come on, tell me."

"It's Vera. Why would anyone adopt her in the next two weeks if no one's looked at her in the past six months—no matter what I do?"

"What if we foster her?" Jake asked.

Sophie stopped in her tracks and faced him. Her jaw hung open. "What?"

"What if we foster her? You said that she gets along with other dogs, right? Tess and Lola would be OK for a while. We'd need to make sure that they do well together first, but then we could at least try it."

"But three dogs, Jake. That adds a whole new dynamic for the girls." She was silent for a moment, a kaleidoscope of scenarios rushing before her. "Yeah. We could try it. That would be fantastic!"

They walked for a while, Sophie caught up in a fantasy of taking Vera on regular walks, giving her a quiet, safe place to sleep, providing her with a family to love and care for her, sisters to play with.

"When?" Sophie asked.

"When what?"

"When could she meet the girls?"

"Well, we could go out there after we finish this walk, I

guess," said Jake.

"And maybe I could catch Emma and talk to her about it," added Sophie. "Now" wasn't soon enough. Her chest was bursting, her skin itching with adrenalin. She wanted to wrap it up yesterday. She wanted to talk to Leah. She gave Jake a big hug.

They walked on, the girls bounding ahead of them on the trail, which soon gave way to a small beach on the lake. The morning sun danced on the water. Tess and Lola waded in, mercurial ripples flowing away from them. Sophie found a stick to throw and Lola plunged after it, swimming with deep, sure strokes.

Tessie barked a few times, then followed her sister, long coat floating around her like a veil, plumed tail held high above the water. She stood still for several seconds, then shook off before pushing into a short, arcing swim back to shore. Reaching solid ground, she trotted up to Jake, laughing all over her face. And when he tried to leap out of range, she shook herself, a curtain of water flying from her coat, soaking his jeans and jacket. Sophie laughed.

"Good to see you can still smile," Jake said. "Even if it is at my expense!"

"Well, what do you think?" Sophie ignored the comment. "Can we go to the shelter now?"

"Sophie, we just got here. Let's at least take them to the first bridge."

"OK." Sophie gritted her teeth and called the girls. She knew Jake was right, but she felt so desperate to get back to Vera. "What if we bring Vera home today?"

Jake stopped and looked at her. "Wow, you're really into this, aren't you?"

Sophie gulped, afraid she'd been too eager, too pushy. She shifted her weight back and forth trying to calm herself.

"What if she doesn't get along with the girls?" Jake's voice was still reasonable. "And what about a bed and all the other things she'll need?"

Sophie's heart skipped and pounded in her chest. "She'll get along fine with the girls, and I can get everything I need from the shelter." She looked up at Jake and gave him what she hoped was a convincing smile. "And it's not like we don't have a ton of dog beds at home."

"I haven't even met her yet, Sophie!" Exasperation in his voice.

Sophie froze. Jake had suggested it, so he couldn't back out now—could he? In an effort to lighten things up, she put her arm through his and snuggled close to him. "Yeah, but you'll love her. She's so sweet and smart. You'll probably like her more than I do."

"Have you thought about where she'll be when we go to work? We can't leave her at home with Tess and Lola."

But Sophie had an answer for this, too. "I'll just drop her off at the shelter in the morning and then pick her up on my way home. That way, the public will still see her for adoption."

"Well, OK. But only if I like her, and only if she gets along with the girls. We can't bring her home tonight—it would be too rushed. You can pick her up tomorrow morning so she'll have some time to adjust during the day." Jake squeezed her arm. "We'll work it out, don't worry."

"Thanks, babe." She took his hand. The high, green canopy rustled overhead, and the lake spread like an expanse of glass beside them in the cool morning air. "We can take them for a long walk together on Sehome Hill before bringing her home. I'm supposed to work on Monday, but I'll call in sick. And the shelter's closed on Mondays, so she won't be missing anything in the way of adopters."

Sophie looked down at Tess. She paced beside them, seemingly lost in thought. Sophie wondered what passed through the collie's mind as she walked, her head slightly bowed, ears tilted back, body relaxed. Lola was off exploring the steep, wooded hillside above, watching for the perfect moment to dive-bomb them. Sophie wondered how it would be for the girls to have a third dog around for a while.

The last dog they'd fostered had been a ten-pound devil called Wally, who within the first hour had stacked the girls' toys under the coffee table and attacked them viciously if they even looked his way. Tess had refused to have anything to do with him, leaving the room when he entered.

Twice in the two weeks he'd lived with them, Lola had been forced to lift his bald, squirming body in her jaws after he attacked her face. He had squawked and growled until he realized she wasn't going to give up, then the moment he'd relaxed, she'd let him down. There hadn't been a mark on him.

Sophie marveled that Lola had such good control of those jaws—jaws that could press up to four hundred pounds of pressure per square inch. The lesson of the correction hadn't lasted long, though, and Wally had been back to his obnoxious habits two days later. Sophie had taken control of the situation by making him work for everything—meals, affection, treats. But his presence had still been a burden to the girls. Sophie hoped that Vera would be a much better foster child than Wally. Thankfully, he'd been adopted by a neighbor and Sophie still took Tess and Lola to visit him from time to time—they actually liked him now that he didn't live in their home.

Sophie's reflections were brought to a close by Lola trotting alongside her, tail wagging and ears back. "Hey Lu! Having a good time?" She stroked Lola's head, scratched behind her ears, and gave her a cookie before the dog romped off again. This time, Tess broke her meditation and raced after her sister at full speed.

By the time they arrived at the shelter, it was three thirty on Saturday afternoon and Emma was crossing the parking lot to her car. The shelter closed at five.

"Emma, I talked to Jake, and if Tess and Lola get along with Vera, we're going to foster her—if that's OK," The words tumbled out all at once and Sophie was aware of the high, frantic quality of her voice. "We have Tess and Lola in the car, so we can test Vera now and take her home tomorrow. I'll bring her back before work each day and pick her up each evening. That should at least give her a break from the stress of the shelter. What do you think?"

Emma gave Sophie a long, level stare before answering. Sophie fought to hold her gaze. She held her breath, tucked her hair behind her ear, tapped her index finger on her thigh.

"Well, OK. But you need to fill out the paperwork first. And if someone's interested in adopting her, you know you'll need to bring her back, right?"

"Yes, I know." Sophie resisted the urge to hug Emma. "Thank you, Emma. I'll do the paperwork." She ran back to the truck barely touching the ground.

"She said yes!" she told Jake. "I need to do the paperwork—no, maybe we should see how they do together first."

TESS AND LOLA

Tess and Lola were confused. They had been taken for a walk on their favorite trail, but it had been cut short compared to all the other times they'd ever been there. Now, here they were, in a parking lot outside of a low, dark building, with the sound of dogs barking uncontrollably inside. Jake had leashed them up, asked them to jump down onto the pavement, and kept them there, just standing around, not even allowing them to sniff the grass—which was just out of reach.

Next to the building was an enclosure that contained two dogs barking directly at them. The girls turned away and licked their lips in unison. Tess was tempted to bark back and give the dogs a piece of her mind, but Lola was calm and steady, and for once, Tess took her cue from her sister. The place reeked of frightened dogs and other animals, and Tess wasn't feeling quite as sure of herself as she usually did.

"Good girls. Good quiet," Jake murmured. His voice helped Tess to settle even more.

There was a loud bang, and through the shelter door appeared a young dog with Sophie in tow. They knew she was female from the air currents swirling between them. And they recognized her scent from Sophie's clothes.

The dog's ears were forward, tail high above her back, and laser eyes directly on them. Tess turned her back and sniffed the ground. She took a few steps away, giving the dog more space, giving herself more space. Lola licked a couple of times, then sat on the ground and scratched her face. She, too turned away from the dog. They were used to Sophie working with strange dogs in the classes she taught, but this was a brand new location.

"Girls," called Sophie, "you're doing such a good job!" Then she stepped backward, leading the dog away from them. They could tell that Vera was more relaxed when she approached a second time—her tail was lower, her eyes softer, and her trajectory toward them wove from side to side. Sophie said something to Jake and he turned and walked them toward the road.

Now that they were putting more distance between themselves and the building, the girls felt more at ease, and they sensed that Vera was more relaxed too. Still, the stuttering, prancing gait of that dog behind them was a little unnerving. They checked in with each other—a ritual of ear snuffles and exchanged glances—and forged ahead.

Before they knew it, the dog was trotting next to them—just a few feet away. Tess threw her a look; a subtle invitation to communicate. But instead of turning her head away in respect, Vera let out a sharp bark and landed face to face with Tess. A moment later, Vera's paw batted her shoulder. Tess knew the act was playful, yet the pressure and pounce had an echo of intimidation too. She angled her body further away from the dog, herding Jake to the far side of the road.

Tess was now on full alert, her body tingling with awareness. She knew what she needed to do. For the rest of the walk, she would assess, teach, and coax the shepherd to respect and communicate. She would read and answer every subtle flick of an ear, every blink, every sweep of the dog's tail.

And second by second, she would unroll a path of firm direction, teaching the shepherd to fit in. Tess had done this with dogs for as long as she could remember and it was as natural to her as breathing.

Other than a few sidelong glances in the girls' direction, and her high, poised tail, the dog wasn't threatening, Tess decided. She was easy to read with those big ears, bright, direct eyes and long expressive tail, and by midway through the walk, Tess was confident she could handle her. The collie knew she radiated poise and confidence, and she threw out an ongoing monologue of signs to the dog. She calmed and reassured the shepherd every step of the way.

Lola paced along beside Tess and ignored the dog. As far as she was concerned, she would tolerate this walk and avoid the shepherd for as long as she could. In fact, as long as Tess was between them, she could pretend that the dog wasn't even there.

But when Sophie eased her course closer to the girls once more, Lola stopped to sniff, losing herself in the vivid odors of the dogs who had passed there before her. She moved on, distracted by a movement in the grass a few feet away, and to her delight, saw that Vera pulled over to investigate the spot she had just vacated, nose buried deep in the grass. Lola tried this again. Sniff, move on, and watch. Vera mirrored her movements precisely.

She walked a bit further, and Vera followed. And just like that, a flurry of warmth and anticipation flitted through the golden, an unexpected delight in this dog who, out of the blue, afforded her such admiration.

"They're doing really well," Sophie said to Jake. "Let's put the girls back in the truck, so that you can meet her properly." Tess and Lola whirled around and headed back to the shelter, interpreting Sophie's phrasing and turn of voice with ease.

They trotted back down the road shoulder to shoulder, their collective gaze directed forward. They moved smoothly, and when Vera threw them a confrontational stare or lunged in their direction, they looked away or slowed, noses to the pavement. When they finally jumped into the safety of their truck, Lola pawed at her bed and settled down with a groan of contentment, relieved to be free again. Tess, however, sat tense and poised, eyes riveted on the shepherd, following every move she made until she disappeared from view—still attached to Sophie.

SOPHIE

Sophie studied Jake surreptitiously, trying to figure out what he was thinking. She knew that he wanted to like Vera, and that he ultimately didn't want her to be euthanized. But would it be enough? Especially after their experience with Wally.

"Are you ready?" Sophie asked.

She walked Vera over to him. He gave the dog a liver treat and she took it from him with her front teeth, then backed up.

"She sure is gentle. Lola never takes treats like that," he said. Sophie let out her breath. That was a good sign, wasn't it?

"Let's walk a bit," Sophie said. "Here, you take her." She handed Jake the leash and Vera strode out in front of him, pulling ahead, but not too hard. Sophie hoped it wasn't too hard, anyway—Jake had a thing about dogs who pulled. With the girls mature and well behaved, she'd forgotten how strict he was.

"Vera, come," he said suddenly. Vera was distracted by something at the side of the road and pawed at the ground, consumed by some invisible smell or creature. But when she heard him, she turned away from it, sat in front of him, and met his gaze. "Wow, she's really smart!" He gave her a cookie. "OK, Vera, let's go." She strutted ahead again, ears forward and tail high.

They walked along in silence for a while, Sophie stealing glances at Jake's face, but he didn't give anything away. Finally, he reached forward and stroked the dog's shoulders. Vera glanced back at him—whether with interest or irritation Sophie wasn't sure. "She sure is dirty—shedding a lot too," he said. He made a face and tried to brush a clump of fur from his hand.

Jake was so damned fastidious. Sometimes it irked Sophie. "She's shedding like crazy, but I can bathe her tomorrow. That'll get rid of her loose hair. I've never seen a dog blow its coat like this before, but that must be what she's doing. In two days, she went from normal-looking to this." She gestured toward Vera's tufted, moth-eaten coat, aware that she was babbling. She needed to shut up and let Jake make his own decision. A loud truck roared past and Vera looked at it, but otherwise didn't respond. "What do you think of her?" Sophie asked when she couldn't stand it any longer.

"She's fine. Let's see how she does at home."

Sophie couldn't believe it. She would have jumped for joy, but she didn't want to overdo it. "Really? I owe you! I'll do the dishes for a month!"

"Can we go back now?" Jake had apparently reached his limit. He seemed tired of the dog, the walk, the whole situation. He had that look on his face where he was losing interest, tuning out—"shutting down" they would say in dog-handling language.

"Sure. But you have to meet Sarah before we leave." She'd never even got him out here before and she didn't know if he'd ever be back.

"OK, but just for a minute."

They turned back toward the shelter, and Vera stayed with them. She no longer pulled, and from the way Jake smiled and spoke to her, Sophie wondered if he was actually starting to like her.

"Let's meet at the Arboretum tomorrow to re-introduce her to the girls. It'll be a neutral environment for all of them," Sophie said. "I'll pick her from the shelter and you can bring Tess and Lu."

As soon as Vera stepped back inside the kennel, her paws traced a circular pattern, and within seconds, they picked up speed until she leapt up one wall, then the opposite wall in a wild circle, her bark unnerving. Sophie watched Jake watching Vera. She hated to admit it, but she was relieved to see his shoulders slump and his features contract in shock.

CHAPTER 12

VERA

Vera awakened from a furtive sleep. She was filled with unease. At the sound of the doors clanging, she started her mind-numbing dance of leap-bounce-leap.

Rob appeared. She stopped circling and sat, knowing that this action, more than anything else, would get immediate results. When he opened her kennel door she followed him down the corridor to the yard. She knew every pebble there now, and had sniffed every sparse blade of grass an infinite number of times.

The only reprieve she had was Sarah, and Sarah wasn't with her this morning. She squatted and relieved herself, and when Rob led her back to her kennel she resumed her dance.

She had just finished eating when she heard Sophie in the corridor. Again she stopped circling and sat, like clockwork. She could tell that the woman was excited by her tone of voice and her scent. And Vera also smelled the potent odor of the dogs she'd met the day before. Sophie harnessed her up and led her out of the building.

But instead of heading out the driveway and down the road like they had always done before, they walked over to a truck in the parking lot. With a bang, Sophie opened the back and motioned her up.

"Vera, jump!"

The roof over the truck bed made the space look small and contained and safe to Vera, and when the back closed behind her, she checked out the space carefully—a rubber floor liner, a bowl of water, a bed, a stuffed toy, bits of food.

With a dull roar, they started moving. Vera had felt this sense of motion on her trip to the shelter all those months ago, and when she went to the vet every other week to donate blood. At first, the tendrils of those frightening associations alarmed her.

But all of a sudden, the novelty of driving away with Sophie took over, and she ran from window to window as the world fled past. They drove for a long time, changing directions and speed, but eventually the sound of the traffic faded, and the truck stopped. She could see parked cars beside her, and woods beyond.

Outside, footsteps padded to the back of the truck and with a squeak, the hatch opened, and Sophie stood before her, inviting her to jump down. New, fresh smells accosted her nostrils, and the trees above sang with wind and birdsong. Jake appeared. He smiled and gave her a cookie. He was calm and steady, and had a voice that made her feel warm inside. Standing there by the forest, encapsulated by kindness, wolfing down cookies, she felt like she was the center of everything.

Then Jake reached up and opened the back of the car. Lola.

To Vera, the golden was a pale blur. One second she towered above, the next she loomed in Vera's face, larger than life—and Vera stood helpless, trapped by the leash. With no hope of escape, she lunged, grabbed Lola's neck, and took her down in one fast, seamless motion. Her own strength and agility surprised her, and she let go just as suddenly as she'd taken hold. In an instant, Lola scampered off to the edge of the forest. Vera glowed with confidence.

She heard excited chatter from Sophie, felt herself pulled backward, then saw Tess hop down, trot in a wide circle and approach from the side. The collie stood tall, her head and tail high and poised, completely self-assured. Vera was fascinated. She didn't feel threatened when Tess grew close, sniffed her nose at an angle, then trotted off down the trail. In fact, Vera hit the end of her leash, trying to rush after the collie, longing to join her.

But Sophie kept her close, and a moment later, varied scents and images assaulted Vera's senses in a way that made her brain spin. Plants on either side of the path clawed at her, tore at her ears, her face, her eyes. She blinked and ducked and plastered her ears to her skull. Tess and Lola temporarily forgotten, she clung to Jake and Sophie.

And then two people with a dog appeared.

Tess swept forward to greet the dog, and Vera watched the arc of their bodies, the touch of their noses, the sweep of their tails. In that moment, the dog was magnetic, and she careened down the path, pulling Sophie behind. She reached him—tail wagging, ready to sniff and curve and paw…but in a moment of panic, all she could do was crouch and grovel, then rush past to safety.

Sophie

Sophie buzzed. Her whole being hummed with pride watching Vera navigate the woods. The shepherd seemed to be lost in some kind of nirvana sniffing the edge of the trail. The three dogs had been fine together after the initial scuffle, and Vera had been polite with the couple and their dog—if a little unsure.

Still, Sophie had a persistent, niggling concern with how Vera had greeted Lola. She knew that the current philosophy on dog-dog interactions was to let them work out social disputes without human intervention—it let them establish status, and prevented complications later on. And in spite of having an aversion to conflict of all kinds, Sophie had let Lola work things out with Wally, and that had seemed go all right. But Vera was no ten-pound scrapper.

They followed the trail back to the parking lot, the girls running ahead while Vera explored the edge of the path, still on her leash. Sophie made a mental note that Vera had not peed since leaving the shelter.

Thirty minutes later, when Sophie pulled into their driveway it was quiet, with a light breeze moving the cedar fronds above. They decided to walk the girls one last time before introducing Vera to the house, and watched the shepherd follow Lola, mirroring everything she did, just like she'd done at the shelter. Any animosity between the two dogs seemed to have dissipated. But by the time they got back to the driveway, Vera still hadn't relieved herself.

Approaching the house, Sophie was wired with anticipation—she'd imagined this moment a million times in the past twenty-four hours. Jake put Tess and Lola on the deck, and with a flourish, Sophie opened the mudroom door. For a moment, Vera seemed spellbound.

VERA

Vera drank in the room in a state of bliss. She glowed with a comfort she had sometimes experienced when she first awakened. She hadn't liked Sophie wiping her paws, but she'd known Sophie for so long now that she wasn't afraid—she just didn't like the way it felt.

She had enjoyed her walk with the girls, and meeting the dog on the trail left her curious; she'd discovered that if she wasn't sure how to act, she could copy Lola and everything would be all right.

And now, here she was in a safe, confined space with Sophie and Jake. It was quiet, steeped in the scent of dogs and people, devoid of fear.

With the leash unclipped, she sensed her freedom and trotted away. The room expanded around her, and her nose went into high gear. She couldn't believe the complexity of the space. She raised her eyes and saw the ceiling angle high above her. Things were suspended in the air and stacked against the walls. One area smelled strongly of food, another of dog toys.

She checked for the dogs. They were blocked from her by an invisible barrier that she didn't completely understand, but they left her alone, so she could concentrate on her exploration.

Inch by inch she investigated everything: the kitchen cabinets, the objects on the bookshelves, the piano, the couches, the wires under the desk in the office, and the bathroom with the bowl of clear, standing water. She smelled the dog bowls on the shelf in the mudroom, and the basin of water on the floor. She tested it with her tongue. When she was finally done, she became aware of Jake and Sophie watching from a distance.

"Vera, come upstairs," Sophie said, and climbed what appeared to be a cliff of some kind. Vera paced back and forth; she had never seen stairs before.

With much trepidation, she let Sophie coax her up one step at a time following a trail of salmon cookies. When she reached the landing, she shook off in a storm of excitement, bathing in Sophie's praise and the delicious sensation of a hand caressing her ears.

After that, she ventured up the second set of stairs with relative ease and arrived at the top, overjoyed. With exquisite care, she explored the upstairs loft office with its wooden chest of drawers and the large, overstuffed chair. In the bedroom, she tensed and barked when a large dog stepped in front of her, reflecting every move. But when she realized it had no scent or sound, she decided it was of no consequence.

An hour after she had started her mission, she was finished. She was bursting with life, burning with excitement, and with a devilish energy, tore down the stairs and raced through the living room.

CHAPTER 13

LOLA AND TESS

Trapped on the deck, Lola was not amused. She didn't like the sounds of the neighborhood that kept her awake, nor the feeling of vulnerability. And she liked her bed—inside, in the front hall where it had been for as long as she could remember. She had been staring at Sophie and Jake through the glass doors for a long time. She was sure they had seen her, but thus far, they had completely ignored her—a huge betrayal. And all the while, that new dog had been sniffing around inside. It was a good thing the dog hadn't curled up on her bed!

Irritated, Lola lay down on the hard wooden deck. She didn't worry about the dog; she knew it would be gone soon. Other dogs had come and gone over the years. She rarely liked them, but she tolerated them as best she could, did what she could to keep the peace, and went about her day.

Tess was unconcerned about her banishment. She loved the deck and could lie for hours watching the day go by, keeping an eye on the birds, the squirrels, and the deer.

Deer were a species that definitely required her attention, and she would wholeheartedly deliver a burst of high-pitched barks, leaping and dancing, intoxicated by their presence. The deer often ignored her, but sometimes they bounced away, sending her into an absolute frenzy—until Sophie or Jake interrupted with "Tess, quiet!" She would stop barking long enough for them to go back inside and leave her alone; then she'd get back to work.

As for the new dog… Tess felt its presence ease through the house, and was curious, delighted really, to rise to the challenge.

Finally, Jake opened the door. Lola got to her feet, shook herself off, and was just getting ready to meander inside, when a rush of black and grey flashed into view. There was the dog, poised and eager to interact just inches from her face. Taken aback, Lola froze. Without warning, Vera jumped away and leapt on top of the hot tub.

Lola was fascinated. She'd never thought of anyone jumping onto the hot tub before. She hadn't even considered it an option.

Tess watched from a distance, not sure what to make of the dog either. Every fiber in her being was attuned to reading Vera, and at the moment, she wasn't sure that she liked what she saw. The dog was young, powerful, and impulsive, and her level of excitement was over the top. Tess didn't like her manners either—the way she had charged into Lola's face just then was downright rude. Tess felt compelled to take Vera down a notch, but was uncertain about the wisdom of confronting such a dog. For now, she would keep her distance and be patient, using her skills of negotiation to maintain peace.

A few seconds later, Vera bounded off the hot tub, landed halfway across the deck, and launched herself onto the bench. The girls watched in awe. The dog barked a few times, her strong voice echoing down the meadow, then trotted back into the house, head high, clearly pleased with herself.

The girls had just followed her into the dining room, curious to see what she'd do next, when Vera whirled around, pawed at Lola, collapsed into a play bow, then reached up and mouthed the golden's face.

Something about the energy of this dog intrigued Lola. The way Vera had followed her on their walks and mimicked her behavior made Lola less wary than she would have been with a complete stranger. She pawed and mouthed back, and a moment later they were engaged in a wild romp, roaring and wrestling in the dining room, bumping up against the chairs.

Tess wasn't so sure she liked this. So much action in the middle of her living space was too much. And she wasn't sure of this dog; of the noise, of the electricity jolting off of her. And

Lola. She'd never seen her sister behave this way with another dog. This was out of line. She barked—a high, controlling volley to rein them in.

Just then, Lola stopped. And demanded that Vera do the same. With her solid frame anchored to the carpet, she lowered her head, hunched her shoulders, and wedged herself against the couch. She'd enjoyed the strength and youth of the dog, reveled in the slam and bump against her flank. And yet, though appealing, the sum of it was rapidly overpowering—and Lola was done.

But Vera didn't stop—not right away. The shepherd's mouth found Lola's neck, paws clawed her shoulders, the jolt of hips slammed her ribs. But finally, Vera gave up, Lola raised her head, and the dog made a beeline for Tess.

Tess turned away when Lola liberated herself from the dog. She didn't consider herself a target. She had dismissed Vera with a sweep of her tail and was lost in finding niblets on the kitchen floor—when powerful jaws closed on the back of her neck.

For a second she froze—radiating indignation, then rage—a clear warning to Vera to stop.

But Vera didn't move, didn't silence her growl or release her neck. Cobra fast, the collie whipped around, a fury of sharp barks issuing forth, expecting—no, demanding—that Vera leave her be.

"Good girl, T…" She was vaguely aware of Sophie's voice… then Vera stiffened and the shepherd was on top of her—the whole sequence no more than a blur. The hardwood floor slammed into her back, Vera's teeth gripped her throat. The brute force of the animal crushed down on her, and with a sinuous strength, Tess thrashed, kicked, erupted with screams of outrage. She twisted her head, writhed to escape, to catch Vera in her jaws. But she couldn't do it. She was overpowered.

An instant later, the dog was gone and Sophie's screams filled the room. Tess clambered to her feet, limbs shaking, heart like a train in her chest. She wanted to take that dog down. *Now.* But with a deep sense of self-preservation, she rushed to the guest room to regroup.

Tess was a bold dog and she was not afraid of Vera. In fact, the only time she'd been scared in her life was when an Orca breached beside the sailboat in which she dozed. But although she was not afraid, she was not happy either. She licked her lips and sulked.

CHAPTER 14

SOPHIE

Sophie found Tess nestled on the futon in the guest room. The collie didn't look up—she kept her head anchored to her paws. Sophie worked her fingers through the collie's snowy ruff looking for blood and was ridiculously relieved when she didn't find any. No punctures—Vera had some bite inhibition, anyway. Maybe even good bite inhibition.

Sophie pulled the collie into her lap and massaged her back, trying to make sense of it. Why would Vera have attacked? Tess had given her a clear, respectable message and the dog completely ignored it. Sophie would have thought that even a poorly socialized dog would have understood—but apparently not.

"She's OK," she called to Jake. But Tess looked dejected and upset—her ears back and her body frozen in place. "I think they're just working things out." The words felt dishonest, but she couldn't give up already. She became aware of the tremor of adrenalin still in her hands and arms as she stroked Tessie.

"I'm leaving Vera in the mudroom." Jake's voice had taken on a brittle edge. "I don't like the way this is going, Sophie. I want to give her a chance, but not if she hurts the girls."

Apprehension fled through Sophie. She worked her hands through the collie's coat. "We *have* to give her a chance, Jake. If this doesn't work out they'll kill her. I can't be responsible for that. Can you?"

Jake stood in the doorway, his face contorted. "Don't try to blackmail me, Sophie. I said we'd try this, but not at the risk of this family."

There were no good answers. No right answers. "No, but…"

She needed to get out, needed time to think. "I'm taking the girls out. I'll be back soon. You'll be OK with Vera?"

He grunted and disappeared into the living room.

Sophie loaded up the girls and drove down the hill to the local cafe. She was exhausted from Vera's antics and sick to death of walking. She left the dogs in the car and sat at a table by the window, hands wrapped around a steaming mug of coffee, and with the aroma of fresh espresso filling her senses, she felt the knots in her shoulders ease.

She forced herself to be objective—she couldn't afford to freak out right now. She had to fix things. She closed her eyes and breathed in deeply, stretching her lungs to capacity. Why was she so upset?

Well, for one thing, she was pissed at Jake for being so disgustingly logical. But when it came to the squabble—Tessie hadn't even been hurt. And it was Vera's first day: the dog had never been in a house before and never lived with other dogs. Maybe Sophie was expecting too much to think that the three girls would be polite to each other. If she could convince Jake to keep Vera for a few more days till they knew her better, they could do it. They could find her a good home. The right home. She knew they could.

She just needed to keep a cool head, even if things got more challenging. And she would do everything possible to make things work out between Jake and Vera—and, of course, the girls and Vera. She couldn't consider taking Vera back to the shelter permanently, especially after seeing what a vibrant dog she was.

But what about Tess and Lola? Through the window, Sophie watched cars rush past the golf course.

Lola seemed to like the shepherd well enough, and Vera hadn't actually hurt Tess—just her feelings. And Tess wasn't just any dog—she was well-balanced, tough, and fully capable of looking after herself. In fact, she was the most confident, socially-savvy dog Sophie had ever known.

And this was a temporary situation. She needed to get over

her unease and push forward. Throughout her life she had taken on many challenges that most people wouldn't have considered, and she'd done well. But conflict and unrest at home? It terrified her.

She stayed at the cafe for thirty minutes, then took the girls to the dog park. When they were tired and relaxed and Sophie was ready to face Vera again, they drove home.

After Sophie put the girls on the deck, she went to check on Vera. She saw at once that Vera wasn't in the mudroom—instead, she lay on the living room floor with Jake stroking her face and chest.

"How long have you had her out?" Sophie asked. She tried to make her voice upbeat.

Vera smiled, walked over, and flopped down at Sophie's feet. Then she rolled onto her back, and wagged her tail. Her big, cinnamon paws curled onto her chest and her hind legs flopped apart to expose a pink tummy. Like a slow metronome, her tail swayed from side to side. Sophie melted, and crouched down to stroke the creamy fur.

"About fifteen minutes. She was quiet in the mudroom, so I decided to see how she'd do."

"What do you think of her, Jake?"

"I like her a lot. The dogs'll work it out. We just need to be careful at first." He smoothed the fur on Vera's face. "She's so sweet. I can't imagine taking her back."

"Thank God for that!" Sophie said. She leaned over and kissed Jake's cheek, gave Vera a final scratch behind her ears, and stood up. "I'm going to change before I give her a bath. Sorry I was such a bitch." She started up the stairs.

Like smoke the shepherd flowed past her, barely touching the steps, paws silent on the carpet—the effect was eerie, otherworldly. Sophie motioned Jake over to watch, and for the next five minutes they called her up and down, speechless at her panther-like grace.

On a whim, Sophie decided to try something. She had trained Vera to "stay" at the shelter, and was curious to see if she could do it now. She gave Vera the hand signals for "down" and "stay" at the top of the stairs and ran to the bottom.

"Vera, come!" Jake called when Sophie reached the final step. But instead of running down the stairs, her head and front paws appeared over the half-wall of the landing. She stared down at him, head cocked to one side. Jake looked back at her and growled—a deep threatening sound from the back of his throat. And then, to Sophie's horror, his eyes locked with the shepherd's and he glared at her.

"Jake, stop it!" She grabbed his arm. "What are you doing?"

Vera's expression changed to laser-focused and hard. A low growl followed by a string of forceful barks tore out of her. She disappeared behind the half-wall and shot down the stairs.

Instinctively, Sophie stepped in front of Jake. The dog charged around the corner—ears forward, teeth bared, hackles raised. "Sweetie, it's OK." Sophie's voice was low and honey smooth. The shepherd's eyes met Sophie's—and like a switch had been flipped, she collapsed with puppy-like softness to the floor. Sophie swallowed again and again, her mouth chalk dry.

"It's just me, Vera. It's all right." Jake's voice was gentle and silken behind her.

Sophie moved aside, and Vera rolled to her back at Jake's feet. He knelt and stroked her face and tummy. "Jake, what the hell were you thinking? That was stupid!"

"I was just playing," Jake said. "I guess she didn't think it was funny."

"No, I guess not!"

What had just happened? Sophie'd never seen such a sudden, dramatic shift in behavior in all her years of dog training. How the hell were they going to manage this dog? *Jesus!* She looked up at Jake, trying to read his expression, but his attention was focused on Vera—rubbing her face, crooning to her. She tried to still the trembling in her hands.

When Sophie let the girls back into the living room, they greeted Vera with a quick nose-to-nose sniff. Sophie had never seen Tess forgive anyone this quickly. Ever. The collie usually held grudges for weeks, if not months. Surely that meant that Tessie had not been so traumatized after all. Sophie felt like she was keeping a tally sheet for Vera, with "good" in one column and "not so good" in the other. It was filling up fast—on both sides.

The bath that followed went smoothly, though it took both Jake and Sophie's expertise to execute it. Sophie was silent and withdrawn, and in spite of wanting to vent to Jake, she was filled with such conflict she couldn't trust herself to say the right thing. So she focused on Vera and did her best to minimize the dog's emotional trauma.

Vera's coat was dense and fine, and absorbed the water and shampoo like a sponge. She shook herself off every few seconds, and before long, all three of them were soaked and soapy. She hated having her back-end handled—probably the result of her injuries—and Sophie gave up trying to dry her.

"Sorry, Vera!" Sophie tossed the towel by the mudroom door. "I can't do this any more either. Let's go for another walk—you can air-dry instead." The walk that followed was uneventful—but though Vera sniffed and sniffed, she still did not pee.

VERA

Vera was wired. She was so excited she could barely stay still. Her coat felt oddly damp, but not uncomfortable. She watched the girls carefully, learning how they navigated the house and paced themselves, how they managed space and toys. She recognized the dog toys, but she wasn't interested, and she noticed that the resident dogs weren't, either. In fact, they didn't pay attention to anything in the room at all.

At one point, she had reached up to take a cursory bite at a chair, but Sophie had given her a stern look and said "leave it"—a phrase she had learned at the shelter—so she stopped. She wanted to please Sophie and Jake, to hear their voices rise in praise, to hear the breath of their laughter.

And she craved Tess and Lola's acceptance. She liked being with them, reading them, and occupying a place in their lives, but she was uncertain of how to avoid conflict.

Most of all, she didn't want to get hurt.

She followed Sophie's instructions as much as she could during dinner and mirrored Tess and Lola when she wasn't sure what to do. At one point she got a sharp look from Sophie, but then she tried something else and was praised.

The evening was a blur. She observed her new family, and through trial, error, and careful observation worked out territorial issues and space. It was a huge puzzle to her, and when Jake placed her back in the mudroom, she lay on the mat in front of the door, eyes staring into the darkness, mentally exhausted.

Later, Sophie walked her again, and when they returned, the girls touched her nose with theirs and ambled off. Not knowing what else to do, Vera pranced into the living room behind them, found an empty place on the carpet, and lay down.

She tried to stay in one spot, but the incessant noise of the television battered her, and she was too wired to stay still. She jumped up and walked over to Jake. He sat motionless, staring straight ahead. With a fiery intensity, she willed him to look at her. Finally, he glanced down.

"Vera, go lie down." She cocked her head to the side and tried to understand—but nothing happened. He went back to looking straight ahead. She glanced around the room and her gaze fell on Lola sprawled on the love seat. She felt a quickening in her limbs and trotted around the coffee table. She released a loud, sharp bark in Lola's face.

Lola opened one eye and groaned. Nothing else happened. Vera raised her front leg and pawed at the golden, scratched at her face—and barked again. She was burning with disquiet, desperate to act, to do anything; to move, to run, to play, to shed the dreadful anxiety that tormented her. In the shelter she'd had no choices, but here the options were unfathomable. She had no idea what to do next, so she bit the golden's head.

Heavy with sleep, Lola rolled off the couch and mouthed Vera back. Vera felt her excitement build, then spin out of control. She jumped on top of Lola, tried to pin her down, bit at her neck. She leapt away, then pounced on her again. But as their play escalated, instead of becoming more frantic, Lola refused to continue and stood motionless, her head down. In a fit of desperation, Vera chewed on Lola's leg. She raked at the golden's shoulder with her claws. She waited. But after several seconds of no response, she gave up.

And walked back to Jake.

She sat in front of the man, staring as hard as she could at his face—but he ignored her. She whined, a high-pitched keening sound, certain to get his attention. But he still didn't respond. In frustration she raised her paw, long nails extended, and scratched him firmly down his leg.

"*Ow! Jesus, Vera!*" Jake's voice hit her like a hammer and shattered any sense of peace she had left. She fled up the stairs to the glass doors of the bedroom balcony, and let her anguish punctuate the night.

CHAPTER 15

SOPHIE

The next day proved to be much easier and more straight-forward than Sophie had dared to imagine. She set the alarm to awaken her every two hours throughout the night, and Vera finally peed at three o'clock in the morning, eighteen hours after she'd left the shelter. After that momentous event, Sophie was sure the rest of their time with Vera would be easy in comparison.

In the morning Sophie was tired, but also happy to be spending the day with the three girls instead of heading off to work. Lola and Vera had two relaxed play sessions while Tess cheered them on; there were no squabbles between the dogs; Vera wasn't destructive when Sophie left her alone to take Tess and Lola for an off-leash hike; and the shepherd did not have any accidents in the house.

Vera seemed to remember everything she'd been taught the previous day—in fact, her manners were impeccable. And most importantly, Tess and Lola seemed to enjoy her enthusiasm. She certainly challenged the girls, but they held their own, and were patient and diplomatic. Maybe Vera was actually going to be good for them.

Sophie did learn a couple of new things about Vera. The first thing was that Vera and Lola liked to be walked together. Vera mimicked everything Lola did, and though the golden looked aloof, she seemed very pleased with herself in her new role. The one time Sophie tried walking Vera and Tess together, two deer appeared at the end of the driveway and Tess redirected her excitement onto Vera's ear with a sharp snap. In a moment of chaos, the shepherd retaliated by baring her teeth and lunging at the collie, and Sophie barely had time to step between the two dogs before a fight broke out. After that, she walked them separately, each accompanied by the calm, poised presence of Lola.

The other thing Sophie learned was that Vera did not like to be brushed. In spite of endless patience and a river of treats, Vera struggled through the entire grooming session, leaping to her feet every few seconds, bumping Sophie with her muzzle, and working her back legs like pistons when Sophie tried to comb the fringe of fur on the back of her hind legs. The result was still dramatic: Vera's clean, brushed coat gleamed like plush velvet and was so soft and thick that Sophie had a hard time keeping her hands off it.

All in all, it was a good day and Sophie was satisfied that it had more or less gone according to plan. When Jake got home that evening, Sophie regaled him with the details of their day.

"So you think it's going to work out?" Jake turned toward Sophie just before turning out the light that night. He moved a strand of hair from her face and tucked it behind her ear.

His touch still sent a thrill down Sophie's spine, and from it she absorbed all the strength she needed. She searched his face for any sign of doubt and couldn't find it. She would try to forget the events of the previous day and move on. "I'm not looking forward to taking her back to the shelter in the morning. But yes—I think she's going to be amazing."

CHAPTER 16

SOPHIE

The next morning, Sophie closed the canopy hatch behind Vera and drove north. She tried to keep her voice light and upbeat, but she was filled with dread as she walked Vera into the shelter. It quaked with the barking of dogs—scared dogs, angry dogs, bewildered dogs. She couldn't imagine what Vera was thinking. How could she possibly understand what was happening? Sophie prayed that the transition back to her kennel wouldn't be too traumatic. "Vera, you'll come back home tonight, I promise. And maybe you'll get to see Sarah today."

But the minute Vera stepped into her kennel, she started her dance—her big, creamy paws arced into a circle, then picked up speed, driving faster and faster until her voice exploded from deep in her chest and she ricocheted up and down the walls, over and over. Sophie ducked back through the door into the office, swallowing the bile that rushed into her mouth. What was she thinking, bringing Vera back to the shelter during the day? It was crazy, a completely insensitive and thoughtless idea.

"She's spinning again already," Sophie choked out to an animal care worker. "I'll be back to get her in a couple of hours."

She drove back to the freeway and sped south toward work. The road faded, and all she could see was Vera spinning and spinning in front of her. Her nails dug into the steering wheel, her arms and shoulders shrieked with tension. Finally, after several deep breaths, she forced herself to relax enough to think.

The day was grey and cool so far, and rain was in the forecast. Since she had desk time scheduled for the afternoon at the clinic, she could conceivably drive back out to the shelter at lunchtime, pick up Vera, and leave her in the truck for the afternoon. She knew Jake would understand. There was simply no way that Vera could stay at the shelter ever again. Period. It would destroy her.

She rushed through her morning at work and for once, her patients were straightforward and she finished her schedule right on time. Grabbing her lunch, she ran to the truck and flew out to the shelter. She went straight to Vera's kennel. The minute Vera saw her, she stopped spinning and sat. She looked freaked.

"Vera! You're coming with me!" Sophie unlocked the kennel door for what she hoped was the last time.

The afternoon at the clinic passed slowly, but finally it was an acceptable time to leave. With a twinge of guilt, she snuck out the door without helping staff finish up with their patients at the end of the day—something she'd never done before. She sprinted to the parking lot afraid of what she would find.

As she approached the truck, she strained her eyes to search for any sign of movement. She couldn't see Vera's big, pointy ears through the windows. And it was quiet—no explosive barks echoed across campus.

She held her breath, peeked in, and relief melted her—the dog was lying on her bed with her beautiful head cradled on her paws. The shelter toys Sophie had left were in the same pattern of disarray as when Sophie left, Lola's bed was intact, and the bowl of water upright. When Vera saw her, she stood up, smiled, and shook herself off—as if waiting for Sophie was the most natural thing in the world.

VERA AND HER SISTERS

Vera was overjoyed to be back in Sophie's truck. She had been distraught when she found herself back in her kennel at the shelter. But now all that had changed again. She felt the truck pull into the driveway and stop, and she sniffed the air, nostrils flaring. She knew she was home.

When Sophie stopped at the mudroom door and fiddled with the latch, Vera crowded in front of her, willing it to open. She could hear Tess barking right on the other side, and she tensed, giddy with anticipation. She had no doubts about this reunion at all. She was primed.

Tess tingled, every fiber in her being singing a welcome when Sophie's truck pulled into the driveway. She barked and spun, and when the door was flung open and Vera bounced into the house, Tess glowed with the thrill of it, nuzzled the dog's face, and trotted off.

Lola lifted her head. There was something different about Sophie's arrival and she paused, weighing the significance. Then a burst of energy filled the room, a dark dog smiled and pranced, and Lola's twinge of uncertainty blossomed into a flood of delight. She stood and shook off and in a luxurious greeting, stretched into a full bow before she sauntered up to sniff noses. She was reassured to see that Vera's presence was soft and polite. In fact, everything about Vera made Lola feel good: the tipped ears, the long mouth, and the laughing breath panting out of her.

Then the three girls were romping through the living room together, Tess barking with abandon, and Lola and Vera dipping and bowing to one another in delight.

Sophie

"Sit!" Sophie shouted above the uproar. The three dogs turned to her and sat. "Down!" They dropped to the floor. Sophie felt like a conductor with a powerful, sinewy orchestra in front of her. This was amazing. "Sit!" The girls sat in unison. "That'll do." She released them.

The girls went back to their greeting, more poised than before, and when Sophie started up the stairs, they flew past with Vera in the lead.

Sophie didn't have a clue how she was going to deal with all this energy, but she'd have to figure it out. And soon. And she needed a plan for tomorrow as well—for the rest of the time they fostered Vera, actually. They couldn't leave her inside all day—they didn't even know if she was house trained. Vera hadn't peed in the house the day before, but then, she'd been walked every two hours. After some thought, Sophie decided to call Miriam, a dog-walker friend, to take Vera out during the day. At least for the first couple of weeks.

Vera

A sharp rap at the mudroom door caught Vera's attention. She had no idea what had caused this unlikely sound, and she charged, angry vocalizations erupting from deep in her chest.

She slammed her paws up high on the door, glowered through the window, and found herself eye to eye with a stranger. She was vaguely aware of Tess shrieking behind her, and Lola's deep, forceful barks to one side. Her whole being urged her to keep the intruder out.

Sophie growled something and pushed into her, blocking her access to the door and forcing Vera and her sisters out of the mudroom. The shepherd allowed herself to be herded backward by Sophie's insistent legs, but she didn't like it. She couldn't take her eyes off the strange form looming though the glass.

"Girls, down!" Sophie's presence was tall, stern, and intimidating, and Vera dropped to the floor in silence.

The door opened, and a short, stocky woman stepped into the room. Energy sparked off her, and Vera's heart pounded at the novelty of the invasion. The shepherd lifted her nose and sniffed, trying to glean clues from the air currents.

"That'll do!" Sophie's words startled her and she sprang to her feet followed by her sisters.

"Vera," Sophie said, "Miriam's going to take you out this week." Tess circled and wagged, laughing up at Miriam, but Vera stayed by Lola, watching.

Now that the woman was inside and the girls were happy, Vera was curious. She liked people, especially women; but she held back, sticking by Lola. She watched the woman lean over and scratch Tess's back and ears, and when the collie curved and danced, Vera relaxed further, safely outside the woman's sphere of attention.

Then, without warning, Miriam stepped forward, crouched down, and stoked Vera's head. The woman's eyes, only inches away, locked onto hers and she darted back, panic flaming inside her. She licked and licked and looked away, struggling to stay in control—until Lola saved her, stretching and bowing and gliding into the space between them.

"Lola!" Miriam said. Her voice was lower than Sophie's and carried more heft, and Vera weighed the impact of it. The woman scrubbed Lola's back and ears till the golden walked away, then she stood up and turned her attention back to Sophie.

Without the direct, hard stare of the woman boring into her, Vera's curiosity got the best of her, and she took a few tentative steps toward Miriam, stretching her nose forward, her back legs still anchored well behind her.

"Now she's coming around," Miriam announced. "It's always better to ignore these dogs at first. She'll be fine."

SOPHIE

"Well, she's an honest-to-God German shepherd, isn't she?" Miriam said. Sophie winced at the tone of her voice. Why couldn't Miriam be a little more measured? Sometimes she seemed so brash and besides, she was scaring Vera. "She's such a good-looking dog, too. Sure you don't want to keep her?"

"I'd kind of like to, but it's so much work, and I don't want to deal with all the doggy politics—Tess and Vera already had one squabble."

"They seem fine now."

"I know, but Vera's a different kind of dog. She's…"

Miriam laughed. "She's just a German shepherd! Sure, I'd love to take her out during the week when you're at work. We should take them for a hike with my boy, Baker. You know how good he is with other dogs. We could take them up the Galbraith logging road."

Sophie showed Miriam Vera's harness and leash, where the treats and plastic bags were kept, and they made arrangements to meet on Saturday morning for a hike.

Sophie checked her watch as soon as Miriam left. Five-thirty. Well, thank goodness she'd taken care of all that before Jake got home. She wasn't worried about it exactly, but still. Just then, she heard his car pull into the driveway.

She went out to meet him, closing the door carefully behind her. "Jake! You're home!"

"Is anything wrong? You look worried." He reached back into the car to get his bag from the passenger seat.

"Well, not exactly. But we can't leave Vera at the shelter during the day any more. She started spinning the moment I put her back in the kennel." Sophie tried to still her fidgeting hands. She really didn't want to have another argument about Vera.

"What did you do?"

She recounted the day, emphasizing Vera's anguish at the shelter. "Miriam will walk her three days a week and I'll take her to work with me on my half-days off. Here, let me take that." She relieved him of a stack of folders.

"What about Tess and Lola? We definitely can't leave them with Vera."

"No, but Vera hasn't jumped the baby gates yet, so I think she'll stay in the mudroom. And with any luck, she won't be here for long."

The moment Sophie saw Jake and Vera together, she knew it would be all right. "Hi, Vera," he said after greeting Tess and Lola. "Did you have a hard day?" He crouched down and rubbed her chest and face. "Be nice to Tess and you can stay for as long as you like."

CHAPTER 17

SOPHIE

On Wednesday afternoon after work, Sophie took all three girls to the local dog park by the lake for the first time. She couldn't think of a better way to see how Vera would act around strange dogs when off leash, and she wanted to try it in a large, open area before meeting Miriam and her dog on the narrow logging roads of Galbraith Mountain.

She was reassured in that Vera had been appropriate with dogs in the neighborhood when she was on leash—a good indicator of how she'd react to them off leash. Dogs tended to be much more defensive when restricted by the leash than when they were free to express themselves unencumbered. And Tess and Lola were solid dog-park dogs: reliable, playful, and they knew exactly what to do to stay out of trouble. They would take care of Vera.

Sophie and the three girls arrived at the park in early

afternoon. Although it was a beautiful spring day, there were only a few dogs chasing a ball into the water. Sophie watched them for a few minutes. They didn't worry her.

The huge field was a brilliant green, and swallows darted everywhere, cutting and twisting as they hunted. Vera was alert, eyes tracking the swallows, tail high. A piercing whine of excitement gave way to sharp, staccato barks.

Not sure how best to proceed, Sophie unclipped Tess and Lola first, holding Vera at her side until the sisters rollicked off together. Vera strained forward, frantic to join them, her attention on the birds temporarily disrupted.

"Vera, sit!" Sophie waited for the shepherd to comply and make full eye contact with her. Then she held her breath and unclipped the leash.

Lola saw her coming. She crouched, braced herself against the onslaught, lowered her head, and froze. The shepherd slammed into her, pounced onto the golden's back again and again, and mouthed her neck. Vera looked obsessed.

"Vera!" Sophie shouted the dog's name over and over. She jumped up and down, waved her arms, ran toward the lake—anything to distract the shepherd into chasing her. But Vera seemed glued to Lola's unmoving form—using her teeth, her paws, the bump of her body to get Lola to react. "Vera, come, you'll hurt her!"

Suddenly, the shepherd looked up, focused, and charged—her body a missile aimed straight at Sophie. Sophie turned sideways and bent her knees, prepared for certain impact. But Vera dodged past—and raced after a swallow. Her head lowered, her front and back legs stretched out parallel to the ground, and then her body was moving like a wave across the grass, each leap covering, what? Ten to fifteen feet? Sophie had never seen a dog run like this. She was so fast and sure, wolf-like and predatory. And yet, Sophie was pretty sure the shepherd had never done this before in her life.

Vera chased the swallows for an hour without interruption, the birds seeming to dive in front of her face, to goad her ever faster, cutting and turning. She ignored the dogs that came and went from the park. She ignored Tess retrieving her Frisbee from the lake. She ignored Lola playing and hopping in the tall reeds, trying to tease other dogs into chasing her.

Finally, exhausted, she trotted to the beach and followed Tess into the water. A strange dog wandered by and she looked at him, then splashed deeper into the lake, biting and pawing at the wavelets.

"Good girl, Vera!" Sophie waded in to join her. Vera panted, her face beaded with water droplets, her eyes wild. "Come on, girl. Time to go home."

As they walked up the beach together, a black lab trotted up to Vera. He looked friendly enough with his loose body and soft eyes, and Sophie was eager to see what the shepherd would do. Vera stood on her toes, reached her head as far forward as she possibly could to sniff the dog's nose, then whirled away to join Lola.

Not the best greeting in the world, Sophie thought, watching Lola and Vera meander off together along the shore. But at least she'd been respectful. Walking back to the car, Sophie tried to ignore the fluttering unease she felt in the pit of her stomach—there had been no conflicts that she could pinpoint. And yet, she had the distinct feeling that something was wrong.

By Saturday morning, however, the feeling had faded, and Sophie felt much better about Vera's experience at the dog park. She was bursting with anticipation—Vera would meet a new dog and go for an off-leash walk on the logging road close to their house. And Jake had agreed to come along for moral support.

When they arrived at the trailhead, Miriam was already there with her five-year-old lab mix, Baker. He was bouncy and sleek and a little submissive, and when Tess and Lola leapt from the back of the truck, he slowed and arced and bowed a welcome. The three dogs mingled and sniffed and trotted off up the track together. Forced to stay in the truck, Vera whined, her voice a pitiful squeak.

"Why don't you let her out?" Miriam asked. "She'll be fine.

Baker can look after himself."

"I think we should take it slowly with Vera," Sophie said. "This is so new for her,"

"The leash could be a problem," said Jake. "Why don't we call Tess and Lola back and let her out while Baker's up ahead? The girls can help Vera meet him."

Sophie was starting to regret the whole process, her feelings from Vera's recent experience at the dog park resurfacing. By nature she liked to be cautious, and she didn't want Vera to scare Baker—or worse—by unleashing the shepherd too soon in a brand new place. Technically, as a foster dog, Vera shouldn't be let off the leash at all—but it was too late for that now. Decisions. And no time to process. *Damn.* She should have thought this out more carefully before they arrived.

"Sure," she said finally. "OK, Vera." Vera soared out of the truck. "Sit!" Sophie put a piece of cheese in front of her nose just as she hit the ground, and obediently, Vera sat. She was tense, eyes focused on Sophie's, brow furrowed and ears erect. But she was responsive, and the leash was loose.

When called, Tess and Lola bounded back to her, joyful and panting, paws muddy from the ditch that edged the dirt road. "Here goes!" Sophie said under her breath. She unclipped Vera's leash. "OK, girls, go play!" The three dogs tore off up the road in a wave of excitement.

Baker was occupied by something further up the track, and when he heard the girls, he turned to greet them. Tess and Lola reached him first and sniffed noses briefly before racing on. Then Vera, who had been distracted by a squirrel, arrived. She surged into Baker's face, tail high, weight forward, and Baker was suddenly on his back, hind legs splayed, frozen in place. Vera's head darted down, her muzzle pressed to Baker's neck.

The world stopped for Sophie—her vision narrowed, her stomach clenched, her hand flew to her mouth. She held her breath, afraid to move, afraid that any movement would trigger the worst. The seconds stretched and still Vera's jaws hovered over Baker's throat.

Then Tess and Lola were trotting toward the two dogs. And

Vera, hearing their footfalls, looked up, beamed a smile, and with great élan, bounded over Baker and raced up the road, the lab in hot pursuit.

"Jesus!" Sophie's heart pounded. She was such a wuss when it came to conflict.

"See?" Miriam said. "She's just a German-shepherd punk. I don't know why you're so worried about her. She just needed to show Baker who's boss."

Sophie took her hand away from her mouth—the one that had been ready to stifle a scream. She sucked in a lungful of air and blew it out slowly. Vera was turning out to be all right with other dogs after all—in spite of her early history at the shelter and her spat with Tess. Sophie didn't really know why she was so concerned. There had been a few little incidents, sure, but they didn't warrant this level of discomfort. She gripped Vera's leash more tightly and tried to shake it off.

"What did you think of that?" Jake asked when Miriam walked ahead.

"I didn't like it, but she did OK. That dog is so intense—I always expect the worst of her."

They watched her trot after Lola. Vera had a prancing gait, throwing her front paws out in front of her, head held high. It made her look somehow angelic and vulnerable. She ignored Baker, but forced her way into something Tess was sniffing, pushing the collie aside. Tess woofed indignantly, and trotted off to join Baker.

Lola swaggered ahead of Vera, checking on her with a coy glance if the shepherd lagged behind, swishing her long, golden tail. Once she had Vera's attention, she broke loose to chase after something deep in the bush far more important than her foster sister.

Sophie had to admit that she was enjoying Lola's relationship with Vera. Lola was such an introvert for a golden retriever, and didn't make friends easily. Deeply thoughtful, she observed and appraised her environment quietly, and had she been human, Sophie surmised, she would have been a philosopher or a scientist with the brute strength of a Sherman tank. Vera's fascination with Lola was touching, and their playfulness with each other, though too rough and noisy for Sophie, was well matched. This was probably a good thing for Lola.

They walked on, breathless on the steep road. The valley spread out below them; Lake Whatcom a deep-blue jewel, Mt. Baker towering over the foothills, glacier-capped and brilliant. Taking in the scene of the dogs chasing and playing around her, Sophie had an inkling, just for a moment, that they should consider adopting Vera.

She watched the shepherd race after Baker and mouth his neck, twirl to follow him when he spun away from her, stop to sniff when he lifted his leg on a rotten stump—then bound off again. They traversed a stream, vaulted over a pile of logs, and ended the chase back at Lola. Tess stayed close to Jake, seeking protection from all the activity.

"Sophie, maybe we should adopt her," Jake said.

"Well, why not?" Miriam chimed in. "I mean, just look at her. Why wouldn't you?"

"We aren't supposed to have more than two dogs in Sudden Valley, for one thing—and I don't want three dogs. And I worry about Tessie. Tess and Vera haven't bonded the way I'd hoped."

"Don't worry about Sudden Valley," Miriam said. "I have a friend there with six dogs and no one cares. And if you have two dogs, what's the difference with having three?"

"She's a great dog," Jake said. "I can't imagine her living with anyone else."

Sophie was silent. She knew how long dogs lived. It wouldn't be a matter of a few months, it would be at least six years of caring for three dogs—if Tess and Lola had long lives. The thought overwhelmed her. Once she'd made the commitment, she knew there would be no backing out no matter what happened. She watched Lola, enjoying her careful exploration of the weeds at the edge of the track. For such a big dog, she had a delicate grace about her. It fascinated Sophie.

"I'll think about it."

The golden stopped, raised her head, scented the air—and

was gone. Vera followed her, a fluid streak disappearing into the gloom. The forest seemed to close behind them.

Uncertainty shifted inside Sophie, but she didn't want to appear to overreact—not with Miriam there. She trusted Lola off leash in the woods without question, but Vera was a completely different matter.

"Vera!" She shouted the name, put everything she had into it in hopes that Vera would stop, leave Lola and come right back. As soon as Vera's name left her lips she realized how silly that hope was. No dog in her right mind would forgo a chase so quickly. Especially a dog with as little experience in the world as Vera.

"Don't panic," Miriam said. Her face had that "chill out" look that drove Sophie crazy. "Lola will take care of her. You know they'll stick together."

This was true, Sophie thought—or at least hoped. But three minutes later, Lola reappeared alone, her face jubilant. She trotted off to sniff with Tess.

"Lola, where's Vera?" Lola looked up at Sophie with a blank expression on her face as if to say "Who?" Had she dumped Vera on purpose? The thought flashed through Sophie's mind. "Lola, search! Go find Vera." Her voice was firm, insistent. But Lola continued to look back at her as if she didn't understand a word Sophie said. Lola knew those words. They had trained her to "search" years ago. Sophie was baffled.

"Vera!" Sophie yelled. "Vera!"

"Sophie, calm down," Jake's voice had a sharp edge to it.

She hated to be told to "calm down". "Vera!" Her voice was almost a scream now.

"Lola and I will go up the road and call her. Sophie, you and Tess stay here. And Miriam, take Baker back down the road to look for her."

The moments crawled past. "Tessie, speak!" Sophie clapped her hands and Tess looked up, bright-eyed, and let loose a loud, sharp bark. "Good girl, Tess! Speak!" Sophie and Tess wandered up and down the strip of road, Tess barking, while Sophie searched for any movement in the ferns and bushes that lined the track. They wove through the edge of the woods, but the brush was dense and difficult to navigate. They could hear Jake and Miriam calling up and down the mountain. But there was no sign of the shepherd.

Then she heard a "yip" in the distance. Surely that couldn't be Vera so far away. But how far could an athletic dog travel in five minutes? One mile? Two miles? It was mind-boggling how much distance a dog could cover—especially Vera.

Thirty minutes had passed. She'd seen signs posted on trails for years pleading for the return of lost dogs. She'd always asked herself how anyone could lose a dog. It had been beyond her comprehension—but also, when she imagined it, her worst nightmare.

"Vera, come!" She was in a full panic now. How could she have let this happen? And to poor, sweet, abused Vera; so new to the world, so naïve. What if she were badly injured, a broken leg, or worse? She couldn't imagine that Vera would leave Lola's side on purpose.

The day wore on. Jake and Miriam joined her again, and for a while they wandered up and down the road together, calling, beseeching Vera to come back. What if this was it? What if they never saw her again? By now it was late afternoon. What about water? Vera must be thirsty and scared. Maybe she had found a stream. The air was chilling off and Sophie was cold. She was numb, horrified, desperate.

By eight o'clock, the light was starting to fade in the deep shadow of the mountain where they searched, and they decided to make one last sweep before returning home to make "lost dog" signs. Sophie and Tess stuck to the same area they had patrolled earlier, walking up and down, up and down, calling and barking.

A rustle of branches sounded just up the road. Tess alerted, her ears swept forward, eyes fixed on the spot. Did that hemlock bough just tremble? It fell like a curtain beside the road, obscuring the forest beyond. Had the breeze disturbed it? Had she imagined it? But no, Tess heard it too.

With the collie at her side, she ran forward and arrived at

the branch just as a bedraggled, trembling German shepherd crawled from beneath it. Vera looked exhausted, barely able to stand. With great effort, she dragged herself to the middle of the track and collapsed, shaking. Sophie cradled the beautiful head in her arms and yelled to Jake and Miriam.

She stroked Vera's sleek face and smoothed her back with long, massaging strokes. "It's OK, sweet girl, you found us." How far had she run? It was conceivable that she hadn't gone any distance at all. Vera was so panicked it occurred to Sophie that perhaps she had barely made it off the road when, overcome with terror, she had frozen. At that moment, Sophie couldn't imagine giving her up.

But when they got home, there was a message on the answering machine. "Sophie? This is Jessie from the shelter. We have someone who's interested in Vera. They want to see her. Can you call and arrange a meeting? They're an older couple with a home business and acreage. Sounds like a good fit for Vera."

Sophie's stomach lurched. This was it. Exactly what she wanted. So why did she feel like calling back and saying that they'd decided to adopt her? Period.

Then she was crying uncontrollably. She felt like a beetle pinned through its thorax: no decision was the right decision and she was painfully, unbearably immobilized.

The next morning, after Jake had held her and calmed her down, and after they had talked the situation into the ground, Sophie called back.

"Jessie? This is Sophie. Can you give me the phone number of the people interested in Vera?"

CHAPTER 18

VERA

Vera couldn't understand it. She had been soaring, full of new sensations and experiences, surrounded by her sisters, Jake, and Sophie.

And then without warning everything changed.

She crouched on a blanket in the corner of a strange room, images of the past twenty-four hours crowding her brain… great sadness in Sophie and Jake, a long car ride, new people, a new place, and new smells.

Everything familiar was gone.

A woman walked toward her past a high counter, a table, chairs, things that were familiar, but the room filled her with dread. The woman was kind, but anxiety poured from her in a caustic river and Vera absorbed it into her fragile being like a sponge.

"Don't you want your dinner, Vera? What will I do if you don't eat?" The woman hovered over her, crowding her space.

"Stop worrying about the damned dog, Kate. She's OK. Just leave her alone." The voice was deep and gruff; the man huge, his hands enormous, and a beard obscured his face making his features difficult to read.

Vera had liked him at first. His voice had been kind and gentle. His large, strong hands had stroked her face and chest with such care and warmth that she had been lulled to sleep. But now that Sophie was gone, he was always angry. He shouted rather than talked, sometimes at the woman, sometimes at her.

"Doug, lower your voice. You're scaring her."

"Jesus Christ! What's wrong with this fucking dog?" He stomped out, slamming the door behind him. Vera cowered further into her corner.

"It's OK, Vera. He doesn't mean anything by it. It's just the way he is."

Kate offered her a piece of ham and she snatched it from the open palm, studying the woman's lined face. She still didn't know what to think.

That night, Vera lay in the room by their bed—afraid to move.

The next morning, Kate got up at first light and took her for a walk in a field of tall, sweet-smelling grasses by the house. Small creatures hid and scurried beneath her feet. Vera stalked forward in slow motion, head cocked, alert to the sound of tiny paws clawing and pushing their way through the earth. *Now!* She'd spring, all four paws leaping high in the air, landing where she thought the creature should be. She was barely aware of the sharp jerk on the leash from behind. Kate talked to her in an unrelenting drone that she found comforting at first, then annoying. She tuned it out.

Later, after she'd sniffed her breakfast and gone back to her bed, the man growled into the room and clipped a leash to her collar. She followed him, afraid to resist.

He led her to a building that smelled of oil and metal. She didn't want to go inside. It was dark and forbidding. Huge, strange objects hung from the ceiling, lined the walls, rose up from the floor. He dragged her through the door and, tail tucked, she lay tethered to the wall.

Suddenly, a deafening noise blasted her, pounded into her brain. The sound went on and on. Sometimes it stopped and she'd start to relax, only to explode again with crushing intensity into the stillness. She retreated into herself.

Much later, Kate came and untied her. Again, they walked through the field, and Vera sniffed and listened to the ground. Consumed by the hunt, everything else faded away, but once they reached the house, she ached for her sisters, and for anything familiar. Kate's kindness eased her discomfort, but the world still buzzed with the woman's anxiety, and Vera recoiled from it.

That night, the air prickled with ozone. Rain and thunder and wind battered the house, tore at the roof, slammed the walls. Only once before had she experienced such a storm, and the violence of it terrified her. She crawled to the bed where Doug slept and tried to leap to safety.

"What the fuck?"

She clawed and strained to get purchase against the sheets, the pillows, his arms. His shouts punctuated the darkness. Fists pummeled her face. She yelped and fled to an open closet in the center of the house where the noise was less deafening and the flashes couldn't reach her. She curled into a ball, and for the rest of the night, she watched and listened, heart racing.

The days passed, and she became more familiar with the daily routine. Every morning the man grumbled and blustered, and left—slamming the door behind him. Later, the woman walked her to the shop where she was tethered for hours. She became more accustomed to the bang and crash of the equipment, to the odors that clung to her coat. Large men came and went, boots clomping on the concrete floor, voices loud above the ever-present clamor.

Then, one day, the man untethered her.

"OK Vera. Let's see what you can do." His hand reached down and rubbed her face and chest. She groaned in pleasure. He didn't touch her much, but when he did, his warmth connected with her and she drank it greedily. She felt him unclip the leash from her collar and she stood still for a moment, not sure what to do.

She took a tentative step forward, then sniffed her way along one wall. She smelled mice and oil and the fading scent of a dog.

"Good girl, Vera!" She glowed in his praise and continued her investigation.

"Doug?" Male voices filled the shop entrance. She darted further back into the building to avoid them, but an ear-splitting sound exploded in front of her as a machine kicked on. Trapped, she fled toward the light—but a cluster of men blocked her exit.

Laughter splintered the air, their eyes preyed on her. A man moved toward her, reaching out, fingers only inches from her muzzle. She barked and barked, shouting at him, at them, to get back, to leave her alone, to let her pass.

But he kept coming, his hand outstretched. She backed up, barking louder, each bark more frantic than the last. She couldn't run further away; the sound still crashed from the darkness behind her. She didn't know what to do. In a desperate effort to clear her path, she snarled and snapped.

"Holy shit!" the man snatched back his hand.

A fist grabbed her collar, twisted, and jerked her off her feet.

She landed on her left side. Her still-tender ribs connected with the pitted concrete floor and she yelped. Doug's fury bore into her. She was on her side, sliding out of control, dragged by her neck.

He clipped on her tether and then the men were gone. She faced the wall, and shook.

After that, her apprehension bloomed into terror. Every day, Doug took her to the shop, and as time crept past, the pressure to defend herself—from the constant flow of men who moved through the shop, and from Doug himself—mushroomed, until she felt she would explode.

She had felt safe for periods of time in her original home, and at the shelter, and certainly with her sisters. But here she felt threatened with crushing consistency.

Doug's patience was short, and every time she shrank from him, every time she cowered from sudden sounds or movement, her fear was met with a volatile verbal rebuke and sometimes physical assault. The more she cringed and the more she warned his customers away, the more severe was her punishment.

CHAPTER 19

Tess and Lola

Tess moped. She missed Vera. There was something about the shepherd that had intrigued her in spite of the friction, the ongoing conflicts, and the moment-to-moment challenges. The spontaneity of the dog, their shared energy, and Vera's naivety had nestled into her soul in such a way that without her, Tess pined. She didn't miss the stalking, the constant vying for Lola's attention, the concentration it took to avoid conflict with the dog. And yet…in the short time they'd spent together, Vera had grown on her. But by degrees, as the days turned into weeks, the ache and the emptiness became an echo, and she slowly regained her effervescence.

Lola mourned too. She had known few dogs in her life that

she truly adored. Few that she felt comfortable with. Not even Baker achieved the status of a true companion. But Vera had. Her absolute devotion, and her willingness to mirror Lola's every move and share every experience had rocked Lola's foundation. Lola's bond to Vera was now so strong that the dog's absence was physically painful. Even the shepherd's rough and tumble play, although sometimes difficult to control, had endeared her to Lola. Who else could she romp with in such a way?

Time passed and Lola clung to Tess. She spent more time curled up by Sophie and Jake. For Lola, the shadow of Vera's absence lingered on.

Sophie

It had been almost a month since Vera left, and Sophie and Jake had had endless conversations about Vera's new home. Sophie tried to envision her being pampered and well cared for, conjured images of her running in the large orchard behind her home, imagined her daily hikes in the foothills of the North Cascades: all the things the couple had promised. But Sophie couldn't suppress the feeling that she had committed the biggest betrayal of her life by sending Vera away. The feeling gnawed an unrelenting assault on her gut. Tess and Lola missed her too— she could tell. They were withdrawn and quiet. Even Tess was subdued, and would lie for hours on the deck without so much as a woof.

Sophie threw herself back into her shelter work with renewed passion. She spent most of her time following through on her plan to take Sarah out in the community, and with the help of Leah and a third volunteer, would take three dogs for long walks in the parks of Bellingham, armed with "Adopt Me" jackets for the dogs, and packets of adoption information.

Sophie also worked with Sarah on her CGC training, and the dog made progress—but still no adoption. Sarah's main challenge was staying calm in the presence of new dogs, so they practiced it relentlessly when they got together. Sophie had started the CGC program with other dogs too, but they had been adopted before she got very far.

She also kept up with the Open Paw classes, but her enthusiasm had started to wane. She didn't have the drive to fight the administration any more and without their concrete support, it had started to feel like a weight dragging her down. Her heart just wasn't in it. She missed Vera desperately.

"I'm going to call Kate and check on Vera," Sophie said one evening. "I can't stand it any more." She was proud of her discipline—it had been two weeks since she'd last spoken to Kate.

Jake nodded. "Good idea."

Kate answered with an airy "Hello?" But when Sophie asked about Vera, there was a long, weighted silence.

Sophie held her breath.

"Um…well…she's not doing so good." And then words spilled from the phone in a rush. "Doug shouts at her a lot. He's older, and doesn't hear so good. He expects the dog to do what he wants, when he wants, and he just doesn't get it that she's sensitive and he can't yell at her like that."

"He *yells* at her?" Sophie couldn't hold it in. Being hard of hearing was no excuse.

"She cowers in the corner and she won't come into our room at night any more—that's where her bed is. And yesterday, she growled and barked at a couple of clients who came by the shop. You know, we can't have her barking at our clients—so Doug hit her."

"He *hit* her?" Sophie couldn't believe what she was hearing. "You need to bring her back."

"I don't think he'd go for that. You know, it's a male thing. He wants to make it work."

"Kate, let me think about it. I'll get back to you."

When Sophie hung up the phone she was pale and shaking and nauseated. She couldn't believe that Vera was living such a nightmare in her new home. Talk about a betrayal! She dialed Emma's number and the director answered.

"She's cowering and growling at people," Sophie said.

"Get her back. Tomorrow. Before she bites someone," Emma said.

"Bites someone?" Sophie echoed. She hadn't really considered that to be a risk with Vera. She was more worried about Vera being in an abusive home. Sophie knew that if any dog got scared enough they would bite, but it occurred to her for the first time that she didn't know what "scared enough" meant for Vera. She sat and thought about this.

"What did she say?" Jake asked.

Sophie related the conversations.

"Well, bring her back here then. However you can do that. When can you get her?"

A flood of gratitude swelled in her chest, but then her breath caught. There it was again—that creeping anxiety about canine politics. "But what about the girls?" She had hated the friction between them. What if they couldn't find Vera another home?

"The girls will be fine. You worry too much!" His words were light and teasing, but they still irked her.

Given the circumstances, she chose to ignore them. "I'll see if Kate can meet me at the dog park after work tomorrow."

This was getting more and more complicated. Sophie had to go to the clinic in the morning. Then she had the thirty-minute drive home to pick up the girls so she could drive another thirty minutes to Jake's school. They had planned a special presentation with the girls for Jake's students to celebrate the last day of class. Actually, to celebrate the last day of Jake's elementary school teaching career. But now, what about Vera?

She called Kate.

"Kate? The shelter wants you to return Vera. It doesn't matter what Doug says, it's a safety issue. If she continues to live in her current situation, she'll bite someone." ˙

There was a sigh on the other end of the line. "Will you still foster her? I don't want her to go back to the shelter. Can't you adopt her?"

There it was again. "We'll take care of her until we find someone who will. I can meet you at the Bloedel Donovan dog park at one o'clock." She gave Kate directions, hung up, and turned to Jake. "We're getting her back!"

Sophie had never been so excited. For a second she

remembered that Jake would be leaving for Mexico in a few days, where she would be joining him in a month—but she pushed it out of her mind. She didn't want to think about it.

"I've really missed her," Jake said. "I love that dog."

CHAPTER 20

SOPHIE

Friday was Sophie's last day at the clinic before her summer break. Since most of the students had moved out till fall quarter started, she was able to leave work right on time. Back home, she gathered leashes, beds, treats, and water for the girls, and loaded them into the truck.

They pulled into the dog park just behind Kate, but by the time Kate opened her car door, Tess and Lola were already in the field. The three girls came together in a tumult of joy, and Kate and Sophie cheered their chase around and around the field, clapping as the dogs barked and pawed and mouthed one another, completely oblivious to everyone else in the park.

"Seeing that, I know I'm doing the right thing, though I don't know what I'm going to tell Doug," said Kate. "He doesn't mean to scare her, he's just hard of hearing and he doesn't understand her."

Sophie didn't know what to say. This had more to do with who Doug was than just his hearing loss. "You're doing the right thing, Kate. It's just not the right home for Vera. Doug needs a bullet-proof dog who doesn't care about his tone of voice." She faced Kate and held her gaze. "But he should *never* hit a dog— no matter what."

She jogged over to where the girls played together at the edge of the lake. As Lola dug—powerful shoulders working, her face a mask of concentration—Vera pounced on the spray of sand and water that arced from between Lola's hind legs. Tessie circled and barked.

"Girls! Let's go! We'll be late!" She had to shout to be heard above Tess's voice, but still they ignored her. Vera was now peppered in sand and water droplets, her face eager. "Girls, come!" Sophie sprinted across the field, and a moment later they were prancing beside her.

Kate's face relaxed into a smile when they reached the parking lot. "They sure look happy together!" she said. "Let me know how Vera does. I'm going to miss her. She's a good dog."

Sophie found herself lost in a fantasy on her drive to Jake's school. The freeway faded in and out as visions of the three girls hiking and playing together on mountain tracks unfolded before her. She soared as she drove into the school parking lot. This time, she knew she'd done the right thing for Vera.

When Sophie unloaded Tess and Lola from the truck, Vera whined. And when the three of them walked toward the school, the whine escalated into a high-pitched shriek. Sophie had been careful to park in a deeply shaded spot at the side of the road, close to the area where Tess and Lola would be demonstrating their talents. But although she had left fresh water and a large treat for Vera, she was consumed by guilt.

The children were already assembled in a large circle on the lawn and as Sophie approached, she heard Jake issuing instructions on the noise level, good listening skills, and how to be respectful of the dogs.

The early afternoon sun beat down, but in spite of the warmth, there was a freshness to the air. Delighted with the audience, Tess and Lola nuzzled and pawed one another, and the collie barked a greeting. The children murmured, raising their hands to tell stories of their dogs at home, giggling when Tess pranced up to lick their faces, their hands reaching out to stroke her thick, white ruff. Lola swaggered past them, apparently pleased to be the center of attention, but not so interested in being mauled.

"Girls, down." Sophie instructed. The dogs dropped to the ground and looked up at her. In the sudden silence, Sophie could hear Vera crying in the truck.

The whole class began buzzing with excitement about the third dog.

"You have another dog?"

"Can we see him?"

"Where is he?"

"She's a special dog," Jake explained. "She's had a hard life and a big day so far. She might be scared having so many kids around her."

"We'll be careful."

"We promise."

"Pleeeeease, we really want to see her."

With each bark and whine, Sophie's desperation rose until she was choking on guilt. "What if I got her out, Jake? You could just hold her off to the side while the girls and I do our demo. I don't want her to feel abandoned. I'm sure she'll be all right with Tess and Lola here."

"All right," Jake said to the class. "Sophie will bring Vera over, but until we see how she's doing, I don't want anyone to go near her. Give her lots of space, and time to get used to being around you. Got it?"

Twenty-five wide-eyed faces nodded back at him.

Sophie waited till Vera's cries ebbed for a few seconds, then opened the truck. Full of excitement, Vera ducked her head through the harness and jumped down. As soon as she touched the ground, she sat without being asked, and walked calmly on leash over to the group.

Tess and Lola trotted over to greet her, sniffing and pawing her face while she stood tall and proud, absorbing the attention like a queen. Lola chuckled and bowed in front of her, heavy tail swishing.

"Vera looks like she just arrived in paradise," Jake said.

"All right, everyone," Sophie said. "I want you to leave Vera alone until we give you permission to greet her, then you can come up and pet her gently. Move very slowly, one at a time. Jake will give you cookies to feed her. Does anyone know why I want you to move slowly?"

Sophie started her lesson. She pointed out canine communication signals using Tess and Lola as models. She talked about the body language of dogs, Tess and Lola's large English language vocabulary, and how dogs learn. She emphasized the importance of kindness to animals; that animals have feelings just like people; that even shouting can be terrifying to them. She talked about Vera's past and how much it had affected her. When Sophie was ready, Tess and Lola performed their repertoire of tricks and skills under her guidance while the children stared, transfixed.

All this time, Vera lay at Jake's feet looking relaxed and happy. It was uncanny to Sophie how she could look so at peace after the last month.

"All right, everyone. You can approach Vera now, one at a time. You need to move slowly. Remember? We talked about that. Pet her on her chest and shoulders and give her a cookie. Don't touch the top of her head because it might scare her. If Jake asks you to go back to your place, you need to do it right away."

One at a time, the children crept forward, talking to Vera in soft tones, oohing and ahhing over what a beautiful dog she was, and how they would like a dog just like her. They fed her salmon cookies and stroked her chest, their small hands fluttering through her thick, black-and-cinnamon fur, their high voices seeming to mesmerize her. She lay quietly, bathing in the attention. Tess and Lola watched, taking it all in.

Then the bell rang and the spell was broken: the children went back to their places on the lawn, the girls made their final round of goodbyes, and Vera stood up to shake off and prance.

It was the end of an era. Jake was retired.

Later that night—after the retirement party at a local wine bar, after the long drive home and the girls' joyous romp through the house; after dinner, and the decision that Vera would sleep upstairs as part of the family—Sophie lay awake with Lola in her arms and Jake pressed against her back, thinking. Jake was leaving in two days for Mexico, and four weeks later she would be joining him there. What then?

CHAPTER 21

SOPHIE

The drive back from the airport was packed with silence and the unknown. It was always awkward after Jake left. The air felt different, even sound didn't resonate the same way. It wasn't necessarily bad, just foreign and empty, and it took Sophie a day or two to adjust. Thoughts drifted by of Vera and the girls, visions of them playing and hiking and lingering together.

She thought about Sarah back at the shelter, too. She still managed to visit Sarah three times a week, and take her on walks around town wearing her "adopt me" jacket—sometimes alone, sometimes with Leah. Sarah had thrived on these outings and Sophie was determined to keep the trips going—no matter what transpired at home—until Sarah got adopted.

Sarah had been at the shelter for seven months now, and Sophie loved her more than ever. Part of Sophie wished for Sarah in her life instead of Vera...she had never fallen completely in love with Vera, but rather felt an overwhelming sense of responsibility for her. If only Vera had gone to a good home, then she could have adopted Sarah. Maybe.

A car pulled out in front of her, too close for comfort. *Better concentrate on driving.*

LOLA

Lola was jerked out of a deep sleep by a series of sharp, forceful barks followed by Tessie's yips. It took her a moment to orient herself, but when she opened her eyes, she realized she was alone in the bedroom. There was no sound of Sophie flying to the rescue—then she remembered that Sophie and Jake were out.

Vera! That's what the commotion was about.

She leapt from the bed and trotted down the stairs, her thoughts a whir. Rounding the corner, she tensed, uneasiness making her hesitate—Vera's jaws were clamped firmly around the collie's head and Tess stood with legs splayed, her stiff posture shouting out that she was unsure of what to do next.

Vera glanced up and loosened her grip, allowing Tess to jerk back. Lola saw her opportunity. With a rush of confidence she raced forward, and just when she found the point precisely between the two dogs, she stretched into a bow; golden legs reaching before her, tail high behind. She held her position while the seconds ticked by—statue-still, head low, willing her sisters to withdraw. She felt strong and complete and utterly calm. She sensed Vera's resolve falter and heard the whisper of Tess's paws on the carpet as she sidestepped away. Only then did Lola move, turning first to greet Tess, and then Vera. Once she knew that the tension had dissipated, she sauntered off to her bed in the front hall.

Vera's presence kept Lola in a constant state of conflict. She enjoyed the shepherd's companionship, glowed when her foster sister followed and mimicked her. But now that Vera was back full-time, the dog pushed her constantly. Vera never negotiated for space, and would even jump right over her rather than find some other path to pass by. To Lola, such an invasion of air space was monstrous, a violation of some universal law. Even she and Tess would go to great lengths to respect each other's invisible boundaries; they would never pass each other with only inches to spare.

But now, Lola was always on guard, always watchful for infringements on Tess's space as well as her own, always cautious of giving in, of pushing too hard, of relinquishing too much status to the shepherd.

When Lola reached her spot in the front hall, she groaned and stretched her legs, delighting in the thick softness of her bed. But her eyes were watchful, and she listened for yet another infraction against the collie.

TESS

Tess recoiled when Vera released her head. It was all she could do to control herself. Any other dog, and she would have lunged, snapped, and let loose a barrage of verbal corrections as she backed the dog off. Then she would have trotted away with a swish of her tail and her back turned—triumphant.

But this dog…the more she studied her, the more worried she became. In spite of the dog's poor vocabulary, Tess sensed a complexity, a depth of response, a maneuvering of boundaries, a lack of control.

So she deferred—she had tested other options, and deference was her only choice. She would watch and wait and manipulate where she could. And if pushed too far, she would fight. She didn't think these things through—they were a part of who she was, of what she knew. For now, she would avoid Vera. She would lie by the glass door and watch the world go by. She would wait for Sophie and Jake to return and rely on Lola to protect her.

Sophie

Lola and Vera were lying by the door when Sophie got home, but there was no sign of Tess. Sophie looked through the entrance hall and into the kitchen and dining room, then peered through the dimness of the narrow hall to her right. There was Tess's sweet, expressive face peeking around the corner.

"Tessie! What's the matter? Do you miss Jake already? Come here, girlie." What was going on with Tessie? In all these years, the collie had never hung back. Did she know that Jake had gone on an extended trip? Sophie reached into her pocket and pulled out a beef treat. That got Tess's attention, and a moment later, all three girls were sitting in front of her looking eager and relaxed. She studied them carefully and hoped that nothing bad had happened while she'd been gone.

"OK, girls, let's play." Spontaneously, she pulled a clicker from her jeans. Playing always grounded her and occupied the dogs. "We might as well start whipping Vera into shape with the clicker, hey girls?" Three faces looked up and Sophie laughed. "Girls, down." The dogs responded in unison. She clicked, ready to reward them with kibble when, without warning, Vera skulked from the room, tail tucked and ears pinned to her skull. Sophie looked on, shocked.

The clicker-training method had always worked for her— both in the classes she taught, and with her own dogs. Tess and

Lola had been exclusively trained with it. She didn't use clickers at the shelter because the timing of the click followed by the treat was critical, and she felt it was too complicated to teach to volunteers. So this was new to Vera—but still.

She had never had a dog fearful of the clicker before, though she knew it could happen. She just had to accept that things she'd taken for granted with other dogs could be challenging with this one.

She found some cheese in the fridge and cut it into tiny pieces. "Come on, girls, let's try this again with yummier treats and show her how it's done."

This time, she held the clicker in her pocket to muffle the sound. Ignoring Vera, she focused on Tess and Lola. "Girls, down." The girls lay down. She clicked and gave them each a piece of cheese. Out of the corner of her eye she saw that Vera had joined them again and lay next to her sisters, looking up at Sophie with interest.

"Good girl, Vera!" Sophie omitted the click, but rewarded her with a cheesy treat. "Girls, stand." Tess and Lola stood, side by side. She clicked, again followed the click with a treat, then lured Vera into a stand and fed her a cube of cheese when she was in position. "Well, at least you can be in the same room with the clicker now." She leaned down and stroked Vera's face. "Don't worry, you'll grow to love this. We'll do some more tomorrow."

Just then the phone rang and Sophie answered it, putting the rest of the cheese in her fanny pack. "Can you go for a walk on the North Shore Trail? We're just heading out." *Miriam.*

Sophie was about to respond when Vera and Tess erupted. Their barks echoed through the house, bouncing off the high ceiling, ricocheting from the windows. They tore back and forth from the huge living room windows to the glass doors, hackles up, tails flagging.

Lola's bellow joined in, as loud as a foghorn, and then Vera was charging full tilt past the couch and coffee table tearing around and around, Tess snapping at her as she passed, Lola looking on in stunned amazement. Sophie tried to block her, but the shepherd feinted to the left to avoid Tessie, and knocked the phone from Sophie's hand.

"Vera! Stop!" It would have been funny if they'd been out-side, but with the shepherd's arousal level sky-high in the small space, Sophie worried that—what? That she'd break something? Or worse, that there'd be a fight? She banished the thought as soon as it entered her mind, grabbed a handful of cheese from her pouch and stuck it in front of Vera's face the next time she raced past. Miraculously, Vera stopped. The other two girls sat beside her. And it was over.

Sophie calmed her breathing and looked up, just in time to see a deer disappear into the forest on the far side of the meadow. Oh, so that's what the fuss had been about. The perfect formula for chaos—a collie, a shepherd, and a deer.

She didn't have a clue how she was going to handle the energy and politics of all three dogs while Jake was gone—and she'd been back from the airport for less than an hour.

She retrieved her phone from the carpet. "Hey, Sophie, you still there?" Miriam's tinny voice quavered forth. "What happened?"

"Yeah, I'm here. Vera just had a bad case of the zoomies. Deer." She scanned the meadow to be sure nothing else had appeared. "In answer to your question—sure, I'll be there in fif-teen minutes."

CHAPTER 22

LOLA, TESS AND VERA

Lola was perturbed. Tess's bark, echoing in the back of the truck, was earsplitting. And now, with Vera added to the mix, the two herding dogs had actually stepped on her tail and tripped over her back legs as they paced. Vera barked some-times too; that powerful staccato bark. Lola didn't like it.

The air blowing through the screen in the back of the truck was now sweet with the smell of grass and the freshness of the lake, and Tess inhaled deeply. Yipping with the thrill of the ride she twirled, bumped into Vera, and compensated by looking away at the critical moment. Vera barked and spun, joining the frolic. In spite of the confined space and commotion, Tess nuzzled Vera briefly, touching her nose to the shepherd's ear.

The truck stopped, the back opened, and Sophie stood in front of Vera, blocking her way out. The woodsy smell of the forest filled Vera's nostrils, and with Lola and Tess waiting beside her, she felt her confidence soar—and then Sophie lowered the tailgate.

Vera leapt. She angled around Sophie and stretched her long legs before her, eating up the trail that led away from the parking lot. Her paws drummed on the cool path and the breeze whistled in her ears. Her limbs drove her faster and faster. She thought she heard Sophie's voice, but when the world came into focus, she was alone in a strange place.

"Vera. Come!" The voice reached her again from far in the distance. It carried a tone of desperation, almost anger. She stopped, afraid to move toward the anger, afraid to stay away. "Vera!" The tone softened, and she caught a glimpse of Lola charging toward her. Then she was moving again, racing past Lola and toward Sophie, excitement spurring her on.

She barged back into the parking lot just as Baker, the black lab, trotted up to Tess. Vera slid to a halt, watching Tess prance toward him; neck arched, ears and tail high in a poised greeting.

The collie circled the lab and sniffed, a radiant confidence about her as their steps intertwined. Then they raced off together, fused in a game of chase; his black body flying after hers, Tess galloping back and forth on the trail, coat streaming, mouth open, ears tipped back with excitement.

Vera was like a sponge these days, absorbing everything she could from her sisters. She loved to watch other dogs from a distance, loved to study their language—her language. She drank in all she could. But as much as she recognized and used it, she was not sure of it. Her eighteen months of isolation as a puppy had made her timid and awkward, and Tess was a hard act to follow—her greetings were complicated and fluid, out of Vera's league.

Vera hung back a moment longer and saw Lola walk

forward, sniff noses with Baker, and move on. She recognized a certain lack of assurance in Lola, a holding back, a shyness with new dogs, and these greetings were something she felt she could mirror.

Although dogs often scared her, she had met Baker once before and followed Lola's lead. She walked up to him, sniffed his nose, and joined Lola at the edge of the trail, her heart racing.

SOPHIE

Sophie watched Vera approach Baker. The shepherd looked a little stiff and worried to Sophie, ready to leap away if Baker so much as blinked.

"Cool!" said Miriam. "Your girl is learning. Have you adopted her yet?"

"Miriam, we just got her back a couple of days ago, and now Jake's out of town."

"Yeah, I know, but you're going to, right?"

"God, I don't know. Let's just say we're considering it. But I want to see how she does on this walk. The last thing I need is a dog with issues on trails!"

By the time Sophie and Miriam reached the lake a few minutes later, Baker and Vera were caught in a wild chase while Lola crashed through the woods by herself. Tess trotted and sniffed beside Sophie, avoiding the mayhem as much as possible.

Sophie was intrigued by Vera—after only a few minutes, she seemed to be relaxed and playful with Baker. And from what she could tell, the lab was holding his own with her; she seemed to be listening to him and responding to his requests, retreating when he suggested it and then launching into unabashed play when he invited her back.

There was an easy give-and-take to their interaction, peppered with play bows and pauses. Vera didn't seem to be as pushy with him as she was with Lola, and Sophie pondered this, but decided that Vera was still on her best behavior with him. Well good. She'd take that.

Sophie grabbed a stick to throw into the lake for the golden, but with Vera actively trying to snatch it from her hand, Lola lost interest and trotted up the shore to explore. Sophie finally managed to toss it, but once the stick was floating, Vera waded out, then jumped back to shore like a deer, all four legs springing free of the water at once, her lithe body twisting in the air to get back to land.

"Not sure of the water today, Vera?" Miriam asked.

"Maybe it's too cold. Tess, go get the stick!"

Tess surveyed the situation carefully, decided that Vera had lost interest, and with great poise waded into the lake, shook a few times, then pushed off and swam out to retrieve the stick. She grabbed it, spun deftly, and started back to shore. Vera charged into the lake, pulled the stick away from her, and dashed back to land, dropping it en route.

Now the stick was floating in four feet of water. There was no way Tess would attempt to get the stick again. Not with Vera there. Sophie sighed. She hated anything to interfere with Tess's games.

"OK, kids, let's go!" Miriam strode ahead of Sophie, her gait strong, arms swinging loosely at her sides, voice filled with confidence.

In spite of her small stature, the woman had an authoritative air about her, like she knew everything there was to know about dogs. Sophie shrank in her presence, felt fragile in comparison. She stood up straight and pulled back her shoulders. She knew what she was doing with Vera. And what she didn't know, she'd just have to fake around this woman.

The trail was glorious: a high, thick, green canopy of maples flanked by the deep jade of the lake on one side, and a steep forested hillside on the other. Carved from the remnants of an old rail bed, the way was straight and wide enough for them to walk side by side. The dogs sprinted ahead, shoulder to shoulder, then fell apart to pursue their own interests.

Tess matched her stride to Miriam and Sophie's, steering clear of the crazy play of the shepherd and lab. Lola charged up the hillside, climbing high, high above them, her strong haunches driving her over fallen logs and boulders. Once satisfied, she'd leap and fly back down to the lake, clearing logs and small cliffs with her bounds, only choosing her footing once she was airborne.

"I wish she wouldn't do that," Sophie said, holding her breath for the hundredth time as Lola flew over a stump, landed on a log, and sailed onto the trail.

"You could keep her on leash," Miriam said.

"No way. Running is her passion. If anything happens, I'll just have to deal with it. At least I have a cell phone now, so I can call for help if I need to."

Miriam laughed. They chatted on about their summer plans; hikes they wanted to take with the dogs at Mt. Baker, the pros and cons of adopting Vera.

"I want to adopt her," Sophie said. "But I don't want to have to change anything in my life—like this, for example." She gestured to the dogs playing ahead of them.

"Doesn't look like you'd need to, does it?" Again, that know-it-all tone. Sophie ignored it and focused on the trail ahead.

Two big dogs trotted around the next corner, their owner not yet in sight. Miriam smiled, her face as relaxed as always, her composure completely unruffled. "Let's see how she does."

Sophie made a feeble attempt to absorb Miriam's nonchalance and make it her own—it was so different having complete responsibility for a dog compared to giving advice to clients or friends.

She strained her eyes to see if she could make out the breed and body language of the dogs. They were at least a hundred feet away. She glanced at Vera who was still engaged with Baker. They trotted along in the lead. Other than Vera's tail, which was high above her back, she looked fine. Come to think of it, she hadn't seen Vera's tail down once—except when she was scared—and Sophie wondered if the "mix" part of Vera's lineage was Husky. The approaching dogs looked relaxed and playful— Sophie swallowed.

TESS AND LOLA

Tess's head came up and she scented the air. Ah, company. A rush of exhilaration swept through her the moment she caught sight of the dogs; her legs tingled with excitement and she pushed on into a swift trot. At the perfect distance, she slowed and angled sideways, her head raised, neck arched, and her tail like a flag, waiting for the dogs to bound up to her. A calm, commanding energy suffused her, and the dogs—adolescent males, she decided—settled and greeted her politely. Congenial trust flowed between them, and they sniffed and curved around each other in an expertly choreographed dance. Once Lola drew closer, Tess melted into the background, content and fulfilled.

Lola approached the dogs because she had to. She had never been fussy about dogs she didn't know. Although she understood their language as well as Tess, she had no interest in them other than a superficial greeting. She arced up to them slowly, sniffed noses at an angle, endured the scent of youth and braun, and with great purpose mingled with relief, moved on. The dogs looked up—directly at Vera.

VERA

The dogs seemed loose and easy, and Vera hung back and watched with rapt attention while first Tess greeted them, then Lola. In a moment of uncertainty, the world constricted as the dogs loped toward her. But then, like magic, she found her rhythm: she curved away as they drew near, arced back to sniff noses—and escaped.

She was so consumed with her success that she barely experienced their odor, their stance, their subtle communications. Another challenge—and she had survived. Intensely proud of herself, she raced down the trail after Lola.

She had just settled into an easy trot when a bicycle flew past. And then another. They came out of the blue, a whir of sound spraying from the wheels. The first one startled her and she sprang to the side of the trail, tail tucked and terrified. But when she noticed that the other dogs trotted on with no change in stride, she followed suit, struggling to do the right thing. After that, with the dogs flanking her, she barely noticed them.

During the seven-mile lake walk, she encountered dogs of all sizes and breeds. Bicycles sailed past as she walked and splashed, pranced and played through the afternoon. By the time she got back to the parking lot, Vera had greeted at least fifteen dogs, and while she hadn't lingered, she had managed to go through all the motions. She zinged with excitement, was gilded with pride.

"I don't know how Vera did so well on this walk," Sophie said to Miriam when they reached the parking lot. "It's crazy that she's adjusting to everything so easily."

Vera heard Sophie's voice, heard her name, heard the joy in it. But as she turned to Sophie and smiled, the deep rumble of an engine caught her attention. A door opened beside her and she heard Sophie gasp. A large, black dog dodged around the truck and stormed into Tess's face. The sharp odor of musk and thunder poured from his muscled body. He was a monster of a dog. Vera flinched, indecision immobilizing her.

"Max, get over here!" A shout from behind the truck sent a bolt of dread through Vera.

Max pushed closer to Tess and the collie side-stepped, held her space, then greeted him with confidence—she was tall, assertive, matronly, and completely in control.

Then the dog barged forward and stopped in front of Vera. He towered over her, muzzle quivering, weight forward, body stiff. Panic raked her limbs and she did the only thing she could—she lunged, drove him back. Once. Twice.

It didn't last.

A second later he was on her, his teeth a vise on her neck. She cringed at the stink of his breath, the vibration of his growl— and then she was fighting for her life. She was on her back, the dog at her throat, at her belly. She tore at an ear, snapped at his face, bit down and tasted blood. Sophie screamed, a hand grabbed at her collar—and then the dog was simply gone and she was drowning in fear and confusion.

CHAPTER 23

SOPHIE

Sophie held it together until she had dropped off Miriam and Baker, but after that, the afternoon played over and over in her mind, filling her with dread.

Vera had done so well with everything—until the fight. Sophie kept asking herself the same question: *Did it mean anything?* Miriam had been adamant that Vera had been standing up for herself against a big, rude dog. "Just chill, Sophie. It's what any self-respecting German shepherd should have done," she'd said, that cavalier arrogance creeping into her tone. Sophie really wanted to believe her.

But had Vera started the fight? It had happened so fast. Maybe Miriam was right. Maybe the other dog *had* started it. Miriam had seen it from a different angle, had been closer to Vera when the dogs got into it. And as long as there hadn't been any injuries, and she was pretty sure that was the case, it was actually just normal dog behavior, right? Did it really matter who had made the first move? She relaxed, little by little, as she analyzed it, rationalized it.

That evening, she sat at her computer in the upstairs loft. Tess and Lola slept behind her, and Vera, she hoped, was still asleep in the mudroom. She'd removed the baby gates, sure that Vera would doze the evening away. The dog must be exhausted.

Sophie was lost in her email to Jake, describing her walk with the dogs—how magical the lake had looked in the late afternoon sunshine, the way the dogs had played and greeted...

"Ouch!" Four razor-sharp nails sliced down her leg. Vera sat facing her, claws extended like a cat, ready to rake Sophie again. Four threads of blood oozed from welts on her thigh and the skin was already darkening into a bruise around them. It hurt like hell.

"Vera, no!" Sophie's voice was sharp, but instead of backing down, Vera pawed more seriously, her brows knitted into a frown. Sophie jumped back. "Stop it! What are you doing?" She grabbed the paw to place it back on the floor, but Vera whipped it away and reached out again, catching her leg a second time. This time even harder.

"You're going back to your room!" Sophie fumed.

What was that about? Her thigh burned, and blood dripped from the lacerations. She was shocked. What did Vera want? She wasn't hungry. She didn't seem to crave physical attention. She didn't need to go outside. She'd had plenty of exercise and socialization. Yet in spite of everything, the thought of sentencing Vera to isolation in the mudroom yet again, filled her with guilt. Still, she led Vera back downstairs and closed her off.

She finished her email to Jake, leaving out the fight and the clawing episode. She didn't want to tarnish his pristine image of the shepherd—and besides, Sophie hadn't decided if the incidents were all that significant. It *had* been a big day for Vera. And she probably missed Jake. A lot. Sophie could think of many reasons why Vera might be confused and more stressed than she would be under normal circumstances. Still, the dog didn't have to rip her leg open! That was just weird.

A few hours later, she walked the three drowsy girls, then led the way to bed. Vera could sleep upstairs with them. Maybe it would assuage the guilt of banishing her to the mudroom for the rest of the evening.

The three dogs settled, each finding their own space—Lola lay in the middle of the queen-size bed, of course. Reassured, Sophie checked her email inbox a final time. A message from Jake opened on the screen and she felt a thrill when she read it. He'd had a good flight down to Mexico and the commute to San Miguel had been beautiful. The dry air was rich with the scent of the high desert, and their house was just as he remembered. His email hummed with excitement. It was one of the things she loved about Jake—his childlike enthusiasm for life.

Vera

Vera lay, panting, several body lengths from the bed. She was exhausted, spent, fried, but the day popped and fizzed in her brain—a kaleidoscope of dogs and humans, scents and sounds and water. And although her time in the mudroom had helped to quiet her frantic energy, seeing her sisters drove it higher once again. Still, she glued herself to the carpet and forced herself to mimic the two dogs lying calmly in their places.

The golden lay stretched on the large, human bed. Sophie was in the other room and Tess was by the window, but for now, they didn't interest her.

Then Lola wagged her tail. One beat. Vera stared at it. She felt an urgency to pounce as if it were prey. Another beat. Now the golden was flailing, writhing, throwing herself around and around in a circle. From her sphinx position on the floor, Vera levitated and landed on the bed beside her sister. She roared, caught the golden's fur in her mouth, spun and rolled.

Lola's body was strong and supple against hers. She bathed in the pleasure of the rollick and slam of flank to chest, in the bump of shoulder to hip, in the feel of Lola's breath hot on her neck. But the speed intensified and Lola grew reckless, her strength insurmountable, and for the first time, Vera wavered, a spindle of doubt wending its way through her stomach, into her chest, down to her toes. She fought, struggled to maintain the balance of play with the limber, shark-like whip of her body.

She was screaming now, her voice matching Lola's roars. Sound choked the room. The wildness of the day, the noise, and the battering threat forced her to the edge, her muscles hard as steel, her voice a feverish pitch, her momentum now pure survival. Just as her lip formed a snarl, just as she poised for attack, Sophie's voice sliced through the room. Vera clung to it like a life raft.

"Stop it!"

Vera leapt from the bed. The floor was solid under her paws, Lola sturdy beside her, and her harsh, panting breath was one with her sister's. She stared at Sophie, taking in the tall, alert form that filled the space before her—the square stance, the direct gaze. Tension drained from her body. Her breathing slowed, and she sank to the floor. With Sophie there, she knew she was safe.

"Vera, come. You're sleeping downstairs tonight." The voice

was neutral, calm. It was just what she needed.

In the mudroom, Sophie knelt beside her. Hands caressed her ears, stroked and rubbed her face. She groaned in ecstasy.

"Sometimes you're so amazing, baby girl. Then you freak me out. I was thinking about adopting you, but after today there's no way. You're way too much for me, Vera. Way too much."

Sophie's voice was soft and musical. It soothed the itch in her limbs, the confusion in her head, and she finally relaxed onto the mat in front of the door, drifting blissfully on Sophie's presence. Sometime later, the woman walked upstairs leaving her alone in the dark.

CHAPTER 24

SOPHIE

The next morning Sophie awakened at six o'clock, refreshed. Yesterday seemed to settle into normalcy, and she didn't know why she'd been so upset. In daylight, after a good sleep, and with the welts on her leg hidden under a bandage, Vera didn't seem so unpredictable after all.

Ah, no work, no plans. She jumped out of bed and checked her email. Nothing new from Jake. Email was incredible. Only a couple of years before there had been no email, and their communication had been solely by planned phone calls and letters. It had made it hard to be apart for weeks at a time while Jake traveled—she often chose to stay home with the dogs.

Today she ought to make a decision about who would care for the three girls when she joined Jake in Mexico. She didn't really feel that she should leave at all; but she and Jake had bought the house there two years before, and they'd promised themselves that after Jake retired, they'd have at least two weeks together in San Miguel. She'd lined up a college student to take care of Tess and Lola, but she wasn't sure about leaving all three dogs with this girl.

Vera couldn't go back to the shelter—Sophie was sure that as soon as she was safely out of the country, Vera would be euthanized. Or at least, would have two weeks of sheer hell back in her kennel. The possibility of a good adoption before Sophie left was pretty much zero. And there was no way the shelter would allow her to leave Vera in the custody of a college student for two weeks. Well, that narrowed her options a little. She'd have to think about it.

After taking care of the dogs and eating her cereal while curled on the couch, she called Lucy, the college student.

"I need to talk to you about the dogs. You can still take care of them for two weeks next month, right?"

"Sure, I can't wait!" The voice was bursting with enthusiasm. She sounded about ten years old.

"How much experience do you have with dogs, Lucy?" She'd talked to Lucy about this before, but at the time had considered her as a pet sitter for Tess and Lola, not for Vera too. Vera changed everything.

"Oh, lots and lots. I had a ton of dogs growing up, and me and my roommates just got a puppy. It's so cool! He's soooo cute."

Sophie cringed. College students and puppies were not a good combination at the best of times. "We're fostering a German shepherd," Sophie said, "and if she doesn't get adopted before I leave, I might adopt her. What would you think about taking care of three dogs instead of two?"

"Sure, that would be fun. I love German shepherds!"

"I'd show you exactly what to do with her. She's only two years old, so she has more energy than Tess and Lola, and you wouldn't be able to walk all three dogs together. We'd pay you more, of course."

"Wow! That would be great! I just graduated and I won't be working much, so it should be fine."

"When can you come out to meet her?" Sophie looked out the kitchen window at Vera lying on the hot tub. That dog was a beauty with her head high and alert, big ears pivoting to catch every sound in the neighborhood.

"This afternoon? I can borrow my roommate's car."

Sophie organized the day in her mind. She needed to train

Vera, but she could take the dogs to the dog park as part of Lucy's orientation. She'd just have time for a quick trip out to the shelter to see Sarah before Lucy arrived. She'd better get busy.

She gathered her clicker and a baggie full of treats, as well as some string cheese for Vera, and started training Tess and Lola. Before she knew it, Vera was joining in, tentatively at first, then with more confidence. Sophie decided to work on "heel" with Vera. The girls demonstrated it one at a time for the shepherd, then Sophie lured Vera into position with a cookie. The problem was that each time Sophie tried to focus on Tess or Lola, Vera would insert herself into the middle of the exercise and take over, in spite of being instructed to stay on her mat and reinforced with lots of treats for holding her position. This meant frequent interruptions and increasing frustration for Tess and Lu who took their work very seriously. Sophie was tired of it.

"This dog is driving me nuts," she said to the girls.

Then she had a thought. Vera had probably been living in a dog house before she went to the shelter, so maybe she'd like a crate. Sophie had one stored under the deck from crate-training the girls. It was huge—big enough for Vera.

She crawled under the deck to retrieve it. It was covered in spiderwebs and pollen, but she hauled it up to the dog-wash area, scrubbed it off, and dried it. Then she carried it to a corner of the living room, put a dog bed in it, and admired her work. "Vera, I'm going to leave this here to see if you like it."

Tess and Lola ignored the crate and continued with their training, but Vera lost interest in Sophie. Out of the corner of her eye, Sophie saw her exploring it carefully. The next time she glanced over, Vera was lying inside, looking utterly content. Sophie closed the crate door. Problem solved!

Later, heading out to the shelter to see Sarah, Sophie realized that she actually felt optimistic.

Sophie arrived back home just in time to greet the girls before Lucy arrived. It had been a wonderful visit with Sarah. Whenever Sophie drove into the parking lot now, Sarah recognized the truck from the outside exercise area, and the dog's unfettered excitement melted Sophie to the core. God, she loved this girl!

They spent forty-five minutes together, walking, running, training and playing. The thing that Sophie enjoyed so much about Sarah was that they were completely attuned to each other—just like she was with Tess and Lola. She didn't like to compare, but the better she knew Vera, the more complicated Vera seemed; fluctuating between being overwhelmingly happy, withdrawn, unpredictable, and pushy; and if Sophie really thought about it, she never seemed very interested in interacting with Sophie or Jake unless they had food.

For instance, she wouldn't come up to them just to say hello, or to ask for attention except for giving "claw treatment", and she rarely wagged her tail—a signal showing that a dog wanted to interact. Granted, she flopped onto her back in front of them for a belly rub, but that sometimes seemed manipulative and attention-seeking. She essentially blocked their way and would sometimes do it over and over as they tried to cross the room. And she followed Sophie everywhere, always keeping her in sight—a habit Sophie wanted to break. If Sophie crouched down to stroke her, she'd get up, walk away, and lie down somewhere else. Sophie sighed.

A knock on the door interrupted her thoughts, and she looked up to see Lucy's silhouette through the window. Vera erupted in a volley of barks, charged past Sophie, and put her paws up on the door—going eye to eye with Lucy through the glass. Tessie's voice joined in and Lola threw in a couple of baritone barks.

Sophie signaled Lucy to wait, called the three dogs over to her, then waved the girl inside.

Lucy stepped into the mudroom, miniskirted and wearing a clinging, cleavage-revealing T-shirt. On her feet were a pair of sparkly flip-flops. Sophie made a serious effort not to roll her eyes. The miniskirt and T-shirt Sophie was used to from working at the college, but the flip-flops were going to have to go.

"Oh my God, your dogs are really cute!" Lucy said.

Sophie watched the girl crouch down, fingers deep in the dogs' coats, grinning from ear to ear. All three girls clearly loved her. She squealed when Tessie bounced up to lick her face.

"Well, they sure seem to like you," Sophie said. "Let's go into the living room and I'll have you put them through their paces. Then we can take them around the neighborhood before driving down to the dog park."

Sophie had Lucy ask the girls to perform their basic skills—sit, down, stay, come, and "watch me"—and the tricks that Tess and Lola knew. The girl laughed when they did the exercises in unison, clearly delighted at how responsive they were.

Lucy put on all three harnesses under Sophie's direction. "Make sure the label is in your right hand when you harness them," Sophie explained. "They wear the same size, so don't worry who gets which one."

Sophie asked the dogs to sit, then opened the mudroom door. They waited until she released them with "That'll do".

"Wow, they're so good," Lucy said, her voice excited. "I hope my puppy turns out like this."

Sophie turned her head away and grimaced. She doubted that Lucy understood the years of work it took to teach a dog reliable behaviors. "It's not safe for you to walk all three dogs at the same time, so you'll need to walk Tess and Lola together, and Vera by herself. She's been a good girl, but you'll need to have both hands free to work with her because she likes to chase squirrels—and she's *really* strong. Is that going to work for you?"

"Oh yeah. I don't mind." Lucy giggled and ruffled Tess's ears, miniskirt bobbing. "I just love walking dogs."

Yeah, and cruising the neighborhood looking for guys, Sophie thought with a smile.

The dogs were all well-behaved on the walk. Against her better judgement, Sophie had Lucy handle Vera, and in spite of the flip-flops, she seemed competent.

"I'll leave you the truck so you can take the girls to the dog park." Sophie explained their dog-park rituals. "How often do you think you'll be able to take them?"

"Oh, pretty much every day. It'll be fun!"

There were only three dogs at the park when they arrived, and Vera, true to form, flew after the swallows, checking in with Tess and Lola from time to time. She was polite to the strange dogs who were playing by the water, but other than a cursory greeting, ignored them. Tess and Lola played and swam, and all in all, it was a pleasant time.

"You'll need to check out the park when you arrive before you unload the dogs," Sophie said. She watched Lucy closely and was pleased that she was paying attention. "If there are groups of dogs playing rough, take the girls back home again and walk them in the neighborhood. Vera's still new to this and I don't want her to get scared or get into a fight. That would be awful for her and scary for you, too." Sophie smiled at her. It seemed like a lot of information.

"Sure, that's not a problem."

"And Lucy, you'll need to wear better shoes when you're out with them. You could easily trip or lose your footing wearing flip-flops."

"Oh yeah, I would never wear these walking the dogs on my own," she said, her eyes wide. "I guess I just didn't think about it today. Sorry. "

As they drove back to the house, Sophie wondered what else Lucy wouldn't think about. But after making arrangements to visit again in a couple of weeks before Sophie left for Mexico, Lucy drove away, apparently thrilled with the prospect of pet-sitting the three girls.

Later, Sophie wrote to Jake: *I think Lucy will work out OK. She has a natural ability with the girls and seems to care a lot. But she's just so young and girly. At her age I'd finished nursing school and was working nightshift as the only RN in a county hospital, so I guess she can look after three dogs for a couple of weeks, right?*

Jake wrote back: *Sophie, she'll be fine. When are you going to adopt Vera? What if someone else adopts her first and we lose her? Do it tomorrow!*

CHAPTER 25

SOPHIE

Sophie lay awake for most of the night thinking about Jake's email. She hadn't told him about her concerns—Vera's aloofness, her inability to settle well in the evenings, the way she'd raised her paw and shredded Sophie's leg on more than one occasion, and the scuffle she'd had in the parking lot. But in the scheme of things, these seemed to be relatively minor details. Dogs could be trained. She knew that.

But three dogs. *Jesus!* Maybe they could find her another foster. *Ha!* There was just no way—she was running out of time. And really, every time Sophie thought about giving up Vera, she was torn apart by guilt and grief.

She must have worked something out in her sleep because she awoke the next morning with a feeling of optimism and anticipation bubbling inside her. She had made up her mind.

She was going to do it.

She walked the three girls, fed them, ate her own breakfast, then tried to read. Vera and Lola wrestled in the living room while she drank her coffee. Tess's high-pitched cheerleading destroyed any hope she had of concentrating on her book. Ah, life with a new dog. She was going to do *what* today?

She picked up the phone and dialed the shelter. "It's Sophie. Believe it or not, I'm going to adopt Vera!"

After her trip to the shelter, after signing the papers and spending time with Sarah, Sophie drove home and settled down with the three dogs. It felt profound to take on something she knew would change her life in ways she couldn't foresee. But she felt like she'd finally done the right thing.

Her moment of reflection, hands entwined deep in Tess and Lola's red and golden fur alternating with Vera's black and tan coat, didn't last long. The phone rang. She should ignore it, but she didn't. It was Miriam.

"Guess what I just did?"

"Well finally! I think we should celebrate. Baker can't wait to see his girlfriends."

"What about Cedar Lake? I have to stop on the way and get Vera a new collar now that she's no longer an orphan—a symbol of her new status in the family." Sophie watched Vera trot over to Lola and start mouthing her head. Lola rolled onto her side, pawing Vera's face. Tessie had moved outside and lay on the deck, watching the world go by, the sunlight and shadow playing on her coat. Sophie felt a warm glow well up in her. If only Jake were here—he would love to celebrate this with her.

She ran upstairs and when she was finally able to get online, fired off a quick email to Jake: "*Congratulations! You are now the proud father of an 80-pound, smart, sweet, beautiful GSD (German Shepherd Dog)!*"

She called Leah, bursting with excitement. "I did it!" she announced when Leah answered the phone. "We adopted Vera. Now nothing else bad can happen to her."

"I knew you would! I guess it just had to be the right time. The bad thing about her not being at the shelter any more is that I don't get to see her as much."

They decided on a date for Leah and Jim to come for dinner the following week. Now that Vera was one of the family, it was time to invite people over—the last thing Sophie wanted was for her to become territorial.

An hour later, Sophie picked up Miriam and Baker. The three girls rode in the back of the truck together, and Baker sat behind the seat in the cab.

"I just don't understand why it took so long for you to adopt Vera," Miriam said. "It seemed like the perfect solution all along. Why didn't you?"

"Because, first of all, we're not supposed to have more than two dogs in this community. And second, Vera's a handful. She's so intense, she harasses Tess and Lola, and she doesn't seem to be bonding well with Jake and me. And then there's the fact that she's a German shepherd."

"Yeah? And?"

Sophie gave Miriam a barbed glance, but her friend was looking out the window. Sophie's throat constricted in annoyance. It was almost impossible to get any compassion from Miriam and sometimes it just pissed her off. "They're supposed to be protection dogs as well as herding dogs, and that's a whole other issue I don't want to deal with."

Miriam nodded. "I kind of see your point. But she's a good dog."

"I know, but she's still a challenge. Have you ever experienced a situation where you want to do the right thing, but it seems overwhelming?"

"Yeah, when my mother-in-law came to live with us for a year." She went into a detailed account of the situation, and Sophie hoped that things would settle down with time as they had for Miriam. Before she knew it, they were at the pet store.

Perusing the collars, she found one that was a beautiful weave of black, violet, turquoise and purple.

"This is it!" she declared to Miriam. And when she returned to the truck, she placed it ceremoniously over Vera's head. "Your days of orphanhood are over, Miss Vera! You're home!"

CHAPTER 26

SOPHIE

When Sophie finished packing, she gazed down at the three dogs. Overall, Vera had done pretty well in Jake's absence. She had welcomed Leah and Jim for dinner, and a few days later, seemed thrilled with a visit from their neighbor, Frank, and his wife. She'd been on her best behavior for the first hour, and when she got too rambunctious with her sisters later on, Sophie had put her in the mudroom and she'd settled down right away.

Walks with the three girls had been reasonably successful— no more lost dogs, no more fights, and Vera had had numerous meetings with strange dogs over the past four weeks. It had been busy with the addition of Vera, and there was still tension between Tess and the shepherd, but considering everything, Sophie felt that things had been better than she'd dared hope.

The second session with Lucy had gone well too. Still

miniskirted, the girl arrived in sneakers instead of flip-flops or sandals, and focused her attention fully on Sophie's instructions. She was given a list of numbers to call in case of emergency, including Leah's, their neighbor Frank's, and their house phone number in San Miguel de Allende. She had demonstrated a number of skills with all three dogs, and had promised to email Sophie in Mexico every day. What else could Sophie ask for? And really, what choice did she have at this point?

That night, she wrote her final email to Jake. She noticed for the first time since Jake left that the girls weren't engaged in their routine of wrestling and barking on the bed. The room was strangely silent.

She looked over her shoulder to check on their whereabouts. Lola lay on the bed as usual, but Vera was nowhere to be seen. She crept downstairs and found the shepherd lying in front of the mudroom door. Come to think of it, they hadn't played the night before either. Maybe this was a new pattern. Perhaps they'd got all that crazy bedtime rowdiness out of their systems. If so, it had happened just in the nick of time.

She made a final check of her bag. It was ready except for her toothbrush. Tomorrow was the big day, and she was leaving the house at five AM.

CHAPTER 27

VERA

Vera knew something was wrong. Sophie was gone—and had been for days and days. Lucy was there at night and for a short time in the morning each day, but otherwise Vera was home alone with her sisters. They'd been to the lake a couple of times—but not for long—and Vera had filled her time chasing swallows and avoiding strange dogs.

Dogs worried her more and more lately. Lucy had been taking her for walks with Tess and Lola—she liked this because she clung to her sisters now, not sure what else would change in her life. But her sisters always approached the dogs they passed in the neighborhood, wagging and prancing up to them—and Vera would be forced to follow. At first she did as Lola had taught her—sniff and move on.

But today she was on edge and they were approaching a large, male dog. Vera cringed. She felt the proximity of the dog like a wall in her face, and with her sisters crowding her and the leash attached to her harness, there was nowhere to go except directly up to him. She hesitated, but the pack pushed her forward.

She lunged closer to the dog, and a sharp volley of barks forced him back. Confidence punched through her. She felt Tess glance at her, sensed the collie's annoyance, and was again dragged toward the dog. But Vera refused to let it happen a second time; this time she lunged again and again, snapping the air with conviction.

"Oh, she just does that sometimes," Lucy said.

The voice was irrelevant to Vera, a mewling sound that irritated her ears. But she could smell fear wafting from the other woman and her dog, and with satisfaction, she watched them retreat.

"She's just happy. She didn't mean anything by it." Lucy giggled and they moved on.

Vera was proud of herself. She had inexplicably gained control of the situation, and the sense of accomplishment buoyed her. She turned to Lola and snuffled her ears, then did the same to Tess. She felt Lola's mouth on her neck and wheeled back toward her, pawing and nuzzling.

Behind her, Tess erupted in a flare of commotion. The leash caught on Vera's back paw and she whipped sideways, throwing Tess off balance. She heard Lucy gasp, heard Tess's correction in her ear, then Lola was racing down the road, leash flailing behind her.

"Lola!" Lucy's hands were wild in the air. "Come!"

The golden stopped and looked back. She stood on her toes, balanced for a chase. Vera couldn't bear it. She strained after Lola, yipping a sharp, demanding bark and felt Lucy jerk back on her leash. At that moment, a squirrel flashed in front of them, and ignoring Lucy, she charged it, pulling the woman off her feet. Tess joined in and they raged after it together, dragging Lucy in their wake.

"Stop it!" Lucy screamed. "Bad dogs!"

They reached the base of the tree where the squirrel now sat on a branch, chattering at them from above. Vera could almost taste it, it was so close. Tess whirled in beside her from the other side of the tree, and they pursued it together, front paws high on the trunk, nails clinging to the bark. Then Lola crowded beside her, bellowing and laughing. Vera felt pressure on her leash, heard the scolding voice of Lucy, and they moved on, the three dogs radiant.

"No dog park for you today," Lucy said. "Bad dogs! I thought this was going to be fun." She sounded angry. But Vera tuned out the anger—she had heard it from Lucy so many times—and bathed in the jostle and bump of her sisters—so familiar, so precious.

When they returned to the house, Lucy filled the water bowl, slammed the door, and was gone. Vera lay for a long time in the mudroom, the excitement she'd felt earlier replaced by confusion. She had no bond with the woman who lived here now, no desire to pass time with her. She felt abandoned, lost. She listened for Sophie and Jake in every sound she heard—the cars on the street, the wind in the trees, the creaks and shifts in the core of the house.

Sometimes a physical pain overtook her, a deep ache in her chest, but at other times her muscles squirmed and itched, and she had to move. She would turn her attention to her sisters, to the windows, to anything that distracted her from her loss, from the endless passage of time. She paced and panted, barked and whined until her sisters hid from her. Lola would pad up the stairs to stretch out on the large bed, Tess would often curl up on her bed in the hall.

As the day progressed and the air in the house grew stifling, Vera found Tess panting in the dining room, gazing through the glass doors at the meadow. She wanted the observation spot for herself, but more than that, she gained status from simply displacing the collie, which gave her immense pleasure. Vera

stood over her, her body stiff and imposing. She even squeaked
a high, demanding yip. Tess ignored her for as long as possible,
but finally stalked away.

LOLA

Lola dreamed. She dreamed she was running, bounding
after deer with Vera, playing in wild abandon with Tess. She
dreamed of romping through grasses, and of Jake and Sophie.
She lay undisturbed on Jake and Sophie's bed. Vera had once
tried to join her, but Lola had glared at her and Vera finally
retreated and wandered off to lie elsewhere. So now Lola had
the room to herself.

She stretched; front toes pointing far ahead, back paws
reaching way behind, luxuriating in calm and comfort. She, too,
missed Sophie and Jake. She ached for their love and attention,
for the laughter they brought her.

Lucy didn't interest her in particular, other than for what
she could dispense—walks, treats, dinner. But her presence was
minimal, and so Lola coped by closing her eyes and drifting,
waking only to check in with Tess, and sometimes Vera, when
the shepherd wandered into the room to gaze out the glass door
to the upstairs balcony. If Lola hopped down from the bed, they
would touch noses and smile, and sometimes paw and mouth,
but Lola never allowed play to go further than that. She would
freeze and hop back on the bed, out of range.

TESS

Tess missed Sophie and Jake, missed the playtimes, the
walks, the love and care and attention. She missed everything
about them. And she didn't always feel safe with Vera. The dog
still stalked and harassed her, loomed in front of her, bumped
against her, demanded her spots in the house. But Tess wasn't
willing to fight, to put herself at risk. So she licked her lips and
moved away, and did quick little look-aways to make Vera feel
at ease. She was a social wizard, so she always deferred.

The girl who was staying with them was young and inexpe-
rienced, and Tess had a handle on her—she had figured out how

to get the most treats and attention possible. But Lucy wasn't around enough, didn't take them out enough.

Tess's bladder was full now, and she didn't know when she'd have a chance to relieve herself. And it was hot. The blinds were open and the sun streamed in, forming scorching-hot spots on the carpet. She didn't remember the sun burning into the house in such a way before.

After a while, even her favorite place in the hallway got too warm, so she wandered into the guest room and hopped onto the futon. The air was cooler here and a breeze moved the curtain. She put her head down, and was just drifting off to sleep when she heard a sound and looked up.

She saw with a shock that Vera stood on her back legs with her paws on the windowsill. Tess stared, her head fuzzy from sleep. And then Vera was gone—her haunches vanishing behind the curtain, her tail flashing from view. Tess jumped off the futon and barked. Once. It was an indignant bark, meant to bring Vera back. She paced back and forth, expecting the dog to reappear. She heard Vera's bark, but no dog surged back through the curtains. Puzzled, she jumped back on the futon, put her head on her paws, and waited, gaze glued to the window.

CHAPTER 28

SOPHIE

Sophie's reunion with Jake filled her with hope. They talked for hours about the girls, especially Vera.

"One thing I don't like about her is her name," Sophie said. They were talking over breakfast in the courtyard of an outdoor cafe. A few small wrought-iron tables lined the terrace and a red-clay fountain murmured in the background. Nestled under palms and bougainvillea, it gave the place the feel of a grotto. "It sounds like the name of someone's ancient aunt. And it makes me think of her time at the shelter, which was horrible—especially toward the end." Sophie's gaze rested on a huge, split-leafed philodendron, its leaves a lush green against the red-brick walls.

She breathed in the scent of the cafe—fresh coffee, baked goods, the heady perfume of flowers. She loved San Miguel—a good thing, since they now owned a house here.

Watching him across the table, Sophie could see clearly that Mexico was a part of Jake's spirit. He had traveled here, lived here, studied Spanish here. The heat of the place was in his blood. He loved the gentle nature of the people, their music, their art, their culture. She heard him fantasize about it during the cool, rainy Bellingham winters, and secretly watched him packing months before his day of departure. For the past three years he had spent summer weeks down here by himself, while Sophie stayed home to care for the dogs.

Sophie, on the other hand, was a part of the Pacific Northwest, her heart captured by the cool green of the mountains, the islands, and the inland waters.

Yet over their thirty years together, they had found ways to compromise, and pursued the things they both enjoyed. They had backpacked in the mountains, traveled by motorcycle through Europe, lived in Germany, and scuba dived in Mexico and Belize.

But Sophie always returned to her passion for dogs and running, and Jake always yearned for his guitar—and Mexico. The house in San Miguel was part of their compromise. Vera was the other part—Vera was for her. She knew this in spite of Jake's interest in the dog. In exchange, Sophie needed to hold up her end of the bargain. She had to like Mexico—a lot.

"What if we call her V-dog?" asked Jake. "She looks just like a Velociraptor when she stalks Tessie—and she's so stealthy. And V can also stand for 'vicious', 'violent'…"

"No way!" Sophie laughed. "She's not vicious or violent. But I like 'V'. It can stand for 'Velociraptor' and 'Vunderbar' and 'Very beautiful' and 'Very smart'. This coffee's delicious!" She put down her cup and looked at Jake. His face was so relaxed, his lean, tanned body so at home in shorts and a T-shirt and sandals. He did look like he belonged here.

Her stomach gave a lurch. She really didn't want to move to Mexico, and yet the idea simmered in the air around Jake. The house was a larger-than-life manifestation of it.

"Well, OK, then. V-dog it is!" Jake smiled at her, a wide, content, slightly impish grin.

A dog wandered into the cafe and lay down beside their table. The rippled outline of his ribs punched through the skin and his neck was scrawny and naked—no collar graced it.

"Our dogs don't know how good they have it!" Jake said, staring at the dog.

A sudden lump in her throat made Sophie check her pockets for treats, but for once they were empty. The only other thing she could do was to balance her water glass on the cobblestones beside the table and offer him a drink. But the dog danced backward and eyed her from a distance. "He's so cautious. Such a survivor. I wonder what his life is like."

There was a sudden flurry of Spanish as their waitress shooed him away. The animal darted behind the wall that bordered the cafe, and disappeared. The young woman set a plate of *huevos rancheros* in front of each of them, and Sophie was hit with the sharp aroma of salsa and eggs, cheese and chiles.

"What do you want to do with the girls when we get home?" Jake asked.

"I can't wait to take them hiking in the mountains together." Sophie took a bite of the eggs and her mouth filled with the perfect balance of flavor and heat. She closed her eyes and floated on it. "I really want to get Vera into agility. She's so athletic." In her mind's eye she saw Vera soaring over jumps, scaling the five-foot A-frame, leaping through tunnels in two strides. That dog would be a star.

The stray dog was back beside them, sitting four feet away and Sophie tossed him a forkful of eggs. He caught and swallowed them in one gulp and resumed his vigil. He was very polite. She tossed him another forkful.

"Sophie! You're encouraging him."

She ignored the comment. "Maybe I'll even have Vera compete in agility. Wouldn't that be something! I bet she'd do well." She flicked another forkful of eggs.

Jake smiled at her, a smile that filled her with love and

excitement and anticipation. "Whatever you want to do with her, Sophie, you should do it. She's amazing."

After breakfast, they wandered through the open-air market and bought tomatoes, white Mexican cheese, and rolls for lunch. Sophie's mouth watered. She'd never known tomatoes to be so fragrant.

Jake found her a handmade silver necklace and a pair of earrings crafted by a local silversmith. They didn't usually like to shop, but the attentiveness of the merchants and the quality of the goods made this market irresistible. Then they hurried past the open meat market, and finally climbed the curving steps back to the street, ready to wind their way home through the blinding midday heat for lunch and a siesta.

Sophie found herself in awe of the street dogs. "Let's watch them, Jake." She stopped on the sidewalk and observed a scrawny, yellow dog begging from a tourist—he was so skilled— never getting too close, yet close enough to be noticed. Another dog trotted along the raised sidewalk, hopped down to the cobblestone street to avoid pedestrians, then waited for a car to pass before crossing to the other side to greet another dog. They sniffed and arced around each other just like dogs did at home, then went their separate ways.

She'd read about these "village dogs" in Raymond Coppinger's book, *Dogs: A New Understanding of Canine Behavior, Origin, and Evolution*. They had never belonged to anyone, and over time had evolved to survive in increasingly complex societies. She was completely captivated by them.

"Here's an Internet Cafe." Jake grabbed Sophie's hand and pulled her out of her reverie and through a low, dark doorway. "Let's check email. We haven't heard from Lucy in days."

Sophie's fingers were slick with apprehension when she typed in her password, and her sandaled feet beat a steady rhythm under the table. Finally, a brief note popped onto the screen. "Everything's fine. The dogs are really happy." That was all it said. It was only the second time they'd heard anything from Lucy.

"Damn her!" Sophie spun around to face Jake. "What's

wrong with that girl? Why can't she just let us know what's going on? She promised!"

"Don't worry, Sophie. At least we know we can still travel and leave them at home with someone." Jake pulled Sophie close, but she struggled against him.

"Jake, I'm pissed. It's just not right."

"Look on the bright side—it doesn't sound like it's been a disaster. It's all right, Sophie. We'll be home in a few days."

They passed the long afternoon in their high sunroom overlooking the valley, snoozing, reading and watching desert storms slide past in the distance. Later that afternoon they climbed the steep, dusty road behind the town to explore the high arboretum. A panorama of colonial architecture glowed in reds and golds below them. Deep shadows traced the buildings, and they could follow the winding city parks in hints of dappled green. After the previous months of stress from work, the trials of the shelter, then Vera's saga, Sophie floated, breathed, let in the heat and the color, and drifted into a state of absolute contentment. "I love you, babe," she whispered. She took Jake's hand, kissed his fingertips, and realized she was ready—for anything.

CHAPTER 29

VERA

The moment Vera's paws touched the ground, she knew she'd made a mistake. She heard Tess bark, and spun around to leap back through the window—but it was too high above her. She reached up as far as she could with her paws on the rough cedar siding, and barked. But Tess didn't answer.

The world loomed around her. The deer, whose scent had propelled her out the window, had vanished, its essence lost on the air currents that rustled the leaves above. She walked toward the road, testing each step. Without her sisters or her people beside her, without a tether, she was lost. She looked around, wild-eyed, and when she reached the end of the driveway, she crouched and dug her nails into the gravel. She heard a rumble, then a roar as a beast of a truck charged toward her and raced past. Wrenched into action, she chased it away, roared back at it, felt the satisfaction of the race, the hunt, the game. And then it was gone.

She looked around, hot and winded. The air here was still and stagnant. She was at the end of the neighborhood and it felt like the edge of the world to her. The houses stood as they always had. The pavement burned her pads. She was thirsty, and alone. She lowered her head and sniffed the urine of a dog who had recently passed by, then another.

She wandered and sniffed, and soon she was in a place she'd never been before; behind a house, beside a fence, beneath a deck. She froze. There was no one to direct her, and an infinite number of places to explore. Here, there wasn't even an echo of her sisters' scent. But curiosity got the best of her. She moved forward, sniffing and wandering, nose to the ground, lost in her own universe.

Finally, she looked up. Nothing was familiar. Anxiety tiptoed through her, swelled, and with a final jolt, set every nerve ending on edge.

She turned to follow her track back home, but it shifted and swam, her scent an ethereal mist on the stirring breeze. A presence made her whirl.

A dog loitered beside the nearest house. He was large, male, and familiar. She had backed him off once before with her lunge and bark. He stopped, looked away, then arced toward her, moving closer and closer. She sniffed the ground, turned her head away, and licked her lips, but he moved closer still.

Then he was too close.

Fear careened through her. Her heart battered her chest, her muscles screamed. She growled, lunged, snapped, and when he stood on his toes and whipped his tail high over his back to retaliate, she ran.

She felt his snarl behind her, felt his heat bearing down on her. Her limbs burned, stretched, shrieked, and she raced as fast as she could, even after he no longer chased her.

A screech of brakes, people shouting, and she was flying faster still, fleeing a man and the familiar words: "You goddamned dog!"

And like a beacon, there it was. Home. Relief tumbled through her, her heart sang. She rushed through the cool of the carport. She barked, whined, clawed at the door. But no one opened it. She heard Tess bark back at her from within. She ran to the gate on the deck, but it, too, was closed. She barked again. Silence. Finally, she curled up in the shade of the steps, alone and afraid.

She lay that way for a long time, ears pivoting, listening for something, anything familiar. Then, from across the street, came the sound of water, the scent of a man she knew, familiar footfalls. She raced across the road, tail wagging frantically. She bounded up to the neighbor, laughed at him, circled him, and fell into a deep curtsy. She was beside herself with excitement, with joy, with the knowing that she had been found, been saved.

"Vera!" the man said. "What are you doing here?" He rubbed her hips, her face, her back, and she pranced for him, bowed again, and danced for him. "You're awfully pleased with yourself."

She stopped and looked up, panting. She cocked her head, hung on every sound, but only understood her name.

"I'm sure you're not supposed to be here. You look hot. Thirsty?" He filled a bucket with water from the hose and she drank, the coolness and flavor of it transporting her into flawless bliss. He took her by the collar and led her home, up the steps, and onto the deck. He closed the gate behind her and was gone.

When the glass door leading from the deck to the dining room was opened hours later, Vera rushed in. She raced past Lucy. She didn't even stop at the water bowl, although she was once again frantic with thirst. She greeted her sisters, bowed and twisted and cavorted with Lola, snuffled Tess's ears and pawed her ruff.

"How did you get out there?" Lucy studied her, making Vera's hackles prickle. "I know I didn't leave you outside." After a few minutes, the woman walked back to the TV, parked herself on the couch, and stared straight ahead.

That night, Vera slept next to Tess in the room upstairs, her head only inches from the collie's back. She smelled the sweetness of her sister, heard the evenness of her breaths, and when the balm of Lola's rhythmic breathing reached her, she closed her eyes and fell into a deep sleep.

The next day was just like any other. The sun rose and the house warmed, and when Tess wandered toward the guest room, Vera followed her into the hallway, considering a stalk-and-charge maneuver to break the boredom. But when Tess crossed the threshold of the guest room, a web of distress seized Vera and held her captive. She saw the window, saw the curtain stirring in the light breeze, saw beyond it an endless nightmare. Stalk and charge forgotten, she wheeled around and ran to the comfort of her crate.

Then one afternoon, something changed. Tess and Lola paced and stewed, nuzzled Vera, pawed her. Something was about to happen. Vera could feel it.

And then she heard a car in the driveway.

Jake's car.

Tess and Lola crowded the door, their barks resounding through the house. Vera ran to join them. The door opened, her heart leapt, and just like magic—Jake and Sophie were home.

CHAPTER 30

SOPHIE

The morning after Sophie and Jake returned from Mexico was glorious. It was late July, the sky was brilliant, and a light breeze sweetened the air.

"Let's go to Fragrance Lake today," Jake suggested. "I want to see how V-dog does off leash."

"I don't know." Sophie looked down and pushed her hair

back from her face. "Maybe we should wait a few days. It's such a busy trail. I worry about V."

"What do you mean? They need a good hike and I haven't been up there for ages." He sounded so confident, his face portraying the same relaxed, unconcerned expression as his voice.

He was probably right. Vera had done so well all summer that there was no reason to worry. She'd pretty much proved herself on trails before Sophie left for Mexico, though V had never been on a trail as steep, narrow and winding as this one. How would she negotiate oncoming traffic on a trail this challenging with limited opportunities for evasion? Sophie stifled the thought. It would be great for Jake to see how far Vera had come. Presumably, all had gone well with Lucy, though Sophie hadn't been able to get hold of her since they returned.

Sophie took her time packing water and sandwiches, treats for the dogs, leashes and poop bags, a nagging reluctance stirring her thoughts. But finally everything was ready, and they loaded the three girls into the back of the truck.

The parking lot was a flat strip of gravel squeezed between the steep, wooded slope of Chuckanut mountain and a busy road. They unloaded the girls with care, kept them on leash until the first set of switchbacks, then released them. The dogs sprinted off with Vera in the lead, full of flair and life. The air was warm, the path cool and earthy underfoot, and a canopy of giant maples rustled above them in the breeze. It really didn't get much better than this.

Still, with each step, Sophie felt a wisp of uncertainty gain form and momentum. She knew what Jake would say if she mentioned it, but finally, her discomfort outweighed her desire to please. "Maybe we should put Vera back on leash—at least for a while. I mean, we haven't been around her for a couple of weeks and I haven't talked to Lucy yet." She could hear an edge to her voice.

"She'll be fine. Tess and Lola will take care of her. She hasn't run off since we adopted her, right?"

"I know, but still..." Sophie's face flushed. She was sick of being cast as the alarmist, the over-cautious coward. She bit her tongue and picked up her pace.

For now, however, Vera stuck to the trail, eager and happy. Sophie admired her black and tan coat in the patterns of sunlight and shadow as she trotted up the path. She had a confident, panther-like gait, sinewy and fluid, her long tail perfectly balanced behind her. For all the problems that Vera had had in the past, she was rising out of them like a phoenix. Sophie had to admit that she was falling head over heels in love with this dog. They had done the right thing by adopting her after all.

When the first strange dog of the walk appeared ahead of them, Vera hung back; a subtle hesitation, Sophie noticed, but it allowed Tess to greet the dog first. While Tess was occupied by her visit, Vera arced past, expertly avoiding any confrontation, then trotted by the owner and focused on something further up the trail. Sophie was proud of her, appreciating how she had finessed the encounter.

With Lola back on the path after some wild exploration, Vera seemed even more relaxed; she greeted the next two dogs briefly and ignored their owners. Sophie heaved a sigh of relief—shepherds were supposed to be aloof, and it was better to be aloof, she decided, than to jump on everyone like Tess had done as a youngster. That had been a hard habit to break.

"Look how well she's doing," Jake said when they stopped for water. "You worry too much. Can you believe what a great dog she is? I love this dog!"

"I know," said Sophie, catching her breath. "She's beautiful, sweet, smart and just totally adorable. We lucked out."

VERA

Vera was having the time of her life. She felt light, almost giddy, her sense of vulnerability evaporating. There was something so magical, so airy about having her pack together again. She felt it like a burst of light in her being. The path floated beneath her, her paws danced on the earth. She was with her family; she was home.

She raised her head from the scent she'd been studying at the edge of the trail. How had Lola sprinted so far ahead? Her eyes focused on her sister and with alarm barreling through her chest, she forged ahead, almost desperate to reach her.

She was halfway there, when a man appeared from around the next bend. He was huge, towering, and he thundered down the trail toward them. The man's hand reached toward her sister and Vera slowed, her sense of well-being vanishing, her gut contracting into a painful ball. Completely mystified, she watched Lola trot past him, golden fur floating around her in slow motion. And then the golden was beyond him, unharmed, trotting away.

But the man was approaching Vera very quickly, his strides shrinking the distance at brain-numbing speed. He came on like an avalanche, terrible and inescapable. She wanted to run away, but the brush on the side of the path crowded in on her. She had to pass him. Panic stormed her brain, froze her thoughts. What had Lola done? Do the same!

His hand bore down from above, first a shadow against the trees, then a solid mass, then a weapon. She knew what must follow, felt the blows before they landed.

She knew this man. Almost.

A kaleidoscope of past beatings and pain blinded her and she did the only thing she could.

Sophie

They were on the last switch-back of the hike when a bearded man with a walking stick appeared. Lola was in the lead, and Sophie saw that the golden would brush right past him.

"Hello there, boy." He reached down to pat the top of her head.

Lola ducked and pointedly ignored him. Sophie smiled to herself—it was so Lola.

Vera trotted about fifteen feet behind her sister, comfortably mimicking her behavior. A burst of pleasure flashed through Sophie. For the first time, she was confident the shepherd would be fine—she had come a long way in trusting V.

She could finally relax with Vera around people and dogs—at least off leash.

She watched the man lower his hand to stroke Vera's head and a glow of warmth filled her chest. She was back home, in the forest, hiking with her dogs. Life didn't get much better.

The shepherd's muzzle jerked, and a glint of white flashed in the dim forest. Sophie strained to see what was happening. For a moment the dog seemed to be attached to the man—a bizarre trick of the light. Then Vera trotted on again.

"*Fuck!*" The man leapt away, clutching his left hand. "She bit me!"

Everything stopped.

She couldn't have bitten him.

It was impossible.

Sophie's gaze slid to the man's hand. Blood? Was that really blood?

Goose bumps iced her skin. She was acutely aware of the silence, of the sunlight and shadow playing on Vera's back. Jake stood locked in position down the trail from her, and the stranger was frozen several feet up the hill, his face twisted. Behind him, the three girls posed in an artistic tableau of innocence.

Then everything was moving fast, too fast.

Vera

Vera sniffed the ground beside Lola, nose to nose. She was lost in the scent of coyote scat and the comfort of being with her sister.

A sudden hiss of movement split the air above her and she jumped sideways, pain glancing through her haunches. She whirled, the stink of the man thick in her nostrils. His hard stare glared back at her, and she caught the flash of a weapon above his head. Her heart raged against her ribs and she crouched, teeth bared, body braced to strike again and again.

A jerk on her collar threw her sideways. She writhed, scrambled, her focus steel-tipped. *Get that man! Now!*

But Sophie held tight, dragging her further up the trail. Vera roared, coughed, fought for breath. The man strode toward Jake now, and the sound of his anger tore into her, ripping loose her past.

"Vera! Sit!" Sophie's voice was sharp and desperate.

Vera gasped between barks. She jumped, lunged, twisted, fought. Then Sophie's palm was cupping her nose and for an instant she drowned in the scent of hot dogs. She didn't care. Food bounced off her chest, off her scrabbling paws.

But the smell blossomed.

Gained strength.

And she was wolfing down her favorite treats, gulping mouthful after mouthful.

"Good girl, Vera." The voice was smooth again, the panic gone. Vera's fury ebbed. And Sophie guided her up the trail.

SOPHIE

Sophie's hands shook. She had been barely able to attach Vera's leash, and though she felt a modicum of relief when Vera settled, she was afraid that the dog would slip her collar. Sophie had never seen Vera like this. The shepherd had been in a frenzy of pure rage. She struggled to put on Vera's harness, her hands fumbling as she tried to thread the quick-release clip together without allowing the leash to slip her grip. It finally snapped shut, and she was able to stand upright.

She took stock of Tess and Lola. There they were, just up the trail staring at her, their bodies rigid. She made eye contact with them and then crouched over Vera, leash short and tight. She ran her right hand over the shepherd's back and down her hips. The dog flinched. *Shit.* She was hurt. Why the hell had Vera bitten him in the first place?

She heard shouting behind her and stood up. It had started with a blur of male voices. Now insults lashed back and forth. *Men! Jesus.* From where she stood, the man's back blocked her view, but it seemed like he was bearing down on Jake, ready to knock him over backward. He was taller than Jake, and broader. No wonder V had been scared of him. Another wave of adrenalin slammed through her.

"Crazy fucker!" The man's voice boomed and echoed though the forest.

Sophie had to get down there. Had to put a stop to it. Somehow. With Vera in her harness and in a relative state of calm, she dragged the dog with her. What if the man hit Jake? It was the only thing she could focus on now. But what about Vera? She *had* to think about Vera. It was like having a self-detonating bomb attached to her. So that meant she couldn't get between the men—V would almost certainly attack him, especially now that he threatened Jake. She couldn't tie the dog to a tree—what if someone else came along the trail?

One thing at a time.

Sophie left the trail and stumbled downhill through the underbrush until she was parallel to the men. She was still twenty feet away, hoping she'd think of something, anything, to diffuse the situation.

The stranger gestured now, hands stabbing the air, his face only inches from Jake's. "What the hell are you doing up here with that crazy dog? You should be locked up!" She strained to see whether his hand was bleeding, but she was still too far away, and he moved it too much to be sure. She inched closer. Vera had tensed up again, and strained against the two inches of slack Sophie had given her. She could feel the vibration of a growl against her leg. Sophie stopped. Any closer and she risked losing control.

"Get out of my face!" Jake's voice fractured the air. His features were wild, distorted, outraged. She'd never seen this side of Jake. She had a mad impulse to drop the leash and run off with Tess and Lola. Let the lot of them work it out on their own.

The man took another step toward Jake, forcing him to stumble over a root. Jake caught himself on a tree branch and leaned right back in the man's face.

"I'll nail you for assault if you don't get the fuck away from me!" Jake spat. Sophie was close enough now to see spittle fly from his lips. He looked rabid. "And how dare you hit my dog, asshole!" Jake's weight was forward, his feet planted, knuckles white. Sweat soaked the back of his blue T-shirt.

"That dog should be put down." The man took a step away from Jake, but his fists were bunched, and a vein was pulsing and pulsing in his red, bloated face. There was a dark stain on the side of his khaki pants—blood from his hand? Oh no!

If he touched Jake...she burned with indignation, the shock and denial that had shackled her at first, gone. "Stop it!" she screamed, shocked at the shrillness in her voice. The men stopped and stared at her. "Let me see your hand." She forced herself to speak in a confident, reasonable tone. "I'm a nurse. Jake, come over here and take Vera so I can check his hand." She thrust the end of the leash toward him, careful to restrain Vera by her harness. Control the dog, control the men. *Jesus.*

"What?" The man seemed confused for an instant, suddenly deflated. He looked down to examine the wound and flexed his fingers a few times. She could see blood on the back of his hand.

"It's bleeding," she said. "Let me check it out and I'll give you our phone number." She handed Jake the leash, started to walk toward the man and reached out to examine the bite. "Jake, do you have a pen?"

"Forget it." The man stuck his hand in his pocket. "Just stay away from me. And do something about that fucking dog." He turned and stalked off down the trail.

"Go to your doctor," she shouted after him. "Dog bites can be bad, especially on the hand. You need to get it taken care of. Soon!"

Jake and Sophie stood motionless for a few moments, watching the man disappear around the next bend in the trail. How could things change so fast? Sophie's heart pounded. She felt cold all over in spite of the heat of the day.

"Can you believe that guy?" Jake stared down the trail. "What a complete jerk! He hit Vera!"

She gawked at Jake. She didn't know what to say. "Yeah, right. After she bit him." Jake would have hit Vera too if the tables had been turned. That bite must have really hurt. Finally she said, "Are you OK?"

Jake didn't answer. He seemed like a stranger to her. She didn't know whether to soothe him, be angry with him, or just leave him be. She felt lost, wanting to yell at him for being so insanely defensive, wanting to comfort him, wanting to scream at Vera for putting them in this impossible situation. She stood still, trying to sort it out.

Slowly, she gathered her wits and after a long silence asked, "Did you see how bad the bite was?" They were still standing in the middle of the trail. It felt like they'd been there for hours and hours, but it must have been less than five minutes. She sent out a silent plea that Jake would respond to her.

"No. I just saw blood," Jake said. The words came out slowly, as if he were weighing their significance. Then he faced her, eyes hunting for answers. "Jesus, Sophie, Vera bit him. Shit!"

A thread of comfort crept through Sophie when Jake spoke, and her anger started to drain away—drop by drop. His voice always did that to her. She needed to know what he was thinking, to reassure herself that he wasn't sinking into that shell of isolation where he seemed to find such solace. As long as he would talk to her, she could still feel a thread of connection to him. "I just hope he gets it checked out. Maybe I should go after him."

"No, Sophie, I don't want you going near him! It might not be that bad."

"But it could be!" She tried to breathe, tried to get her head around this thing. "I don't know what else we could have done. He didn't even let me look at it."

"The guy's an asshole!" Jake shifted his attention to the shepherd. "And what the hell were you thinking, Vera?"

She stared back at him, wide-eyed. Her head tilted slightly to the side, adjusting a little with each word. She crouched, her back rounded.

Sophie looked into Jake's pale and stricken face, and her heart sank. Further up the trail, Tess stood rigid, staring at Sophie, and even Lola looked concerned, her black eyes searching Sophie for some kind of explanation. A woodpecker hammered above them, a sharp, insistent tap. It echoed through the silence. She looked back at Vera. The large, expressive ears were plastered to her skull, her gaze glued to Sophie. There was no sign of her tail, which meant it must be tight on her tummy. Jesus, what a mess.

"Goddamn it! I can't believe she did that," said Jake. "It changes everything."

CHAPTER 31

SOPHIE

The walk back to the truck was a nightmare. Every muscle in Sophie's body screamed. No matter which way she looked at the situation, she couldn't make sense of it. Vera had been off leash, so she could have cut through the woods to avoid the guy if she was scared; she had not been cornered, and she'd been with her beloved sister, Lola. Granted, the man had been walking down a narrow trail toward her from above and had reached out to pet her on top of her head, something that almost all dogs disliked; but that was no excuse. And with that beard, Sophie wondered if he had reminded Vera of the adopter who'd yelled at her and hit her, what was his name? She couldn't remember. But that was no excuse either.

She walked on in silence, not sure what to say, not sure how it changed things, but realizing more and more with every step that the changes were going to be monumental, whatever they were. Vera strained at the leash, whining to join her sisters.

Jake jerked back. "Vera, stay close." Sophie couldn't remember handing the leash to Jake, but apparently she had.

"I feel like I'm walking a kid with a loaded gun." His voice was leaden, flat. Then, with another burst of anger. "Last time anything like that happened I was eighteen years old and drunk out of my mind. Christ!" He handed the leash to Sophie. "Here, you take her."

Sophie reached out and slid her arm around Jake. She needed the contact, to feel the strong and benevolent force he'd always been, solid at her side. But there was no give in his rigid body, no acknowledgment of the gesture. Ice crept down her spine and she stepped away, took the leash, and hung on to Vera with white-knuckled desperation.

VERA

Vera was ready to explode. Her thoughts swarmed, and the blood in her veins burned, acid sharp. The man's assault played over and over in her mind. Her hip and lower back ached with a deep pain, and worst of all, Sophie had shouted at her in battering waves of disapproval. She was held tight at Sophie's side, yet Sophie felt impenetrable to her, a world away.

Vera needed to join her sisters, to find some calm, to pound into Lola and exorcise the madness that inhabited her, to bump into Tess and feel the collie's matronly cockiness. Instead, she minced along beside Sophie, craving freedom, but bound so tightly that she could barely move.

TESS AND LOLA

Tess and Lola paced ahead in silence, shoulder to shoulder. Behind them, chaos enveloped Vera like a storm, and they clung to each other, aware of the shift and bump of each other's bodies. They had never known such violence from a dog or a human, had never heard Jake shout in anger, had never heard Sophie rail against another dog—or anyone.

Tess shivered to her core and glanced back at Sophie and Jake. She couldn't stray too far, bound as her heart was to them, but she feared moving closer. Lola hung back with Tess, reluctant to allow even a few inches of separation from the dog who had been her life for as long as she could remember. They buried their noses in the weeds only millimeters apart, seeking out the mystical scents of mice and squirrels, the odors transporting them to another time, when life was normal.

A sudden force crashed between them. Vera. Larger than life, jolting them apart. Lola felt a paw hard on her back and Tess cringed, the shepherd's muzzle snapping a whisker-length from her face. They fled, rushing further down the hill, leaving Vera to hit the end of her leash behind them.

SOPHIE

"Vera! Stop it!" Sophie jerked Vera back to her side—the shepherd was so strong. Sophie wouldn't allow the dog to harass her sisters. It was supposed to have been such a good day for them all. She felt sick for Vera, but she was also sad for Tess and Lola. This had to be excruciating for them. She thought about their faces and her heart wept.

Sophie finally broke the silence. "I feel so stupid." Her foot caught a root in the rugged trail and she almost dropped the leash. "Shit! Vera, slow down."

Jake grunted. "Get control of her, Sophie."

Sophie sucked in her breath through clenched teeth and continued talking. "I don't know anything about aggression. I don't know if this means she'll bite again; I don't even know if we can train it out of her." Her voice was loud, her thoughts consuming. She barely noticed when they turned right onto the narrow, paved road that led down a curving, two-mile course to the parking lot. "I mean, would she be all right on wider trails? Is she still OK at the dog park? Maybe the trail was just too narrow for her." She was silent for a minute before continuing on as an afterthought, "And to pet her on top of the head—what was he thinking?"

"What are you saying?" Jake interrupted her train of thought. "That it was his fault? The guy was a complete nutcase, but he didn't do anything to Vera—at first. She had a right to bite him after he hit her, but not before."

Sophie stiffened. "No dog likes being patted on top of the head! She's a German shepherd, not a lap dog." Her voice had a hysterical edge. "That guy was walking downhill on a narrow trail directly toward her from above. Do you realize how threatening that could have been for V?"

"Sophie, it's normal to pet a dog on the head, for Christ's sake. Look at Lola. She didn't like it, but she didn't bite the guy."

"I'm just saying it wasn't all her fault, Jake." She said his name in a cutting, "fuck you" tone. She didn't mean to be quite so nasty, but what the hell. She was pissed too.

"Fine. Just don't expect her to be allowed off leash on a trail again. Or anywhere else. Ever."

Sophie clamped her mouth shut and stormed ahead. She focused on Tess and Lola. They seemed to have recovered from

Vera's intrusion, and were trotting ahead, sniffing the grasses at the edge of the road. Sophie tried to focus on the pale gold and red of their fur, tried to drink in the essence of their sweet, gentle spirits. Yet even they seemed subdued and quiet. Vera was overwrought, chaotic almost, and pulled with all her strength to catch up to them. Jake was in such a bad mood that Sophie didn't dare suggest that he take the leash again lest his frame of mind become darker still. She couldn't stand it when he was angry, and he seemed to be getting worse by the minute. Her arms and shoulders ached from Vera's pulling and jerking.

She tried to remember the man's hand, tried to visualize how severe the bite was. Her mind tumbled into a morass of bite stories she'd heard over the years, and images played before her like a film: the man who had been bitten by his dog while breaking up a fight, his hand requiring multiple surgeries; the man who was mutilated when his German shepherds attacked an innocent dog on a walk. In the tumult that followed, they'd turned on him instead of the dog. She shuddered.

Had Vera's bite been deep enough…to what? Sever tendons? And were there two punctures? Four? She didn't know. And what if the punctures got infected? She could see his hand swelling, red and painful even as she thought about it, the infection traveling over his palm and up the tendon sheaths into his wrist and arm. What if he got toxic? *For goodness sakes,* she told herself. *Get a grip. He'll get help: antibiotics, and whatever else he needs long before that—but Jesus—what if he doesn't?* Maybe she should have chased him down after all.

She snapped back to the present when Vera lunged ahead in a final effort to reach her sisters. They were approaching a curve in the road. She'd been so deep in thought that she hadn't even noticed a woman approaching with two children. Vera looked pleased with herself now, interested in something Tess and Lola were investigating, and had somehow managed to drag Sophie over to her sisters and burst in-between them again, nose to the ground. Sophie jerked the shepherd away.

"Your dog is so pretty. Can we pet her?" the children asked, moving closer.

"No!" Her voice was loud and shrill and she rushed away, dragging the dog after her. The alarm she felt at the thought of someone approaching Vera was crushing. She glanced at the shepherd and was suffocated by dread. She looked away.

She needed a plan. That was how she'd always coped before. Before Vera. And she needed to breathe. And give Jake a break. She gulped the warm, summer air, blew it out, filled her lungs more slowly the second time, the essence of the forest filling her with relative peace. She focused again on Tess and Lola, keeping her eyes averted from Vera as much as possible. What should they do next? Think. *Think.*

"We need to find a trainer who knows about aggression," she said to Jake. She felt like a child announcing that the world was round, but surely that would be the best place to start and it felt good to verbalize it. Vera was way out of Sophie's league.

Sophie considered the local trainers she knew. There was Josie, the woman who ran the training center where she taught obedience classes. But Josie would tell her that Vera would be fine—that she just needed some work. And maybe she did, but Sophie wanted an unbiased answer, the black and white truth, unembellished. She wanted to know just how dangerous Vera was, and if she could be cured. She needed someone who would be impersonal and objective. What about Georgia? She had been training for years. Sophie didn't know her well, but for that very reason she could be a good choice.

"I'll call Georgia when we get home," she said aloud. "She can give us a better idea of what to expect."

"Whatever," Jake said. "But I don't like this. I really don't want to own an aggressive dog. I hate the idea of having a dog who could hurt someone, and I *really* hate being forced into confrontations with assholes like that guy—it was all because of her." Jake gestured toward Vera with his chin. His shoulders were hunched forward, his head down.

Sophie shrank inside. She rarely saw him this way. She wanted to comfort him, but at this moment had no idea how to do that. "I know, babe. I'm sorry."

"What the hell are we supposed to do till then?" His voice was loud. "She's started lunging at dogs in the neighborhood, she ran away when we fostered her, and last night she intimidated Tess—again. And oh yeah, she just bit someone." He counted the points off on his fingers one by one, his voice rising in volume until he was shouting. "What's next, Sophie?"

"In case you've forgotten, she's done well with a lot of people *and* dogs since we've had her. And the man she bit looked a lot like the guy who adopted her before we did—and he scared her to death." She could hear her own voice rising but couldn't control it. She stopped walking and turned to face Jake. "And she's still recovering from our trip to Mexico. That has got to be part of it."

A tidal wave of guilt crashed through her. She dug her nails into her palms, clung to Vera's leash, and tried to breathe. "We should never have let those people adopt her and I should never have gone to Mexico. It's all our fault." Tears burned her eyes and she wiped them away with the back of her hand.

"Sophie, I'm not saying that we shouldn't do anything about it, I'm just saying I didn't sign up for this. *You* didn't sign up for this!"

"I know, Jake." She was aware of a small group of people approaching. She pulled Vera close and lowered her voice. "But she doesn't have any more options. We're her last stop. If she goes back to the shelter now they'll kill her, and no rescue will take her with a bite history."

"I can't think about that," Jake said. "But I'm not sure that that guy wasn't right."

"About what?"

"About her being a dangerous dog." Jake turned away from her and strode down the road.

"How can you say that? You're talking about our sweet Vera!" Sophie called after him, but she cringed at the words "dangerous dog". Deep in her heart, the words resonated.

PART 2:
THE GUARDIAN - 2006

CHAPTER 32

SOPHIE

Jake and Sophie drove along in silence. The county roads were long and arrow-straight, dissecting vast, golden fields. Sophie barely noticed the horses and cattle that grazed and snoozed in the midday sun. She thought back on the past three days. After a lot of soul-searching, she had decided that her loyalty had to be with Jake and the girls and what was best for them. In the week since they had returned from Mexico, Vera had started lunging and barking at dogs in the neighborhood every time they walked her. She'd also creep toward Tess, then charge in to grab the collie by the neck, and she'd pummel Lola relentlessly to get her to play until Jake or Sophie pulled her off. Vera seemed to take great pleasure in her games, but Tess and Lola were visibly disturbed.

"Are you ready for this?" she asked Jake. They turned onto a smaller side road and a rush of nausea made her cradle her stomach. She wasn't sure she was ready.

"Yeah. I just want to know what we're up against."

Sophie studied Jake's profile. She would support him, no matter what. She had put a lot of thought into this and she'd made up her mind. She knew how much he cared about Vera, and she knew that he would be fair.

But what if he decided he didn't want to keep V? The thought sent a bolt of pain through her head. She felt hot, trapped. She rubbed her eyes and let her hands drift down to her neck. Her fingers felt cool and reassuring and she let them rest there.

"I worry about the girls as much as anything," she said, trying to be honest with herself. She cringed every time Vera made a beeline for Tess. "She puts so much pressure on them. They're always aware of where she is in the house—just like we are. It must be exhausting for them." She frowned.

"She intimidates them, but I think they like her. What really bothers me is her aggression on walks," Jake said. "It's getting worse."

"Yeah, I've noticed that too." He was right. In the past week, in spite of asking V to make eye contact, and feeding her a stream of hot dogs or cheese whenever they passed another dog, Vera would often break her focus on Sophie and go berserk.

Consequently, Sophie now found herself holding her breath on walks; the moment she saw a dog appear in the distance, she'd feel her muscles tense and her heart go into overdrive. Vera picked up on her fear instantly, as if it slid up from her solar plexus, out through her pores, and down the leash like some primal serpent. No matter how hard she concentrated, she couldn't control her reaction. Dammit. She didn't know what to do. Vera's issues were well beyond her level of expertise. At this point she found it laughable that she had ever considered herself a dog trainer.

Far in the distance the North Cascades glowed in blue and white against the silver horizon, Mount Baker dwarfing the world. She thought about Vera who stood in the back of the truck, sniffing the air. This could be familiar territory to her, and Sophie wondered if she felt unsettled.

Jake pulled into a driveway marked "Hound Heaven" and parked by a barn that had been transformed into a training center. They left Vera in the shade of an apple tree, and went to check in.

The training room was large and clean, and agility equipment lined the walls. Georgia smiled a welcome.

Jake shook her hand. "I hope you can shed some light on Vera's behavior. It's very disturbing."

"Why don't you bring her in and tell me what's going on?"

Georgia was a large, rugged woman, and a baggy black T-shirt and cargo pants gave her a formidable appearance.

Vera walked into the barn at Sophie's side dressed in her new collar and leash. If she wasn't with the girls, she didn't pull any more—unless there were strange dogs in the vicinity.

Georgia sat on a table and gestured to two chairs opposite her. "Have a seat." The woman was friendly, but in-your-face loud, her eye contact intense. Sophie wondered what Vera thought of her.

They related Vera's story as succinctly as they could: they outlined her history at the shelter, the significant incidents they were aware of, and answered Georgia's questions. When they were done, Georgia started talking. She talked for what felt like hours, her loud voice battering them with anecdotes, examples, facts and thoughts.

"How did she do when you were on vacation?" Georgia asked.

"She escaped once that we know of."

Georgia's lips pinched together and she visibly paled.

Before the woman could respond, Sophie continued. "We were lucky—it worked out all right. She visited our neighbor and he put her back on the deck." Sophie talked quickly. Georgia's brow was now set into a frown, her right hand pressed to her mouth—she was probably wondering how such a vicious dog could have escaped and why Sophie had left Vera with such an irresponsible sitter.

"When I asked the petsitter about it, she didn't have a clue how it happened, so obviously the dogs didn't get the right kind of supervision. But when we tried to get more information, all she would say is that Vera was happy and did really well."

Sophie filled Georgia in on details she'd gleaned from the neighbors—that Lucy had walked all three dogs together against Sophie's advice, and that Vera routinely lunged and snapped at any dog she'd passed. Lucy had apparently explained to them that Vera wasn't aggressive—she was just "happy"—and after the first few days, the neighbors started to avoid them.

In actual fact, Lucy had been a disaster. She'd damaged their truck, left a friend in charge of the three girls for a few days while she went to Seattle, and if she'd cleaned up the house before she left, it was difficult to tell. Sophie didn't have a clue what it had been like for the girls, but she suspected the worst and felt sick about it.

While they talked, Vera paced back and forth, or lay at Sophie's feet and ate the hot dogs Georgia tossed her. Once or twice she stood between Jake and Sophie and watched the woman with interest. Finally, she sat and barked once at Georgia as if to say "OK, enough is enough. Aren't we done yet?"

Georgia's eyes widened and she jerked backward. "See? I could make her bite me right now."

"Are you kidding me?" Sophie said it before she could stop herself. "All she did was bark!" Was this trainer that scared of her? *Jesus!*

Georgia ignored her and pounded on, each word a sledge hammer. "This is a dog who will be fine until she isn't. There are enough good dogs in the world that I don't spend a lot of time on the bad ones. My recommendation is that you take her back to the shelter, but you're probably too bonded to her for that."

"Are you serious?" Sophie was incredulous. "You don't think there's any hope for her? If we take her back to the shelter, they'll euthanize her."

Georgia shrugged. Her indifference drained all color from the room. "But that's not your problem, is it? Sure she could improve. And Sophie, you probably have enough training experience that you could learn how to handle her. But it would be a lot of work—more than most people are willing to provide."

"I'll do it. Whatever it takes," Sophie said, holding Georgia's gaze.

"I will too," Jake said.

"OK then. There are trainers who specialize in aggression, but I'm not one of them and I don't know of anyone in this area who is. I could ask around and let you know if I hear of someone."

"That would be great." Sophie started toward the door and Vera followed—poised, collected, perfectly controlled. "Before we leave—do you have any idea why she bit that man? It doesn't make any sense to me."

"She was probably scared—he reached for her and she protected herself. It's that simple. And now that she's learned that it works for her, she'll bite again."

They were silent as Jake backed out of the parking spot. Sophie was numb, and the inside of her head felt like an echo chamber, Georgia's words bouncing from wall to wall.

Finally, she was able to speak. "Is Georgia right?" She choked out. "Should we take her back to the shelter?" The thought suffocated her. She was devastated by Vera's behaviors—and now this. But how could they take her back to the shelter? She had no idea how to deal with a dog who was already hard to handle at home, and now had a bite history.

"Of course not." Jake's voice grounded her.

Options flitted through her mind, none of them good. Her head ached. She reached out and grasped Jake's hand where it rested in his lap. He twisted, and for a moment she thought he had pushed her away. And then their palms were together, fingers interlaced, his warmth spreading through her hand. Her headache ebbed, the burning anxiety abated, and she began to breathe.

"We've seen what a great dog she is," Jake said. "We'll find someone to help us. Remember, I'm retired now so I can work with her while you're at the clinic. It'll be OK."

His words buoyed her, like he'd thrown her a lifeline. "What did you think of Georgia?" she asked.

"I don't think she liked V-dog. She didn't do anything except talk *at* us and toss Vera hot dogs. She didn't do any training or evaluation. I think Vera did really well considering the situation, don't you?" He checked the traffic before turning south onto the busy highway. "And then she tells us that Vera should be euthanized? Based on what?" He caught his breath—a deep, shuddering intake of air.

"Her history, I guess." As much as Sophie didn't want to admit it, Georgia's concerns mirrored her own. They needed help. Now. "I'll call Josie at the training center when we get home." In that moment, Josie's positive attitude felt welcome. She certainly knew dogs and was passionate about them, and if, in Sophie's opinion, Josie was sometimes overly optimistic, it would balance out Georgia's dismal prognosis.

When they got home, they left Vera in the truck and greeted the girls alone. It felt so simple to enter the house with those happy, gentle faces welcoming them—Tess's obnoxious bark and Lola's easy, wagging tail. After Jake made a fuss of them, Sophie ran to the couch.

"Girls, time for couch cuddles!" The two girls ran after her and jumped onto the couch. Sophie's hands found their favorite spots—ears, faces, chests, shoulders and hips—and they moaned, the collie purring with pleasure, Lola stretching and laughing under her touch. She kissed their noses and foreheads, and hugged them, feeling their firm, silky bellies. It had been months since they'd indulged in this ritual.

"What are we going to do about that sister of yours, girls?" The dogs laughed back at her, bounced onto the carpet, and stretched luxuriously. Then Tess whirled around, romped over to their toy box and grabbed one of the rope toys.

"Whoa, Tessie, you haven't played with that for ages!" Sophie grabbed the other end, tugged furiously, and fixed her eyes on the collie's. Tess beamed, braced her long white legs, and leaned back; her growl fierce, her jaws clamped hard on the fabric, her head jerking to and fro.

LOLA

Lola saw her opportunity. She had missed playing with Tess. It was not only the joy of it, it was the intimacy, the physical tumble, the natural swoop and weave against the body of her soul mate. Even Lola's mouthing of the collie's familiar, sweet-smelling ruff would invite an all-out assault by the shepherd. So now they no longer indulged.

When Lola snatched the toy from Sophie's hand, Tess

redoubled her efforts. Lola braced, growling and tearing at it with every ounce of her strength. On impulse, Tess let go and Lola fell back for an instant, then pounced, grabbing Tess's ruff in her jaws. Tess twirled and spun, snapping at Lola's flank, nipping her legs, biting her neck. Lola was in heaven—the strong, lithe body of her sister twisted against her, outmaneuvered her, made her whole. She roared at Tess and the collie took her down in a torrent of yips. But Lola didn't mind. She laid her head on the carpet, let Tess grasp her muzzle, and basked in their connection.

SOPHIE

"They're playing!" Jake said. "I haven't seen them play since we got V-dog. Come to think of it, that's pretty weird."

Sophie watched, her thoughts caught up in Georgia's words—defensive, but also aware of the vast contrast between Tess and Lola when Vera was with them—and when she wasn't.

"Let's see what the girls do when Vera comes in," Jake said. "If they're totally stressed by her, we should probably take her back to the shelter."

Sophie gasped, her head bursting with excuses for V, reasons to keep her. But she was speechless.

When they led V inside, the girls trotted up to her, greeted her nose to nose, snuffled her ears, and romped after her. And Vera, head high, pranced into the living room like a princess. There was some low-key growling, Lola and V bumped and bowed, and Tessie danced and barked around them.

"I guess we have our answer for now," Jake said. "They definitely like her."

"Tessie and Lu can play on their walks if they want to." Sophie trailed her fingers over Tess's back as the collie romped past. "And we don't need to decide anything today. Right?" Sophie couldn't make a final decision. She needed to soften it, blur the edges, make it a concept rather than an ultimatum.

"Call Josie. Maybe she can help, or at least give us some pointers." Jake walked up behind Sophie and wrapped his arms around her. "Don't worry, babe, we'll work it out." She absorbed his warmth and melted into him. Yes, they'd work it out. They had to.

As Sophie had suspected, Josie was much more positive than Georgia had been.

"There's a lot you can do," Josie said. She recommended a couple of books, and suggested they take Vera to an area with lots of people and leashed dogs. "Just sit on a bench with Vera beside you and feed her super good treats when people and dogs approach her. Stop feeding her when they walk away."

This approach seemed reasonable to Sophie. She had done this with Tess in the neighborhood and it had helped—except with Tess it had been the desire to get closer to people and dogs that made her lunge and bark in frustration, not an effort to keep them away.

"And there's a trainer I just heard about who works with aggressive dogs. I can give you her name and number. I don't know anything about her, but you could give her a call if the classical conditioning isn't working."

A slow effervescence spread through Sophie's chest, the bubbles tingling, tickling, expanding, floating, till she bathed in the intoxicating euphoria of hope. "Josie thinks we can fix her!" she called up the stairs to Jake. "We can start tomorrow!"

CHAPTER 33

SOPHIE

Sophie surfaced slowly, drifting from the depths of a comforting sleep. A sense of dread suffused her growing awareness, and frantically, swimming into full consciousness, she searched for the source.

Oh yes. Vera. That was it. The details flooded back.

The night before, V had been distraught: going after Lola mercilessly, scratching Jake's leg with her talons, refusing her Kong, jumping on the couch by the wall of windows and barking with deranged intensity down the meadow. Sophie had put her in the mudroom, but even there she was restless. At first, she whined and paced. But then, much to Sophie's dismay, she started spinning.

Desperate to make her stop, Sophie took her out for a walk—but that hadn't helped either. She finally settled, but the rest of them were exhausted. They had left her in the mudroom overnight.

Why had she been so crazy? They'd taken her to Fairhaven Green—a grassy, picturesque town square—to watch people and dogs. Could that have had such a huge impact on her? It was supposed to help Vera. Josie had been sure about that.

Sophie squeezed her eyes shut, trying to make it all go away. Lola was snuggled up next to her, usurping half the bed, and Tessie slept stretched out below her on the floor. At the risk of disturbing Lola, Sophie reached down and caressed Tess's impossibly soft ears and ruff. "Such good girls," she crooned.

Jake was still asleep behind her, his arm circling her waist. The warmth and contour of his body against hers was comforting, but she felt trapped between the man and dog. She shifted her weight. As Jake rolled away from her and groaned, she took the opportunity to stretch.

"I just don't know how long I can go on doing this," Jake said.

"What do you mean?" Tendrils of dread constricted her throat, her voice barely a whisper.

"I hate it when she scratches me—there's nothing I can do to stop her and it hurts like hell. Then I get mad and that doesn't help her either." He threw off the bedclothes. "And she's disruptive. Night after night. It's not fair to us or the girls."

"Maybe she needs more exercise. There's no way she can get enough of a workout on leash." It had been two weeks now since the bite. "What if we take her to the dog park for a while before going to Fairhaven? I took her down there in the early afternoon all summer and she did great."

"And if she bites someone?"

Sophie turned her back to Lola and rolled toward Jake where he sat on the edge of the bed. "She'd have lots of space to stay away from anyone she's worried about. We could even have people feed her cookies—if there's anyone there. I'll run with her first and we can take Tess and Lola along so she feels safe."

Jake considered this for a moment. "I guess we can try it." He sounded dubious.

VERA

After going for a neighborhood run with Sophie, Vera was thrilled to find her sisters in the truck waiting for her. For the past several days, she'd been taken out by herself to places that terrified her. But today, her sisters were going along too. Tess circled and pranced, and even Lola stood and paced and sniffed the air.

When the truck stopped a short while later, she breathed in the familiar scent of the lake and the enormous field where she had spent so much time chasing swallows in the past few months. But unlike the times she'd been here before, she was forced to stay in the truck and watch her sisters bound off together. Abandoned, Vera spun around and around, and while she spun, she barked.

"*Please* don't do that!" The sharpness in Sophie's voice stopped Vera in mid-stride. The truck was open now, Sophie blocking her access to the field. Her spirit burned to chase after her sisters—but she stopped, poised for further direction. "That'll do." Vera soared, but the instant she was in midair, she heard Sophie redirect her with "Sit!" She sat when she hit the ground, fighting to do the right thing, every muscle in her body quivering.

"Good girl, V! Now, go play!" Sophie released her collar and she exploded into a dead run. Scanning the field, she saw Lola. She charged, bowling her sister off her feet, then grabbed the roll of skin at the back of her neck with her teeth. The smell of fur and the texture of flesh in her mouth thrilled her. She wanted her sister to play, and the more Lola asked her to stop, the more she demanded it; biting, pouncing, pawing at the golden's face. But Lola's inertia was unrelenting. It rose up like a wall against her, and slowly she became aware of Jake's voice.

"Vera, easy! Come!"

After a few more cursory lunges at Lola, she sped off after Jake, then caught sight of Tess in the lake. She rushed into the water and barked at the collie. Tess ignored her, swimming and circling just out of reach. A whitecap slapped Vera in the face and she pounced on it, snapping and swallowing; then was caught up in a frenzied game with the waves, chasing back and forth, the sand soft between her toes, the water cooling her legs and chest.

"No swallows today," Sophie called to Jake. "It may be harder for V."

At the sound of Sophie's voice, Vera lost interest in the water, scanned the field and made a beeline for Lola. The golden turned and fled, tearing ahead of her. But the shepherd drove faster and faster, her paws skimming the field, the air a wind in her face. With a magnificent leap she surged forward and reached out her paws. She imagined Lola's collapse under her weight, the joy of success, the status. But when she landed, Lola had vanished.

Vera stopped, disoriented. A blur behind her made her whirl, and the chase was on again, the golden flying before her. Then Lola stopped and sniffed the ground, her back to Vera. Vera pounced—and was ignored. Confused, Vera slammed Lola again and again, her frustration building and building. She mouthed, grabbed, pushed and pawed at Lola—she growled, she threw herself against her sister, she bit at her with her teeth.

Sudden, frantic movement and a dog blasted into their space, inserting himself into her game. She felt his eager breath, his paw on her neck, his hip bumping her sideways. Startled, she lashed out, snapped at his face and her fangs made contact. He screamed and ran.

"Vera!"

She glanced in the direction of her name to see Sophie charging toward her. "What did you do?" Sophie was angry again, her face contorted, her mouth short and set, eyebrows together. Vera crouched as low as she could. She felt Sophie's hands grab her collar, felt the leash jerk at her neck, and shaken to the depths of her being, she followed Sophie back to the parking lot. Enclosed in the safe haven of her truck, she circled, waiting for her sisters.

SOPHIE

"That didn't go so well," Jake walked up to the truck with Tess and Lola. Sunglasses obscured his eyes, but his lips were thin and taut, his jaw rigid.

"Was the dog injured?" Sophie's voice was almost a shriek. What was happening to her? To them? What was Vera doing to their lives?

"A deep scratch on his face. His owner checked him over after you left, but she didn't find any other marks."

Jake seemed older, tired, and Sophie was struck with how defeated he looked.

"I gave her our phone number in case she needs to take him to the vet." His voice was quiet, matter-of-fact, devoid of emotion. His face said it all. "She was pretty upset. That's it, Sophie. We're never bringing Vera back here again. Ever. Are you sure we should still take her to Fairhaven?"

"It can't hurt. The more practice she gets, the better. We can keep it short."

They dropped Tess and Lola off at home and drove to Fairhaven for the sixth time. Parking could be hard to find in August, especially in the shade. Luckily, they found a spot not far from the Village Green.

They unloaded Vera and kept her on a short leash, scanning for people on the sidewalks and doorways of the small, artsy shops. Suddenly, Vera pulled to a halt and stared at the sky. Following her line of vision they saw the long arm of a construction crane. It was maybe 300 feet away, reaching high above the buildings. Vera growled and pulled back.

"I didn't know dogs could see that far," said Jake. He squinted into the distance. The crane was the size of a fingernail.

"How could she be afraid of something so tiny?" Sophie studied Vera. Her laser stare was still fixed on it.

"Damned if I know."

"Let's go, V." Sophie moved forward, luring her ahead with a small piece of cheese. Finally, V took one small step, then another, stretching her neck out and grabbing the cheese each time before advancing again. Eventually, she allowed herself to be led along the sidewalk.

They sat on their usual bench, thinking that Vera would be more comfortable in a familiar spot, and began the exercise.

"V-dog, down." Vera complied and held eye contact with Jake until he rewarded her, then settled in to watch the flow of people.

VERA

Vera had done this exercise several times before in this exact spot, and now that the monster in the sky was gone, she could begin to relax and watch the world go by. It was one of the things she did best—she watched until something didn't fit, threatened her space, or made eye contact with her, then she'd take care of it however she could. She didn't think about what to do, she just did it.

She watched a group of legs scissor past, scuffing the ground, heads and hands bobbing above. Sophie fed her scrumptious treats when strangers approached, then stopped after they passed her. Another group ambled by. Again the treats flowed from Sophie.

There. Something in the background caught her eye; different in shape and movement; fast, and smooth. And then a disturbing whirring sound buzzed her ears. She warned Jake and Sophie; she closed her mouth and tensed, ears forward. When they didn't try to stop her, she plunged to the end of her leash. A sharp bark from Jake followed.

"Vera, down!"

She sat.

"Down!" She walked her paws forward one by one into a sphinx position and looked up at him. His bark hadn't made a bit of sense. She licked and looked away.

"Good girl." She took the small piece of cheese from his fingers with her teeth. "Ow! Easy, V-dog."

"That's nuts," said Sophie. "I just don't get why she'd bark at a bicycle. She did so well with them all summer."

Vera heard Sophie's voice, but didn't pay much attention—a dog pacing toward them consumed her senses. At first he ignored her, his eyes focused elsewhere. But then, he drew closer. His tail wagged—a neutral tail—and his gaze met hers. Vera tensed, her mouth sealed shut—until she smelled the strong, meaty odor of hot dogs pulling her away. She flicked her eyes up at Sophie.

Warmth spread across Sophie's face. It felt like the sun reaching out to save her. "Good girl, V. That's what I want." Vera took the cascade of treats that followed—but the people, the dog, and the bicycle all started to melt together into a sea of noise and movement and potential threat. The dog passed without incident, but when Vera lay down, she turned her back and lost herself in the dingy murk below the bench.

SOPHIE

"I think she's had enough," said Sophie. Let's take her for a short walk before we head home."

Keeping a handful of treats ready and Vera on a very short leash, they walked with great care to the Interurban trail. Massive trees arched over them forming a high, cool canopy, and shadows and sunlight ebbed and flowed on the packed gravel surface of the trail.

Again, they fed Vera when people and dogs drew near. Sometimes Vera tensed and licked her lips, and Sophie would move away from the path, brushing past shrubs to find a secure spot. Occasionally a dog passed with a low tail and averted eyes, and Vera tolerated these creatures without much trouble—a "watch me" cue, a couple of treats, keep to the far side of the trail, and they were good.

Other dogs caused her to tense up fifty feet away and they would need to get far off the trail and feed her treats continuously to prevent a reaction from Vera. Sophie didn't get a chance to study these dogs since she was paying such close attention to the shepherd.

They were on their way back to the truck when Vera glanced upward—and froze. Puzzled, they strained their eyes toward the sky and there, through a break in the canopy, soared a jet. It was barely a speck in the brilliant blue, and the sound had not yet reached them. They searched for some other oddity that could have spooked Vera, but there were only the green, dappled maple leaves, the blue sky—and the jet. They glanced at Vera again and sure enough, her eyes were tracking it, ears forward, and tail tucked.

"That's impossible!" Jake said. "Why would something that far away in the sky freak her out? It's even smaller than the crane."

"I think we should take her home." Sophie studied the dog. Vera's pupils were dilated, changing her eyes from amber to black, and her face was tight—no, more than just tight. The dog was panicked. She was hyper-everything—hyper-vigilant, hyper-sensitive, and probably had hyper-acute hearing too. Sophie felt a sudden, desperate urge to get her back to the truck before something bad happened. She did not have a good feeling about this.

They focused back on the trail, rounding one curve, then another—and then two off-leash dogs sprinted out from behind some bushes. The dogs cavorted up to Vera, all softness and smiles. Sophie pulled back hard on the leash, but instead of bringing Vera to her side, the leash was wrenched through her hands as Vera stormed forward. A sharp pain shot through her index finger, up her hand, and into her wrist, but somehow she managed to hang on. The dogs fell back.

"Sorry!" The owner came into view and hurried up to them. "They're friendly."

"But my dog isn't, and this is an on-leash area." Sophie's voice attacked the woman. "Leash them. *Now!*" She was aware that she was shouting.

The woman glared at her, clearly taken aback. "You shouldn't have that dog on this trail," she said. "I would *never* own a dog like that."

Vera still strained at her leash, desperate to get at the dogs.

The woman had tethered them, but for some ridiculous reason was walking toward Vera again. Sophie's hand throbbed.

"Let me get her out of the way!" As much as Sophie wanted to strangle the woman, she forced herself to attend to Vera and half dragged, half walked the shepherd off the trail. "Vera, leave it. Watch me!" She tried to sound firm, tried not to lose herself in the tears that were just a breath away. Vera's stare stayed riveted on the dogs.

Jake stepped between them, his glare as much a barrier to the woman and her dogs as his body, and somehow they made their way back to the truck without further incident.

"I don't think I can do this anymore," Sophie's voice was a whisper. "Those were nice dogs—Tessie and Lola-type dogs. We're always on guard. There's always one more conflict. There's always one more thing we need to think about so that she doesn't hurt someone. And this time I think she broke my finger. I mean, where does it stop?"

"She broke your finger?" Jake glanced over, and carefully took her injured hand in his. It hurt, but his touch eased her.

Sophie looked down to see a bruise blossoming at the base of her right index finger. It was swollen and red and excruciatingly painful. But she didn't want to spend the time to get it x-rayed and evaluated. "Yes, I'm fine. I'll ice and splint it when I get home. It'll be all right. It just hurts. A lot."

What was bothering her more than her finger was Vera: Sophie's resolve was finally starting to waiver, and that realization in itself was crushing. "I don't know, Jake. Maybe we should look into rescues. This is getting to be too much."

"Let's just think about it for a minute," Jake said. He reached over and stroked her face. "Remember, we're in this together."

"But how did she get like this?" Sophie finally lost it. Her months of determination cracked and gave way, and with her hand shrieking, she leaned forward and wept.

When had all this crazy behavior started with V? Things had seemed to be going so well when they first brought her home as a foster. She'd hung out with Jake's kids at the school, and she'd passed what? fifty? a hundred? dogs on their walks all summer with only one tussle. She'd *greeted* them, for God's sake, and played happily with Baker. And she'd met Miriam and Miriam's husband without any problem, passed loads of bicycles, explored several trails.

There'd been small things—the scuffle with Tessie, her ongoing intensity, and her restlessness at night, but how the hell did she get to this point? Maybe her problem was related to leash reactivity. Leashes limited a dog's options, prevented them from running away from things that made them uncomfortable. But she'd been off leash when she bit the man. And today she'd gone after that poor dog at the dog park when she'd been off leash with Lola, her security blanket. So obviously it wasn't just leash reactivity.

And now it wasn't just reacting to other dogs, either. It was reacting to humans, and cars. It was barking out the car window at anything that moved. It was pushing her sisters around, confronting Lola over her bed, stalking and charging Tessie, and trying to manipulate Sophie.

Every moment of every day seemed to have become a challenge with Vera. Sophie had tried everything she knew as a trainer—techniques that had always worked for the dogs she'd trained over the years—but for the first time, these things hadn't helped. She had no idea that a dog like Vera could even exist. She'd always thought that consistency, limit-setting, patience, and positive-reinforcement obedience training could solve any problem.

Apparently, she'd been wrong.

Sophie stared out the window. She felt flat, the wind that had propelled her thus far, dead. A woman walked three dogs along the sidewalk beside her and Vera stormed at them like a rabid wolf, the truck rocking and bucking under her weight. Sophie longed to be that woman—the dogs trotting at her side barely glanced up.

Sophie had been so sure they'd get to that point…now she doubted it would ever happen.

"Why don't you call the woman Josie told you about?" Jake

suggested. "We need to take V-dog to a trainer who specializes in aggression before we make any major decisions. She's trying so hard. Look at all the amazing things you've taught her to do."

It was true. Vera didn't jump up on people or dig, she wasn't a resource guarder, she stayed off the furniture, and she wasn't the least bit destructive in the house. She'd completely house-trained herself, even though she had never lived inside before. She could even be described as fastidious—she certainly didn't roll on nasty things like Lola did. And she was a remarkable student. She observed Tess and Lola carefully and could mimic them perfectly when it was her turn in their training sessions. In fact, she made Sophie feel like a talented trainer. And she could be cute. And funny. And sweet. If it weren't for the rest of it, she was the perfect dog.

Sophie rummaged though her purse for the phone number Josie had given her, being careful to protect her finger. "I'll call her as soon as we get back."

All the way home she clutched the scrap of paper in the palm of her hand like a prayer.

CHAPTER 34

SOPHIE

The phone was ringing when they walked into the house.

"This is Teresa from the shelter. Sarah's been adopted!"

Sophie's heart leapt. She really needed some good news.

"They're a retired couple," Teresa continued. "We think it'll be a good fit for her. She's going home in about two hours if you want to say good-bye."

Sarah was in her kennel and crazed with excitement when Sophie arrived. Sophie took Sarah's massive head in her hands, kissed her black forehead, and ran her fingers through the coarse, shiny fur. Sarah sat, willing herself still.

"OK, girl. One last fling." Sophie slipped the harness over Sarah's head and attached the leash. "After this you'll have your own family—you'll have the time of your life." They ran through the parking lot, and Sarah struggled toward Sophie's truck. "No, sweetheart, you don't get to ride in my truck any more—from now on you'll have your own car to ride in."

They jogged up the road like they had done countless times before—playing, training and snuggling. Sophie couldn't help but wonder how things would have been different if she'd adopted Sarah instead of Vera. Vera would be dead—that went without saying. And who knew if Sarah would have done as well with the girls as Vera had. Three female dogs in any household were a lot. And based on the conflicts that Vera had had with super-social Tessie, she wondered if Sarah's larger-than-life presence would have been even more overwhelming.

Anyway, it was a non-issue. Sophie would never have adopted Sarah in the first place. Vera was a "failed foster" because she'd had no other options. In contrast, Sarah was a well-balanced dog who hadn't needed Sophie to rescue her. Still… Sophie was going to miss her.

By the time they returned to the shelter, Sarah's new family was waiting in the office.

"She's an amazing dog," Sophie said, handing over the leash. "You're going to love her." She knelt down and cradled Sarah's head in her arms. "Bye sweetie. Maybe I'll see you again sometime." She turned and strode away, her legs feeling foreign and barely responsive. She struggled to keep her poise all the way to the truck.

CHAPTER 35

SOPHIE

Sophie drove home with rollercoaster memories of the summer whirling in her mind. The past eight months had been crazy. But they were entering a new era now that both Sarah and Vera were safe. Well, Sarah, anyway. What was going to happen to Vera? Sophie swallowed hard.

She was also conflicted about the shelter. The passion that had driven her forward with the Open Paw program for the past eight months was flagging. She was frazzled, absorbed by Vera and the girls. No one else had taken up her cause, and after all this time she'd been allowed only one meeting with the staff. Trying to maintain that program by herself was like hauling a sack of cement on her back. She had to decide: Vera or the shelter. She realized that now. She couldn't manage both with Jake, the two girls, and with all the overtime, a full-time job.

Her mind made up, she focused on the freeway. The next thing she needed to do was to make an appointment with that aggression specialist.

She arranged to meet with Nancy, the trainer, the following Wednesday.

"I'll send you an intake form. Get it back to me as soon as you can," Nancy said. "And bring a lot of high-value treats with you. You'll need them."

The form was long, filled with questions whose answers could divulge a lot about Vera's temperament and behavior if answered carefully. Even though the trainer had seemed flat on the phone, she did appear to be seeking a depth of information about V that Georgia hadn't requested. Sophie spent over an hour on it, answering each question with care.

Later that night she tossed and turned, trying to put her mind to rest. There was something she needed to do, but she couldn't quite think of it. Then she remembered—she should call Jane, a dog-trainer friend she had known for fifteen years, but had had little contact with recently. Jane had always owned German shepherds, and ran the obedience program for the local dog club where Sophie had once taught classes.

When Jane heard about Vera's behavior issues, she didn't seem at all surprised.

"Sophie, she's a German shepherd. She'll never be a Tess or a Lola. You'll never be able to trust her at the dog park and you'll always have to be careful with her. She's hardwired to protect you and her family."

"But all shepherds aren't like this."

"Sure, but shepherds aren't supposed to be friendly with

strangers. In fact, they get docked points at AKC trials if they're too friendly."

Sophie was shocked. "Please tell me they're not supposed to bite." Sophie looked over at the three dogs stretched out on the deck in front of her: Tess and Lola were dead to the world, while V lay with her head on her paws, eyes tracking every movement Sophie made.

"Of course not. But you'll need to keep her on leash and far enough away from people so she doesn't feel she needs to protect you." Jane's voice sounded distant and tinny.

"We're going to take her to a trainer who works with aggression next week. I'm hoping to get her past that." Sophie said.

"She'll never get past it." Jane's tone was resolute. "But you can bring her to the Rally-Obedience class on Tuesday nights at seven-thirty if you like, and work with her around the edge of the room. I won't charge you. And if there's any way I can help with Vera, just let me know."

"We'll bring her tomorrow and see how she does," Sophie managed. She was stunned. How could Jane possibly say there was no hope for V without even meeting her?

The next evening, Sophie walked Vera up the hill by their house before leaving for class. It was gorgeous, the low angle of the sun casting a warm glow through the trees. The forest was silent around them except for the echoes of robin song. Vera meandered ahead, sniffing the grasses, tail swinging rhythmically behind her.

For the first time in what seemed like a long, long time, Sophie relaxed. They wandered back toward home and she daydreamed that Vera was normal after all—friendly, trustworthy, not aggressive—that all those hopes she'd had for the shepherd had been realized.

Then Vera lunged.

Sophie felt the sting of adrenalin, fought to catch her balance, and somehow managed to haul the shepherd to a standstill. A neighbor, his dog at the end of a long Flexi leash, appeared on a side road below them, looking up to where Vera shrieked like a rabid wolf.

"I'm sorry," Sophie called out. "I didn't see you." She fought back tears, backtracked up the hill and made Vera sit. She was starting to feel like the neighborhood's crazy dog lady.

"Don't worry," he called over his shoulder, his dog now trotting beside him in perfect heel position.

But Sophie could sense his disapproval.

Jake parked the truck as close as he could to the entrance of the building to minimize their chance of an encounter with an off-leash dog. Ironically, the building where the training classes were held was located at the same dog park where she had met Kate, Vera's previous adopter, just a few months ago; where Vera had romped and played with her sisters before visiting with Jake's students on his last day at school. Sophie shuddered at the thought: what if V had bitten one of the kids? That would have been a great way for Jake to end his twenty-five year teaching career. *Jesus!* How could they have been so naïve?

"I'll check with Jane before we take her in," said Sophie.

The Rally-O class was starting when she entered the hall. It was a huge room with only six dogs in the class, so it would be perfect for V. Moreover, the dogs were confined to rubber mats that had been placed on the floor to improve their footing, so their location would be very controlled. Jane saw her across the room and nodded.

"OK, Jake." Sophie opened the back of the truck, her voice strong and confident, defying her shaking hands. "Let's do it."

She checked the environment for loose dogs, and harnessed V with her head collar. Vera walked toward the building between them; tail and ears up, laser eyes scanning the parking lot.

"This is going to be interesting." Sophie placed one foot in front of the other and straightened her back.

VERA

Vera stood in a small, dark room with an open doorway on one side of her. Beyond the doorway, she saw an enormous room. She heard dogs—lots of them—and one of them was vocalizing with an incessant, nagging bark that put her on edge.

Sophie and Jake hadn't yet allowed her to see the dogs. They kept her leash short, limiting her freedom. It made her anxious because she really wanted to see beyond the doorway into the whole room. She strained and whined, then sat and looked up at Sophie. She heard a click, and an injection of brightness trilled through her as she anticipated the treat. Hot dogs. She loved hot dogs.

Then they were walking, Jake leading them into the large, bright room. Her heart bounded in her chest, her panting deafened her. She closed her mouth and listened.

Dogs. She stopped in her tracks. They were large and small, more dogs in one place than she'd ever seen before. No one looked at her; but just in case, she tensed, threw her tail above her back and glared. She stood on her toes, hackles prickled along her back. She smelled the strong scent of hot dogs, but she wasn't interested.

"Here, Vera. You're all right." Sophie's voice echoed as if in the distance. It didn't calm her, but an instant later she was guided away; Sophie putting pressure on the head collar and Jake moving into her, blocking her from the dogs. Then she was back in the small room again, the dogs out of sight. Like a cool river, relief eddied through her and the scent of the hotdogs jumped to life again. She sat and looked up.

"She wouldn't even take treats that time," Jake said. "Let's give her a few minutes to calm down and try again." His hand was strong and steady on her face and neck. "It's all right, V-dog. They're not going to hurt you."

She listened to the padding footfalls of the dogs in the adjacent room. Beside one of Sophie's shoes was a dark shape that she suspected might be a treat. She stepped forward cautiously and sniffed it, but the scent repelled her and she jumped back.

The next time they led her into the hall, the treats smelled good. She snatched them with reckless determination from between Jake's fingers. She buzzed inside, every fiber vibrating with a mixture of excitement and fear, but now she knew what to expect. She fixated on the dogs, calculating the risk of attack. She was wired, her muscles coiled so tightly that she could barely stay still. She gobbled treats for several seconds in the dogs' presence before she was led away again.

The third time, when Vera stepped into the room, Sophie kept the leash short, but loose.

"Watch me," Sophie instructed. When Vera turned her eyes upward, the dogs disappeared. All that filled her vision was Sophie's face—lit up for her, completely there for her. She ate the tiny pieces of hot dog, one after another.

"This way," Sophie's voice directed her. She smelled cheese in front of her nose, saw Jake's tall, confident form split between her and the class, and she was led back into the small, dark, safe room. She was confused, spent. She ached with fatigue. Voices volleyed back and forth above her, then dropped in conclusion.

Sophie took a step toward the exit. That was all Vera needed. She bolted forward, crammed herself against the door and didn't stop her furious charge until the back of the truck enveloped her. She could hear Jake talking outside, words a jumble, but voices urgent, worried.

"What did you make of that? She could barely handle five minutes."

"I know," answered Sophie. "Thank God we have that appointment tomorrow."

Tess

Tessie had been lounging in front of the sliding glass doors, gazing out at the meadow when she heard the crunch of tires on the gravel driveway. A bolt of joy brought her to her feet, and she trotted to the door, her voice a high-pitched welcome. She loved it when Jake and Sophie came home, and it was her job— had been her job for her whole life—to greet them.

The door opened and Vera strutted into the house. Tessie touched noses with her, and when Vera ignored her, she barked and circled between Sophie and Jake, her flexible spine curving around and around their legs, their hands warm and loving in the weave of her coat. She bobbed her velvety ears up and down:

up when they spoke to her, catching the words and deciphering them, then back into a grin, matching their smiles.

It didn't bother her that Vera barely acknowledged her. Although it was the prerogative of the dog reentering the house to flaunt her status, Tess wouldn't have cared anyway. Vera was still the punk adolescent, and Tess knew it. She just didn't like Vera's threats.

Tess was distracted again by Lola's appearance, and glanced up just in time to see Vera prance over to the glass doors where Tess had spent a good part of the evening. To her dismay, the shepherd circled once or twice, lay down, and groaned.

Now what? Tess fumed. Irritation nattered away in her head, fizzed through her limbs. She scanned the room and thought for a moment.

She had it.

With a burst of energy, she ran up the stairs and barked at the top of her lungs out the glass door in the bedroom. She heard the drum of Vera's paws on the carpet as Vera charged up behind her to check things out. And with a glow of satisfaction, the collie turned tail and trotted back down to once again claim her favorite spot. She sighed and turned her head toward the meadow, bathing in gratification.

Still, it was tiring, this constant game she engaged in with Vera. Vera was always challenging her, pushing her, and confronting her, even if it was just to claim a certain place. And that dog still had absolutely no respect for personal space. But Tess was working things out, learning ways to outsmart her, ways to maintain her own status and to keep the dog where she belonged. She put her head down on her paws and dozed.

CHAPTER 36

SOPHIE

The next day, they drove down the long driveway, past the "Private" sign, and into a parking area designated by a handwritten sign "Park here". Sophie was excited—or scared. She didn't know which. She just knew that her teeth itched and palpitations were somersaulting in her chest. With any luck, this trainer would be able to help.

A lean, middle-aged woman with a cap of short, silver hair walked toward them. There was a studied, calm expression on her face and she looked confident and in control.

"Hello. Jake? Sophie? I'm Nancy." Her voice was measured, and when she smiled, only her mouth moved. The rest of her face stayed flat and devoid of emotion. "So that's Vera back there?" She gestured to the masked face peering out of the canopy window.

"Yeah."

"Well, get her out. I want to meet her," the woman said with a flourish. "I'll stand over here so I don't crowd her."

Nancy took several steps back from the truck and turned sideways. She'd obviously put some thought into how to greet Vera and what body language would make the dog comfortable. Sophie was impressed.

Sophie harnessed Vera in her head collar, her fingers fumbling with the clasp. She hadn't realized how nervous she was—how much she'd anticipated and feared this moment. What if Nancy thought there was no hope?

"That'll do!" Sophie tried to keep the anxiety from her voice, tried to be strong and assertive. Tried to make Vera believe she was confident. Vera sat as soon as her paws hit the grass.

"She's very well-behaved, very polite," said Nancy. "Hello Vera." The woman's voice softened when she spoke to V, but she didn't reach out. She didn't stare at the dog either. She just stood there, smiling and talking to V, her eyes focused on something far away. "In case you're wondering—I'm being indirect to make her more comfortable."

Vera stared at the woman, ears back, heavy tail wagging. She pulled toward Nancy, and it was all Sophie could do to hold her back.

"V, sit!" Sophie said. She could hear the unintended sharpness in her voice and Vera responded as if she'd been hit. "Watch me." Vera's head snapped up and their eyes locked. Confident that she had Vera's complete attention, she gave her permission to greet her new trainer. "That'll do, V."

Vera raced up to Nancy and sniffed her hand, her jeans, her sleeves, and finally, her shoes. The woman stood still with her arms at her sides until Vera had finished her investigation. Then Nancy handed V a treat.

"Well, at least she likes people," Nancy said, laughing. "I brought her roast chicken."

Relief raced through Sophie followed by a welcome tingle of hope. She loved this woman! V loved this woman!

"Let's take her into the fenced area," Nancy said. "I'd like to observe her off leash." They walked into a large, flat, grassy enclosure bordered by a six-foot cyclone fence. Enormous oak trees lined the field, their leaves turning to gold, the ground beneath them littered with acorns.

As soon as Vera was unclipped, she trotted off. They watched her inspect the perimeter of the area, then check out the assortment of agility equipment scattered across the field.

"She's much more confident than I expected," said Nancy, walking to the middle of the yard. "Look how far out she's exploring without you."

Sophie glanced over at Nancy. The woman's eyes were narrow, tracking Vera's movements. Sophie was struck with the inferences Nancy was making from Vera's behavior—she guessed that she herself did the same thing with her medical patients, but for some reason hadn't applied the same behavioral interpretations to dogs.

"Let's see how she does with recall," Nancy said.

"Vera, come!" Jake called. Vera turned from the tunnel she was sniffing and charged the seventy-five feet to sit in front of Jake, her gaze glued to his. "Good girl, V-dog," he said, and gave her a small piece of hot dog.

"Wow!" Nancy said. "I can tell you two have worked hard. She's really bonded to you." Again, the woman smiled. This time her eyes crinkled and smiled too.

"Really? It doesn't seem that way to us. We don't know what to do with her," said Sophie. In light of Vera's flawless greeting, the comment seemed silly as soon as she said it. She palmed her burning cheeks with an icy hand, a clumsy attempt to cool her discomfort. She felt like a hysterical novice owner instead of a trainer consulting another trainer. *I refer patients to medical specialists all the time,* she reminded herself. *It's exactly the same thing.* She squared her shoulders and looked Nancy in the eye.

"What's bothering you the most?" Nancy asked.

"The bite was the worst thing," Sophie said. "But it's also her reactivity to dogs, and her behavior in general. We've had her for about three months now and she's getting worse instead of better—in spite of all the work we've done."

"Obedience training isn't going to fix this," Nancy said, shifting her focus from Sophie to Jake and back again. "You have to change her emotional reaction to the things that scare her, not just her actions. So all the skills you've taught her— sit, down, attention and so on—are going to give you a foundation to work with, but they aren't going to change how she feels. Aggression work is a completely different type of training."

Sophie wasn't surprised. "We've tried classical conditioning." She looked at the ground. Why didn't she really know this stuff? All these years as a dog trainer and she couldn't even make classical conditioning work. The dog now lay at her feet—a picture of well-behaved loyalty. "It didn't help."

"If it didn't work, you probably did too much too fast."

Sophie thought about how careful they'd tried to be on Fairhaven Green. "She has so many things going on that we don't know where to start." She could hear her voice rising. "Evenings are especially bad—she's been scratching Jake on the legs when she finishes her Kong, then she jumps up on the hide-a-bed and barks out the window or attacks Lola, our golden— she's being playful, I guess, but for Lola it's way too rough. And she won't stop."

Now that Sophie was talking, emotion streamed out of her and she felt a beachball-sized sob rise in her chest. It wasn't just the avalanche of behaviors that was bothering her. It was the fear of not knowing where it would end.

"She also bullies our collie, Tess, as much as she can get away with, and she's blocking us from Tess and Lola when we want to give them attention. The only thing we can do is to put her in the mudroom behind baby gates." Sophie caught a flash of movement over Nancy's shoulder and was surprised to see Vera trotting out into the field again. She was such a stealthy dog—silent, swift, intelligent—and Sophie never knew what to expect next. "Putting her away by herself makes me feel so guilty."

"I think she's telling you that she *wants* to be in the mudroom," Nancy said.

Sophie stared at her. "You're kidding!" She thought for a minute, fiddled with the leash, then shifted her gaze back to Vera. "Maybe you're right. Sometimes I'll take her out for another run, or play with her some more to tire her out. But it doesn't seem to help. If anything, it makes her worse."

"That's what I'm saying." Nancy's tone became more urgent. "She's overstimulated. From what you said on her intake form, she was either chained up or at the shelter until three months ago. Now she's exposed to the real world; she lives with two dogs and two humans and sometimes it's just too much for her." The woman shrugged as if the explanation should be obvious.

Sophie swallowed. All the shenanigans they'd had to deal with started to make sense.

"You need to understand that three months is no time at all. She's overwhelmed and doesn't have a clue how to deal with it. You need to teach her how to behave." Nancy's eyes seemed to be searching, probing, trying to figure out if Sophie and Jake had it in them to do the work. To understand this dog. To turn her around.

"That's what we're trying to do," said Jake. He was leaning forward, and Sophie could tell he was eating up every word, his attention riveted on Nancy. "What should I do when she scratches me? I've tried telling her 'no', 'leave it', and 'uh-uh' and it just makes her do it more. Then I get mad at her—I can't help it."

"Try changing the picture," said Nancy. "First of all, it sounds like you need to put her in the mudroom as soon as she finishes her Kong. Just say to her in a light voice, 'Vera, let's go to your room.' Walk her over to it, close the gate behind her, and give her a special treat. She'll do fine."

Sophie and Jake exchanged looks. It seemed way too simple a fix.

"And if she does try to scratch you before you take her away, hold her paw gently in your hand, stroke it, and say something like 'What is it, Vera? Do you want to go to your room?' And then take her there."

"You make it sound so easy." Jake said.

"One thing I want to be really clear about." Nancy fixed them with a hard stare. "Treating an aggressive dog with aggression only makes it worse. So verbal or physical corrections of any kind are verboten." She looked back and forth, her lips pinched together like those of an angry parent. "If you get upset with her, leave the room, but don't direct it at her."

"That makes sense," said Sophie trying not to feel like she'd just been scolded. "We'll be really careful. We never use physical corrections, or 'no', but sometimes I use 'uh-uh' with the girls." She laughed as Vera popped out of a tunnel fifty feet away.

"You can't do that any more," said Nancy, shaking her head. "You'll sabotage her progress."

Sophie looked at the trainer, an undercurrent of wariness making her squirm inside. There was something about this woman that she liked, but distrusted—maybe it was the woman's confrontational style, or her detachment, or her know-it-all delivery.

Sophie ran through Nancy's suggestions in her mind. Everything the woman said made sense—and they were running out of options. At least Nancy seemed to know what she was talking about and used positive methods—no punishment allowed—which suited Sophie. Vera was such a sensitive dog in spite of her crazy behaviors.

"One other thing I want to mention." Nancy's terse, humorless voice interrupted Sophie's thoughts. "I noticed on your intake form that you had a question about medication. Just so you know—I don't use drugs in my training."

"Really? I've read that antidepressants can help to reduce

aggression." In fact, medication for Vera was something Sophie had hoped for. She had prescribed antidepressants for her patients for years and had seen remarkable changes in their quality of life once the medication took effect.

"Not necessarily," Nancy said. "And the last thing I want to do is to interfere with her brain function."

Sophie either needed to trust this woman and try out her methods, or find someone else—and they were running out of options.

VERA

Vera tensed when Nancy reappeared with a large, male dog. From his musky odor she could tell he was intact. He was tall and dark and light on his feet, and he trotted beside Nancy full of confidence. He ignored Vera, which put her at ease.

"Prince and I are going to walk back and forth in a line about forty feet away from you. When Vera looks at Prince, I want you to click and treat. If she licks her lips or looks away, tell me and I'll move back."

Vera licked her lips and looked away from the dog. She observed that he was on leash. She understood leashes—they kept dogs away from her.

Nancy and the dog started pacing back and forth, back and forth, yet they didn't appear to be coming any closer to her. She licked again and again.

"Vera, watch," said Sophie, and Vera raised her eyes, comforted by Sophie's smile, the click, and the forthcoming pieces of hot dog. She held Sophie's gaze for a while, then, when she couldn't stand it anymore, she looked back at the dog. He was closer. She knew it! She stood on her toes as tall as she could, raised her tail above her back and let out a mighty "woof".

"You should have clicked when she looked at Prince and then had her look right back at you before she barked," said Nancy.

"Oh, sorry, I didn't realize..." Sophie's voice faded, and Vera looked back up at her to see what was going on.

"It's OK, V, good watch." V heard the click and anticipated

the treat, mouth watering.

Vera was careful to check back on Prince more often. She didn't like anything sneaking up on her—her whole life she'd worked hard to refine this skill. She glanced back at the dog, got a click, and then looked up at Sophie. Hot dog. It worked! She glanced back at Prince again. Click. At Sophie. Treat. Excitement flitted through her. She could actually make Sophie click and give her a hot dog whenever she wanted!

Her gut uncoiled. She lowered her tail from its perch over her back. She was aware now that Prince was moving closer, but it was so gradual, and she was keeping such close tabs on him, that she continued to unwind.

To a point.

Then he entered her bubble. She had no idea what defined her space, and it changed from second to second depending on a million factors, but at this moment, with this dog, it had been breached. She licked and licked, looked away, glued her eyes to Sophie, and finally, in response to Jake's voice, Nancy stopped advancing and took the dog away. Vera felt the unbearable pressure dissipate. Her oasis of safety was restored.

Sophie

"Can we meet again next week?" asked Sophie. Nancy and Prince had advanced to within twenty feet of Vera—without Vera lunging and barking. "Can we practice this during the week with friends? Is there anything else we can work on?" She was speeding down a highway to Vera's recovery, her brain spinning out of control. "What do you think her prognosis is? Do you think she'll get better?" Sophie felt all the distress of the past months spilling out of her in a flood of excitement.

Nancy laughed. "I like your enthusiasm." The woman hesitated and a downward twitch of tension distorted the corners of her mouth. "Vera did so well today that I think it'll take her a year at the most—then she should be back on trails and playing at the dog park." She swiped at her nose with her index finger.

A prickle rose on the back of Sophie's neck. Was something wrong?

No. She was being silly, overreacting again—she had just been told she was going to get her life back! A surge of relief quelled her doubts and she threw her broadest smile at Nancy and then Jake. "Really?"

"Sure," Nancy said. "I'll give you some exercises to work on, and you can set up a context just like we did here today with any dog she knows. Just make sure the person follows your instructions. I wouldn't usually recommend that after the first lesson, but with your level of expertise and Vera's skill level, you'll do fine. "

"She has one dog that she plays with. Should we still let them play together?" asked Jake. "And we've started taking her to a dog class." They explained the procedure they'd gone through the night before.

"Yes, you definitely want to maintain any relationships she has. And the class sounds like a good idea. Try to get at least three dog-dog interactions a week. The class can be one of them, and you should try to have her play with her friend at least once a week too." Nancy reached down to stroke Vera's face. The dog ducked and stepped back. "Oops. I guess she didn't like that. Anyway, that leaves one additional interaction for you to set up with a person and a well-socialized dog. Otherwise, keep her away from dogs and strangers. Every encounter has to be carefully planned. And remember—things will probably get worse before they get better."

CHAPTER 37

SOPHIE

Over the next week, Jake and Sophie fell into a routine, realizing how important it was for Vera that her life be predictable. Sophie ran with Vera on the roads of Sudden Valley early in the morning, scanning constantly for off-leash dogs. When she saw someone approaching with a dog, she slipped into the woods bordering the road or retreated up a driveway, or even retraced her steps to a crossroad where she could maintain a safe distance. Sometimes this worked, but at other times Vera was overwhelmed, especially if the dog stared at her, and she would erupt in a burst of vocalizations and lunges.

After Vera's morning outing, Sophie took Tess and Lola on wild, off-leash runs on the Beaver Pond trail where they played and romped, unencumbered by the whims of their sister. Afternoons were spent training Vera, or working through an exercise with one of Sophie's friends and their dog. With the distance between the dogs carefully controlled, there were no reactions from Vera.

In the evenings, Sophie trained and played with the girls for thirty minutes. This was the highlight of their day. They bathed in Sophie's undivided attention and showed off to each other. She worked on Vera's obedience skills, but also set up a variety of games such as catch, fetch with a selection of objects, "find it", tricks, and puzzles. The muffin-tin game was one of her favorites because it combined a variety of skills.

Sophie was always astounded at how much she learned from watching the three dogs. They had such different learning styles and ways of approaching problems, and she drank in every action, watching them not only working, but observing each other. Vera, however, was an ongoing concern. The muffin-tin game was a perfect example.

LOLA, TESS AND VERA

The girls watched with growing interest as Sophie brought out the balls and placed the muffin tin on the floor. It was one of their favorite games, and Lola knew she was the best.

"OK, Lu!" Lola jumped to her feet. Consumed with concentration, she stared at the balls. Before one was even out of Sophie's hand, Lola was off, the ball whizzing in a blur down the hallway before her. She snatched it up, and with the rough texture of it grasped firmly in her mouth, she trotted back and deposited it carefully in one of the muffin-tin holes.

"Good girl, Lu!" Sophie threw the second, and the third, and finally, the sixth ball. Lola only misjudged placement of one ball, and positioned it with more precision the second time to be sure it fell into its target. Then she lay down in her favorite sphinx position, ready to leap to her feet if necessary, staring at the muffin tin and willing Sophie to place a cookie under each ball.

When Sophie was finished, she went to work. She loved the feel of the balls on her nose when she scooped them out one by one to find the treat hidden beneath. It was so satisfying. She was finished before she knew it, thrilled with her perfect performance.

She loved these games and the competition between herself and Vera. She loved showing that dog how to execute complicated maneuvers, loved to outdo her. She settled down to watch Tessie, but anticipated Vera's turn with glee. Sometimes she learned from Vera, but more often, seeing the dog perform made her itch to show Vera the right way to do it.

Tess wasn't as captivated with this game as her sister. She didn't care that Lola was better than she was. And Sophie always did exactly what Tess wanted her to do, anyway. She loved the retrieving part and the cookies part, and Sophie made the other part easy for her. She bounded after the balls, coat flying, cut back to Sophie from the narrow hallway, then tossed the ball directly at Sophie, not even trying for the muffin tin.

"Put it away," Sophie said, holding the muffin tin toward her. Tessie sighed to herself, picked up the ball, and Sophie caught it in one of the holes as it dropped to the ground. Five more balls and she scooped up her prize, burrowing her slender nose under the edge of each ball to lick out the treat.

She leaned against Sophie when she was done and felt a protective arm encircle her. The power of her sister Vera always made her wary, though if any part of that dog touched her during the game, she wouldn't hesitate to correct her. It was Tess's job to keep her in line.

Like Lola, Vera loved this game, but her level of excitement sometimes alarmed her. She knew she didn't want to cause any conflict, but once aroused, she couldn't control it—especially with Lola. And especially outside. Even when she played fetch or chase just with Sophie, she would feel a surge of something wild inside her that drove her to the edge of the abyss. She'd go into a tense "down", her whole being filled with a frantic energy, and stay there, clutching the ground with her toes and nails, until the feeling subsided. Sophie never pushed her.

When playing with Lola, though, she couldn't stop herself. She would just push harder and harder, excitement and anxiety overtaking her until finally Sophie or Jake stopped her, or Lola fled. Or froze. Or fought.

Tonight, though, she wanted to outdo the golden. She was patient. She liked that Sophie locked her in her crate during their games. It removed her options so she could relax and study the other two girls until it was her turn. She had learned a lot that way.

Sophie emptied the balls onto the floor in front of her, and Vera crouched, gaze glued to Sophie's hands. A ball shot through the dining room and into the kitchen, and Vera soared after it, the table and chairs fading into nonexistence. The ball expanded, swelled, darted, took up her entire focus. In two bounds she was in the kitchen, snatched up the ball, and with claws skittering on the hardwood floor, skated backwards, trying to maintain her speed. She deposited the first ball cleanly into the muffin tin—without any help from Sophie.

"Yay V!"

Sophie's voice was happy, delighted, and V crouched for the second ball. It whipped down the hall. She leapt over Tess, grabbed the ball and flew back into the room, depositing the second ball in its spot.

She was on a roll now, her excitement climbing higher and higher.

She heard Sophie's voice soothing her, but it wasn't enough to overcome the almost hysterical enthusiasm she felt, crouched and ready for the next ball. Sophie tossed it, more gently this time, just across the dining room. Vera turned, pounced, and leapt back at Sophie in one movement. She was so close to bursting she could barely control it. In a final effort, she crouched into a down, toes gripping the carpet as hard as she could.

Lola and Tess looked on, poised to act. They recognized the hair-trigger state of their sister, knew that with a glance, with a careless move, she could lose control. They lay like statues, eyes averted.

"Good job, baby girl!"

Vera trembled, watching Sophie place cookies under the three balls in the tin. As soon as she extracted the food, she raced to the comfort of her crate, the walls safe and familiar. Slowly, her breathing returned to normal, Tess and Lola relaxed and rose from their sheltered spots by Sophie, and the tension in the room evaporated.

After playtime, the girls were given their stuffed Kongs. By now, Vera was an expert and could empty a Kong faster than Lola. She had figured out how to bite down hard on the narrow end of the toy, roll it with delicate precision, toss it end over end, and eventually extract each tiny morsel of food from deep inside. Then she'd jump on the hide-a-bed under the large living room window, bark at the meadow, and make a beeline for Jake. It was a pattern she found comforting. It gave her structure when the evening's entertainment was over—and tonight was no different.

However, this time when Vera finished her lament and headed for Jake, instead of seeing his familiar irritation and recoil, his face softened, eyes warm with reassurance. She raised her paw like she always did, poised to claw his leg—to make him do something, anything, to ease her distress. But tonight, she was disarmed. He was so changed in his expression that she didn't really know what to do.

She hesitated for a moment, paw suspended in the air like a puppet. Then Jake took her paw in his hand. She barely felt him touch her pad, and his warm fingers smoothed the back of her wrist with the gentlest of pressures. His velvet voice filled the air around her. She recognized her name and the phrase "little room". She cocked her head, snatched back her foot, and trotted toward the mudroom.

CHAPTER 38

VERA

The next afternoon, Vera found herself in the back of the truck, and she was happy. She had no idea where they were going, but her sister Lola stood beside her, sniffing the air that wafted in through the canopy windows. She adored Lola. She wanted Lola to be hers. All hers.

The truck came to a stop outside a small house with a fence around it.

She jumped down from the truck, glanced up at Miriam and was pleased to see that the woman was talking to Sophie and barely noticed her.

"So, how's she doing?" Miriam asked. "Have you cured her yet?"

"Yeah right! It's going to be a long haul." There was something about Sophie's voice that made Vera cringe, that sent a crawling sense of discomfort down her spine. She shook off.

"Vera's just a punk. She'll be fine. Bring her in with Lola and I'll get Baker."

At the familiar tone of Miriam's voice, Vera shifted her attention and barely heard the ongoing mumble above her. She focused on the child across the street, the cat at the end of the road, the blur of a squirrel above. She'd been here before—an enclosed area with bushes and lots of good smells—and that other dog. She liked to play with him sometimes, but he still made her anxious, especially in this space where he exuded ownership and a certain undercurrent of threat. She turned to Lola and snuffled her ear.

A door opened, and Baker trotted into the yard, head high, tail up. He curved around her and sniffed the ground. Tangled sensations of delight and distress clouded her thinking, and a flare of adrenalin needled her skin.

She needed to act.

He was turning back toward her—now! Vera leapt; and in a flash she had him on his back with her teeth at his throat. Instantly, her position established, she let him go. Then he was on his feet again, running madly around the yard.

"Get him, Vera!" Miriam shouted.

She heard the fever in Miriam's voice and sprinted after Baker. In an instant she was on top of him again and they were wrestling, his body tense and hard against hers. He barked at her, a rapid-fire cacophony, the sound increasing in pitch and volume with each second.

"Go Vera!" Miriam's shriek splintered the balance. Everything changed. She felt Baker's energy shift. His body, his jaws, writhed to subdue her. She screamed back, and, desperate to protect herself, her teeth found his throat. She clamped down.

"Vera!" She barely felt Sophie grab her collar and haul back. She heard Lola belt out loud, baritone roars. She was aware that Baker disappeared into the house, aware of Sophie's anguish when she was led out the gate. Alone, she cowered in the back of the truck.

SOPHIE

"I am so sorry," said Sophie. There were four punctures in the shiny black fur of Baker's neck, and one of his long, delicate ears was scratched and bleeding. Her heart sank. If only there had been no injuries. "We'll pay for any vet bills," she said, stroking Baker's sleek coat. "Poor Baker. He's such a sweet boy. Why the hell did she attack him? I thought they were friends." Sophie was devastated. Nancy was right. Things were definitely getting worse.

"He'll be fine. The punctures are shallow. It could have been much worse." Miriam examined the damage. "Let's see how they do together now that they've calmed down."

Sophie was appalled at the prospect, but finally agreed. "OK, but let's keep them on leash."

She needn't have worried. When she brought V back into the yard, the dogs ignored each other and sniffed the ground, then finally touched noses and after that stayed apart. Lola lay in the shade and watched, and after a few minutes Vera joined her.

"Well, I guess we'd better go," Sophie said. "I'm sorry that happened. I feel sick about it. I don't know what we're going to do with her."

How would they ever get past this? Like Jake had said, the shepherd was a time bomb.

CHAPTER 39

SOPHIE

On the drive back to Nancy's training center a few days later, Sophie felt somewhat hopeful about Vera's progress. The week had certainly been a mixed one, but they had learned a lot. She tried not to think about Vera's fight with Baker and focused instead on the shepherd's success—at least with dogs—in class the night before.

When they arrived, Nancy was working with her dog in the driveway. For a moment she disappeared into the small training facility.

"How did it go?" she asked when she joined them.

"We had a pretty good week," Sophie said, glancing at Jake. "She did well in class last night except when she snapped at a woman who approached her. She also reacted to two dogs when we were walking in our neighborhood...and she had a fight with her friend, Baker—maybe it wasn't such a great week after all."

Nancy stiffened. "Maybe I wasn't clear last week. Every time she reacts she gets a bath of chemicals that will stress her out for the next eight to seventy-two hours making it more likely to happen again."

Sophie cringed and reached down to stroke Vera's solid, smooth back.

"It's bad handling to let her react," Nancy continued. "Tell me what happened with the woman in class."

"V did a nice job of greeting the lead trainer, but when the assistant walked up and held out a treat, she lunged and snapped." Sophie stared at the floor, then glanced up at Nancy.

"She looked happy at first—wagged her tail and smiled—then without any warning, she switched into aggression."

"And what did you do?" asked Nancy.

"I pulled back on the leash," Sophie said, feeling a familiar rush of heat to her face. "In the moment, I didn't know what else to do."

"Oh my God! That's just about worst thing you could've done. That's how you *create* a reactive dog, not treat one," Nancy leaned forward, and Sophie could feel an invisible admonishing finger waving in her face. "Any time you treat aggression with aggression—jerking, yelling, hitting—you're going to make it worse. I told you that last week. You do know that a wagging tail doesn't necessarily mean that the dog is friendly, right?"

Sophie stepped back. What was *that*? Had she just been reprimanded? And was Nancy really questioning her knowledge of a tail wag? Sophie suddenly wanted to leave. But they needed a trainer. This trainer. There was no one else to turn to. It was Nancy or nothing. *Shit!*

"I know that," said Sophie, keeping her voice level. "But what would you have done in a similar situation?"

"I would never have allowed the situation to occur in the first place. That woman should not have been allowed to approach Vera. She isn't ready to greet strangers yet, but we can work on it today if you want to."

Sophie swallowed hard. "Yes, that would be great. Thank you." She tried to read Nancy's expression, but the woman's face was impassive.

"What should we do about off-leash dogs?" Jake asked.

Nancy shrugged. "We talked about this last week. You need to take her places with good visibility where there aren't many dogs or people. That way you'll have time to hide or get Vera behind you if you see a loose dog."

"We can try walking her at the cemetery. It should be quiet there," Jake said, glancing at Sophie. "And what do you think about the fight? Why would she have attacked Baker? We thought they were such good friends."

"She was too aroused." Nancy's stern face challenged them.

She sounded frustrated. "When dogs are overstimulated, their excitement can turn to aggression. We talked about this last week, too—you need to start writing things down."

Had they talked about it? Sophie had no recollection of it or of the alleged discussion of off-leash dogs. And how were they supposed to write things down when they were outside working with Vera?

The trainer released an exasperated sigh and looked away. Sophie thought how much like Vera she was—maybe she would lunge and bite, if Sophie pissed her off enough—or, with more control, lick her lips, yawn, and turn away. Maybe that's why she understood reactive dogs so well.

"You need to keep her as calm as you can. That way she'll be less likely to aggress or react."

"But I thought you wanted her to play." Jake's voice had an edge to it. Sophie shifted her feet, hoping Jake wouldn't just walk away. He had an intolerance for arrogance, and avoidance was his default for dealing with it.

"Not if her arousal level gets too high." Nancy's posture softened and she backed down. Sophie envisioned hackles smoothing out on the back of her neck. "I know this isn't easy, but you just need to continue to work with her and she will improve."

"I don't think we'll let Baker and Vera off leash together again for a while," Sophie said. "Maybe we'll just do exercises with him. On a brighter note, evenings are much better; she's stopped clawing Jake, and we don't feel guilty putting her in the mudroom any more. That's huge for us."

They spent the next thirty minutes teaching Vera how to meet and greet strangers appropriately—practicing it over and over, first introducing her to each other and then to Nancy. For the second part of the class, they ran through another exercise with Prince, took a short break where they worked on impulse control, then repeated the exercise. This time they started thirty feet apart and by the end of the lesson, Nancy and Prince were able to get within ten feet of Vera.

"Another good session," Nancy said when they were ready

to leave. "You're doing excellent work. But remember, you must *not* let her react. If she does, it's your fault and she won't get better."

On the way home, Sophie's thoughts ricocheted inside her head. It was so hard to feel good about Vera for any length of time. Why couldn't she just improve? In everything? All at once?

"What's it going to be like for you when I go back to work next week, Jake? Are you going to be OK?" This thought had been haunting her for the past six weeks, ever since "the bite day". She hated the thought of leaving him alone with all three dogs the first September of his retirement. It didn't seem fair.

"Sure, it'll be OK. The dogs are different with me. They're calmer. I think there's less competition when you're not around. I'll be fine."

Well, thank goodness for that. The days were rushing past and Vera was still a handful.

CHAPTER 40

SOPHIE

For the past week, Sophie had been back at work: getting up at four-thirty in the morning to run with Vera and walk Tessie and Lu, then dashing off to the clinic. By the time she made it to her desk, she was ready for a nap. And fall quarter hadn't even begun.

The early morning runs with Vera in the pitch black had been an ongoing drama. Most dog walkers didn't wear lights in the dark, and a few had strayed too close before she saw the mesmerizing gold or turquoise glow of the dogs' eyes in the light of her headlamp. Vera, of course, had exploded, flooding Sophie with adrenalin and sending her into a panic of guilt. Nancy's words, "It's *your* fault if she reacts," played over and over in her mind like a mantra.

But as hard as she tried, it was impossible to reach her goal of no reactivity with the shepherd. Driving to the clinic for the first day of appointments fall quarter, she realized yet again she was relieved to be leaving the house. There was something not right about that.

She spent the first ten minutes at work catching up with staff she hadn't connected with in the last week. After checking her mail cubby, and with a cup of strong coffee in hand, she settled at her computer, scanned her emails, and updated staff records—the past week had been spent doing CPR and skills review.

At nine o'clock, she checked her patient schedule—all "same-day" appointments. The first day the clinic opened, patient load was usually light. Not so today, apparently. Her morning schedule was already packed, chief complaints ranging from "cough," to "abdominal pain," to "headache." Pretty routine stuff.

That said, any one of those complaints could be something life threatening, and she needed to approach each patient methodically—rule out the bad stuff, narrow down the diagnosis through history, physical exam, blood work and imaging when necessary, then treat the most likely thing. Since medical diagnosticians couldn't see inside their patients without extensive studies, primary care providers almost always worked in shades of grey—at least at first. She would have been much more comfortable working in black and white.

Her first patient of the day presented with a cough. The phrase "cough for two days" on the student's intake sheet lit up her mind with a huge array of possibilities. Having done this work for so long, a list of potential causes came to mind automatically without the painstaking exercise of mentally ticking through the list of differentials before she entered the exam room.

She introduced herself. The young woman was pretty and petite, makeup meticulously applied, clothes impeccable. But her skin was ivory pale. Sophie glanced at the electronic medical record in front of her.

The student's P02—the level of oxygen in the blood—was ninety-four percent. In a healthy college student it should be ninety-seven or higher, so it was low.

Sophie sat up straighter and glanced at the girl. Yes, she was definitely pale, her breaths rapid and labored.

The girl had a history of asthma, which would explain the low reading and shortness of breath. Her temperature was 101, respiratory rate, twenty-four—both elevated. Sophie glanced at the student's medication list...prozac, birth control pills, albuterol—a medication that treats asthma.

"When did this start, Beth?" Sophie asked.

"I got a sore throat a couple of days ago and yesterday I got this cough." She erupted into a deep moist cough that left her gasping for breath.

"Have you used your inhaler?"

"No, I left it at home in Seattle." Gasp. "I usually don't need it."

This was no time for a lecture about keeping a "rescue inhaler" for her asthma on hand at all times.

"I'll have a quick look at you, then get you started on a nebulizer treatment and we'll talk some more when you feel better. Has this ever happened to you before?"

The girl nodded.

"Ever been hospitalized for asthma?"

She shook her head.

The girl's lungs wheezed and popped under Sophie's stethoscope, but the sounds were faint—not a lot of air going in and out.

"Wait here, Beth," Sophie said. "The nurse will be right in with a nebulizer and I'll be back to check on you in a few minutes. You'll feel better soon."

Sophie whipped into the hall to see her nurse standing at the desk, the nebulizer set up beside her ready to head to the room. "Thanks," she said. "She sure needs it."

Back in her cubby, she scanned her next patient's medical record. The student was male, nineteen years old, and had never been to the clinic before. "Headache with vomiting" was his chief complaint.

Sophie opened the door. A young man was curled on

the table, one arm wrapped around his head, the other hand clutching a basin. The exam room was dark, indicating to Sophie that his eyes were sensitive to light,

"Hi Saul," she said. "I'm so sorry about your headache. When did it start?"

Saul cradled his head while he provided a verbal history. Two red flags jumped out at Sophie: the headache had awakened him in the night, and it was the worst headache he'd ever had. She should probably send him for an MRI. But did he have insurance? She'd figure that out in a minute after doing a physical exam. She excused herself to check on Beth.

Beth was breathing more easily as the albuterol, mixed with cool, moist air, relieved the spasm in her air passages. "I'm glad you're starting to feel better, Beth. I'll be back in fifteen minutes to check on you again."

She raced back to Saul and noticed that her next patient was already in her third exam room. She glanced at her watch. Yikes. She was already twenty minutes behind schedule.

"Saul, can you sit up now?" He moaned, and eased himself into a sitting position, eyes tight against the light of her computer screen. "I'm going to do a neurological exam now. And I'll need to look into your eyes with a light. I'm really sorry."

He squinted at her, then squeezed his eyes shut again. She fell into the familiar rhythm—cranial nerves, coordination, strength, balance. Everything was normal. But there was still that history of the worst headache ever, and the fact that it had awakened him in the night—both potentially indicative of an intracranial mass.

She reviewed her options: the cost of the MRI was in the thousands, but a CT scan would be a less expensive option. Still, other than the two red flags, it sounded like he had a classic migraine—nausea, vomiting, photophobia, and he'd had similar headaches before, just never this bad. On the other hand, he'd never been scanned before. Arg! There was no clear answer—to scan or not to scan.

"Saul, do you have medical insurance?"

"Uh, yeah. I think so." He slowly extracted his wallet from

his back pocket, and checked each card. Finally, he handed her one. Blue Cross Blue Shield. Good.

"I'm going to make you an appointment for a CT scan today. I think it's a normal, super-bad migraine, but I'm worried about the fact that it woke you up in the night and that it's the worst headache you've ever had."

"Well, I guess I've had one this bad before, and it didn't actually wake me up if I really think about it. My roommate woke me up and..."

Sophie saw the structure of the diagnosis she had created shift and mutate. An adjustment in one tiny piece of the puzzle, and the outcome evolved from possibly malevolent to manageable.

"You're sure," she said.

"Yeah. He was banging around in his closet."

"OK then. I'm going to move you to the observation room and we'll give you some medicine to help with your headache and the nausea. Just try to sleep." She grabbed his pack and jacket. "Come this way."

After he was settled in bed and medicated, she hurried back to Beth, making a mental note that he'd need to be educated about migraines and their triggers before he left the clinic. And he'd need some medication to take with him.

Beth's P02 was up to ninety seven and she was no longer fighting for each breath. With the increase in airflow, Sophie heard rales in the bases of her lungs as well as the popping, squeaking sounds common to mycoplasma pneumonia. Sophie reassured Beth, prescribed antibiotics, steroids, and two inhalers, talked to her about each separate medication, made her an appointment for the next day, and fled to her next patient.

It all flooded back to her. She loved her job and thoroughly enjoyed the students and the staff, but seeing a new patient every fifteen minutes was impossible; it was like running on a treadmill at full speed for ten hours. She knew that today she'd have no time for breaks or lunch and would get out from work at least an hour and a half late. She felt defeated before she even started. She set her face and opened the door to the next exam room with what she hoped was an empathetic smile.

"Hello, Joyce," she said. "Tell me about your abdominal pain."

On her drive home from work that night, she turned on NPR and listened to an interview with George Bush—something about the ongoing trial of Saddam Hussein. Presently, though, her mind wandered back to the dogs, and she found herself dreading her arrival home. In all these years, she had never experienced anything like this.

When she opened the door, Tess accosted her—a flurry of red fur, bouncing, barking, and laughing—and Lola and Vera smiling up at her, not as animated, but crowding her, nevertheless. A second later, Vera growled at Tess and jumped on Lola, Tess snarled at V, and all hell broke loose.

"Sit!" Sophie shouted. "Now!" she screamed when they didn't respond. They sat. But V jumped up again, pounced on top of Lola, and bit her on the head. In a rush, the golden twisted around to mouth her back, and before Sophie could get out another word, they were all going at it again in the small space of the mudroom. The noise was deafening.

Then Tessie whirled to go after Vera with the same matronly animosity she used to display with Lola. Sophie reached in, grabbed Tess by the ruff with one hand and V with the other and hauled them apart. "Enough, girls! Down! Jake, get Vera out of here!"

Tess and Lola dropped to a down, and Jake called Vera into the living room. "Stay!" they said in unison. Sophie had enough presence of mind to put up the baby gates, then walked into the kitchen, leaving Tess and Lola in the mud room. She ignored V.

"So, Sophie," Jake pulled her into a hug. "How did it feel to have patients again?"

"It was a really hard day, but way easier than coming home! How did you do with the dogs?" Cords of tension seared down her neck and shoulders. She put down her bag and hung up her coat. "I hope it was better than this!"

"It was fine. They slept a lot and I walked them a couple of times. I took V on a long walk and nothing bad happened. They were just waiting for you to come home so they could go nuts." He beamed at her.

"Great," said Sophie. She felt like hitting him. What was it about her that made the dogs so crazy? Maybe she should just stay away! She felt like crawling under the house.

"Tell me about your day." Jake finally seemed to realize how distraught she was. "Sit down and I'll get you a glass of wine. The girls are fine where they are."

In spite of the out-of-control greeting, the rest of the evening went by smoothly. They noticed that after Vera enjoyed playtime with her sisters and Sophie, and after she emptied her Kong, rather than heading for Jake like she'd always done before, she made eye contact with Sophie, then trotted to the mudroom asking to be shut in. In some ways, they were starting to get their lives back.

At least that's what she thought.

CHAPTER 41

VERA

Vera adored Sophie. An attachment that had evolved since the day they met at the shelter had now blossomed into infatuation. She followed Sophie from room to room, studied her, ached for her when she was gone. Part of that bond meant that she craved Sophie's presence and attention—however and whenever she could get it.

From watching her sisters, she knew they could influence Sophie—could make Sophie do what they wanted. But nothing had worked for Vera so far. It became a personal challenge, and she watched with studied intensity for any possible crack in Sophie's armor. Sophie had been poised and cool with her and could not be coerced into doing anything out of the ordinary. They had a complicated relationship, and Vera wasn't entirely sure what she wanted; she just wanted a change.

On this particular day in October, a new woman came to the

house. Vera was introduced to her in the way she was always introduced to new people: Sophie put her in her kennel, the stranger entered the mudroom, talked to Sophie, met Tess and Lola, and then sat at the island in the kitchen. That way, V had a clear view of the stranger from her crate.

She liked to observe visitors' body language, to read their level of tension, to attend to their voices, to scrutinize their smells. She always felt more relaxed with women than men, but learning as much as she could before she met them helped to relax her, no matter what the stranger's gender.

The scent of the woman, mingled with a faint odor of strange dogs and new dog cookies, wafted through the room to her kennel. There were other odors too, but she dismissed them. A trill of jealousy needled her skin when the woman leaned close to Sophie and laughed, praised and petted her sisters and fed them treat after treat. She shifted and stirred in her crate, the cool, metal texture of the door hard against her pads as she pawed it again and again.

Irritation popped like fireworks inside her. She needed to join them. Then she remembered her trick from the shelter. She sat still and silent, with only her panting breath scratching her throat—and right on cue, Sophie released her. Vera barged from the crate, vaulted up to the woman, and crowded into her.

"She's so beautiful and soft," Cindy said, her hand stroking V's neck and chest. Her touch was pleasant, but the contact pushed her, drove her over the top. She gulped a handful of treats, then pounced on Lola and bit her solid shoulders. When Lola ignored her, she paced and barked, and paced some more.

Sophie put her back in her crate, and with the four walls boxing her in, she felt less addled.

Eventually, she was released. Time passed. Sophie stayed focused on her friend. Tess and Lola slept. The women talked and talked, an endless jabbering noise that made Vera's flesh crawl.

When the light started to fade, however, she'd had enough. She stood, faced Sophie, and let out one sharp, ear-shattering bark. Vera was sure she saw Sophie flinch; and just for a moment,

Sophie's eyes flicked to hers and her face tensed. Another sharp bark confirmed Vera's suspicions.

"V, done!" Sophie said and led her to her crate. V liked her crate, and walked in willingly, but she burned with interest, eager to try the bark again.

Finally, the woman left, and V was free. She paced from the glass doors to the large living-room windows and back again, driven to relieve her sense of disquiet.

She scanned the room. Lola was asleep on her bed, and Tess snoozed on the deck—no distractions there. She wanted Sophie to play with her, to run her fingers deep through her fur. She wanted Sophie.

She walked up to where Sophie stood at the kitchen sink and barked—once. Sophie didn't flinch or look down at her, but when Vera saw the muscles in her back tighten, she felt a surge of triumph. She barked a second time, testing it. Hearing Sophie draw in a slight, sudden breath, she barked again. Sophie didn't move.

Frustrated, she barked louder and faster, pounding her voice into Sophie's back, demanding that she pay attention. She felt powerful, wild, in control. Still nothing. Vera walked around Sophie and stood beside her so she could see her face. It was mask-like. Frozen. Vera knew that look. She barked and barked to break the mask, to have Sophie reach out to her. And then, without so much as a glance in her direction, Sophie turned away, climbed the stairs, and disappeared.

SOPHIE

"I don't know what I did," Sophie said to Nancy over the phone three days later. "But she's been barking at me. We are so careful not to reinforce any unwanted behavior." Sophie was desperate. Vera's bark deafened her, blinded her almost. Vera didn't bark at Jake, thank goodness, but although he teased Sophie about it, it was starting to wear on them both.

The barking would start when Vera's eyes locked onto Sophie's—intense, hard, demanding eyes; not the soft amber eyes she'd grown to love. Then V's mouth would pucker and she'd start her incessant barking. "I'm ignoring her, but it's not slowing down," Sophie said. "She walks in front of me to block me, and if I accidentally make eye contact with her, she starts up. It's awful!"

"I don't know why it started, but it's definitely something *you* did," Nancy said. Sophie rolled her eyes. She was getting used to this—Nancy always tossed out blame. Sophie just let it roll off her most of the time.

"You're doing the right thing by ignoring her, Sophie, but don't challenge her or give her any attention. It may get worse before it gets better, but hold your ground no matter what. Use ear plugs if you have to, but don't give her any attention for barking at you."

Until this barking phase started, things had been going relatively well with V. Sophie searched her memory for the moment she had reinforced this behavior, but couldn't find it. It had definitely happened while Cindy was there—but she'd been so engrossed in the visit that she was completely unaware of what she'd done. There hadn't been much time for friends since V had come into their lives, and seeing Cindy had been a special event.

This was the fifth day of Vera's barking. They had all eaten dinner, the girls had had their playtime, and Sophie was preparing to settle on the couch, expecting the worst. She didn't know how much longer she could go on doing this. What if the barking didn't stop? She didn't want to think about it, but she knew she couldn't live like this forever. And the barking had an aggressive edge to it. She wasn't afraid of V—yet. But what if this escalated?

Well, here goes! She placed the earplugs in her ears and picked up her book. It was helpful to have the trainer's support, to know that Nancy felt she was handling it correctly. Any feedback V received for barking, including scolding or putting her in her crate or the mudroom, would give Vera the attention she sought and thus reinforce the barking even more. All Sophie could do was ignore it.

Right on cue, just as Sophie sat down, Vera's eyes burned

into the side of her face and the dog erupted. This time, Sophie timed it. She opened her book and read, turning the pages definitively, one after another. Her head exploded in V's blasts in spite of the earplugs. She felt like screaming at V to shut up. She felt like throttling her. Vera's frustration was so thick you could almost see it like a dark wind in the air around her.

"I can see her blowing your hair back," shouted Jake over the barrage.

Sophie didn't look around, but she could feel V's breath on her neck, perhaps one foot away. *Jesus wept!* She glanced at her watch. Ten minutes since this onslaught had started and V was still going strong. She could just imagine Tess and Lola hunkered down, paws clamped over their delicate ears.

Sophie stood, book in hand, and walked to the stairs. Without so much as a glance at Vera, she blocked the bottom step with a baby gate and fled.

Head throbbing, she turned on the bath, added some bubbles and switched on her favorite music. She sank into the heat; the fragrance and music and silken water transporting her somewhere tranquil and sweet. Surely things would get better. She did not want to live this way.

An hour later she emerged from the bathroom feeling refreshed and relaxed. She'd taken time to paint her nails and even trimmed her bangs and used some special leave-in hair conditioner that she'd forgotten about.

Sophie stopped when she opened the bathroom door. She heard Vera crying at the bottom of the stairs, her whines plaintive and sorrowful. *Too bad, V!* Sophie settled down on the bed to read. It was a book her mother had given her—a British mystery, a delicious escape. But after fifteen minutes, V's cries escalated into a series of spins. Fighting down a wave of nausea, Sophie flashed back to the shelter. *Dammit!* She was trapped. That dog always got her way. She walked down the stairs, removed the baby gate, took V's head in her hands, and kissed the black diamond on her forehead.

"Don't ever do that to me again, V."

Vera turned her head away, but eased her back against

Sophie's leg. Sophie stroked the shepherd's beautiful face, ran her fingers over the velvet ears, caressed the cinnamon chest. She wanted so much to love and trust this dog. But Vera couldn't seem to let it happen.

After that, Sophie and Jake scrutinized Vera second by second. They analyzed every move she made, trying to curb any weird behavior patterns before they took hold. Sophie never knew if their efforts paid off—how could you possibly know what disasters had been avoided? But, as time passed, she and Jake seemed to get better at spotting things that could lead to trouble, and on the whole, Vera improved. Unless she got stressed or her routine was altered, life became somewhat more tolerable. And, to Sophie's relief, Vera's verbal demands for attention didn't recur.

CHAPTER 42

Sophie

The quarter passed quickly for Sophie, and the routine they had established for Vera at the end of the summer held—for the most part. They found that Sophie's return home after the long work day was an ongoing challenge. So, with misgivings, Jake isolated Tess in the hallway behind baby gates when Sophie first got home to prevent the dogs' arousal levels from going through the roof. Tess's feelings were hurt, but Lola and Vera were calm without the collie's antics, and Sophie always spent a special, quiet time with Tess once everyone was settled.

On Tuesday evenings, they attended the Rally-O class, and on Thursdays, made the long drive south after work to continue private lessons with Nancy. Vera seemed to be making progress, but life with her was still complicated and stressful. Sophie and Jake hadn't discussed Vera's fate for several weeks, but their decision still hung in the air, unresolved.

Every Wednesday and Friday, Vera went to work with Sophie and stayed in the back of the truck in the mornings.

When Sophie was finished at the clinic, the two would drive to Fairhaven and run for miles on the wide, mostly straight, Interurban trail where Sophie could spot trouble from far away. Through September and October, Sophie watched the leaves in the high, cathedral canopy turn from green to brilliant golds and then, as the days drifted into early November, to a deep, tawny carpet underfoot.

Running, she felt much more in control with V. She could dart out of situations easily to keep Vera safe—most of the time. Every time V reacted, which happened maybe once or twice a week, she felt overwhelmed with guilt—but she *had* to exercise V. From the reading she'd done, she knew that exercise increased serotonin levels in the brain and would help lower Vera's anxiety. She had tried throwing the ball for V, but after two or three tosses, the shepherd lost interest, so it was up to Sophie to find other ways to get her the exercise she needed.

The Wednesday afternoon before Thanksgiving was cold and wet. The trees, once so lush and golden were now skeletal outlines against the slate-grey sky, and the trail underfoot had turned to a slick, decaying brown. A steady rain fell and Sophie shivered, zipped up the collar of her red running shell, and pulled down her hat.

By the end of the first mile she was warm, and with the trail deserted, she was able to relax. In the past, she had enjoyed those warmer, sunny days for her runs; but now, the worse the weather, the better. Rain meant that she and V often had the trail to themselves.

They had just turned around at the two-mile point and were heading back to town, when Sophie noticed two men in the distance. They seemed to be shouting at one another, jostling back and forth across the trail as they approached. She stopped and strained her eyes, trying to focus more clearly, but her glasses were streaked with raindrops. Was it good-natured banter? She wasn't sure. Were they drunk or stoned? Possibly. By this time she was soaked to the skin and very cold in spite of running, and the thought of retreating further from town worried her. She glanced down, and for once felt the thrill of having a powerful and loyal German shepherd at her side. Vera sat in heel position, back straight, face tilted toward Sophie's. Their eyes locked.

"Well, V-girl. How shall we handle this one?" Vera stared back at her, eyes glass-clear and intense through the rain. "I think we'll pull off to the side of the trail. Then I'll feed you thousands of treats when they pass so you don't bite them. Maybe they'll have settled down by then—but if we need to, we can run past at full speed. What do you think? Not a great plan, but I'm freezing!" Vera looked steadily back at her. She took everything so seriously when they were out together, just the two of them. And right now, Sophie thought, that was just what she needed.

They were running again, their pace faster than normal, but Sophie's breathing was steady. She had switched Vera to her right side, away from the men, and though V seemed uncomfortable there, she held her position. The men were pushing each other, shouting obscenities. They seemed younger than she had thought at first, possibly even college students. She felt instantly relieved, and with new-found confidence, decided to jog past them. But at a distance of twenty feet the men stopped their jostling and focused on her. And Vera.

"I used to have a German shepherd," shouted the larger of the two to his partner. He wore a heavy, black hoodie and sagging jeans. He was tall and bulky. What could possibly have made her think they were college students?

"Oh yeah?" answered the other. She could see him clearly now; long hair streaming with water, eyes squinting against the rain, his face with that lean, hard look of the street.

It was too late to turn back and Sophie made a split-second decision: she ran like she had never run before. She could feel Vera straining to get between her and the strangers. A few more strides and they'd be past. Her breathing was harsh now. It caught in her throat.

VERA

Vera was not happy about the strangers. These men moved erratically, and as they drew closer, she smelled a sharp, pungent, human odor—and something else that set her even more on edge: when Sophie spoke, her voice was tight and strained. Sophie was scared.

"V, right," Sophie cued her. Vera wanted to stay on the side where she could best protect Sophie, but she hung back, crossed behind, and pulled up on Sophie's right. Her awareness soared, each cell quivering and alert. She couldn't intervene as well from that position, and part of her—no, all of her—demanded that she take charge. A formidable threat loomed before them and it was her job, her passion, to protect Sophie—no matter what. Vera tried to angle past Sophie to her original side, but the leash held her trapped against the edge of the trail where a steep bank fell to the forest floor below.

They drew closer, the scent of the men now overpowering, and Vera's sense of danger exploded. One of them stepped forward, grabbed Sophie's arm, and jerked her away. A streak flashed at the edge of Vera's vision, she heard the thwack of bone on bone, then Sophie hit the ground.

Rage tore through Vera's belly, surged into her chest. Her lungs stretched, her shoulders bunched, and she launched with missile speed. The man crashed to the ground beneath her, crumpling into an inert pile of flesh and stink. With feline precision, she found solid purchase on the smooth trail and towered over him, jaws locked in a vise-like grip on his arm. His scream deafened her. His sweat and terror consumed her. Her rage became a frenzy, and she bit down hard, again and again.

The thick fabric of his jacket tore under her bite. She heard a snap, and something gave way in her jaws. The heavy, sweet smell of blood filled her nostrils. She bit down again, holding the man immobilized, warning him not to move; not a muscle, not even an eyelid—or she would tear him apart. She knew this without thinking. A deadly rumble rose from deep in her chest.

In the silence that followed, Vera listened for the man behind her. With one ear cocked toward him, she heard every breath, every change in position. He stayed back from her, frozen.

Sophie was inching toward her now; she heard her name, barely a whisper. Then Sophie's hand scrambled for the leash and Vera felt pressure on her neck. She bit down a final time, heard the man cry out, turned, and bounded away.

PART 3:
Loss - 2011

CHAPTER 43

VERA

Vera was jolted awake from a deep sleep by the sound of the door handle turning. She leapt to her feet, tail beating, expecting to see Tess and Sophie burst through the mudroom door. But instead, Lola appeared with Jake on her heels. V rushed over and covered her sister in snuffles and kisses. Lola gave her a sideways glance and a tiny wag, then made a beeline for her bed. Buoyant now that her favorite sister was back in the house, she turned her gaze to Jake. His warm hands caressed her face, working their way down to her chest, rubbing and massaging her fur. Her heart melted, and she lost herself in his touch.

When she was satisfied, she trotted to the glass door and sat, nose pressed to the corner, willing it to open. She stayed in position, patiently awaiting Jake's part of the bargain. But no Jake appeared. Finally, she heard the toilet flush, then his footsteps. But still the door remained closed. She barked. A single, sharp note.

"OK, V-dog. I'm coming. Hold on a sec." She understood the intent of his phrases enough to ease her escalating tension.

"There you go, girl!" Jake leaned across her, and as if by magic the door slid open.

She swept outside, and in a single bound landed on top of the hot tub. The meadow stretched before her, the breeze filled her nostrils. She caught the musky scent of deer and scanned the tall grasses, but there were no deer in sight.

What was that? A small, dark form crept through the yellow blades, body glued to the ground. Then the unmistakable smell of a cat. She flew across the deck. Her back paws landed on the bench and her front paws found the high handrail. She loomed over the creature. The cat below her stopped. She could see its eyes burning into her, its tail twitching. She leaned forward and gave it everything she had.

"Vera! Done!" Even in her frenzied state, she heard Jake's voice. But this was a cat! No turning back. Her voice ricocheted down the meadow. Now other dogs in the neighborhood were barking in concert.

"Oops!" Jake's voice was stern. She deflated. There was no anger in his tone, but it defined a distinct line that she couldn't cross. She felt the boundary as surely as if a wall had been placed between her and the cat. She turned, hopped off the bench, trotted past Jake and into her crate in the living room. The crate door closed behind her.

She curled into a ball, put her head on her paws, and watched Jake sit down at the dining-room table. She could just see Lola's nose in the entrance hall where she lay on her bed. Seeing her wonderful Lola, V felt a surge of contentment.

But something was missing.

The growing uncertainty had started when Sophie and Tess disappeared. In fact, a few cycles of meals and walks and sleep had transpired without them. In spite of Jake and Lola's presence, which calmed and soothed her, her world was suffused with an underlying disquiet.

And now, curled up in her crate with nothing to distract her, a sense of urgency welled up. She missed Sophie intensely. And even though she didn't have the bond with Tess that she had with Lola, Tess was woven into the fabric of her life and the collie's absence wound around and through her, bathing her in sorrow. Her heart wept for Tess.

Since the attack on the trail by those men so many years before, Vera had felt an ever-present need to protect Sophie, to know where she was at every moment. If Sophie left home without alerting Vera, she would search the house in a panic, checking everywhere—on top of the furniture, behind the beds, at the desk in the guest room, upstairs in the walk-in closet—her pupils dilated, her breath heavy, her body wracked with tension. When Sophie finally returned home, V would race up to her, tail swinging to and fro, relief flooding her soul.

When they walked together, the shepherd paced beside Sophie like a guardian, matching every step, reading the environment with all of her senses and intuition; ready to take on the world. That said, she had also learned to follow Sophie's lead—to a point. She would watch and listen to Sophie if people or dogs approached, arc around them, and with great restraint, avoid the lunge and bark that were always her first choice.

But if the dog was too intense or the tail too high; if the dog stared or stepped toward her; if he were off leash—or a million other things—her gait would stiffen, and a loud rumble would rise from her chest, the lunge and snap just a breath away. For human strangers, the same applied. A stare, a hand reaching forward, and most of all, passing too close—would set her fear, her anger, her protective instinct into motion.

Presently, Jake opened the door of her crate and she stood and stretched, extending one leg at a time.

"Good girl, V-dog," he said. The caress of his hand down her back centered her again. Lola wandered over, and Vera drank in her sister's solid, steady presence. She watched Lola sit in front of Jake.

Although she no longer felt compelled to mimic Lola like she had in the early days, right now she knew that joining Lola's lead would be to her advantage. So she sat too, temporarily distracted from the distress that haunted her. She stayed in place, gaze glued to Jake's.

LOLA

"OK, girls, what can you do?"

Lola threw Jake a quizzical look. Jake never played with them, and it was out of character for him to start now. But Vera swooped and bowed beside her, so she didn't have a choice. She, too, dropped into a deep curtsy, stretched her forelegs far in front of her, and felt a pull through her tummy, up her back all the way to her hips. She rocked back into a stand.

"Good girls!" Jake's voice encouraged her, and the treats were salmon. Her favorite.

"What else can you do?" She spun in a tight circle and stopped in a sit directly in front of him. Then, seeing Vera march in place beside her, she spun again in the opposite direction. She did not want to be outdone by her sister. Jake handed her another treat.

"What else…" She knew what was coming. She threw herself onto her back and rolled over again and again, carving an arc on the floor, ending up in a stand, laughing at Jake. She could see Vera off to the side, legs braced, ears forward, mouth closed, poised to pounce.

"Vera…" She heard the warning tone in Jake's voice just as Vera collided with her.

She had always loved to play, the physicality of it, the spin and bump and brawl, teeth on fur, rushing and whirling; then the lull. Except with Vera, there had never been a lull. The shepherd's excitement climbed higher and higher until the dog exploded into attack mode. It was this that Lola feared most about her sister.

But today, Lola wanted to play in spite of this. It was why she had rolled over and over on the carpet: she knew that Vera simply couldn't resist such an invitation. She trusted Jake to control V, so she could get a taste of the twist and tumble, and the comfort of her sister coiled and tense against her while they wove and danced together. She loved Vera now, not in the same way that she loved Tess, but they shared a sense of harmony, shared the world together—most of the time.

She felt V's teeth on her neck. She bellowed, feinted to the side, and dropped to her shoulder, felt Vera leap free. Then they were on their hind legs, locked in an embrace, mouth to mouth, heads weaving, darting, attacking with careful strokes. When Lola felt Vera's excitement surge, she leapt away and turned her back, then spun again to resume their gambol, risking everything. For one infinite moment they curled and mouthed, entwined—and then Lola stopped. Within moments her sister started the predictable cajoling; the pushing, poking and biting. But Lola still did not move.

This was always the critical moment.

"Vera, done!" Jake's voice filled her with relief and she felt Vera turn and trot away. As soon as Vera sat in front of him, she knew she was safe—she jumped to her feet and took her place beside her sister. Jake gave them each a treat.

They'd had two fights in the past, both started by corrections from Lola when Vera pushed her past her breaking point. Lola had nursed her injuries for three weeks afterward. Her punctures healed slowly, and her feelings of betrayal and distaste for the dog had overwhelmed their relationship. She had ignored Vera until proximity and the shepherd's persistence won her back. But she would never forget.

"Good girls! She did well, didn't she Lola?" Jake's hand massaged her ears and face and she looked up at him with limpid eyes. It had felt so good to play. But now, she was taken over by Tessie's absence again and it filled her with a heavy, physical ache.

To rid herself of the feeling, Lola rolled to one hip and scratched her face and ear with her back paw—a frenzied hammering of annoyance. Over the years, this action had become a reprieve from the chronic anxiety of living with Vera: the shepherd's unpredictability, the undercurrent of potential danger, and the toning down of all that was natural to her. Lola had learned to be measured in her actions, and it was in her nature to observe and adjust. But it had taken its toll.

"Lola, leave it." She flopped onto her side. It was a constant battle now, this struggle between Lola, and Sophie and Jake. She didn't understand their incessant demands for her to stop scratching, and the conflict would sometimes escalate until she was beside herself with frustration—all she could do was to hide from them and pound and pound away at her head.

VERA AND LOLA

"Are you bored, girls?" Vera looked up at Jake. They had

been doing nothing for hours now, and the girls had been either snoozing or watching him read or play the guitar. He seemed anxious in spite of his stillness. Sophie was always moving, talking to them, playing with them. All at once he stood up and strode away, long legs powering him out the door, voice floating behind. "I have an idea. Be right back."

The girls studied him as he assembled his project—he was suddenly so animated. He stacked up a laundry basket, books, treats, strips of cloth—all things they had seen before, but never in the living room, never like this. They knew that whatever he was doing, it was for them, and they took it all in.

When he was done, they saw an upside-down laundry basket elevated on two small books, one at either end. Then they watched him place two treats under the basket, each laid on a separate strip of cloth. Both strips had an end that poked out from under the rim of the basket, one on either side. They had no idea what to make of it.

"OK girls. You have to figure out how to get the treats without touching the basket." He stepped back and they got a clear view. "Bet you can't!"

Vera watched Lola with rapt attention from behind the door of her crate. After five years of training and playing games together, they had learned to take every clue they could from each other.

Lola walked carefully around the laundry basket, lost in concentration. She pushed at it with her nose, but Jake stabilized it, so it didn't move. She walked around it again and tried to push her nose underneath the edge. She salivated.

Finally, unable to make sense of it, she lay down; front legs spread wide and head planted firmly between them on the carpet—the position gave her comfort when she was stumped. She was not used to losing, and it crushed her. She fixed her eyes on the treats.

"OK, V-dog, you're on!" Vera strutted up to the puzzle. She knew she could do it. She had watched Lola carefully and certainly knew what hadn't worked. She put her paws on top of the basket and posed for her prize.

When Jake laughed but didn't produce a treat, she hopped down and carefully walked around the basket. She pawed at the side, then turned her attention to the bottom rim and dug at the perimeter. Her nails caught one of the strips of cloth, and miraculously, the treat came out with it. She swallowed it, then noticed an identical strip of cloth on the other side. She raced around and pawed out the other treat using the fabric strip. Excitement burbled up inside her and she bounded over the basket and sat for Jake.

"V-dog! You did it!" She pushed her head into Jake's hand and he rubbed her head. She beamed with pride. "Wait till Sophie hears about this," he said. "She'll be blown away!"

By this time, Lola itched for another turn. She could barely hang on till Jake released her from her down. She marched up to the strip of cloth. This time she knew what to do and with complete confidence, pawed at the cloth and accessed the treat. Then she spied the strip on the other side of the basket and pulled that one out too.

"Lola, that was really something!" Jake sounded just as excited as he had been for Vera. Lola bowed and cavorted and snatched the proffered treats with a laugh.

Later, after another walk and a long nap on her hot tub, Vera lay by Jake's feet as he ate dinner at the coffee table. She always lay here when he ate, had done so for as long as she could remember. She liked the way he smelled and the soft, low timbre of his voice when he spoke to her. Sometimes she'd rest her head on his foot, the warmth bathing her head in comfort. Her sister lay across from her, eyes closed. Lola seemed disengaged, and an insidious strand of dread threaded its way through Vera's body, starting at her center and wending its way to her toes.

"You miss Sophie and Tess, don't you, girls?" Jake asked. "They'll be home in a few days. Tess has her surgery tomorrow."

Vera understood "Sophie", "Tess", and "home", and she perked up her ears, felt a jolt of hope, of possibility, saw Lola preen and glow in response. But no one appeared, and eventually, when Jake and Lola made their way upstairs to bed, Vera curled up in the mudroom in front of the door. Waiting. Eyes wide open and head on her paws, she listened to the wind, to the sound of tires on the road, and to the absence of her family.

CHAPTER 44

TESS

Tess didn't know what was happening. Everything was wrong. A deep lethargy haunted her. Her chest ached. She opened her eyes and looked around. Chain link and concrete swam and shifted in front of her. She lay on a thin blanket, and without her bed from home, her back and elbows hurt. She was hungry. Very hungry. The smell of disinfectant and disease hung in the air. Where was Sophie? She whined, the sound high-pitched and pleading. Where were Jake and her sisters? She whined again.

"OK, girl, let's go." A tall, unfamiliar woman clipped a leash to her collar. Tessie stood. It could only mean one thing.

Sophie.

Hope springing through her, she staggered after the woman as best she could, but her legs felt disconnected and she wobbled as she walked. When she saw the room, her heart dropped. The odor of drugs and disinfectant was suffocating. Two strangers stared at her. She wheeled around to get back out the door.

"Uh-uh!" the woman's voice was sharp and unexpected. Tess tensed, clamped her jaws shut, and leaned against the leash even harder. "Tess, stop it! It's all right." She felt herself dragged toward the center of the room. Hands grasped her, forced her into a down, and there she froze. What to do next? She was surrounded, overwhelmed, exhausted. Her spirit faltered. Hands lifted her onto a stainless steel table and held her in a vise-like grip. Something buzzed on the skin of her front leg, then a sharp, stinging pain, a cool rush up to her shoulder, and nothing…

SOPHIE

Feeling sick from guilt and an overwhelming sense of betrayal, Sophie drove away from the OSU Veterinary Hospital and into downtown Corvallis. What if she wasn't doing the right thing? What if something awful happened to Tess during surgery in this strange hospital so far from home? Maybe the cancer was slow-growing and she'd have done better without the surgery. Sophie shook it off and swallowed hard, forcing herself to take deep, slow breaths.

As she opened the door of the New Morning Bakery, however, her rational side took over. "I just have a really good feeling about this one," Dr. Yangtze, the oncologist, had said to her the day before. She repeated this sentence over to herself a few times and felt deliciously light. There was nothing else she could do at this point, so she'd better make the best of it.

Coffee. The smell of fresh-baked goods melted her into a puddle of bliss. She found a table, put down her copy of *The Girl with the Dragon Tattoo*, and made a beeline for the display case, anticipating four of her favorite things—a latte, a scone, a good read, and time to enjoy them.

An hour and a half later, she emerged, realizing that for the first time in years she had a whole day just to herself. No guilt about not walking her dogs or canceling clients, and no pressure to train V. She felt giddy. She had just read, undisturbed, for over an hour. Truly, it had been years since she had experienced such freedom—probably since their last trip to Mexico when they first adopted V.

How had her life spun so far out of control? Since starting her reactive-dog business in addition to her job at the clinic, she had been working, what, sixty hours a week? And then there were the dogs to take care of, walks and training, and Vera's classes. She felt like she rarely saw Jake at all, and when she did, she was bone tired, and probably bitchy.

She found her car and looked at the city map. There had to be a mall around here where she could get a T-shirt. She hadn't thought to pack one—it had been so cold and rainy in Bellingham.

She pulled into the street and tried to focus on driving. Her train of thought had snapped her back to her life in Bellingham and she felt suddenly trapped, backed into a corner. She knew that Jake wanted to support her and always had, but recently he'd been irritable—he did all the laundry, housework, and grocery shopping, and walked the girls when she was gone. She knew he was tired of it. And so was she.

She wished he were here now so they could talk, indulge in the things they loved most, cry together over Tessie. But on such short notice there was no one they could trust to take care of Vera, not even with Lola's help. She tried to stifle the simmering frustration in her gut—she should be used to all Vera's limitations by now. This time was different. Tessie needed them.

The mall appeared on her right and she pulled into the parking lot. It was relatively small, but she should be able to find what she needed. Eager to distract herself and get on with her day, she hurried through the double doors.

On the way back to her hotel, T-shirt in hand, she noticed that *The Girl with the Dragon Tattoo* was playing at the local cinema at six o'clock that evening, and there was a neighborhood pub just down the block. She'd go out for dinner and a movie. Try a new beer! She needed to finish her book before seeing the film, but with the whole day ahead of her, she could do it. She felt like she was skipping out on life, like she was on some kind of harebrained vacation. How pathetic was that?

An hour later, she slipped out of the hotel and jogged to the Willamette River Trail. It was paved, but that was fine. She was used to pavement from running with V for the past several years. Unpaved forest trails were out of the question with the shepherd. They were too narrow, and it was too easy to be ambushed by a dog or a runner.

Still, since the attack on the Interurban trail all those years ago, she had felt naked running without Vera, and her loyalty to the dog had not wavered.

A man on roller skates flanked by a German shepherd flew past, and a familiar pain took hold of her heart, that whisper of regret that she couldn't quite shake. V was too protective of both Sophie and herself for her own good—for anyone's good. Sophie would give anything to be able to take Vera wherever she went. But it would never happen.

Sophie slowed and drank in the array of people around her—kids on their skateboards, students lost in a game of Frisbee, cyclists, walkers, runners. A whole world out here, and all she did was dogs. Aggressive dogs at that. What was she thinking? She did have Tess and Lola, she reminded herself. Without them, she'd lose her mind. A couple of weeks before, she'd taken Tessie to Vera's Rally Obedience class on a whim, and Tessie had literally danced into the building, greeted each dog, made a fuss of their owners, and settled in at her side.

And when it was Tess's turn, they'd sailed through the course together with no leash, no clicker, and no treats. People had actually talked to her, and applauded their success on the course. A far cry from when she was there with Vera—both of them apart and distant, the pariahs of the class. True, Vera could finally stay in the class for an hour on a short leash, Sophie armed with a clicker and a bagful of treats—a world of progress since the beginning. But though she shouldn't compare her to Tess, they were night and day. Night and day.

Sophie ran. The breeze swirled up her arms and lifted her hair. The silent, sinuous river slid past and the sun, so warm on her face, sparked a sudden surge of euphoria. She imagined Tessie trotting into the future, her center sun-bright. She drank in the sweet, heady scent of spring and lost herself on an eddy of birdsong. The miles drifted by effortlessly and finally, her mind cleared.

CHAPTER 45

SOPHIE

Sophie awoke at five the next morning, then dozed off again and dreamed—something about Vera greeting a man and a strange dog. The alarm forced her back to the present. She'd had so many dreams about V being normal. She longed for it. Still.

Tessie! She dressed quickly and packed—Tess's bed, her toys, her bowl and treats—all Tess's special things. She'd have time for something to eat, a few minutes to read, and maybe a run before she picked up Tess and made the long drive home. The phone call she'd had from Dr. Yangtze the evening before was reassuring: the tumor had been removed without complications, and Tess was doing well. She could call the clinic at nine o'clock and, if Tess had urinated, Sophie could take her home. They'd know more when the biopsy results were back.

But by the time she finished breakfast at eight o'clock, she couldn't bear to stall any longer and dialed the clinic. After being on hold for several minutes, the vet tech came on the line. "She can leave as soon as you get here—as long as she pees first." Sophie gulped her coffee, drove back to the hotel, packed the car, and was at the clinic twenty minutes later.

After she paid the bill, an unsteady, disheveled collie with an incongruous plastic cone around her head was led into the lobby. Sophie knelt down and cradled her as best she could, but Tess pulled away toward the door, her head weaving back and forth as she struggled to get oriented.

"You can take her outside to see if she'll urinate." The tech held out a packet of medicine and a sheet of instructions and smiled. "Here are her pain pills. She may need them for the first couple of days. We gave her two at seven o'clock this morning, so she should be good for her trip home. We'll call you when we get the pathology results. Any questions?"

Sophie scanned the discharge sheet and shook her head.

Tess sniffed and wandered, swaying unsteadily, her cone catching on the grass when she lowered her head. Unable to bear it any longer, Sophie stole a glance back at the clinic and removed the collar. With that, Tess squatted.

"All right, Tessie girl. Let's go home to Jake and your sisters!" Tess lifted her head, caught Sophie's eye, and hurried to the car. When Sophie opened the door, Tess scrambled up onto her bed, ignoring Sophie's attempts to help her. With a twinge of guilt, Sophie left the collar off, but Tess paid no attention to her incision, put her head on her paws, and drifted off to sleep.

As Sophie drove north on the freeway leaving Corvallis behind, she realized with a shock that she still hadn't figured out what to do about her schedule. There were only six hours left before she'd be hurled back into the madhouse that was her life. She settled into the monotony of the drive and started to work on a plan.

CHAPTER 46

TESS, LOLA, AND VERA

Lola was bereft. She listened for her sister Tess, searched for her. She walked from room to room, and stayed alert when she and Vera went for walks with Jake. She dreamed about Tess, her paws twitching. She missed Sophie, but Tess—well, Tess was her life.

One afternoon, Lola heard a car turn onto the street a couple of blocks away. Her ears strained forward, her eyes focused on the back door. Shepherd and golden rose in unison, mouths closed, barely breathing. There was the distinct sound of Sophie's car pulling into the driveway. Lola was sure of it. Heart racing, she bounded into the mudroom, jostling with Vera for position.

"Are they home, girls?" Jake opened the door. He held Vera's collar and clipped on her leash. Lola charged out, unfettered excitement bubbling out of her in a chorus of high-pitched yips. Vera strained on her leash—overjoyed, overflowing with eagerness, her tail beating in a wild arc behind her.

Tess knew she was home. She heard Lola before she saw her, then smelled her distinct, wonderful odor, and felt that warm, panting breath on her face. She nuzzled her sister, then relaxed into Sophie's arms. She heard Vera's high-pitched whine, and wagged, feeling a twinge of delight. The shepherd's muzzle snuffled into hers, and she licked and laughed and snuffled back. Jake joined them, and with her family complete, she turned to lead them out of the driveway together to do her business.

SOPHIE

"How did it go with you three?" Sophie asked later when they settled in front of the fire that evening. Tess had managed to finish her chicken-and-rice-stuffed Kong and was stretched out on her bed in the hall. She showed no interest in her sutures, so the Elizabethan collar remained unused. Lola lay on the couch beside them, snoring.

"We had a good time together—we even tried one of those puzzles. I need to tell you about it sometime."

"I bet they missed Tessie." Sophie glanced down the hall to check on Tess. She was in a deep, restful sleep.

"They did. How're you doing? You OK?"

"I'm pretty tired. But in spite of Tessie's surgery, it was a good trip." She sat up and faced him. "And you know what? It felt really good to be dog-free for twenty-four hours."

"Whoa! That's something, coming from you!" Jake grinned and toasted her with his glass of red wine.

"And I've decided to close the reactive-dog business so I can spend more time with you and the girls," she blurted. Her voice was higher than she wanted, a hint of indecision slipping through.

"You're kidding, right?"

"No," she said. "I'm not." She looked down at her lap. "It's just that working two jobs takes up every second I have. I don't want to do it any more." She wouldn't have even considered this two weeks ago, but it felt good to be verbalizing it, to be giving her plan substance. "Would you think I'm a flake if I quit?"

"A flake? No way. It would be the best decision you've made in a long time." Jake gave her a reassuring smile. "More wine?"

"Sure. I'd just die if I missed out on time with Tessie. And she can't work with me any more. Not after this. So I'd have to leave her at home. I think the work's hard on Lola, too. And I can't use V as a teacher dog—she'd *make* the clients reactive." Sophie laughed.

They were quiet for a few moments, watching the fire. The flames played through the room, flickering over the hearth, and the sharp scent of cedar logs reminded Sophie of her childhood.

"I'll finish up with my current clients and not take on any new cases. And as for V, I think she's worked hard enough in her life. I've decided to stop all the extra stuff—all her classes and contexts—just like you suggested a while back."

Jake had pointed out on several occasions that Vera was who she was—that Sophie's contexts, challenging walks, and introductions to new dogs on a regular basis weren't fair, and could actually be holding her back.

But for some reason, Sophie had stuck by Nancy, believing that if she did exactly what Nancy recommended, Vera would be completely rehabilitated. In spite of all the work, however, V's behavior had plateaued, and she hadn't shown much improvement in a long time. At seven years old and after five years of intense training, Vera deserved a break.

Sophie looked up at Jake. "What do you think? You're not saying much."

"I think that's a great idea too," he said. "I should have forced you to take a break from everything a long time ago." He squeezed her hand and smiled.

Vera lay on her side on the dining room carpet; her toes stretching and twitching. She groaned in her sleep. They had noticed her muzzle turning silver in the past few months, and two whiskers on each side of her face were now pure white.

"Can you believe she's sleeping?" Jake asked. "I don't think I'll ever take that for granted."

"Me neither." In the beginning, they had gone for three years without seeing her eyes closed. She must have slept, but so lightly that any slight sound or movement awakened her. "Why did it take me so long to ask the vet to put her on medication?" Sophie asked.

"Because Nancy didn't believe in it," Jake said.

Sophie grimaced. She had always told her students to advocate for their dogs—all the time. But when it came to Vera, she'd completely messed up—and she wasn't proud of it. "Yeah, but I didn't have to do everything she said."

"Don't be so hard on yourself," Jake said.

There'd been other ways she'd screwed up too—so many signs that Vera had problems from the moment they'd brought her home. Like when V had chased the swallows so compulsively that first summer at the dog park. Sophie had discovered from her reactive-dog studies years later that rather than enjoying it, V had been beside herself with anxiety, the act of chasing swallows a mechanism to help her cope.

Sophie's breath caught in her throat. "Maybe if I'd started her off right, V would have had a better chance at being normal." She remembered how V and Lola had played so frantically on the queen-size bed when Jake was in Mexico—the way they'd looked when the sessions were finished—pupils dilated, brows furrowed, staring at her as if they were drowning. She was lucky they hadn't had a knock-down fight when she was there by herself. "What was I thinking?" she said. "Even when they were so wound up that they could hardly keep it together, I always thought they were just having fun."

"But you did the best you could at the time, Sophie. We all did. You need to let it go." Jake raised his wine glass to Sophie's, and their eyes met. "Let's just toast V-dog's sleep, Lola's patience, and a long life for our sweet Tessie!"

CHAPTER 47

SOPHIE

Tess recovered quickly. That first night, she marched up the stairs before Sophie could stop her and stretched out on her large, cushioned bed more relaxed and happy than Sophie had seen her the whole time they were gone.

The days grew longer, and gradually Tess's stamina returned. She joined Lola on her off-leash walks, no longer bounding ahead, but hurrying along at a trot, always keeping Sophie and Jake in sight.

Two or three times a week, Sophie took Tess to the lake. The collie's hind legs had become a little stiff and noticeably weaker in the past six months, but she still loved to swim, and was as determined as always. Without Lola to retrieve the Frisbee for her—Lola's allergies now prevented her from going to the lake—Sophie had to be careful not to throw it out too far, but they managed. They stayed to themselves in a corner of the dog park, Tess ordering Sophie around while Sophie surreptitiously monitored the dogs that came and went.

One day in midsummer, in spite of Sophie checking carefully before crossing the field to their secluded corner, two dogs came charging straight toward them, no owner in sight. Sophie glanced at Tess who seemed completely unconcerned—she paced along in her customary gait with her tail a plume above her back and her nose high in the air. Before Sophie had time to act, the dogs were upon them. Boxers. Tess did not like boxers— and these boxers were out to have a good time.

They pounded up to Tess, bodies tense and muscled, heads high, docked tails pointing skyward. They fell into formation, circling Tess, one on each side of her such that she was contained within their space. Sophie stopped, afraid that any movement on her part might trigger a fight. *Trust in Tess*, she told herself. But Tess was older now and more vulnerable, and every fiber in Sophie's being compelled her to intervene. She forced herself not to move.

The boxers froze perpendicular to Tess, one on either side, their heads placed firmly across her back. Sophie held her breath, steeled for the inevitable.

But Tess was unperturbed. She reached her muzzle around as far as she could without moving her body and greeted each dog, first to the left, and then to the right. Then, with impossible grace, she simply melted toward the ground and floated out from under them.

By the time they realized what had happened, she was gone— dancing toward the lake, laughing back over her shoulder, and prancing as high on her toes as Sophie had ever witnessed— neck arched, tail a regal flag over her back.

The boxers looked at each other for a moment, confused, as if to say "Where did she go?" then raced back to the picnic shelter where Sophie could now make out a woman in the shadows holding a cell phone in one hand and a cigarette in the other—completely oblivious.

Sophie was stunned. She had never seen such poise and elegance in a social interaction in her life. "Tessie," she called out, sprinting after the collie. "How did you do that?"

Tess stopped at the lake's edge, ankle deep, and barked a sharp "Throw it now!" at Sophie, staring at the Frisbee.

"OK, OK, Tessie, but you have to swim out to get it. Lola's not here, you know."

Tess barked again.

"OK, Tessie, but I'm warning you!"

Tess swam, sure strokes pushing her through the sparkling water to grasp the soft, hot-pink Frisbee. Wading to shore she staggered, her coat heavy with water. But she shook herself briskly, and with overflowing enthusiasm barked and cavorted against Sophie's legs before she hurried back toward the water for the next throw.

As Tess swam and retrieved, Sophie thought about the collie's amazing social skills. She might not be an Einstein with Kongs and puzzles, but she was a genius with dogs. She'd demonstrated it a thousand times over the years. In Tess's work with reactive dogs she always knew when to hold eye contact, when to look away, when to lick, or when to move closer or arc away.

Tess had never had a student dog bark or lunge at her, and every dog-aggressive dog she'd worked with over the years had befriended her. Ironically, Sophie thought, Vera had always been her biggest challenge.

Tess and Vera

When Tessie trotted into the house after her swim, Lola and V met her with an easy greeting. Oblivious to their grimaces, she shook herself off, showering them with water. She stretched and spun, shimmied under the delicious roughness of the towel when Sophie dried her, then trotted over to the glass doors overlooking the meadow. She circled and lay down, nestled her chin on her paws, and drifted off.

Then she heard Vera bark. It was an urgent bark that resonated from the tall windows in the living room. She cocked her head and listened, trying to resist the urge to investigate. Based on the timbre of the bark, she wondered if it could be a deer— or even a cat. The bark came again. She couldn't stand it. She

stood up, stiff from her swim, and hurried over to the window
where Vera was focused on the meadow, her body shifted forward, ears erect and tense. One more furious bark unfurled, and
Vera was gone. Tess scanned the meadow. Nothing. She barked
and barked. Nothing.

Disappointed, she trotted back to the window. But that
pushy dog was in her spot. Again! She could share the spot if
she wanted to—but she didn't want to. It was her spot, after all.
She considered her options and decided it was time to teach
that dog a lesson. Again.

Tess swaggered over to Vera's sacred crate, stomped inside,
and dug and scraped with her front paws until the layers of bedding were piled in an unruly mass in the center. Not quite satisfied, she scratched at it some more, fashioning a rough nest, just
the right size to cup her damp body. Finally, head nestled on the
threshold, she closed her eyes, and slept.

Vera lay in front of the glass doors, gloating. She loved to
trick that collie. But Tess moving toward her crate got her attention, and anxiety wormed through her belly when Tess sauntered inside. V couldn't bear her crate to be inaccessible to her.
She licked and licked and glanced away, and a reverse sneeze
convulsed her body. She watched in horror as Tess rearranged
her bedding, then lay down—and stayed there.

But what could she do? After all these years, Tess still worried her. The collie was always one step ahead of her, and she
never knew what Tess would do if confronted directly. Vera
turned her head away from her crate, glanced back, then turned
away again. Finally, unable to bear it any longer, she stood up
and stalked to the mudroom. A moment later, when she peeked
back into the living room, like a miracle her crate was empty,
and Tess was back in front of the glass doors.

CHAPTER 48

SOPHIE

As the summer drew to an end, everything seemed to slow down. The days were hot and muggy, and with Tess's health declining, the world seemed to revolve around her. Although there was no obvious recurrence of the cancer, arthritis plagued her more and more, her liver function tests skyrocketed, and it was clear that her kidneys were failing. The pathology report on the biopsy from her surgery had come back with a poor prognosis.

By October, Sophie had moved into her downstairs office where she slept on a futon beside Tess. Tess's new bed was an elaborate affair of memory foam, with firm pillows placed carefully around the edges to support her back. Tess would doze for hours during the day, paying visits to Sophie, Jake, and her sisters each time she awoke. If she wanted a drink, a snack, or help getting up, she'd call Sophie over with one sharp bark. This same bark would send Vera into a panic, and she'd cringe behind Jake or Sophie, trembling.

"What's the deal, V?" they teased. "Is your blind, deaf, crippled sister too scary for you?" But Vera didn't think it was funny, and she couldn't relax until Tess was once again quiet and settled on her throne.

Under the guidance of a holistic vet, Sophie plied Tess with a home-cooked diet, offering her a variety of supplements in addition to an assortment of cooked beef, chicken, pork, turkey and pureed vegetables. Tessie might eat chicken voraciously in the morning, but later that day Sophie would search in vain for something to pique Tess's appetite. Tess would look up at Sophie with an expressive stare as if to say, "What else ya got?" and Sophie would hurry back to the kitchen to fetch a different treat, then attempt to feed her by hand from a warm pottery dish.

Anna, their regular vet, monitored Tess's acute care, prescribed pain medication, and tracked her progress with labs.

Sophie found strength in Anna's frequent check-ins, and depended on her unfailing support through Tess's gradual decline.

By November, Tess had signs of dementia. She'd get stuck in corners and be unable to find her way out without help. At night, the moment Sophie turned out her reading lamp, Tess would clamber to her feet and start to pant and pace, sometimes falling, sometimes losing herself in a corner. Sophie would leap out of bed, take Tess outside to do her business, then settle her back down again.

After weeks of this, Sophie discovered that a night-light would calm Tess's nighttime anxiety. Still, she got little sleep for months, and although she didn't miss any days at work, she was chronically fatigued. When Sophie was at the clinic, Jake looked after Tess: he walked her several times a day, offered her food and water every couple of hours, and checked on her constantly.

With their attention so focused on Tess, Sophie worried about Lola and V. But Lola got on-leash walks with both Tess and Vera, and when Sophie was off work, she would take Lola on romps on her favorite trails. In addition, Jake and Sophie often combined Lola's special walks at Whatcom Falls Park with Vera's on-leash strolls at the cemetery. They would meet where the trail converged with Bayview Cemetery at its western boundary.

LOLA

Lola sniffed along the edge of the path on the way to meet Jake and V at the cemetery. It felt liberating to be outside and off leash. She'd felt odd lately with Tess's changes. Her collie-sister kept to herself now, sleeping much of the time, and Lola could no longer count on her to make the multiple daily connections she'd always loved—the soft looks, nose touches, ear snuffles, easy wags, and so many other things.

Slowly, since Tess's absence the previous spring, Lola had grown closer to Vera. The tension she'd felt since the shepherd came to live with them so long ago had started to wane. The dog's eyes and body had softened, her ears folded back with pleasure more often. Lola sought her out now, looked to her for companionship.

She caught the scent of something wild and lifted her head from the grasses she'd been sniffing. The intense eyes of a dog-like creature stared back at her. She froze. She had seen such an animal before, but never this close, and never while under its scrutiny. Curious, she held its gaze. It wheeled around and trotted away, its scent drifting behind in a river of mystery. At first, she wasn't sure what to do. But when it stopped to glance back at her with a coy prance and swish of its tail, she couldn't resist. The grasses flicked past her face, the sun warmed her back, and the grey, bobbing haunches pranced just ahead. Then it cut into the dense woods and disappeared.

"Lola!" She heard Sophie's scream, but was so intent on finding the creature that she barely noticed. A scorching excitement drove her forward, and the promise of the coyote drew her like a magnet.

There! It had stopped again. She saw the curve of a back, the flick of its tail, and she could just make out the yellow eyes watching her. The coyote whirled, jumped over a log, and floated off again through the trees. Lola crashed forward. The thrill, the novelty of it, made her increase her pace, and though the stiffness in her back slowed her a little, she didn't really notice it— the coyote kept a constant distance between them, staying just at the edge of her vision.

Then it vanished and an overwhelming odor assaulted her nostrils. Coyotes. Lots of them. She stopped, a curtain of uncertainty blurring the edges of her confidence. The safety of Sophie pulled at her, but at the same time, she could taste the thrill of finding the animal. She hopped over a fallen tree, then hopped over another one, then again, forming a pattern, back and forth.

"Lola!" Sophie crashed into view not far from her. "Come!" Sophie's voice was a scream of desperation. Lola had never heard the sound before. She bobbed away again, disconcerted, not sure what to make of it. Then Sophie's voice reached her again. "Lola, come. I have cheese." The softer voice and the magic word made her stop. And in that instant, Sophie collided with her, grabbed her collar and clipped on her leash. She found herself guided back to the cemetery road, and then Sophie was crouching beside her.

SOPHIE

"Lola, what were you thinking? They could have killed you!" Sophie wrapped her arms around Lola's sturdy chest, and burying her face in the soft, golden fur, drank in her warm, faintly musky scent. "Lola, I would die if anything happened to you."

Lola, however, appeared oblivious to Sophie's display of affection and pulled away. They jogged on, Sophie matching the golden's pace.

"You may not think it's a big deal, Lola, but you need to be much more careful. You're not two years old anymore!"

For ten minutes, the eerie caterwauling of coyotes echoed from deep in the forest, giving Sophie chills, making her skin curl and crawl. At twelve years old, Lola wouldn't have stood a chance against a hungry pack of coyotes. Sophie bit her lip and fought to still her shaking hands.

"Are you all right?" Jake asked when she joined him and Vera by the truck a few minutes later. "You look freaked!"

"We almost lost her," Sophie choked out. "Jesus. Who would have thought?"

"Maybe we should start keeping her on leash all the time," Jake said.

"Yeah, we should. But I just can't—not all the time."

The pale winter sunlight illuminated hundreds of headstones, all different shapes and sizes. Some glowed green with moss, some were ornate—all of them faced Bellingham Bay; a hillside of sentinels.

"I love seeing those two girls as a pair," Sophie said, linking her arm through Jake's. "V isn't left out any more. I know it's at Tessie's expense, but V always longed to be part of the pack."

"I know," said Jake. "Look at them checking out that branch together." The leaves had turned to brown and Lola's face glowed pale gold in contrast. Vera's muzzle was buried in the leaves beside her sister's, just the black diamond on her forehead visible, dark ears looming. Lola snorted, and Vera jumped back in a playful hop, all paws poised in the air before landing with precision and grace; then they carried on together down the road, Lola with her swagger and V with that prowling, panther-like gait.

"How are you doing with Tess?" Sophie asked. "She's going downhill really fast and I'm gone at work a lot..." Her voice trailed off. She looked up at Jake. His forehead was drawn, his eyes distressed, his lips somehow vulnerable.

"It's hard," he said. "I'm fine taking care of her as long as she's OK with it, but..." He stopped and faced Sophie, his voice stricken. "But Sophie, how do we know when to stop?"

Sophie wrapped herself around him, her cheek fitting perfectly into the curve of his shoulder. She felt the rise and fall of his chest, felt his breath on her hair and his arms enfold her. Together, they were a pillar of hope—had been for as long as she could remember. They would get through this.

"I don't know, Jake. But she's still eating, and she loves her walks. She's still bossy as hell when I take her out and she drives Lola and me crazy." She thought of Tess insisting that they climb yet another Sudden Valley hill, even though her back legs were starting to tire and give out. She would sometimes lie down at a crossroad to get her way. "And she still seems to be happy most of the time."

Jake stared at the ground. "But what if she's in pain in spite of the meds?"

"I don't think she is. She just seems tired. She still joins in with the girls at playtime—and she really gets into it." Sophie giggled. She thought of Tess perched on her throne, tapping away at her toy piano with one toe. She'd fix her bright eyes on Sophie—one black, her blind eye ruby-red—and demand payment for her performance.

"Her Kong makes her happy too," Jake said. "And she loves to boss you around—she's always telling you what to do." He looked back at Sophie and joined in with a full, liberating laugh.

"That dog is amazing!" Sophie took a shuddering breath. She had become Tess's private nurse and slave, and she bathed in the privilege of taking care of this dog, of sharing her last days in such an intimate way, of being able to spoil her. And even in her debilitated state, Tess made them laugh.

As far as Sophie was concerned, euthanasia was a gift that guardians could bestow upon their animals. But she knew now, more than ever, that every situation was different, that every dog was unique. In Sophie's world, it wasn't yet time to say goodbye to Tess.

"We should probably go home in case she gets stuck somewhere," Sophie said. They had left Tess on her bed with her water bowl beside her, but they were always worried about leaving her, even for an hour, in case she got lost in the house.

When they got home, however, she was still sleeping on her bed. Her luxurious red coat lay in disarray around her, and her slight body was nestled so deeply into the cushions that Sophie felt a sudden shock of adrenalin. With painstaking care she checked for the rise and fall of the collie's chest, and when she saw movement, found herself shaking.

V stood in the doorway and watched Lola wander over to sniff her sister's long, elegant face, and run her exquisitely sensitive nose over Tess's muzzle. There was no grey in that muzzle, Sophie noticed, and the tip of the collie's nose was as ebony-black now as it had ever been.

Her sisters finally wandered off to lie in their respective spots; Vera by the glass doors overlooking the deck, and Lola curled up on her bed in the front hall. The thought of losing Tess was unbearable.

CHAPTER 49

Sophie

Three days later, Tess awakened Sophie at five o'clock. In the mornings, Tess was full of energy. Sophie was often roused by the sound of her stirring at four or five. "Tessie, what's going on?"

Tess looked at her, smiling and panting. A fan blew the pure white of her ruff back from her face, and her ears flew forward and back, attentive and laughing sequentially, while Sophie spoke to her. Tess couldn't sleep without her fan, even when it was cool in the house.

"Is it time to go for a walk?" Sophie sat up and smoothed back the fur on Tessie's face. "OK, sweetie. Let me see if Lola wants to come too."

Earlier that morning, Sophie had awakened to find that Tess was no longer beside her. She leapt out of bed just in time to see Tessie staggering into the bathroom. She had rescued the collie and massaged her back to sleep, but now Tess was up again, full of drive and energy.

Sophie removed the baby gate she'd placed in the doorway, partly to prevent Tess from getting lost in the house again, and partly to deter sweet Vera from coming into the room to sleep with Sophie. She trudged upstairs to peek at Lola. "Hey, Lu. Want to come out with us?" Lola rolled from her back to her side on Sophie's side of the bed, and groaned. Jake lay on his back, arms flung wide beside the golden.

She glanced over at Vera. "Hey V." Vera looked up, and the tip of her tail twitched in greeting. Sophie caressed her face and ears, then tip-toed away.

She had her answer: no one wanted to join them this morning.

"OK, Tessie, let's go." She supported Tess's weight as they made their way out the door and down the ramp. "Are you sure, Tessie? It's pouring!" Well, maybe it would be a short walk today.

In the past months she had allowed Tess to determine the distance, duration, and speed of their forays. Their walks were often painfully slow and long-lasting, and every once in a while, Sophie would need to phone Jake to rescue them with the car. On these occasions, Tess was thrilled to have her "chariot" arrive, and would clamber into the back seat like a puppy. Sophie had fantasized on buying a little red wagon for Tess, but Tess enjoyed her walks and car rescues so much, and got so much pleasure from bossing Sophie and Lola around, that she had never pursued the idea.

They wandered out of the driveway and into the rain. The droplets fell like silver ribbons in the beam of Sophie's headlamp, settling in diamonds on Tess's coat. Sophie honored every one of these walks now, never knowing which one would be their last. She was imbued with a deep sadness when she considered this, but it somehow made her treasure each moment with Tess even more.

TESS

As Tess wandered out the driveway, her senses drank in the rain. It settled in a cool, soft mist on her face and filled her with the rich scent of dawn. Her world was softened now, wreathed in cloud; sounds were muffled, the edges of objects blurred and indistinct; even her sense of taste was so dulled that she rarely felt like eating. But on this morning, the lethargy that haunted her lifted, and the scent and touch of the rain excited her, pushing her down the road at an alarming speed. When they got to the corner of the main road, she needed to turn left.

"Come on, Tess," Sophie urged. "Let's not go all the way around today. Let's go back now. It's raining too hard for you. You'll get cold." But Tess was adamant. She crouched down, gripped the pavement with her toes, and leaned against the pressure of the leash. This was the only direction she would go today. She had to do it.

"OK, girlie." In these last months, Tess knew that Sophie could read every request she made: Sophie took her wherever she wanted to go, brought her water and treats when asked, and helped to reorient her whenever she got lost. Even Jake had been easy to train lately. Tess didn't know what had changed, but she enjoyed it, finding opportunities to get whatever she wanted whenever she could.

Now that she knew Sophie would take her on her favorite route, she stopped to sniff. The scent of a new dog and the fading odor of a raccoon suffused her brain. The rest of the world disappeared. Inch by inch she made her way forward, the scents opening vast doorways into memory and instinct.

"Sweetie, we have to go. I'm getting cold." Sophie broke through Tess's meditation and the world sprang back at her. She walked forward, stiff after the short break, and continued up the hill, aware of the splash of rain on the pavement and the breeze stirring in the long fur of her tail. She heard the call of an owl. It cut through the rain like a spear—wild and sharp, then guttural. She reached her nose high, scenting the breeze, hoping to catch more information; then let out a string of indignant shrieks. She didn't like that sound and never had. She screamed at it.

"Wow, Tess, I can't believe you heard that!"

Sophie's voice calmed her and she lost interest in the owl. She wandered on.

They made their way down the other side of the hill. Her wrists hurt on the steep incline, but she took it slowly, finding excuses to stop when she found collections of water to lick from the ferns and grasses at the side of the road. She was driven by thirst these days, and any source of water was like a magnet: puddles, containers filled with rain water, leaves that cradled tiny ponds.

At the bottom of the hill, Tess veered left onto a narrow, muddy path—she could have followed this route blind it was so familiar. She led Sophie through a stand of spindly alders to a makeshift plank bridging a wide, swampy creek. She hurried forward to cross it by herself. And stumbled.

"Tessie!" Sophie's firm hands caught her and lifted her to the other side. "You can't do that by yourself anymore. You almost fell in!" Sophie sounded irritated, but Tess shook herself off. She didn't understand what Sophie had said, but it never occurred to her that she had limitations. She did what she needed to do, and Sophie and Jake kept her safe and comfortable and gave her what she wanted. And she had Lola. Even the shepherd was respectful lately. She was content with that.

Now they were on the final stretch. They had crossed the field step-by-step and she was deeply fatigued, but at the same time steeped in a great sense of satisfaction.

And then her back legs gave out.

She sank onto the grass. Coolness shrouded her, and the icy

rain ran through her fur, numbing the ache in her back. She struggled to get to her feet but it was no use.

Through the veil of rain she heard Sophie's voice, then just the feel of raindrops on her forehead and nose and the muted roar of water all around her.

Sometime later, Jake's arms gathered her, and she was lifted against the warmth of his chest. She felt Sophie's hands stroking and soothing her face and back.

The door opened and light flooded over her. A warm towel massaged her back and legs and she was lowered to her bed. She sank into the luscious warmth of foam and blankets and dozed, not aware of Jake or Lola or V checking in on her, only easing awake when the smell of chicken stirred her senses. She raised her head and ate from Sophie's hand.

SOPHIE

When Sophie returned home from work that night, Jake greeted her at the door, looking pale and drawn. "She isn't doing well," he said. "She hasn't eaten since this morning and it's been hard to get her to go down the ramp, even with a lot of support. The last time I tried to lift her she cried, so I just couldn't do it."

"I'll say hello to her and try to get her to eat something." Sophie dropped her bag from her shoulder and fell to her knees to greet Lola and V. "How are you, my beautiful girls? How's your sister Tessie?" She kissed their noses and stroked their ears, Lola's so long and silken, V's so large, erect, and velvety. "Bat ears" they called her.

"Tessie!" Sophie crawled up to Tess where she lay on her bed. "Aren't you feeling so well, sweetie?" Tess looked up at her and wagged, struggled to stand, and failed. "It's OK, sweetheart. You're fine there for a moment. Just let me get changed." She turned to Jake, buried her face in his shoulder, and wept. His body shuddered and his arms enveloped her. They stood that way for a long time while Lola and V looked on, brows furrowed. By the time they drew apart, Tessie had fallen back into a deep slumber.

That night, Sophie dreamed of the three girls playing. They

ran together through a wide, green, green field, sunlight brilliant on their coats.

She was jolted awake at six o'clock by the silence. How could it be so late? She had slept all night without being awakened—that hadn't happened for months. Slowly it dawned on her. She held her breath, turned on her bedside lamp, and looked down. Tess was stretched out on her side. Was she breathing? Sophie watched, her attention riveted on Tessie's chest for several minutes—but there was no movement at all. Tessie was still. She was gone.

And three weeks later, Lola was gone too.

CHAPTER 50

Sophie

The day that Lola died began just like any other. The four of them had driven to Hovander Park for a long, leisurely walk. The park was deserted, the day overcast and still, and they ventured north into the off-leash area. They could see the expanse of it, a hundred yards to the north and half a mile to the south—sweeping green and yellow fields, the Nooksack river sliding past to the west, woods and more fields to the east. Mt. Baker stood stately and glacier-capped in the distance, overseeing it all.

Sophie unclipped Lola's leash that morning, and with a sly look at V, Lola scampered away, Vera lunging after her, her bark high and playful. Later, when V had settled, Lola fell in beside her sister, and they paced shoulder to shoulder across the open field. It gave Sophie hope to see them together again—since Tessie's death, Lola had been too bereft, too fatigued to engage with Vera.

But that evening, Lola refused her Kong. And when Sophie and Jake walked her outside, she started to shake. The emergency vet sent them directly to the Kirkland Emergency Clinic where an ultrasound showed that a tumor had perforated her intestinal wall. Lola's abdomen was filled with pus.

"We can operate," the Kirkland vet had said. "She's in good shape for a twelve-year-old dog. And if she survives the surgery, if she recovers from the severe infection, we may be able to treat the cancer with chemo. If she were my dog, I'd do it."

But Lola was not the vet's dog. To put Lola through all that, then bring her home for a long recovery without her Tessie, was unfathomable.

Lola died on a soft, warm bed in a dimly-lit room with Jake and Sophie caressing her beautiful, wise face. She had already drifted into a comfortable, narcotic-induced sleep—and then she just fell deeper into her slumber.

She died on December 30th, 2011.

It would have been Tessie's thirteenth birthday.

PART 4:
FINDING VERA - 2012/2015

CHAPTER 51

2012
SOPHIE

Watching Vera process her loss had been excruciating. She had licked and licked for days: her lips, the carpet, her paws. Reverse sneezes and hiccups plagued her several times a day for months. It had been agony to see her pace and whine, looking for Tess and Lola each time she entered the house, her gaze resting first on the spot where Tess's hospice bed had been, then on Lola's bed in the front hall. She'd wander into the living room, slump down in her crate and lie there for hours, unmoving.

Sophie found it odd that V never ventured onto Lola's coveted bed in the front hallway, and refused to try out Tessie's beds or even the living room couch—in spite of encouragement. She wondered if Lola had warned V away from these special places so many times that Vera was unwilling to risk her sisters' wrath.

A couple of months after Tess and Lola died, Sophie had fantasized on getting another dog, thinking it might jolt Vera out of her depression.

"I don't want to take the chance," Jake said. "She doesn't make friends with new dogs. Never has since that first summer."

Sophie had to agree. Even after all their work, Vera had never allowed strange dogs into her world after the six months following her adoption. And Sophie wasn't ready to take on the politics of having another dog with Vera, even if their introduction went well. She couldn't stomach the possibility of fights, or the constant vigilance needed to be sure the dogs were always safe. Nor could she imagine the option of keeping them separated—one dog would always feel excluded.

And then one morning, Sophie noticed how relaxed V was around the house. Without the constant negotiation for space with her sisters, she started to invent her own games and spent more time out of her crate. Playtimes, which at first had been so unbearably empty for both V and Sophie, became fine-tuned to Vera's favorite things now that she had thirty minutes of Sophie's undivided attention—twice a day.

Sophie practiced new skills with Vera, spent the entire summer teaching Vera *Treibball*—a German ball-herding sport—and the following fall, delved into the multifaceted *Wag it! Games*. Sophie taught V complicated heeling patterns, how to negotiate a variety of obstacles, and how to herd large, colorful balls through a course and into a goal. And, since Vera couldn't demonstrate skills for Sophie's classes at Josie's training center, Jake made training videos of Sophie and V working together.

Almost a year after losing Tess and Lola, Sophie stood with her arm around Jake, watching Vera lounge on top of the hot tub. Adoration and respect flooded her heart, her eyes tracing the shepherd's alert ears, her thick, lush coat, the sinuous curve of her back. She looked regal in the morning light.

"She's an amazing girl!" Sophie said. "Can you believe how far she's come? The best part is that I feel like I can finally trust her to make good decisions."

"Most of the time." Jake smiled down at Sophie and kissed the top of her head.

They stood a few minutes longer, Sophie drinking in the details of the calm, composed dog before her. Vera was complex, she decided, but not volatile. Unique, but not scary. Opinionated, but not pushy. She may not be perfect—but she was close.

CHAPTER 52

2015

SOPHIE

Sophie strode onto the rocky outcrop of Turtlehead. Below her, Orcas Island fell away to the wide, grey expanse of President Channel, the ghostly outline of Waldron Island barely visible in the mist to her right. Stuart Island was out there somewhere, but for now it was shrouded in dense fog.

Tendrils of mist played in the sunlight around her. A window opened to deep blue above, and far below, the steel-green sea danced in a spotlight of sparkles. Then she was once again wrapped in silver and silence.

She knelt down, traced the craggy rock with her fingers, and inhaled. Exquisite grasses, wet with dew, nestled in the crevices; rocky ridges glowed blue-green with lichen. The air tasted salty and pure—then was momentarily enriched with a hint of spice and warmth when the mist cleared and sunshine spilled onto her face. She sighed deeply, her breath coming easily now. Things didn't get much better than this.

She stood for ten minutes longer, taking in the visual feast of sea and sky and the caress of the breeze through her hair. Then she turned to retrace her steps.

The trail back down was rugged at first and laced with roots, and she was careful to watch her step. But then it smoothed out and cut along the side of a gently-sloping valley. Maidenhair ferns tumbled over outcrops above, and further down the valley, the forest floor was carpeted with thick, bright green moss. Lichen-draped vine maples, their pale leaves like clouds in the dark glen below, glowed under the high canopy of alder.

She thought of Jake and Vera back at the rental cabin: Jake's fingers flying over the strings of his guitar, filling the space with music, the air rich with the aroma of fresh coffee. She guessed that Vera was curled up beside him, listening to his music, large ears swiveling, alert for the sound of Sophie's car bouncing up the long drive.

Sophie was retired now. She turned this over in her mind,

tested it, looked for threads of panic woven through the overall euphoria. How could this be? It seemed only months since she'd started her career as a nurse practitioner. How could it have been twenty-five years of diagnosing MS, brain tumors, colds, pneumonias and a thousand other ailments in all those students on the cusp of their lives? It addled her brain, made her head spin to think of it. Would she miss it? She didn't think so.

Her capacity for compassion had waned, and her motivation to drive herself into the ground with the pace of the clinic had recently eluded her. And now, for the first autumn since she was twenty-one years old, she would not have to return to the insane pressure of the medical field. She could turn her complete attention to whatever she chose: long, dreamy days with Jake and Vera, volunteer work with the dogs at the shelter, teaching dog classes at Josie's, daily hikes. Such luxury seemed unbelievable.

She'd have to be careful with the shelter, she reminded herself. She had no desire to be consumed by it again. She would walk dogs, train dogs, and teach classes. That was it. Period.

A pang of hunger brought her back to the present and she realized she had almost reached the parking lot. In anticipation of breakfast, she quickened her step and drank in the clear morning air.

When Sophie pulled up to the cabin, a smiling, masked face peered out from between the flower boxes on the porch. Jake stood next to V, lean and bearded, a mass of curly, silver hair framing his tanned face. Sophie loved those faces.

"She knew you were here about five minutes ago," he said. "She must have heard the car."

The cabin was built into a barn, an oasis of solitude and good taste, nestled on a fenced, twenty-five-acre parcel of land. The first time they stayed there, Sophie had hoped to find trails winding through the property where they might walk V. But the land was wild, with thick brush and blackberry vines covering much of it. Still, with the fence in place, they had no worry about loose dogs darting out of the woods or strangers approaching the cabin.

"It was amazing up there, Jake." She wrapped her arms around him, feeling the roughness of his beard on her forehead. "If you want to go later, I can stay with V while you hike. The views are spectacular!"

"Maybe. V's happy you're home. She has something for you."

They sat down to fresh coffee and cinnamon rolls, and Jake handed Sophie a card. The envelope said "To Mummie." She tore it open, and there on the front of the card was a photo of a happy German shepherd with the caption, "Happy Retirement!" written under it. She opened it up and inside, it said:

Guess what?
You're MY bitch now!
Love, V-dog.

Hilarity bubbled up through Sophie's chest and escaped in an uncontrolled burst of laughter. Tears rolled down her cheeks. She reached down to scratch V's ears and the shepherd groaned with pleasure and pushed her face more firmly into Sophie's palm. "Just think—in the olden days *I* used to tell *you* what to do!"

V's ears folded back into sheer ecstasy and Sophie wrapped her arms around the powerful shoulders, gave her a squeeze, and kissed the black diamond on her forehead.

With that, V had apparently absorbed enough attention for one morning—she stood up and walked to the door. A flicker of emotion stung Sophie's eyes. For years it had been inconceivable that she could allow Vera to order her around. Yet now it felt so natural and completely without risk.

"See?" Jake said, "I bet you'll interrupt your cinnamon roll to let her out."

"Yup. She has me all figured out!" Sophie opened the door and admired the dog's stride as Vera sauntered onto the porch. They watched her scan the overgrown garden then settle down, nose high, studying the air currents, eyelids at half mast.

"She looks so relaxed," Jake said. "Where do you want to take her today? Swimming?"

VERA

Vera dozed on the porch. She liked this place because it was so quiet—no dogs, no strangers, no traffic. There were only two rooms and one entrance to guard, and she knew exactly where Sophie and Jake were at any given moment. She kept one ear trained on the cabin so she could pick up their voices, and with her chest pressed against the wooden planks of the porch, she could easily track the vibrations their footsteps made on the cabin floor.

"Swimming sounds good," Sophie said. "That'll be safe." Vera pricked up her ears. She recognized her name of course, and the word "swimming" was familiar too. She loved swimming.

Just as expected, Sophie and Jake soon joined her on the porch, clipped on her leash, and led her to the car. She would have trotted there willingly, unattached, but she liked it better this way: joined together by the leather leash so that neither Sophie nor Jake could disappear. They played a "search" game at home sometimes, making her stay in her crate while one of them hid in another room. When called, she would charge about, searching all their favorite places—the office, the bathroom, the music room, the bedroom—until, in a panic, she found the missing person. To have Jake or Sophie vanish here would be almost more than she could bear.

Once the car was underway, she settled into a meditation, eyes half closed, body rocking with the motion. She could glance outside whenever she chose, but most of the time she preferred to lie with her head up and her muzzle nodding downward so that her ears reached just below the level of the window. This way she could relax, but was ready to take action if need be.

Some time later they stopped. The hatchback opened, and when invited she hopped to the ground. Her nostrils flared. The scent of the sea filled the air and she heard the rush and flow of waves in the distance. It had been months since she'd last been here, so with her tail high in the air, she embraced the newness of it and pranced as far as her leash would allow toward the large, grassy expanse spreading down to the beach. She checked out the man walking by twenty feet away, tracked him briefly, then discounted him; he was too far away and uninterested to concern her. She pulled at the end of the leash, shook off, and looked back for Sophie and Jake to join her.

Finally, they followed, and she strutted along the promenade, staying off the grass because it suited her. She enjoyed the smoothness of the pavement under her paws—grass, she found, was often wet, irregular and unpredictable. She didn't pull. If she felt the leash become taut, she adjusted her pace to match whoever was walking her, Jake or Sophie. No one else ever held the other end of her leash.

A strong, pungent odor exploded through Vera's nostrils. She sat, planting her haunches firmly on the ground, muzzle facing the direction of the scent—she did not want her desire to investigate to be misread.

"OK, Vera, go check it out." The tension on the leash loosened, and V walked forward at a stately pace, testing the air until she found what she was looking for—the heady scent of rotting fish—and buried her nose deep in the grass. It opened expansive images to her, and she dove onto the patch of ground, rolling and wriggling with abandon, covering her back with the remarkable odor, all four paws wild in the air.

She heard Sophie and Jake laugh, and squirmed a little faster until she was sure her coat was filled with the fragrance, then shook herself off and trotted on with a glance in Jake's direction. That detour had filled her with satisfaction—but now she was ready to swim.

When they reached the low wall bordering the beach, Vera couldn't contain her excitement. It whirled up from her belly, a tingling fountain of absolute joy. She whined and pulled as hard as she could.

"Vera, stop!" Sophie held her firmly—an arm circled her chest while the other hand fiddled with her collar. Then she was free, the long Flexi streaming after her.

She bounded deftly over a mound of logs and hit the beach at a full run, pebbles spraying behind her—and then the water closed in on her legs, swirling and tugging at her chest, icy droplets spraying her face. She snapped at one of the waves and the salty, cold water nipped back at her tongue.

She wanted to chase a stick—now!

She turned toward Sophie and let loose a series of sharp, staccato barks. Vera could see her scouring the beach for driftwood, gathering sea-smoothed sticks to throw, but she barked harder, louder.

"See, Sophie? She's got you!" Hearing Jake's voice, Vera glanced at him and saw that he held a stick too. She sent a fierce bark in his direction. She needed a stick—now. She didn't care who threw it.

"Is this what you want, V?" Sophie called, waving a piece of driftwood high above her head.

Vera ran to Sophie and jumped high, grabbing the stick from her outstretched hand. But no sooner did she hold it firmly in her jaws, than she dropped it on the beach, ran back to the water's edge, waded in chest deep, and stood poised, staring at the spot where the stick should fall. It splashed down a short distance from her nose and floated seaward. She launched after it, bounding out a couple of strides until the water cradled her body and lifted her paws—the stick just out of reach. Enthralled, she took another stroke toward the stick, then recoiled back toward land.

"V, get it!" Sophie's voice gave her courage, cheered her on. She took one more stroke, snapped, and caught it. With a powerful thrust of her left front paw, she whirled around and headed for shore and safety. Her toes touched down, and confidence restored, she dropped the stick in the water.

Vera trotted up the beach and shook off, then barked at Sophie again, eyes burning.

"V, go out and get it. Go!" A rock splashed next to the floating stick and V surged out, grabbed the stick, and jumped back to shore.

Vera had no idea why Sophie insisted that she bring back the stick: she had no use for it once she had grabbed it and bitten down a few times, enjoying the varied textures in the soft wood, and she knew Sophie could get more.

Sophie threw the stick again and Vera lunged after it, this

time plucking it easily from the waves. She swam and waded and played until her paws were sore and her hips and shoulders ached. When she was done, she trotted up the beach and fell into step with Jake, utterly content. Sophie, she knew, would follow—firmly attached to the leash.

SOPHIE

"Are you tired of swimming now, V-dog?" Jake asked. "I'm hungry. Let's eat!"

They sat on a log to eat their sandwiches, and Sophie poured water into a bowl. Vera drank her fill, and Jake offered her a large, crunchy biscuit which she devoured, carefully searching between the pebbles for any remaining crumbs.

The beach was deserted, the resort almost empty in the off-season. Sailboats rocked and creaked in the small marina to their right, their rigging humming in the breeze. The enormous Rosario mansion dominated the rocky point beyond. East Sound spread before them, a long expanse of blue-grey dotted with whitecaps spotlit by the sun. The sparkles reminded Sophie of Tess.

"Remember mooring out there with Tess and Lola?" Jake asked, pointing to several buoys bouncing on the waves. "They were such good sailors."

"Yeah, I loved those long afternoons—the girls snoozing in the cockpit while we read. And remember their wild romps on the beaches? They lived for those island walks. God, I miss them!" Sophie still pined for them, her pain furtive, buffeting her breath at unexpected moments.

"I know you do, Sophie. But V-dog's really special too." Jake lowered his head, hiding his face from her, and offered Vera another treat.

"You're spoiling her, Jake! I love V to bits—you know that. But I still miss those two girls." Sophie looked down at V and massaged her wet back, dark fur glistening in the sunlight. V laughed up at them, thumped her tail once, and settled down on the pebbles, stretching out her back legs.

Yes, she loved Vera completely, but how much had the

shepherd's adoption weighed on Tess and Lola? She wondered about the bleeding in Tess's blind eye and her hemorrhagic diarrhea. She wondered about Lola's insane allergies and pica—all of which had shown up for the first time shortly after Vera came to live with them. And she wondered about Tess's cancer.

Suddenly, Sophie stopped chewing. "Someone's coming." A young man walked toward them along the promenade above, gait easy, gazing across the sound. Vera saw him too. She was on her feet, body drum-tight, gaze glued to the figure. "Come, sweetie, he's all right." Sophie moved V a good distance from the walkway, fed her treats, soothed and directed her with her voice. But when the man drew parallel to them, Vera launched, voice cannon-loud, body airborne. The man glanced down and swerved, but by the time Sophie had settled Vera, he was gone.

"Dammit!" The lull of the afternoon was shattered, her heart rate skyrocketing. She was angry at herself for being negligent, at Vera for not trusting her. She hated Vera reacting to people or dogs—took it as a personal affront after all the work they'd done together. God knows, she realized this was defensive behavior, but why couldn't Vera tolerate someone that far away? It had been at least twenty feet.

Sophie sucked in a breath and ran through the triggers: he'd carried a backpack, he'd been on a path above them, V was tired and sore from playing, the stranger had been male. She should have taken all this into account and moved further away. Next time she would judge the distance better, she would be more aware of how Vera was feeling, she would use higher-value treats, she would... She let her irritation pass, and focused on V's lovely face. How could she be angry?

Jake took the leash and they walked back to the car. An older man led a yellow lab across the lawn fifteen feet in front of them. The dog's tail wagged in a relaxed arc, eyes fixed on the path ahead. V glanced at the dog, then looked back at Jake for a cookie, and they continued on without incident, Jake's stride was long and confident, the breeze tousling his hair, Vera's form sturdy and loose, large, soft paws pacing at his side. Sophie filled her lungs with the salty, fragrant air and sighed. Sometimes they got it right.

Before she got into the car, Sophie paused for a moment and looked back to one of her favorite trails. It led from the beach up to Cascade Lake and from there climbed to Mountain Lake and the summit of Mt. Constitution. They'd hiked that trail so many times over the years—and always with their dogs. But not with this one. Never with V.

For years, Sophie had yearned to take Vera everywhere with her—into the mountains, running wild on ocean beaches, racing along their favorite trails with the shepherd bounding ahead, unleashed. She still grieved the loss of everything V could have been, should have been—if they'd raised her from puppyhood, if things had been different.

Bit by bit, Vera's world had shrunk to a fraction of what Sophie had envisioned for her. Still, the glass was half full. And it was enough.

CHAPTER 53

VERA

Vera marched up the cabin steps and put her nose to the door. She had been in the car for a while now, and she was ready to stretch out and snooze in comfort. When Jake opened the latch, she stepped inside and waited for Sophie to dry her paws. She lifted each of her back paws with pride, one at a time—she had figured it out all by herself—and, when Sophie was ready, spun around and offered up her front paws. Then she stood still while Sophie gently wiped the salt from her face and rubbed her back and tummy dry. She liked this routine, and giving Sophie easy access was her responsibility.

She found her favorite spot and dozed, ears swiveling like satellite dishes to catch the nuances in conversation. Flames sputtered and crackled in the hearth, punctuating their voices.

Presently, Jake moved to the kitchen, and within moments, the fridge door opened and she caught a whiff of cheese. Her body felt lead-heavy, but she pushed to her feet and repositioned herself a few feet from him.

"Here you go, V-dog." When she caught the cheese easily and stared at him, Jake tossed her another piece. With a groan, she gave into her exhaustion, and stretched out on her side.

Voices murmured a few feet away, laughter fluttered and ebbed, and Vera dozed, the excitement that had fizzed through her during the day now replaced by a deep and satisfying fatigue.

Then, through the buzz and hum of voices, she heard the word "music". She knew over 150 words in the English language now, and "music" was one of them. Jake's articulation of it slowly seeped into her consciousness, and as soon as she heard him move the guitars, she alerted and rolled into the sphinx position. She stared hard at Sophie.

"You heard the word 'music' did you, V? Not too tired for your chew toy?"

Sophie's voice had that playful tone. Vera didn't have the energy to beg any harder, but she made a concerted effort to intensify her stare.

"OK, baby girl." Sophie walked to the kitchen and rustled around in a bag. V scrambled to her feet, scenting the air. "Are you ready?"

Vera lay back down on the hardwood floor, and lifted the unbelievably delicious beef stick from Sophie's hand. The room disappeared as odor and flavor overtook her senses, the texture crunchy and satisfying.

It was gone in less than a minute and she scanned the room to pinpoint the treat-dispensing toy she knew would follow. It lay by the couch. Piece by piece, she extracted each tiny ball of kibble, maneuvering the toy around the room, nose and paws tipping and rolling it, pouncing, nuzzling, spinning it across the floor.

Finished, she surveyed the room. It was hot now, and the two guitars were loud in the tiny living room. She wandered into the bedroom. It was cooler there. And quieter. She sized up the bed. So comfortable. Other than those raucous play times with Lola on the big bed at home in the early days, she had only been on a human bed when Sophie played scent games with her. Echoes of Lola's stern reprimands in the years since had prevented her from venturing onto any bed alone.

She gauged its height carefully, and although it rose above her head, she thought she could make it. She knew she could. She crouched, haunches stiff and trembling with fatigue, and with one magnificent leap, landed perfectly in the center of the snowy spread. At first she circled, preparing to sleep, but the surface was too smooth.

Momentarily energized, she spread her long toes, extended her nails, and dug—raising the comforter into great white folds, sculpting her nest. Then she circled once more and let her weary body sink into the luxury of it.

For a few moments she gazed out the window to the garden beyond, absorbing the sounds drifting in from the living room. Those voices were her universe, and she floated on their rhythmic cadence. The late afternoon spread before her and finally, with a deep sigh, she rested her head on a pillow of down, stretched out her long, weary legs, and slept.

EPILOGUE – 2017

VERA

Annie. Vera heard the word over and over, Jake and Sophie's voices high with excitement when they spoke it. She hadn't a clue what it meant or why it was so weighted with joy.

"Look at her!" Sophie held up a glowing screen to Jake and laughed.

"You really want to bring Annie home?" Jake asked. "What about V? We can't bring a puppy here! Think about it. Vera would be devastated." His hand caressed her ears, his touch fluid and warm, and glancing up at his face she heard her name once again linked with "Annie". His features were happy, but strained, and seeing the discord, her tummy pitched.

The voices became earnest. She tried to decipher their words, but finally gave up, rested her head on the carpet, and dozed. She was vaguely aware of Sophie leaving the house, but after that, sleep overtook her.

Vera was thirteen now, almost fourteen. Her days were a ritual of meals, treats, playtime, walks, and, when she wanted it, snuggles. She managed her life with care, and Sophie and Jake supported her, kept strangers at bay, protected her from dogs, and provided just the right amount of entertainment to keep her happy. Her days floated past, buoyant, airy, and completely satisfying. Almost.

The slam of the mudroom door startled her from sleep and the sound of Sophie's voice teased her toward awareness. She was still bound to Sophie, and each moment away from her felt awkward and empty.

"Vera? Where are you?" A flash of pleasure slid sideways

through her consciousness as she fought to orient herself. The world shifted, righted itself, and she jumped to her feet, shook off, and trotted to the mudroom. Sophie stood before her, bristling with excitement—Vera felt it ricochet like sparks around the room. She stopped, assessed the situation, and ran her nose over Sophie's jeans.

Just what she thought. Sophie stank of dogs again—no, not multiple dogs this time, just one dog. She shifted her weight away, swung her head aside, and was half way to the living room when Sophie called her back.

"Annie." She pointed to her jeans where the smell lingered. Vera reached out her nose and tested the scent again. Female. Puppy. Collie. For a moment an image of Tess whispered before her, then it was gone. Sophie pulled a treat from her pocket and V gobbled it as she sniffed the odor, drawing it deep into her nostrils and blowing it back out the slits in the sides of her nose. The rich scent made her head spin.

"I have something else for you." Sophie tossed a ball of something soft and fluffy onto the floor. "Where's Annie?" V studied Sophie. The woman stared at the ball of fur, a smile lighting her face. "Where's Annie, V?"

The fur lured her closer and she buried her nose in it, inhaled, drifted. There was something about the texture, the sweet collie smell, and the treats Sophie produced that kindled an interest, a hint of longing. This was Annie?

It had been so long since she'd been close to another dog. She had two friends she walked with from time to time, but she would never allow them to get closer than a body's length from her. She had never sniffed with them, mused with them or snuffled them. She sniffed the fur again, grabbed it, and spat it out when the hairs clotted on her tongue.

SOPHIE

Sophie was nervous. She hadn't meant to fall in love with Annie. She had worked with the puppy as a service-dog volunteer trainer, and Annie had caught her attention at one month of age. In the weeks that followed, the furry ball had rocketed to the forefront of Sophie's awareness—she was confident, sweet, smart, happy, affectionate and full of life, and Sophie couldn't deny that of all the dogs she'd worked with over the past few years, Annie was a beacon. Sophie couldn't let her go. They had discussed adopting Annie, but the four-month-old puppy still lived her life as a service-dog-in-training at Brigadoon Service dogs while they figured out how to manage Vera. They had to act soon.

Every night for weeks, Sophie had lain awake, imagining Annie tearing through the house, trying to sort out how they could make things work without putting Annie at risk, and without putting V's final months or years in jeopardy. Since V had lost her sisters, she had never accepted another dog. She was their light and joy—but still a problem with dogs and strangers and still very much a special-needs girl.

"What are we going to do about Annie?" Sophie's voice was higher than normal, a feverish urgency to it. Sophie and Jake were walking Vera in the neighborhood, the first hints of fall cooling the air, the vine maples turning crimson. Sophie had lain awake once again plotting this conversation.

"I think we should adopt her and bring her home," Jake said.

Sophie stopped and faced him. Deja-vu twisted her brain. They'd done this dance before. She was sure of it. "But what about V?" She let her attention shift to the shepherd who was lost in her own world, probably sniffing the scent of a new dog in the neighborhood, judging by the duration and intensity of her focus.

"I don't know, but you love that puppy so much—I think we should do it."

Sophie's thoughts churned. She grasped for answers that didn't exist. "We could fix up the house so that they never get together couldn't we?" Her mind conjured the living room, the hallway, the mudroom, and the kitchen as she spoke. "We could cordon off a large area for Annie, use baby gates in the hall to separate the area where V sleeps, put tie-downs in the kitchen." Sophie searched Jake's face for signs of doubt, but his eyebrows were raised and eager, his eyes lit with possibility.

"Yeah, I think it could work. We would make it work. I just never thought of keeping them separated before," he said.

A few days later, Sophie drove into the cemetery. She had picked up Annie from the kennel and tucked her away in a crate on the back seat. The puppy rode silently, but when Sophie looked in the rearview mirror, she could see Annie's eyes taking in the world through the kennel's wire frame.

This was it. The day V would meet Annie. Sophie had primed Vera for it, brought Annie's fur home for the shepherd to sniff, paired the scent with hot dogs, chicken and salmon, taught her the puppy's name. Today Jake would walk V toward Annie and Sophie—then, when Vera licked or yawned or sniffed the ground showing signs of social discomfort, he would walk her away to give her a break. They would repeat this procedure over and over, being careful to gauge Vera's level of stress, then ease into a parallel walk with Annie.

Sophie needed to remember to breathe. In and out. In and out.

Today was the most important day she could remember since Tess and Lola died.

VERA

There was something different about this day—Jake was anxious. She could smell it swirling from his clothes, hear it in his voice, see it in the tension of his movements. And Sophie was nowhere around.

At first.

They arrived at the cemetery. She viewed it as her property now. She had been there so many times that the strolls they took had melded together. But the odors were always fresh and she could stride out on her long leash and choose which route they walked, which water spigots to drink from, and for how long they roamed. And Sophie and Jake were always compliant. She liked that.

Today they parked in the "meeting people and dogs" spot.

Whenever they met a dog or new person at the cemetery, Sophie would park in this particular place. Her skin tingled, her heart scampered in her chest. She had heard that name Annie so many times today that she just had a feeling.

She jumped down from her crate, and the first thing she saw was a dog in the distance—a startling white ruff, a slender nose, dancing white paws. An excited, high-pitched bark pierced the air. She stiffened, trying to catch the scent of the dog, her mind reeling from the tone of the voice. The package of the ruff, the paws, the length of the fur paired with the bark were so familiar.

Then she saw Sophie at the other end of the leash.

"Hi V!" Sophie's voice followed the dog's bark. "Here's Annie!"

Vera eyed the dog. *Annie?* The dog pranced and wiggled, pirouetted light as air, then turned to Sophie and sat.

V licked.

This dog was definitely a puppy. There was something good about that. When she licked, Jake walked her away.

V thought about the dog as they left Annie and Sophie in their wake. She hadn't seen a dog like Tessie for a long time. She scooped up the treats Jake tossed on the ground, but was seized by an uncontrollable curiosity. She swung back toward Annie and Sophie and strode forward, this time leading Jake. She needed more information.

SOPHIE

They had been working for thirty minutes, and V had not shown any tension in her body since Annie's first bark. Sophie was afraid that in her passion to visit another dog, Annie would lunge and bark at Vera, thus sending V into an uncontrollable reaction. But other than cursory glances at V, Annie was focused on Sophie, gobbling the treats with abandon.

"Can you believe this?" Jake's voice was etched with emotion.

"It's a miracle!" Sophie swung Annie around so she was parallel to Vera. The puppy's tail swished, and she hopped toward Vera, ears back, paws skipping and prancing, then her back was to Vera again and she locked eyes with Sophie. "Annie's amazing, did you see that, Jake? It's like she's already figured this out." A thread of hope sprouted in Sophie's solar plexus, curled and spun its way through her heart. With this puppy, it could work. It could actually work!

VERA

Vera kept an eye on the puppy, watched each tilt of her ear, every sideways glance, every frolicking skip and leap and spin. Warmth stirred through her body, a maternal urgency, a deepening curiosity. The puppy stopped to sniff, edged her way along the base of a stump. This dog had become a magnet—the puppy scent of her, the familiarity.

Vera sniffed the scent of a squirrel on the bark of a tree, left it for the fading odor of urine, followed a path of decaying leaves—and found herself a hair's breadth from the collie's nose. The sniff and blow of her nostrils shared the collie's breath, the feel of the dog stroked her shoulder. And just when she thought she could no longer bear the proximity, the puppy was gone, tail flashing, the air filled with praise from Sophie and Jake, their laughter wreathed around her. Vera bounced in a circle, a spring in her legs, her heart bursting.

And just like that, she was whole.

Acknowledgments

Thank you, first of all, to my husband, Don, for his support, enthusiasm and multiple readings of *Finding Vera* throughout the evolution of this book. I couldn't have done it without him.

Thank you, also, to our wonderful girls, Tess, Lola, and, of course, Vera, who have shared their patience, wisdom, and understanding with us through the course of their lives. Vera and Annie continue to do so—Vera as a wise matriarch, and Annie as a perpetual motion, hopelessly happy puppy. This book would not have existed without them.

Thank you to Sabine Sloley, Lynn Graham, Christina Jallings, Bill Smith, Laura Carter, Jan Houston and Janet Martinson for their friendship, ideas, readings, and enthusiastic encouragement and support.

Thank you to my remarkable editors, Laurel Leigh and Sabine Sloley, who taught me more about writing than they'll ever know.

And finally, thank you to all my teachers, both writing instructors and dog trainers, who have influenced me with their passion, knowledge, and skill over the years. And thank you to all Vera's friends and admirers who loved and supported her on her life-long journey. I will always be most grateful to you.

ABOUT THE AUTHOR

KERRY CLAIRE has worked as a registered nurse and nurse practitioner for much of her life, but dogs have always been her passion. She has been a dog trainer for thirty years, and has spent the last thirteen focused on canine behavior and aggression. She lives in the Pacific Northwest with her husband and their two sweet dogs, Vera and Annie. *Finding Vera* is her first novel.